NO RULES

ANITA RIGINS

NO RULES

Anita Rigins

WARM PUBLISHING
El Paso, Texas
www.warmpublishing.com

Original title: *No rules*
published by Edisource
Paris, France

Copyright © 2019 Edisource
Copyright © 2025 Warm Publishing

Interior design by Warm Publishing
Cover art by Scarlett Lovell
Cover design by Angela Haddon
Art by Scarlett Lovell
Translated from French by Iris Clark

ISBN: 978-1-958447-04-8

TRIGGER WARNING

Although *No Rules* is a romance please note that there are several themes within this book that may trigger you. If you are easily triggered by dark content like violence, sexual assault, drug, or grief, proceed with caution and at your own discretion.

*I dedicate this book to R. who will recognize himself. You
saved my life, and you make it better every day.*

PROLOGUE

IRIS

"Love: the impulse of the heart that carries us towards another. It can be recognized by its intensity, by the speed with which it appears and takes control of our being," and blah-blah-blah. Who seriously believes in this definition?

And then there's that chubby little cupid who shoots an arrow right through your heart, stupidly forgetting that you need it to live.

Do you want my opinion? Love, the real kind, the one that takes you to the gut, it's bullshit.

At least, that's what I thought…until I met Tucker.

1. FIND YOUR PLACE

IRIS

A shrill ringtone echoes through the walls of my apartment as I run to find my damn bag.

I'm late.

I trip in the hallway and catch myself on the dresser with one hand. One more inch and my toe would've hit the corner of the furniture, and we all know how painful that is.

Note to self: move this furniture as soon as possible. Oh, and wake up on time the next few days.

I hate people who are late, and I hate being late myself. I'm usually organized but, go figure, not today. Probably the stress of the move.

The noise continues to pierce my eardrums, and I finally find my phone between two cushions of the sofa. Hallelujah.

"Yeah?" I ask, gasping for breath.

With my car keys in hand, I slam the door to the apartment and hear my Aunt Emma's voice on the other end.

"Your sister had another tantrum, Iris," she begins in her unpleasant voice. "When I agreed to take her into my home, I expected a minimum of maturity from her."

The way she says "take her"—as if my little sister were a stray dog—makes my anger rise, which I am unfortunately obliged to swallow. I rest my head against the lacquered wood of the door and sigh, clutching the phone.

You stupid bitch.

I restrain myself from repeating it out loud and answer through clenched teeth. "She's having a panic attack. Comfort her."

I hear my sister crying behind her and imagine her alone, devastated. Her young age hasn't helped her accept the situation; unlike I thought it would.

"Maybe leaving Portland now wasn't such a good idea," Emma continues in a reproachful tone.

On the contrary, it was the only good idea I've had in the last few months. The only solution that allowed me to keep my head above water. A fresh start to keep me from drowning in my nightmares. If I had stayed, I would have been lost forever.

"Pass the phone to her," I say, running down the two floors in a hurry.

"I've got a meeting in thirty minutes, so fix this," my aunt continues in a tense voice.

No doubt that taking in a nine-year-old girl was not part of her plans. A few months ago—eight, to be exact—her life was turned upside-down while my sister's and mine were destroyed.

Unfortunately, the judge's decision was final. My sister was placed in Emma's care. *Without the financial resources, I was deemed too unstable and too precarious to care for a 9-year-old girl.* The judge's words against me loop back into my head, tightening my throat a little more.

I hear a sniffle through the handset, and my heart squeezes as I settle into my semi-functioning Chevrolet.

"Sweetie?"

The sniffling gets louder, interspersed with heavy breathing.

"Everything is fine, Agnes, okay? Just listen to me. Take a deep breath."

"Mom was supposed to drive me for my first day of school."

I grip the steering wheel tightly when she mentions my mom and try to cut off any thoughts other than my little sister.

"I know, honey. But this year, Aunt Emma is going to take you, okay? It's going to be okay."

"No, I have to take the bus alone."

Damn it.

I put the car in reverse, unable to afford to be any later, and pull out of the parking lot of the off-campus housing. I put on the speakerphone as I search my bag for my schedule.

Criminal Science, lecture hall B4. Nine to eleven o'clock.

Me, who was looking forward to start this class, which was unknown to me until then…In fact, when I was choosing my elective, this subject was the one that intrigued me the most. However, when I saw this word, a lump in my stomach and an urge to vomit instantly came over me.

How could I be attracted to this class after what had happened?

But I thought about it, heard a few students praising the teacher on the first day of school, and finally signed up. It's going to give me something extra for my third year of psychology and it might finally help me understand the behavior of a criminal. I may have high expectations, but if it helps me understand what went on in the mind of the man who killed my parents eight months ago, then I want to be in it.

"You'll make it, Agnes," I continue as I turn a corner, wondering if I'll make it. Fortunately, I'm only ten minutes away from the main campus.

"I wish you were here," my little sister whispers, gradually calming down.

I purse my lips as I finally reach the campus. "I'll see you soon," I tell her. I pull into the parking lot and sigh when I can't find a spot near the entrance. "You know what?" I continue as I finally see a free spot a little further on, the only one. "During the fall vacations, you're going to come here, right?"

"Really? I'm going to come to Denver?"

Her tone squeezes my heart a little more as I pull into the parking spot. Even if I don't get her custody, Aunt Emma will let her come to my house for a few days. "Of course—hey!"

A pickup truck pulls in at the same time as me and nearly rips the front end of my car.

"You bastard!" I shout as the car stops at the same time.

"I thought you weren't supposed to say bad words, Iris?" asks Agnes with a surprised tone.

I mumble between my clenched teeth and look out of the window, trying to see the obviously blind driver who almost killed me, but his windows are tinted. One of them slowly rolls down as I squint, furious.

"Are you a complete idiot?" I yell, opening my window as well.

As the truck starts to move again, I zip into the parking space before them.

I saw it first!

"I have to go," I say to my little sister. "Everything is going to be okay. I'll call you tonight, okay?"

"I love you," Agnes answers me just before hanging up.

I breathe a sigh of relief as I turn off my engine, collect my things, and check in my rearview mirror that my red hair is still in place. The advantage of having a bob, rather than wearing my hair long as it used to be, is that it's much easier to style.

The dark circles under my hazel eyes are quite pronounced due to my lack of sleep, but I'll have to deal with it. As I rub a trace of toothpaste under my lower lip, I notice something in the back of my vehicle. The black pickup still hasn't moved.

I open my door and decide to ignore the dumb person driving it; they'll move eventually.

I start to walk away from my vehicle, but a husky, unmistakably male voice stops me.

"That was my place."

His words sound like a command. He doesn't say anything else, as if those simple words are supposed to make me move. I raise my eyebrows and turn to the guy.

His place?

My eyes fall first on a strong forearm resting on the edge of the door, then I raise my head and, when my gaze finds his, I frown. I had never met a man with different colored eyes before.

Sure, I've seen them in pictures, but I have to say that his blue eye on one side and blue with brown on the other are quite unsettling.

His red and white baseball cap hides his dark hair. I don't look at him any further and take a step in his direction.

"Does it say 'Public Danger' on it?" I reply, pretending to look at the ground behind my car as if I were looking for a name. "No, it doesn't say that, so I don't think it's your spot."

"It doesn't say 'Special Bitch' either," he retorts. He frowns, his mouth puckering in the middle of his three-day beard. A few hours ago, I would have called him handsome, but now I'm not thinking about that at all.

"If you don't want to move your truck, that's your problem," I continue as he stays behind my car. Don't complain when it's ripped off later.

His place? Seriously? What a jerk.

I don't wait for a second and walk away to get to class.

2. WATCH OUT FOR WOLVES

IRIS

OK, B4. Where the hell is B4?! Can't they put up a sign, like in Portland?

Three times I walk down that same hallway and no lecture theatre in sight. I glance at my phone screen. Eight fifty-seven. I have three minutes to get there on time.

A student busy with his phone conversation passes by me, talking loudly and gesturing wildly.

"Hey!" I call out to him tactlessly. "Do you know where is the room B4?"

He looks me up and down, pulling the phone away from his ear. One of his blond eyebrows goes up as he answers me, "Sorry, my name is not Michael Scofield. I don't have a map tattooed on my skin."

Who is this jerk?

In front of my confusion, he sighs with a theatrical air and resumes while clicking his tongue.

"You know, from Prison Break? Where on earth are you from?"

I squint my eyes. "Do I look like I want to talk about a show? The classroom?" I ask again, restraining myself from insulting him.

The student sighs again.

"Next intersection, turn right."

"Thank you," I mumble, walking away as he resumes his conversation as if nothing had happened.

Well, you can't say that the students here seem friendly! But I finally find my happiness when I arrive at the door of the lecture hall. I catch my breath and push back a lock of my short hair so as not to look like a half-dead asthmatic.

The room is a huge amphitheater, completely full. Shit. It's a good thing the teacher hasn't arrived yet. I notice two empty seats in the middle of the lecture hall. Weird. Some students are sitting right on the steps but leave those seats free? Maybe the seats are broken?

"Excuse me," I whisper, making the students in the row stand up and move to one of the seats.

Despite my apologetic smile, a student glares at me when I step on his foot.

Miraculously, I end up arriving at my destination without killing anyone. I fall on a chair and grimace when I feel the wood hit my buttocks with full force. Well, it's in good condition but comfort-wise, not so good. Then again, the lecture halls at the University of Portland are not much better. I won't miss Oregon for that.

Two people in the row in front of me turn around and stare at me.

What, is there something wrong with my face?

They stare at the empty seat to my left, then at the seat I'm sitting in, and whisper before turning their backs to me again. I feel a third look at me. On the other side of the last empty seat is a beautiful black woman who is discreetly analyzing me. She raises an eyebrow, and I am about to ask her if I'm sitting in a cursed seat or something. Noticing my own look, she throws me a little smile before taking her things out of her bag.

People are very strange here.

I let out a sigh and pull out my computer. Near me, the students stand up to allow a latecomer to sit in the last free seat.

"If I tell you that this is my seat, are you going to insult me again?"

I hide my confusion as I discover Mr. Public Danger, an enigmatic expression on his face.

I can't believe it.

"What the hell are you doing here?" I ask.

I try to ignore his blue and brown stained eyes. Real trouble magnets, if you ask me.

I concentrate on the logo on the cap he's wearing, partially hiding his mass of black hair. The guy crosses his arms. The veins of his forearms stand out through his gray T-shirt, and I try not to dwell on them.

The beautiful girl sitting right next to him holds back a little laugh before turning her attention back to the screen of her phone. She's probably one of his friends.

"I could ask you the same question," says Public Danger a little more loudly. "Are you following me?"

My mouth opens wide as I squint. What a cheek.

He cuts me off just before I can answer. "I don't mind. I didn't have many redheads following me."

Seeing his little smile, a sign that he's openly making fun of me and my hair, I'm inwardly enraged but try not to let anything show. I straighten my shoulders and lean toward him. "Wow, your humor almost equals your inability to park."

I ignore the hoarse little laugh that comes out of my neighbor's chest. The two people sitting right in front of us turn around again and stare at me as if I were crazy for talking to him like that. I barely have time to wonder at their outraged looks when the door to the lecture theatre opens with a bang.

A small woman in her fifties, glasses on her nose, walks towards the desk in front of us, a box under her arm.

A guy enters just behind her, a smile on his face as he sees some of his friends among the students.

"One minute later and I wouldn't have accepted you," the professor announces in a sharp voice to the guy who suddenly loses his delighted look.

The students gradually fall silent while the woman seems to be looking for something in her box. Even my neighbor seems to calm down, as if this woman were the devil herself.

She abandons her task with a smile and raises her head to address us. Her gaze is terribly direct as she analyzes us.

"Welcome to my criminal science class. I hope you had a good summer vacation, and I would like to take this opportunity to remind you that your summer vacation is over. Many of you are in your third year and come from different majors. Some of you know me because I have also taught criminal law for many years. I am Professor Richards. I emphasize the 'professor.' I know that many students call their teachers by their simple last name, but don't make that mistake if you want to come out of my class alive. I am not your friend."

"Damn," I whisper at the end of her greeting, as shocked as I am impressed by her oral fluency.

"She's always making an impression," my neighbor murmurs. "A little more terrifying than you."

"I didn't know I'd just started a conversation," I whisper angrily.

"Well, you just did, redhead."

As I sigh, the teacher writes her name on the only board behind her imposing desk.

"They do anger management classes," the insufferable dark-haired man suggests to me with an innocent look.

I turn to him with a squint and whisper quietly, "I don't need to control my anger. I just need people to stop being jerks."

He doesn't seem really affected by my new insult, simply shrugs a shoulder and yawns without any embarrassment. He then runs a hand over his short beard before replacing his cap.

"Some people have only taken criminal science as an elective," Professor Richards continues.

I feel myself being targeted when she says this and turn my attention back to her.

"Others as a required subject. Regardless, I'm counting on you to push yourself throughout the semester. The key to success is knowledge, young people. And money, but that's another topic."

A few laughs come out as she purses her crimson lips. Then she sits on the corner of her desk, with hundreds of students looking on.

"Over the semester, you will have several assignments to complete. Criminal science is an exciting but complex subject. You will be required to complete several group assignments in addition to final exams. If you don't feel you can handle the workload, you should withdraw today."

A guy in the front rows makes a comment that I can't hear from my seat. But Professor Richards seems to hear it because she tilts her head to the side with a sigh.

"Let me be clear with you, we don't pair or trio based on each other's looks. So, no, young man, you are not going to choose your partner based on the size of her breasts. And girls will not choose a male partner based on the size of their penis, but on their brain. Although some of them seem to lack one."

More laughter erupts, and a little smile comes over my face. Well, she doesn't look so evil. What a woman! I have a feeling that this class is going to be…exciting.

I keep feeling my neighbor's gaze on me, but I ignore him blatantly.

After a few minutes, the girl sitting on his other side quietly calls out to him, diverting his attention to the rest of the class.

In the late afternoon, I walk out of my cognitive psychology class, lost in my thoughts. It was a trying day. I am exhausted, and my only desire is to dive into bed and stay there until tomorrow morning. Looking like a normal person, like a normal student, is more complicated than I thought. It's been two weeks since I arrived in Denver, completely on my own, but I don't regret my decision to leave Portland. I needed it.

No one really understood my desire to leave, to put distance between me and my past. The truth is, I couldn't stay there. I tried for months, but I couldn't do it anymore. I had an all-consuming need to get away and rebuild somewhere else.

Denver is a big city—and that's an understatement—with about three million people. Thousands of students, all of whom are still unknown to me, as is their city. But it's thousands of miles away from Portland, from my old life, and that helps me feel a little lighter, as if the weight of reality isn't so strong here.

I wonder what my sister is doing right now. Living with our aunt is hard for her. I know she would rather be with me, but I wasn't able to get custody of her after our parents died. So maybe I should have stayed in Portland and tried to see her when I could. But I couldn't stay in that city that reminded me of so many bad things. Not after all this. Not right now.

I hear screams that seem to be coming from a giant speaker and see out on the quad about fifteen female students who are apparently protesting. I stop to watch, as do several other people, one of them starting to film.

I squint and read one of the signs carried by a tall blonde:

We will not let a destroyer of womanhood
lead us.

I laugh softly as I discover another sign. I finally understand who the students are talking about.

My body, my choice.

I can only agree with them. I raise an eyebrow as two girls take off their shirts. One is in a bra while the other is completely topless.

The first girl, the one who leads the way, screams insanity. Her long black hair shines in the sun, and she throws it over her shoulder, clearing her face. That's when I recognize her. It's the girl who was sitting next to the asshole during this morning's class.

She passes by me and stops when she sees my little smile when I discover that she has a penis drawn on her forehead with a white marker.

"Does my drawing displease you?" she asks me while straightening her head, fixing me with her dark eyes.

I raise my hands as a sign of peace, but I can't help but stare at the fake penis.

"You have my full support," I tell her with an air of encouragement.

This seems to be the right answer because she winks at me and leans in. "I think so too. Even though my boyfriend will probably dump me when he finds out. But you know what they say, 'There are plenty more fish in the sea.'"

I pretend to think while putting my index finger on the bottom of my chin. "Personally, I've never seen those fishes come in and say, 'Hello, sweetheart, we're the fishes of the saying,'" I reply.

The girl laughs softly while revealing a whole row of teeth and seems to analyze me from top to bottom as if she's evaluating me. After a few seconds, she offers me a hand, "You're a funny one. I'm Yeleen."

"Iris," I answer politely.

"You're the chick who sat by me in the reserved seats in the criminology class."

I raise an eyebrow, not sure I understand the meaning of these words.

"What do you mean, 'reserved?' Since when do we reserve seats in a classroom when it's full?"

She simply shrugs her shoulders in response, and I finally realize what she's talking about, or rather who. The different colored-eyed Public Danger. So what, because he's got himself seats, people are listening to him? Who the hell is this guy?

"Wait, are you talking about the full-of-himself guy who came in and said I had taken his place?" I laugh falsely and she stares at me a little more closely, intrigued by my reaction.

"You really don't know who this is, do you?"

"I'm new here. And no, I don't know who that is. But I sit wherever I want, reserved or not."

Yeleen tilts her head to the side, both eyebrows raised.

"You've got guts. It's been a long time since a new girl talked to him like that. I like that."

"And so…who was he?" His eyes so disturbing haunt my thoughts again and I shake my head to clear them.

"What's your major?" she finally says, ignoring my question.

"Psych. Junior year."

She whistles as if impressed.

"And you're sticking with Professor Richards? Good luck with that. Me, I decided to drop out as soon as she mentioned the workload!"

She suddenly turns to the girls still protesting a little further away.

"Stop showing your tits, damn it! We're not doing a striptease for all these jerks. You," she says to one of the spectators, "stop staring at these girls or I'll cut off what's hanging between your legs."

I like her tactlessness.

Yeleen turns to me again. Noticing my scrutinizing look, she squints, "Hey, psychologist lady, I feel you analyzing me."

"Sorry, it's involuntary." I have a habit of trying to decipher the behavior of people around me. But sometimes I get it wrong.

A girl calls to Yeleen, and she says, "I have to go." She starts to walk away and then stops for a moment, giving me one last look. "Watch out for the 'wolves' on campus, Iris."

"Wolves?"

But no answer comes to me as she walks away, giving the finger to one of the guys who is still filming the other topless students.

3. RESCUE THE DAMSEL

IRIS

As I push open the door to High Peaks Bar, a hubbub instantly reaches me. The space is completely packed. The various tables scattered around the bar are all occupied. My eyes land on a small stage at the back of the room, where a man is performing. He is playing his guitar while covering a hit from Imagine Dragons. In front of him, some girls are dancing among themselves, totally enchanted by the singer's husky voice.

I see, on the other side, a bar where two older bartenders are struggling. One guy waves a twenty-dollar bill in the air in the direction of a bartender while another slams his hand on the counter, impatient.

I take a deep breath. Well, it's…lively. Most of the younger people here tonight seem to be students, which makes me feel a little better about trying my luck here. I glance at the small paper half-crumpled between my fingers. High Peaks Bar is looking for someone to serve several nights a week, and I need money.

I play elbows to reach the bar and move hastily, avoiding a young drunk. I glare at him, but he doesn't even notice my presence and moves away, joining a table where several girls are waiting for him, a big smile on their lips.

What a jerk.

I make my way over while crumpling the paper in my right hand. I lean on the bar, trying to attract the attention of a bartender. "Excuse me!" I try.

Neither of them hears me. As I call out to them a little louder, one of them turns his head towards me, his eyebrows furrowed. He finishes serving a drink and approaches me.

"What can I get you?" he asks me as the small bulbs above the bar light up his pierced eyebrow.

I shake my head and look serious. "I saw the job offer, and I'm here to apply."

He frowns his thick, dark eyebrows then purses his lips. "You want to work here?"

He looks incredulous as he quickly ogles me. His eyes land on my chest, hidden under a black T-shirt. It doesn't seem to really convince him. He then observes my red hair and continues, "We're looking for a waitress."

I put my two hands flat on the counter and lean towards him. "And why do you think I'm here?"

I stop myself from rolling my eyes and sighing. He seems to be slowly relaxing. As he lets out a soft laugh, the customers get impatient beside us.

"Wait for me here, I'll be right back," he says, leaving me by the counter.

During the next few minutes, I take another look at the crowd. A girl sits down on the arm of an armchair and grabs her glass. I recognize her. It's Yeleen, the student I met this afternoon.

I hesitate to say hello. In reality, I don't really know her.

"Let's go," says the barman I spoke to earlier.

He places himself in front of me and invites me to follow him. I walk along the bar with him, my steps following his.

"What's your name?" he asks me when we enter a narrow corridor at the other end of the small bar.

"Iris. What's yours?"

"I'm Buck," he says, stopping to offer me his hand.

"Nice to meet you, Buck," I reply, quickly grasping his palm.

"Billy will see you now," he announces when we arrive at a closed door.

I nod and let him knock on the wood.

"Come in," answers a demanding and rather husky voice from the other side of the door.

Buck stares me straight in the eye as I wonder if it was really a good idea to come here.

"It's okay, Billy looks like a jerk, but he's a big, soft bear."

I nod without answering him, watching him walk away to the

bar. I inhale once more. I can do it, I have the skills to do it. Besides, I have to do it to have the "financial resources." When I am ready, when my past has no power over my future, I want my little sister back. Continuing my education will help the judge understand that I am stable now, that my life won't go to hell. But until then, I have to rebuild myself.

I pull down the handle and enter the room. A man in his fifties is sitting behind a desk, his nose buried in a newspaper.

"Uh, hi," I say after a few seconds of silence.

He raises his head, apparently displeased to have been disturbed. "Hello?"

"I'm Iris," I announce in a voice that I hope sounds professional. "I saw the flyer you distributed around campus, and I'd like to apply for—"

"I'm not looking for a waitress," he interrupts.

I frown, squinting my hazel eyes.

"But your flyer does say otherwise."

Billy sighs and mutters into his mustache, running his hands through his graying hair. "You're not the kind of waitress I'm looking for for my bar. You're too childish."

"Wow, your bartender was right, a real jerk," I whisper almost to myself as I made my way to the door.

"What did you just say?" his voice rises behind my back.

I turn back to him, furious. "So what, because I don't show my ass or my tits, I look like a kid? Believe me, I've seen enough in my 'little' life to be considered more than that."

My words hit the nail on the head. At first, he doesn't answer me. But after a few seconds, a sincere smile lights up his face and deepens his wrinkles. "And what did you experience?"

Now it's my turn to be silent. I could say so many things to him, but I remain silent, my jaw clenched.

"Are you in college?" he continues.

I nod my head.

"Junior psych major."

The man nods in turn, seeming to think about his next words. "I need a waitress a few nights a week, depending on the availability of the other waiters. One of my employees is on maternity leave. Do you feel up to it?"

My lips curl gently at the chance that smiles at me. "Yes, I am."

Half an hour later, I sit behind the wheel of my Chevrolet, delighted. Shit, I got the job! But my smile fades when I see my aunt's name on my phone.

"Hello?" I begin, putting the car in gear to leave the parking lot full of cars.

"Iris! I've been trying to reach you for hours," exclaims Aunt Emma, hysterically.

"Has something happened to Agnes?" I worry instantly, as I do every time the fear of losing my little sister overwhelms me.

I hear a sigh of annoyance through the phone. "Agnes is doing VERY well, I assure you. A little too well, in fact! The deal was clear between us, Iris! I accepted custody of Agnes but she had to behave herself. I am a very busy person. I didn't plan to have to chaperone her all the time," she finishes in a pinched voice.

Soon it will all be over. I'll have custody of her. I'll have the resources and everything I need to have her here. I have to.

"What happened?" I finally asked.

"Your sister is 9 years old, Iris. I understand that she is still saddened by the death of your parents, but she must learn to behave!"

"Sad?" I retort with a mirthless laugh. "Damn it, Emma, her parents died IN FRONT of her! She needs time!"

"And I need mine! I had some important clients at home today, and I had to pick her up from class because she got into a fight with a classmate."

As a light rain starts to hit my windshield, I hold back a curse. My headlights light up the small road with difficulty. Damn it, I should have taken the back road to campus! Damn GPS that advised me to take this one to save a few minutes!

I slow down a bit and ask my aunt, "Why did she fight?"

"Do I look like I know? I'll put her on, sort it out."

I hear her call my sister, and a few minutes later her little voice rings in my ear.

"Hi, Iris."

The sorrow in her tone breaks my heart, but I try to ignore it.

"What happened, sweetie?"

Agnes doesn't answer me.

"Agnes, why did you fight?"

I hear her sniffling. "We had to present ourselves in front of the whole class. When it was my turn, I heard Isabella making fun of me for being an orphan."

I squeeze the steering wheel with my available hand.

What a little bitch.

"So," my sister resumes, "I walked up to her and pulled her hair. And I don't regret it."

I try not to smile, without success. I would have done much worse than her.

"Are you going to argue with me?" she finally asks me.

"No, I understand. But don't do that again, okay? I also want you to be good with Emma."

I can see her rolling her eyes from here. I hang up the phone a minute later and throw my cell phone on the passenger seat before braking suddenly for a pickup truck on the side of the road, stopped right in front of me.

Damn! I just got the scare of my life!

The rain is still falling lightly on my windows. From here I can see a body leaning over a flat tire.

Okay, that's not my problem, right? Maybe in reality it's just a psychopath trying to lure a prey?

Still, a part of me forbids me from leaving. With a sigh, I pull up right behind the truck, keeping my headlights on though due to the lack of light outside.

The rain pours down on the back of the stranger bent over in front of me, and I almost feel sorry for him. Almost.

I open my car door and get out without thinking. "Do you need help?" I shout through the rain.

My soaked hair makes me want to get back into my car, but at the same time, the man stands up and turns to me. His black locks are dripping. When I notice his eyes, one blue and the other stained brown, I dig my heels in.

If I was lucky at one point in the evening, let me tell you, I'm not lucky now. The asshole from my criminology class frowns as he discovers me here, as surprised as I am.

"I have a flat tire," he finally announces in a loud voice that hits me hard.

"Do you need help?" I ask again, a few feet away from him.

"Unless you have a spare tire," he spits, "no, you're no use to me."

I raise my eyebrows and mentally curse at him in every language I know. "You're really stupid, you know that? Go ahead, cope on your own," I reply, heading back to my car.

"Hey, calm down."

I hear footsteps behind me but I ignore them.

"When people say that redheads have a shitty temper, I can now confirm that it's true."

Furious, I turn around towards him and almost run into him when I discover him right behind me.

"You've got some nerve, man! I come to offer you my help, and you tell me to fuck off. Do you think I'm going to smile at you afterwards like a simpering idiot?"

My anger seems to amuse him. "First of all, I wasn't telling you to fuck off. I was just stating a fact, that without a tire, you weren't going to be much use. And secondly, I'd love to see you simpering."

I roll my eyes and cross my arms over my chest.

"You're unbelievable," I sigh.

He stares at me without flinching for a second, and I stare back. Then his eyes land on my soaked T-shirt and my hair in the same state. I watch him in turn, analyzing the effects of the rain on him. It's unfair, I'm sure I look like a wet dog when, I must admit, he's still very attractive despite the situation. He seems to pull himself together and runs a hand through his short black beard.

"You're freezing, go home."

Seriously, is he talking about my health? I frown and watch him walk away. So, what? That's it?

"Did you call someone?" I continue, ignoring his command.

His shoulders tense a little more as he turns to me.

"I managed to reach a buddy I was supposed to meet—but who, unfortunately, is drunk—just before my cell phone went dead.

But I'll manage, don't worry about me, I'm not a damsel in distress."

In spite of myself, his grumpy expression makes me laugh. So that's it? He doesn't want a girl to come and help him? I guess that would hurt his male pride. Taking it on the chin, I finally say, "I accept to help you. Come on, get in."

When he doesn't move, I glare at him.

"I can drop you at your friend's house, if you want. You're not going to stay here indefinitely. Your death would be on my conscience."

He's still watching me intensely, as if he doesn't know what to think. I get into the car, slam my door, and turn the heater on full blast while I wait. A second later, the passenger side door opens. He climbs into my car, taking over the whole space in a second. The smell of rain mingles with a more masculine scent, and I try to ignore it as I start up again and his car disappears from our view.

"Shit," he sighs while massaging his temples with his fingertips.

He gives me his friend's address, then a silence invades the car. I feel his gaze on my profile and try to ignore it.

At a red light, I turn to him, wondering why he is staring at me. My eyes catch his. I don't look away, and neither does he. His eyebrows furrow again as he analyzes every detail of my face. I do the same and notice a small cut on his lower lip. I don't ask any questions. We are not friends, he and I. I don't know him, and his life is none of my business.

So I also refrain from asking him his name, not wanting to really engage him in conversation.

I start again and stare at the road, trying to ignore his presence beside me. His hands are placed on his thighs, powerful and wide.

"Where are you from?" he finally asks, in a low but perfectly audible voice.

I run my tongue over my lips, caught off guard. I didn't expect him to start the dialogue, given our previous confrontations.

"Portland."

He whistles softly. "And you came to Denver to get lost?"

"Well, Denver doesn't seem like a lost city to me," I reply.

"Why here?"

I shrug, refusing to answer his question. I don't want to reveal myself, to open up to him. It would give him a power over me that I am not ready to give up.

We quickly arrive in front of his friend's house. Despite the bad weather, the rain has finally stopped, and I see some students partying on the front lawn.

I park and wait for the tall, dark-haired guy to get out of the car. He puts his hand on the door handle, but turns to me.

"Do you want to come?"

I glance outside and shake my head. I know these parties, although the ones I've been to in the past have been way more extreme. He seems surprised by my refusal, as if he's not used to being told no.

I'm startled when someone knocks on the passenger side window.

"Hey, buddy, where have you been?" exclaims a tall blond man, leaning into the passenger seat once the door is open.

The guy then sees me behind the wheel, and his eyes start to shine as he jumps to conclusions. He looks quite tipsy and holds a half-full cup in one hand.

"Oh, I understand…yeah," he says. "You and Tucker were busy. I'm TJ."

Tucker. So I can put a name to the guy sitting next to me. I raise an eyebrow and retort coldly, "Absolutely not busy, TJ. I just played cab driver."

Tucker smiles softly at my grumpy expression but still doesn't move from the seat.

"Oh yeah?" continues TJ as he leans a little further in, "will you play cab with me?"

Tucker pushes TJ away, his hand firmly on his shoulder. "Get out of the way, buddy."

"Hey," exclaims the blond man, straightening up, "that's an attack against me, man."

He walks away and forgets about us, hailing a pretty brunette as he passes.

Tucker stares at me one last time. "Thank you."

I give him a solemn look. "Sure, no problem, I wasn't going to let you play the damsel in distress."

He tilts his head to the side, falsely offended, before asking, "Do I have the right to know your name?"

"You'll know it when I write it on my parking space."

His eyes sparkle for a moment, then he gets out of the car. "Good evening, redhead."

"Screw you!"

He slams the door, muffling my insult, and strides away towards the house.

In spite of myself, a small smile takes place on my face. I start the car again, trying to ignore the last twenty minutes and the tall dark-haired man watching me over his shoulder.

4. THEY ARE HERE

IRIS

Yawning like crazy, I get out of my Chevrolet and slam the door behind me. With AC/DC's "Highway to Hell" playing loudly in my ears, I cross the parking lot in the direction of Lecture Hall B4.

This morning, everything is going wrong. I can't wake up. Caffeine was of no use to me, and my shower decided to piss me off at seven o'clock: the water was freezing. My skin is still shivering!

I turn around a few feet from my car and lock it. A small smile appears on my face. This time, I arrived early, which is more like me. I was able to get the parking spot I was occupying last week…which is Tucker's spot. Oh yeah, there are other spots available. But my bitchy side couldn't resist.

I walk into the building, almost dragging my feet. The hallways are packed. Students are rushing in all directions to get to their next class. As I pass a group, a huge noise explodes behind me. My heart misses a beat as I turn abruptly.

The sound takes me back months and my throat suddenly closes. Was that a gunshot?

But I seem to be the only one who is worried about it. Around me, the students explode with laughter and seem excited by the noise, as if they were expecting it.

What the hell is this crap?!

A few feet away from me, a scream rings out in the crowd. Someone is howling to death, and it sounds like…wait, is he howling like a wolf?

The scream suddenly stops as everyone looks at each other, not knowing who just screamed. Another one is heard, a little further away this time. A student in a blue polo shirt and jeans passes through the crowd, handing out some papers. He greets the people while continuing his way. Once the flyer is in their hands, the students seem overexcited.

As he approaches, I notice his blond hair stopping at the nape of his neck and I recognize him. TJ, Tucker's friend!

His green eyes focus on me, and a big smile appears on his lips as he seems to recognize me in turn. He walks towards me with a much more measured step than the other night. The alcohol seems to have definitely left his body.

"And here is my pretty cab," he greets me cheerfully while standing in front of me.

I take a second to understand the name he gave me. "I am not your cab. I'm not a cab at all, I just helped your friend."

TJ continues to stare at me intently, as if looking for an answer in my face.

"Hum, hum, if you say so."

I roll my eyes and start to walk away.

"Hey!" he exclaims as he places himself back in front of me. "Damn, you're really not kidding, Tucker was right."

I let out a mocking laugh. Well, you learn a lot in a few seconds…

"Did you talk about me?"

"Of course we did. It's not every day that a pretty redhead comes into my life," he says, putting his hand theatrically against his heart.

"Iris. My name is Iris."

He nods, suddenly very serious.

"I'll write it down. I will use this information wisely."

TJ hands me a paper with brightly colored words printed on it.

"What's this?" I ask as I take it.

"That, my dear, is your invitation to push through the gates of hell."

My eyes land on the flyer:

The Pack has decided to expand, who wants to try
to join it?

"Really?" I asked. "Does this have anything to do with that guy who was acting like a wolf earlier? Let me tell you, that was more ridiculous than anything else. And what's this "Pack" thing anyway? Some kind of fraternity where all excesses are allowed?"

TJ gives me a simple wink before answering, "You're a newbie. The Pack…it's just the most influential group in the entire college. Look at all these kids," he says, glancing around at the people around us. "They all dream of being in it. Anyone can try out, but the spots are tough."

I don't really know what to say to him. I stare at him skeptically. Fraternities, sororities, and the like also exist in Portland. Their parties are insane. But I get the impression that Denver's are limitless.

"You have to come," TJ continues with an evil smile. "Next week."

I stare at his departing figure and wonder why everyone wants to join this fraternity. I finally glance at my watch, hurrying to my classroom.

The students are crowded in front of the door. Some exclaim in surprise as they enter, others laugh.

When I enter the lecture hall, I hold my breath. The huge room is filled with cotton balls…and hair? I bend down to pick up a soft little ball.

"It's sheep's wool!" exclaims a girl, on my right, cheerfully.

Disgusted, I drop the ball on the ground. But where have I landed? I thought the atmosphere in Portland was crazy, but the one in Denver is way beyond it.

"Do you know what's going on?" I ask the girl.

She stares at me with big eyes, as if I was stupid.

"The wolves are coming!"

"Then what? What does that mean?"

She approaches me and says in a tone of confidence, "It means that the debauchery starts and that nobody is safe from being bitten."

But what's their problem? I ignore the show and start walking up the stairs, determined not to get into this silly little game, whatever it is. Yet, as I see all eyes converge on the front of the lecture hall, I can't help but turn around.

Which one of you are we going to eat first?

I barely have time to digest the message written in chalk on the board when I feel a presence behind me. A look burns the back of my neck.

I turn around and find Tucker standing there with his arms crossed, watching me. I try not to let him see that his presence disturbs me as his vivid lightning eyes analyze my every reaction. His beard is a little more pronounced today. But why am I noticing all these damn details?

"So, do you have an idea?" he asks me seriously a second later.

He clenches his arms a bit more and I watch his biceps contract.

"An idea of what?"

"Who we're going to eat?" he continues with confidence.

The light turns on in my mind. I lean toward him.

"Wait…are you part of this crap?"

Tucker doesn't answer me. He continues to stare at me intently, and I understand that yes, he is indeed part of it. I remember his surprise when he saw me standing up to him when we met. He's not used to people standing up to him. Well, let me tell you, things are about to change.

Losing my patience, I walk down a row and sit in one of the middle seats, leaving him behind me. I don't have time to waste on a buffoon who thinks he's one of the kings of the campus. The seat I just took is not one of the "reserved" ones for him, so I'm sure he won't follow me. I pull out my computer, ignoring all the students who are slowly calming down.

As the screen turns on, I feel heat on my back, near my ear. Don't tell me he sat behind me!

I don't move, recognizing the masculine smell that imposes itself on me. Little hairs stand up on the back of my neck without asking me.

"It's you I'll eat first," Tucker whispers.

I turn my head angrily.

"Well, I hope you get indigestion, you big jerk."

His eyes almost glow as he settles in comfortably, once again surprised by my tone and the fact that someone is standing up to him. The students seem shocked to see him sitting here rather than in his usual place. Right behind me.

Tucker ignores them, unperturbed by their stares. He puts both hands on the table, like a true master of the place. Suddenly, the sound of Professor Richards' pumps echo through the walls. Finally! We will be able to move on.

"Good morning, everyone. I—did we just shoot a wild animal?" she exclaims, seeing the state of the lecture hall.

No one answers. I try to follow her class, painfully aware of the look on my face.

I have the impression that I have taken part in a little game in spite of myself, the rules of which I do not yet know.

5. GAME

IRIS

"So, back to business," sighs Professor Richards, rolling her eyes. "The other day we were only able to skim the introduction to the great course you are privileged to attend this semester. Now we're going to get to the heart of the matter."

Her piercing gaze rests on the students in the front rows. Her pumps click on the floor as she approaches them.

"You, young man," she announces, pointing to a student in the third row. "What does criminal science look like to your developing little brain? What is a criminologist?"

Just behind me, someone is clicking his pen incessantly. I take a deep breath, restraining myself from choking this "someone" otherwise known as "Mr. I-Want-To-Eat-People."

All eyes turn to the student the teacher has targeted. He seems to be thinking hard, running his hand over his chin in puzzlement.

"I'm not really sure, but…it's kind of like the ones on the show Criminal Minds?"

A few laughs are heard. The student gets a pellet of paper in his ear. He insults the person next to him, holding back his laughter, happy to amuse the crowd. Professor Richards does not seem to share their excitement. She crosses her arms and continues to stare at him, pursing her lips.

Oh, oh, I think that's not a good sign!

"What, what's so funny?" asks Professor Richard. She then addresses the student in the third row. "You're not really wrong, even if this show doesn't match reality."

The clicking continues right behind me, and I clench my fists. If I turn around and claw his eyes out, do I have any chance of getting out of this lecture hall alive, despite the pseudo-servants of the Pack who will no doubt jump on me?

Tucker seems to have taken me for a little lamb to chew on. But I wasn't kidding, I'm not a lamb. So his wolf delusions or whatever, let him stick them up his ass I guess.

I look around me. The noise doesn't seem to bother anyone, or else no one dares to say anything. Or maybe I'm just a little too on edge. I discreetly turn to Tucker, sitting right behind me. As I discover his small smile, I almost suppress a grunt. His different colored eyes seem to sparkle with amusement.

"Stop it," I breathe in his direction.

Both his elbows are resting on the wood, and he's leaning forward, much closer to me than I thought. He clicks his four-colored pen again, raises a dark eyebrow, and tilts his head slightly, as if he doesn't understand my request.

"Stop what?" he whispers to me with an innocent look.

My word, he wants to drive me crazy! I am now staring at him, and his smile widens. He understands perfectly my annoyance but doesn't care. Not being able to stand it anymore and wanting to show him that I am not a fragile little thing, I put my hand on his.

His fingers touch the worn wood. I lower my eyes on our hands with rage. My little hand looks ridiculous next to his much larger one, but I don't pull it away.

"Stop. This," I say again, whispering angrily.

He doesn't move, leaving his hand under mine. I raise my eyes and look into his. A few students are watching us attentively, like we're putting on a show for them. I don't move an inch, and neither does Tucker.

His lips part, and he is about to say something to me.

"Am I disturbing you?" exclaims a stern voice from behind me.

I widen my eyes. Maybe Professor Richards isn't talking to me? Or maybe, if I play dead, she'll forget about me?

"Seriously, this isn't speed dating. Take your fingers off your classmate's, you can resume your…activity later."

My cheeks start to heat up as the entire amphitheater turns to us. Tucker doesn't seem at all bothered. On the contrary, he settles a little more comfortably against his seat back.

"So…" he begins slowly. "Can I have my fingers back?"

Lost, I stare at his hand. Shit. I pull mine away as if I've just burned myself and turn to our teacher waiting on the dais, arms still crossed. I feel like I've become her new prey. She resumes her lecture without further comment, and the others eventually lose interest in me and focus on her words.

"So, as I was explaining, the profilers in this show have a role that is similar in some ways to a criminologist. Every professor of criminology will give you a different definition of the subject. Mine is simple. The purpose of criminology is to try to understand and analyze the implementation of a crime. My goal today is to open your mind. We will try to identify the human being behind the crime. I don't want to study the legal system, I don't want to study the consequences of his act. I want to study his motive."

I am hanging onto her every word. That is exactly why I came here. That is why I chose this subject in my psychology course. To understand the act of the monster who shot my parents. Who shot them in cold blood.

Flashes come back to me, and in each of them, a pool of blood is present. I swallow hard, trying to ignore the images that keep haunting me. Then I feel a cold sweat running down my back. Maybe my aunt was right. Maybe it was too soon to leave Portland? Maybe studying this subject will keep dragging me back into the past, keep hurting me, keep me from moving forward?

Yet my former therapist encouraged me to make these choices. I need explanations. I need to understand in my own way what happened in order to grieve.

Listening to his final advice, I mentally count to ten while closing my eyes. When I open them again, right after, the crisis is over. All is well.

"As I told you at the beginning of the first class, my subject is closely related to psychiatry and sociology, but also to criminal law. You will have to use your instincts and your logic to good effect. The key to understanding is the analysis of behavior."

My breath becomes regular again, but I still clench my fist on the desk.

"Are you okay?" asks my neighbor on the right, a petite brunette with glasses.

I turn to her, simply nodding.

"Okay," she continues gently, "because you look—"

"I'm fine," I cut her off.

Her eyes widen, and she turns her head, ignoring me again.

I hear a low chuckle behind me, proving to me that an onlooker has witnessed our little exchange that was anything but cordial. I ignore Tucker.

"I'm going to tell you something," Professor Richards continued. "Listen and analyze. A few years ago, a young woman named Lise Kosle was assaulted as she left the train station. A group of five men abducted her and took her to a building under construction. Four of the five individuals raped the young woman. The fifth man, when he was about to rape her, renounced his act. He gave up for a rather peculiar reason. When he was about to put on his condom, he had 'an engine failure.' This was a momentary physical impairment. He was still prosecuted. Only this man countered, he said that his momentary physical impairment showed his voluntary withdrawal. What do you think the judges said? Was he convicted?"

Well, I would be tempted to say no. I shake my head like most students.

I hear a slight rustling at my back. A husky voice reaches my ear.

"He's been convicted," Tucker announces, leaning toward me again, "I've heard this case before."

I turn my head slightly, trying to ignore him.

"I don't think so. The man played up the fact that the attempt was not carried out. To have an attempt, you need a beginning of execution and an involuntary interruption. Here, there is a beginning of execution but a voluntary interruption."

Tucker smiles softly. He leans in a little more, his masculine scent invading my nostrils.

"Want to bet?"

I roll my eyes even though he can't see it and give in to the temptation anyway, wanting to put him in his place.

"You're on."

Tucker sits back down in his seat.

Professor Richards finally says, "The man is being prosecuted for attempted rape. To characterize the attempt in broad terms, there must be a beginning of execution and an involuntary interruption. Here, the man wants to show that his momentary physical impairment is indeed a sign of voluntary abandonment."

I smile gently. Bingo, I won.

"However," she continues, "the judges contradict his position. For them, it was indeed an attempt because the interruption was involuntary. It was a deficiency that could be explained anatomically and did not reflect the will of the defendant. End of the story."

"Shit," I breathed to myself.

I can already imagine the delighted look of the jerk behind me, satisfied to have won.

A few minutes later, as the class ends and the room starts to empty, I rush out of the room and run down the stairs, my bag slung over my shoulder.

"Hey, redhead!" someone calls me just as I pass the door.

I stop abruptly and turn towards this so particular look, ready to fight. "What, now?"

Tucker slowly but confidently approaches me.

"I won," he announces to me with condescension.

I put on a bored, falsely disinterested face. "Oh, really?"

"You know," he continues, leaning toward me conspiratorially, "they give private tutoring for struggling students."

My jaw clenches and I try to keep myself from punching him in the face. "If you don't stop, you're going to have to take lessons to learn to walk again because I'm going to break your legs," I spit.

He raises an eyebrow, not worried at all. A guy nearby calls him, but Tucker ignores him, concentrating exclusively on our conversation.

"However, I won the bet."

"What do you want?" I grumble between my lips.

"I want you to come next week, to this little 'crap,' as you called it."

I scoff.

"That thing where the wolves will eat the defenseless lambs?"

I approach him, ignoring the pounding of my heart as it speeds up against my will due to the adrenaline. I'm smaller than him, but I'm not tiny. I stare into his eyes as he tilts his head slightly. His breath comes down on my lips.

"I am not a lamb. You're not going to eat me."

"Fighting lambs are the tastiest," he finishes.

"I don't want to be part of your game."

"Oh, but you just got in."

I can't read him. Usually it's pretty easy for me. People reveal their desires and intentions like an open book. But not him.

I have no idea what he's talking about or what his goal is, but if something stupid is going to happen, I'd rather control the situation. I don't think and retort, "Then let me set my rules."

He shakes his head slightly, and his Adam's apple moves slowly. "Rules are meant to be broken. No rules."

"So…what's the point of the game?"

Tucker doesn't answer me. Am I some kind of…challenge? Does he just want to ruin my life?

I see TJ approaching, a delighted expression on his face. Damn, that's all I needed. I turn around and start walking away, feeling Tucker's gaze on the back of my neck.

"You lost," he says in a loud voice. "Come next week."

Still with my back to him, I raise my middle finger in his direction and continue to walk away.

6. LET'S COLLIDE WITH EACH OTHER

IRIS

"Hey, Mrs. Psychologist!" someone shouts behind my back.

I stop abruptly in the middle of the cafeteria. Several students look around, just as confused as I am. I turn to the female voice, wondering if it's really me they're calling, and my eyes fall on beautiful dark hair. Yeleen. She waves her hand in my direction, and even from where I'm standing, I can see her dark eyes shining with joy. The other girl sitting at her table turns to me, looking inquisitive, as I walk toward them.

"No penis drawn in white on your forehead today?" I tease her theatrically.

She squints her eyes and sends me a fry, mocking the others' gaze. I must admit I like her attitude.

"Sit down with us," Yeleen suggests.

I notice a few envious looks on people's faces. Strange…

I look outside, then at my poor sandwich, then at her table. Without thinking, I accept her offer with a shrug. Lunch with them doesn't seem so bad.

"I'm Sarah," says the pretty brunette sitting next to Yeleen as I take a seat opposite her.

"Iris."

Her blue eyes contrast with her tanned skin, and, to my amazement, she holds out her hand. My gaze wanders to the Rolex hanging on her wrist.

Yeleen crunches another French fry and then rolls her eyes.

"Stop acting so formal," she laughs, staring at Sarah, "you look like one of those cheerleading bitches."

A laugh comes out of my mouth as the brunette shoots her an offended look. "Do I look like I want to wiggle my ass around a field pretending to be happy?" She looks to me then, amused. "Forgive me, I was just trying to look civilized."

"So," Yeleen continues, turning to me, "what were you doing all alone like a lost soul?"

I glance down at my sandwich. "I'm not alone, and I'm not lost; I just came to fill my belly before hunger drove me to steal a snack from one of the little students."

The two girls burst out laughing.

"I'm telling you," Sarah sighs, "I'd like to find a little student for myself too. I'm tired of being in a relationship with the single life, if you know what I mean…"

"I thought you were seeing that guy from the baseball team?" asks Yeleen with a conspiratorial air.

Sarah shrugs a delicate shoulder as she pokes her salad with her fork.

"I still prefer to stay single."

"I could change your mind," TJ's voice rings out right behind her.

"Shut up," Yeleen growls, throwing a fry at him.

He catches the fry on the fly and stuffs it into his mouth with an amplified grunt. When he notices my presence, his eyes widen. "My best friend!" he shouts.

"Please stop with that," I say, holding back a smile.

Sarah and Yeleen watch as TJ walks around the table and sits down next to me.

"You know that little prick?" Yeleen asks, laughing, after a few seconds.

"We're best friends," TJ says without letting me say a word.

I shake my head, silently articulating, "Not at all," to the two girls.

TJ leans toward me. "I will behave, I promise. I don't want to die."

I raise an eyebrow at him. "Who would kill you?"

I don't like the way he looks, but he doesn't answer me. "So…" I continue, "are you three friends?"

They nod and Sarah answers, "I've been putting up with them

for three years, much to my dismay—ouch!" she exclaims when Yeleen kicks her under the table. "We're all part of the same gang."

I freeze, trying to understand her words. The same gang of buddies? I remember TJ handing out flyers a few days earlier.

"You're all part of the…Pack?"

They nod in unison, which is quite disorienting.

Damn, wait, I had to run into the Public Danger group? Am I destined to cross paths with Tucker for the rest of my education or what?

I finally understand the look a few people gave me when I sat down a few minutes ago, the envy in their eyes. They must be wondering what I'm doing here. And I wonder why TJ and Yeleen seem to welcome me so well when the seats next to them are supposed to be so dear?

I'm almost ready to grab my sandwich and make a quick escape when Sarah asks me a question. "What are you studying?"

"I'm a junior in psychology. I have to g—" I start by moving my chair back.

"Oh, interesting!" Sarah cuts me off. "Maybe you'll help me to understand the behavior of my asshole of a father-in-law," she says, laughing softly.

TJ leans in and puts his elbows on the table. "She has a criminal science class with Tucker."

Sarah stops laughing and stares at the blond with a frown. "Oh yeah?" She then turns to me. "Do you two know each other?"

Her totally opposite attitude to the one she had a moment earlier gives me pause.

I choose my words, "Not really."

But TJ intervenes, happy to add his two cents. "Actually, yeah, they know each other. Tucker had a flat tire the other day. She picked him up like a wounded little animal on the road."

I elbow him.

Sarah tries to keep a friendly face, but the signs are clear. She looks extremely serious when she nods. I have a habit of picking up on all the little details that make us *us*, and what I see from her doesn't look like friendliness at all.

Could there be something between Sarah and Tucker?

Immediately, I feel that my body is on the defensive. Yeleen nibbles on her fries and says, "So, where's Tucker?"

TJ glances at me before answering, "He's sorting something out with Dan."

He doesn't say anything more, but the girls seem to understand because they nod with a knowing look, leaving me in a state of incomprehension. But it's not like I should care, right?

I hold back for a few seconds but the questions finally come out on their own, "So, what's with this Pack thing? Is it more than a group of friends?" I admit, I ask more than I wanted to, but curiosity drives me to do it.

"Yeah. You're looking at the kings of the campus, baby," TJ replies.

I raise my eyebrows. I'm not really into this kind of thing, people who think they're the kings of the world or something. Yeleen shakes her head, easing my irritation by cutting off her friend, "I know how we're seen by everyone here, but I promise we're not the kings of the world or big tyrannical snobs! But if these morons want to let us have the best seats in the lecture halls and to polish our shoes, we won't complain."

TJ looks offended for a second before leaning in my direction, "But of course we're the kings of the world and big bullying snobs. You don't get to the top by playing Care Bears. Here it's the law of the strongest. You have to show them who's boss."

I tilt my head to the side.

"Well, it makes you really want to join the TJ Empire," I say.

Yeleen elbows the young blond man to show her disagreement. "Don't listen to this idiot. I assure you we're pretty cool."

"And how did you create your 'group?'"

Yeleen swallows what she had in her mouth before answering me. "Freshman year, I met Tucker and TJ. We started hanging out together without mixing with the others, just the three of us. Then Sarah joined us, and a few others you don't know."

"And we started throwing the best parties ever," TJ continues, his eyes shining. "No limits. No restrictions. The world of nightlife was open to us. Not many students were invited. Rumors started flying and we let it happen. It was kind of fun…and then it got bigger and bigger as it went on."

Parties with no limits. I know I can't allow myself to be attracted to this. I can't attend stuff like this if I want to keep a totally stable life.

"But one rumor is true," Yeleen finished. "If you touch any of us, we will destroy you. It doesn't matter who messed with our buddy. If you hurt one of us, you have to deal with the others. Maybe that's our strength. We stick together."

And I finally understand the meaning of the name The Pack.

I wonder what the sentence on the flyer means. They're letting new people into the group? Why?

But I don't ask them a new question. I'm not looking for a buddy group. I just want to live in peace, to build a new life where my past has no hold.

"So, which player on the baseball team were you talking about before I came in?" TJ says, stifling a yawn before staring at the remains of my sandwich. "Are you going to finish that?"

"No one," Yeleen and Sarah exclaim in chorus as I hand my leftovers to TJ.

"Come on girls, be nice," he almost begs, his mouth full.

"So that you can go find your little teammate and make fun of me? No, thanks."

TJ shrugs his shoulders and takes an innocent air. "Male solidarity, I can't help it, honey."

"Are you on the baseball team?" I ask.

He nods, swallowing his last bite.

"So, have you thought about it? Are you coming to our little party next week?" he asks me.

"I'm not sure she's a lamb," Yeleen cuts him off with a chuckle.

As I am about to answer them negatively, my phone rings. The name of my aunt appears.

Shit!

I get up in a hurry. "I have to go, bye!" I don't wait for their answer and hurriedly pick up the phone, leaving the cafeteria. "Hello?" I ask, catching my breath.

At the same time, a lightning bolt strikes near the campus. Wait…don't tell me I left the convertible hood open on my car, right? Don't tell me it's going to rain just to make my day completely suck?

"Agnes just got out of the hospital," my aunt tells me.

"What?" I shout in the middle of the hallway, just before putting my hand over my mouth. "What do you mean? What happened? Is it bad? I'm going to get on a plane, I can—"

"No, everything is fine, but Agnes had a hysterical fit. I didn't know what to do."

A thunderclap sounds. I have no choice but to turn around and head for the parking lot.

"So you took her to the hospital?"

"What did you want me to do?" she asks me in a stern tone.

"Calm her down! Put her in a quiet place. Sit with her, talk to her. Make her understand that she is not a prisoner of her past but free of her present. For God's sake, she's just a little girl!"

I hear Emma sigh through the phone. I pick up the pace, now furious.

"I didn't know what to do," my aunt finally whispers.

I take a deep breath. I know it's hard for her, having a kid on her hands for a while. I know it is. "Look, I…next time, call me and put her on, okay? I'll talk to her as soon as I can."

"All right," she says. "I'll ask her to call you tonight."

She hangs up without waiting for my answer. I close my eyes and swallow another swear word. I finally get to the exit door and push it open while stuffing the damn phone in my bag.

It is at this moment that I bump into a male torso.

My cell phone lands on the floor, and I almost fall while the man doesn't move an inch. A hand is firmly placed on my right hip, stabilizing me.

Still staring at the ground, I bend down to pick up my phone. "Damn it," I growl.

But thank God it doesn't have any scratches!

"Are you okay?" a male voice asks me.

Still crouching, I hold back a grunt as I recognize Tucker's voice. Seriously? I think the universe is against me today.

"Do I look okay?" I mumble as I put my phone away, securing it for good.

I straighten up, and he gently squints his peculiar eyes, which look slightly wet. A smell of soap wafts from his body as he crosses his arms, and my gaze strays to his biceps under his jacket.

Stop! I have no desire to have my stupid mind disturbed at this moment. Enough of the bullshit.

Still pissed off, I walk to my car. All right, it's not raining yet, that's lucky.

"I'm fine too," he taunts me. "You should watch your step next time, redhead."

I turn around, furious. This is absolutely not the time to mess with me, handsome.

"You're the one who bumped into me," I spit out. "And my hair," I breathe as I approach him, "screws you deeply."

He bends his head slightly, apparently delighted with my answer. Or rather pleased that I'm entering the verbal joust. I get the impression that his goal is to piss me off.

His eyes begin to glow the moment he comes up with an adequate answer, and I purse my lips.

"Trust me, I'm not in the mood."

He must see in my face that I am not joking. He comes a little closer and smooths out my bangs as if he wanted to analyze my hair more closely. What's his problem?!

"Are you alright?" His hoarse voice is serious now.

On principle, I don't back down. I keep my eyes on his as my body tenses. It's my stupid mind acting up again. "Do you think I would tell you if something was wrong?"

Tucker smiles softly, and I notice that his bottom lip is a little fuller than the top one. He runs his tongue over it, as if he's holding back from speaking.

Something splashes onto the middle of my forehead. I touch it with my fingertip: rain. No! As the downpour begins, Tucker pushes me toward the entrance of the building.

"Shit," he growls, "let's get inside before we look like wet dogs again."

The students who were outside rush in with us, some of the girls squealing as they pass. Tucker is about to take cover but notices me walking in the opposite direction.

"What the hell are you doing?" he shouts in a deep voice in my direction.

Under the increasingly powerful torrents of water, I yell, "My car!"

I rush to my Chevrolet as the rain hits the worn leather inside. This car is all I have left of my father. I will never ever let it be destroyed. I'll never let go like that idiot Rose in Titanic did!

"Damn it," someone swears behind me. "You crazy chick."

I hear footsteps pounding on the ground behind me as I finally arrive at my car. I jump into the driver's seat, which is also taking on water, and turn on the ignition. The top goes up a little bit and then stops. It's stuck.

"No, no, come on, baby," I moan, my hair sticking to my face.

"It looks like the rain is trying to send us a message!" Tucker exclaims as he comes up beside me.

"What the hell are you doing? Go back inside, you idiot."

Despite the rain, I notice the small smile on his face, but it quickly fades as I start chattering my teeth, completely soaked. Tucker unzips his jacket and throws it at me.

"Put that on," he commands me as he sits in the passenger seat and tries to find the manual roof mechanism.

Stunned, I don't move a muscle as he manually forces it open. Water drips down his arms in the midst of his effort. I approach him and, without thinking, position the coat over both our heads. Our bodies are soaked but our heads are safe, temporarily.

"Come on," I almost beg, and his eyes suddenly catch mine.

A new thunderclap rings out as the hood finally decides to cooperate. The roof closes slowly.

Nevertheless, Tucker doesn't move, an enigmatic look on his face. Why did he come to help me when he usually enjoys pissing me off? I can't process him, and my brain comes out frustrated. This guy is really too complex.

But isn't complexity what makes things more attractive?

No, no, no. No, no, no. Nonsense. I don't need complexity in my life! I step back and slap his now soaked jacket on his chest.

7. PACK LEADER

IRIS

"Okay, are you ready?" Buck asks me as he walks around the bar to join me.

He doesn't wait for my answer and hands me a tray with four beers on it. I pick it up, trying not to spill anything.

"What? Wait, should I start serving straight away?"

"You didn't think I was going to put you behind the bar? You never know, you might water down a beer, and I don't want to be in trouble with Billy."

I roll my eyes.

Buck smiles softly, digging his one dimple in his left cheek. "Come on, cutie, go charm those big guys."

I hold back a curse at his stupid nickname. His few extra years seem to make him think he can call me anything he wants. But this is my first night at High Peaks Bar, and I don't want to get fired after five minutes of work.

I take a deep breath and head to the table I'm supposed to serve. I'm lucky that I'm not shy, or at least I know how to hide my shyness under a tough cookie look. I get to the table where four local bikers are sitting, each one more serious than the other. They give me a quick hello, and I don't waste any time in going back to the bar.

Buck is serving a pretty blonde who seems under his spell. Once she walks away with her drink, I slap my hand on the counter and place the empty tray on it, a triumphant expression on my face.

"Come on, cutie, give me the next order!"

Buck turns to me, eyebrows raised. "You didn't kill anyone on the way?"

I stop myself from rolling my eyes again as he prepares a second order for me.

The door to the bar opens and a girl from my cognitive psychology class enters, quickly followed by two other girls. High Peaks Bar seems to gather the entire population of the city on Saturday nights, especially the students. Most of them are near the two pool tables at the back of the room. My gaze wanders to them, and it is a completely different student that comes to mind. A far too invasive memory comes to mind: a tall, dark, soaking wet man staring at me with his different colored eyes as the rain pours down on us.

I mentally slap myself. It took Tucker coming to my rescue for me to almost—and I emphasize "almost"—find him sympathetic. As he scrutinized me in great detail the other day, my body seemed in no hurry to escape, as if delighted to remain paralyzed under the spell of his hypnotic gaze.

Wait, did I really just have this stupid thought? Damn it, get me out of here before I become a romance novel heroine!

A tanned hand rises to my face. Buck snaps his fingers an inch from my face.

"Hey," I grumble, stepping back.

"Are you still here?" he asks me. "You weren't listening at all to what I was saying."

I straighten my chin, putting a hand on the back pocket of my tight jeans. "Of course, I was."

"So, take that tray over to the table I just indicated," he teases, handing me the drinks.

I turn to the crowd. Shit, which table did he just tell me about? I hear a laugh behind my back.

"At the end on the right!"

"I knew that," I mumble through my teeth as I walk over to the seven students gathered around a small table of four.

After handing a Coke to a strong-jawed blond man who keeps staring at me strangely, I rush to serve the others to escape his interested gaze. I feel his eyes burn into my back as I cross the room, reaching the bar while tucking a short strand of hair back behind my ear. Do we know each other? No, he doesn't look familiar.

The front door opens once more. I let out a sigh as TJ enters the bar, one hand in his pocket, the other tugging at the braid of the tall brunette accompanying him—Sarah. Yeleen enters right behind him, a tall guy on her heels, her gaze focused on her phone. My eyes linger behind them. Thank God, no sign of Tucker...

The eyes of the students in the bar turn to them. Some greet them while others just observe them. It's crazy how Yeleen and her gang attract attention among the partygoers. They must know that they are dealing with the infamous Pack.

I turn my back on the newcomers. Buck watches me from behind the counter. With a teasing look on his face, he points to the table TJ and company are sitting at. I hold back from glaring at my new colleague and pull out the little notebook stuck in the back pocket of my jeans.

It's only when I get a few steps away from their table that Yeleen, who is fiddling with the hair of the tall guy next to her, finally notices me. The guy with her turns his attention to me. Given his build, I guess he practices a competitive sport and must be a real machine on the field. Yeleen gives me a big smile when I reach the table.

"Welcome," I begin.

TJ turns his head in my direction, his blond eyebrows rising in surprise.

"My best friend!"

I squint as I open the notebook, "Stop calling me that, TJ. I'm not your best friend."

He's amused by my sulky expression, and I can't seem to get mad at him. His pseudo-unhappy expression almost makes me smile. It gets to me.

He laughs softly and crosses his arms, "Or what?"

I snap my pen with a psychopath look on my face. "If you don't stop, I'll poke your eyes out."

"So does that mean I won't be able to look at those two little mandarins standing in front of me?"

Yeleen and the others hold back a laugh as I frown. What is he...? His gaze lingers on my breast until I understand.

My eyes glare at him as I retort, "Well, we understand each other, between fruits."

"Between fruits?"

"My breasts, the mandarins. And I'm sure your balls look like two small plums."

He suddenly stops laughing while the others laugh loudly. To lighten the mood, Yeleen asks, "How long have you been working here?"

"This is my first night, actually."

"I worked here for a few months," says the guy next to her. "The pay isn't great, but Billy is cool, you'll see. I'm Trey," he introduces himself and puts his hand on Yeleen's shoulder. I quickly realize that they are together.

"Iris," I reply.

"Well, for a not-so-great paycheck, you might as well work somewhere else," says Sarah, pursing her lips in disgust.

I turn to her and tilt my head to the side. "Why come here if you don't like it here?" I hate her condescending tone, but I refrain from calling her names out loud. The first thing my mother taught me is that you shouldn't judge a person by their appearance. My psychology classes confirmed this, but sometimes it's hard.

Sarah looks at her friends as if they were the reason she came. I don't linger any longer and take their order before adding in a voice that I hope sounds completely disinterested, "Will that be all…?"

"Uh, yes…four people, four drinks?" Yeleen answers me, lost.

"We aren't expecting anyone else. No one is going to join us tonight," TJ insists, holding back a small smile.

I shrug a shoulder, ignoring his far too scrutinizing look, and walk away from their table. I don't let him tell me about their little party again. The other students have done it enough as it is. All day I've heard them talking about it, wondering if they'd dare go. Even at the fucking library where silence is the watchword.

A few minutes later, after their drinks are served, Buck gives me my first break.

"I'll buy you a shot," he says.

I'm sure my face is filled with horror and I try to hide my emotions quickly.

"I…no, thanks."

"Come on, as a new employee, you get one drink when you're on duty."

"I don't drink," I reply, with a lump in my throat.

"You don't like alcohol?" he teases, resting his elbows on the counter. "Let me remind you that you are a waitress in a bar. A drink is nothing."

I stare at him silently. What's that got to do with it? And what does he care, anyway?

A drink is not nothing. Because one drink leads to another. And then you're in trouble and you're making trouble. I know what I'm talking about. An unpleasant flash comes back to me, like an electroshock. A single image rises in my head, spinning in a loop.

I snap out of my lethargy, and an unpleasant shiver runs up my spine as I struggle to swallow my saliva.

"No, thank you," I refuse a little more firmly before going to get the payment from the first group of students.

When I arrive at their table, the blond guy from earlier keeps on staring at me. Can't he see that I'm not responding at all to his enamored fucking looks? As he hands me a twenty, I lean over and pinch it between my index finger and thumb. His other hand wraps around my wrist.

"Are you new?"

"Take your hand away," I growl.

One of his buddies laughs into his beard like a fool. The blond guy doesn't move an inch. He continues to stare at me, and it's very embarrassing. His fingers squeeze me almost painfully, but I don't let it show on my face.

I'm nice—well, most of the time—and tonight is my first night on the job, but there's no way I'm going to be nice for some asshole to get off my back. I'm about to insult him, even headbutt him, at my own risk, when a deep voice slams into my back.

"Is there a problem?"

I recognize this voice perfectly, but I don't move. I am not a fragile little thing. Life has given me a lot of knocks and I've never broken, so it won't happen tonight. The blond finally looks away to Tucker and crumbles. He lets go of me with a resigned look.

"I was wrong," he laughs softly, apologetically.

"To err is human. Many humans are errors," I finish in a gentle tone.

And you are one, my conscience growls.

I don't hesitate a second, get my change to turn to walk away while he and his buddies leave the table. The blond guy walks by me. I see Tucker whispering something to him as he passes, but I can't hear. His body is completely tense, as if he was about to jump on someone.

"What did you say to him?"

"Are you okay?" he asks me in a low but powerful voice, without answering me.

"Of course. I was handling the situation, I didn't need your help."

Tucker stares at the door behind which the blond man disappears, giving me one last look.

"Matt is a son of a bitch."

My mouth opens in surprise at the harshness of his words. Both his fists are clenched and the long-sleeved black top he wears does nothing to hide his tense muscles.

"Do you know him?"

"Listen," he says, running his hand over his unshaven cheeks, "stay away from him."

His sentence sounds like an order to my ears and leaves no room for an answer. I don't even have time to react when he walks away and joins his friends on the other side of the room. His broad shoulders help him to make his way between the people who are starting to indulge in some dance moves. My eyes go down by themselves along his legs that his jeans mold perfectly to.

I stare at his buttocks without restraint before mentally slapping myself.

After a few seconds, TJ turns his head in my direction, losing his smile while Tucker seems to grumble something. What's their problem? TJ nods his head seriously as if he is drinking Tucker's words greedily. The latter crosses his arms, making no effort to integrate himself into a possible conversation. But when he opens his mouth for a second, his tablemates give him their full attention. It's almost as if he gives off an aura around him, attracting all eyes, as if he rules over this small piece of territory.

And then I understand.

I've just found the leader of the pack.

8. FALLING INTO HIS TRAP

IRIS

Another one?!

I don't need to look at the poster in front of which two students are standing to know what it is: the same stupid ads for people to gather at the wolf party this weekend.

"I don't want my roommate to go," one girl whispers to her friend. "She gets all starry-eyed talking about it, and it pisses me off."

Finally, someone who is not totally overexcited about this?

I walk towards the black and white poster, pretending to be interested in it while listening to what they are saying.

"I hate this stupid stuff," sighs the other. "TJ is always bragging. We all know how the manhunt ends. Last year it ended badly. One of us ended up in the morgue and no one seems to care."

What?

My mouth opens by itself, "Excuse me, do you know what this party is about, exactly"

The little brunette stares at me strangely.

"Do you want to go?" she asks, still staring at me.

I shrug one shoulder, pretending to think. In reality, I'm not planning on it.

"Maybe I do."

Her friend laughs sarcastically, "A word of advice, don't go. Trust me, you don't want to get involved in their little games. I wonder what they have planned this year…"

I frown, confused. What they have planned…? It's just a stupid party between students who have to drink more alcohol than they should, right? I don't see what could happen to me—I mean, besides ending up in the morgue, apparently.

"You said a girl died at this party. What exactly happened? What's with the manhunt?"

Neither of them answers me. I lose my patience, "Damn it, girls, this isn't Twilight. Am I going to run into Jacob Black or what?"

They raise their eyebrows at the same time, not finding my joke funny at all. I guess the important thing is that I think I'm hilarious?

They walk away mumbling, leaving me with my questions. Why do most of them seem eager for the evening to arrive and others totally repulsed by the idea? And Tucker, Yeleen, TJ, and the whole gang are connected to the death of a girl? What happened?

I shake my head and enter the B4 lecture hall, trying to forget about this crap for the moment.

I purposely choose a seat on the right side, avoiding the spot where Tucker usually stands. I don't want to be near him right now, not when I'm wondering what the fuck his role in all of this is. Maybe he's more dangerous than I thought. But he's a student, damn it. What could he possibly be doing that's so dangerous?

The class goes on in a rather unnerving calm. Professor Richards's lecture is interesting, but my eyes keep wandering down the rows near me. They search for a single person, who seems absent.

No sign of Tucker.

It's only when I get to my car an hour later that I run into him.

Tucker is leaning against his pickup, arms crossed, staring at me. A rather tall, angry guy is talking to him with big gestures. Tucker continues to stare at me though. I attempt a small smile in his direction, just to be polite. After all, we are on good terms, right? Despite his caveman behavior a few days ago at the bar, he still saved my car.

The guy in front of him sighs and turns his head to look at what Tucker is staring at, which is me. Tucker mutters something, and his friend finally gets into the pickup, slamming the door. Who was that? Another member of his group?

Tucker doesn't take a step in my direction. Arms still crossed, jaw still clenched, he watches me intently, as if waiting for I don't know what.

So I do what I do best. I turn my back on him and climb into my car, ignoring him.

Tonight is my first time behind the bar. Thanks to my success last weekend and this early evening, Buck seems to have decided to trust me. So here I am, serving a pint of beer to a guy who grunts a "Thank you" when I hand him his drink.

A throaty sound catches my attention. I turn around slowly, a polite smile on my face…a smile that quickly turns into a grimace.

"Are you following me?"

With a wry look on his face, Tucker raises an eyebrow as he parks himself on his stool. "I'm not allowed to come here to drink on a Friday night?"

I lean over the counter and sigh, keeping myself from rolling my eyes, "Don't take me for a dummy, it doesn't say 'dumb' on my forehead."

As Tucker leans over, he scans my forehead, as if he's trying to read something.

I straighten up and mime, "Idiot," with my lips.

"Buck will…take care of you," I try to say, pointing to my colleague who is now at the other end of the room, in the middle of a flirting session with a beautiful woman. "Well, what can I get you?"

"Actually, I didn't come to drink."

No kidding? See, I was right, this asshole is following me. Upon noticing my irritated look, Tucker points to a couple of guys by the pool table behind him, "Relax, redhead, I'm with friends."

"Go back to your buddies, then."

A small smile appears on his face. He passes his hand over his unshaven cheek and continues with a teasing voice, "But I'm fine here."

A chick a little further away stares at him without discretion. I'm sure he's noticed her, but he doesn't seem to mind.

"You seem to have a new fan," I laugh.

He shrugs.

"A lot of people think they like me. Others hate me. And you want to know the good news, Iris? I don't give a shit."

I resume, "Well…I have to work."

He seems to like the stern tone of my voice even more, as if he was delighted to piss me off.

"Then accept it," he suddenly and firmly orders me.

I frown, puzzled, "Accept what, exactly?"

"Come to my place tomorrow night," he says.

I hold back a little laugh. "Seriously, does this usually work? You put on your tough guy face, and the girls come running like little bitches in heat?"

He nods, clearly admitting it to me.

"I won't come to your place. Besides, aren't you having your little party tomorrow or something?"

"Exactly," he replies. "This is all happening on my property."

I raise an eyebrow. His property?

Tucker leans in, his different colored eyes staring at me as if trying to undress me. "I want you to come over."

I'm not going to say I'm not curious, because that would be lying. But the truth is, I can't. I can't get into their games and see what they have planned. And anyway, I have things to do: homework, laundry…yeah, my weekend is going to be exciting…

"And what exactly is going to happen?"

Even if I don't go, it doesn't hurt to find out, right?

"You'll only find out if you come."

"On the posters, you say you want to recruit new wolves. So, what, you're going to hold trials to get your Pack to grow?" I suggest, not really believing it.

Tucker doesn't answer me, telling me I'm on the right track. I can't believe it. What the hell is this shit? So that's it, they're doing some kind of job interview?

I decide to hammer the point home and get him to respond, "Some girls said something about a manhunt."

He squints his eyes. His jaw becomes a little more square while his broad shoulders tighten. "Oh, really?"

"They talked about something else too," I whisper, approaching. "A girl who ended up in the morgue, any word on that?"

He steps back as if I've just hit him.

"That's bullshit," he spits, now furious.

Oh oh, I seem to have struck a chord. His reaction doesn't tell me anything. He's hiding something, and I'm not sure it's in my best interest to find out what. But another question keeps running through my head.

"Why do you insist that I come?"

My question seems to calm him down a bit. He's focused on something else now: me. "I told you, I want to eat you."

His sentence should repel me, but it doesn't. Not entirely. His words warm my skin in ways that shouldn't be allowed.

"What if I don't want to be eaten? Has it ever occurred to you that someone might not want to be part of your Pack?"

My defiant look fuels him even more, I can see that, but I can't seem to stray from it.

"Are you sure about this? That you don't want it? *'It's our choices that show who we truly are, far more than our abilities,'* you know. So choose wisely."

I burst out laughing, unable to hold back at those words.

"Are you quoting Harry Potter to me now?"

"Don't insult Dumbledore."

Tucker leans a little closer to me. His face is only a few inches away from mine, but there's no way I'm going to move back first. I stare at him without flinching even though my heartbeat is racing against my will. I don't know what's going on but I don't like this at all. I don't like the attraction that exists between us at this moment. It is dangerous. It means trouble.

He too seems disturbed. He frowns, still close to me. His hot breath falls on my half-open mouth. His pupils almost dilate.

"Come over," he whispers. "Unless you're afraid?"

I can see that he thinks I'm going to refuse again and I don't want to prove him right. And at the same time, I know that he is setting a trap for me by challenging me, by provoking me to make me look like a coward if I say no. So I decide to fall into his trap willingly, ready to turn it all against him as soon as possible.

"I'll come," I say in a determined voice as I stand up. "Let's see if the wolf isn't really a big doggie in need of affection. I'll bring some kibble."

He starts to back away, a little smile on his face. "Your little body will be enough."

Then he walks away, joining his friends on the other side of the room.

9. THE HUNT IS ON

IRIS

The road is rather slippery tonight. Through the windshield of my car, all I see is black. Absolute blackness.

I thought several times about hitting the brake pedal and turning around. But finally, here I am about six miles from the address that was indicated on the posters. At the beginning of the evening, I had changed my mind and decided to stay home. And then, at seven o'clock sharp, a number sent me a text message.

[Don't be afraid, little lamb.]

I quickly realized who it was. I wonder how that bastard Tucker got my number!

Now there was no way to give up, the part of my brain that loves adventure had taken control of my body, guiding it through mechanical gestures.

My car left the busy avenues of the city a few minutes ago. As I drive along a road trying to see signs of life outside, I almost miss a narrow passage on my right. I slam on the brake, stopping on the roadside.

Crap. According to my GPS, I'm supposed to turn here to get to the party venue. Is this a joke?

The headlights of my Chevrolet light up the road as I drive over it. Strangely, it's not in bad shape. I'm expecting my car to get tossed around between potholes on a dirt path, but the ground is covered with a mixture of tar and gravel that makes my tires squeal. After a hundred meters, the path widens a bit. I am in the middle of the woods and still nothing on the horizon. I already have in my mind dozens of horror scenarios in which I get slit or disemboweled at the end.

The road forces me to turn right. My headlights illuminate a huge black wrought iron gate.

But what…who would come to live in the middle of a fucking forest? Why not have an apartment in the heart of the city, where there are signs of life, you know?

The gate is open, like some kind of direct invitation from Lucifer. Okay, I lose focus. With my car still at a standstill, I lean over and squint to read what is written above the gate: "Bomley Property."

I hold back a grunt. I don't even know the last name of the intense-eyed idiot. I may actually be entering the domain of an old psychopath who will greet me with a rifle and a scream.

Come on Iris, you're not a wimp!

After all, I'm the one who played it smart by accepting Tucker's invitation. Besides, I want to know what's going on over there…

But a bad feeling comes over me, as if I'm not going to find a simple crowd dancing and drinking cheap beer.

A bang a few hundred feet away shuts down my thoughts. I jump and hold back a curse. Was that really a gunshot? It can't be!

Before I chicken out again, I go through the gate and follow a second gravel path. There is an alley of trees surrounding it as if to hide the view of the whole surrounding landscape from us. Finally, lights dot the sides of the road.

In another minute, I arrive in a circular drive. In the center of this driveway is a huge fountain, currently dry—let us note the utility of the thing. The structure represents a naked woman looking straight ahead.

Here is the wolves' domain.

Behind the statue, a huge mansion stands. Its structure reminds me of the buildings of the Victorian era. The large white walls and the dark roof are held by large columns, also white. The numerous windows do not let me see anything of the interior. Only one of them is lit, probably with good reason. I take a look around. There are no cars here except mine.

I roll down my window and hear noises in the distance. Music, laughter…I see another path, on the right, which goes around the house, and I take it.

Believe me, the owner is going to pay me for a full tank of gas.

The noises get a little louder. Along the road, dozens of cars are parked directly on the lawn.

Okay, so is this a garden party, or what?

There are a few streetlights planted here and there on the estate, allowing me to see my surroundings. I park next to a Cadillac and start walking towards the lawn when I hear some female laughter. Two girls are kissing—wait, two girls share a man's mouth against the door of a car, three feet away.

If I've just been invited to an orgy, thanks but no thanks. Genitals that go everywhere don't enter mine. I don't want to turn into a walking STD.

Noticing the girls' outfits, namely, their tiny dresses, I think that my shorts jeans and black camisole might not have been the right thing to wear, but never mind.

A light wind blows my red hair out of my face. Luckily my hair is short. I'd hate for it to tangle up like spaghetti in the slightest wind.

I don't recognize most of the people I walk by. Most of them are overexcited and shout to communicate.

"Hello, beauty," a pretty brunette greets me while passing by, her eyes full of lust.

With a pinched mouth, I nod and go on my way. The road stops. My boots sink into the lawn. I swear to God that the first person to step on me will end up castrated.

My eyes suddenly lock onto a spot in the distance, right in the middle of the estate's lawn, where a huge fire is burning about 100 feet high. Are we all supposed to burn the forest together, or what?

Music coming from who knows where roars over the small crowd. Alcohol is flowing. Some are dancing. A girl is sitting on the lap of a guy sitting on the ground, making out with him as though nothing is happening around them.

I search the place, looking for a familiar face. I see TJ from afar, but he seems busy. He goes from group to group and whispers something to some, whose faces light up. The others are obviously waiting for TJ to lean in as well, and they hardly hide their disappointment when he walks away. The few chosen ones to whom he has spoken go towards a small path, further away, and I follow them for a moment with my eyes before returning my attention to the flames, which I move a little closer to. I'm cold, and it's none of my business where those people are going.

I'm starting to think that it's not so bad after all, when I hear a crack right behind me.

I'm sure someone is standing right there, unabashedly staring at my back and neck. I don't turn around, instead listening for the slightest noise. It's like a presence is filling my whole living space without asking permission. And I've felt that way before, when a slightly too sexy, different-colored eyes asshole was around.

At the risk of sounding like a weirdo, I cross my arms, pout skeptically, and loudly declare, "So, this is the little party? Easy girls and easy guys stripping on the floor? I've seen worse." No one answers me. I continue, still staring at the flames, "Is Mr. Grey hidden between the trees, ready to give us a little demonstration?"

Finally, an answer comes to me: a deep, powerful laughter sounds right behind me. Bingo.

The footsteps come closer. Tucker doesn't touch me, but he may as well. The heat of the flames warms my face, and the heat of his body warms my back. Unable to bear it, I take a step to the side and turn toward him.

His arms are also crossed over his broad chest. His head is tilted to the side as he analyzes me. His black hair is slightly wavy, and his beard is a little longer than usual. His torso is molded by a simple black T-shirt and his thighs in denim.

No weird cult outfit or anything. That was a close shave.

"Hi," he finally says, in a loud voice, after a few seconds.

I was expecting a pique or even a line from Harry Potter, not for him to greet me like we were old acquaintances or buddies. Which we aren't.

With a skeptical pout on my face, I turn halfway to the fire, still keeping him in my sights. I point to the flames with my chin. "You invited me to a campfire party? Gee," I say with a fake look of sadness, "maybe I should have brought marshmallows?"

A muffled noise sounds in his chest. "Come with me," he orders me as he moves closer, ignoring my joke.

I ignore him. "What's the program? Are we going to hold hands and jump around the fire singing cheesy songs?"

My tone is teasing, but deep down, I am somewhat relieved. I was expecting something fishy when I came here, only for it be not that far from a normal student party, except for a few details.

His hand rests firmly on my hip. He leans into my ear and whispers, "Come…with…me."

I run my tongue over my lips as his palm practically burns my skin through my top. As he pulls away, a strange feeling of emptiness washes over me. Eyes on me, he waits with his hand out for me to respond to his invitation. I ignore the hand and invite him to show me the way. I don't need his fingers to not get lost.

He walks around the fire and heads for the way used by the students TJ talked to earlier. So what, is this some kind of selection process? Those who take this path can still expect to be part of the Pack while the others just have to comfort themselves by partying around the fire with some free beers?

"Where are we going? To find out about the little game everyone was talking about without really mentioning the rules?"

Tucker stops for a moment and glances at me. "Not yet."

"What do you mean 'not yet'?" I grumble behind his back. "Look, it's nice, the grass…and the trees. But I didn't sign up for a field trip. In fact, I even hate flowers."

Why am I telling him this? As if he's interested! But even if a part of me is intrigued and wants to follow him, another part is almost…anxious— hence the verbal diarrhea coming out of me.

And that's when I notice an old chapel about 30 feet away. Well, that's pretty weird…

"Hey, man, is this some kind of religious thing? Oh, I'm not even baptized," I add when he doesn't answer.

The closer we get, the louder the music gets. I understand that it comes from this half-decrepit chapel. A girl, bursting with laughter, with a glass in her hand, passes through the small door.

"I'm pretty sure this is all a huge sacrilege," I whisper to myself.

A guy stands at the entrance of the chapel, a box at his feet. When I discover that his face is hidden, my heart misses a beat. A wolf mask covers his eyes and nose. A fucking wolf mask like the few guys back in college who enjoyed howling while promoting the party. He straightens up when he sees Tucker coming.

The latter picks up a mask. Just as I think he's about to put it on his face, he hands it to me. I step back.

"I don't think so."

He moves closer to me and whispers so only I can hear him. "If you want to go in there, you have to wear a mask."

"I just saw a girl walk through the doors of the chapel and she didn't have a mask on," I say, crossing my arms again.

"Not wearing a mask gives you a specific label down there. So does wearing one. Trust me, you have to wear one. Pack members wear them."

So, TJ, Yeleen, and their friends will be wearing masks. Is this some kind of protection? Or a sign that they belong to the same group? And what does it mean for the people who don't wear them and enter the chapel?

"But I'm not a member of your pack," I say.

Tucker gives me a teasing look. "But you're going to fight to be a part of it, right?"

I have no desire to be part of their pack. The rational part of my brain forbids me to even consider this idea. And yet, here I am, letting my curiosity consume me. I should run away but I can't.

So, the ones not wearing masks are the ones who want to join Tucker and his friends. Even if I were fighting to be in the game, I shouldn't be wearing one. So why does Tucker want me to have one?

I don't have time to think about it before he reaches for me. His fingers rest on the back of my head as he gently puts the mask on me. My breath hits his face directly.

I've got a wolf mask on my face, guys. Yeah, this is serious!

He runs his index finger through my red hair, and I ask him firmly, "And you? Don't you wear one?"

He leans towards me, his piercing eyes searching mine.

"I don't need one. I'm the leader of the pack, but you already know that, right?"

He doesn't wait another second, instead grabbing my hand without asking and dragging me toward the chapel. The guy waiting at the entrance nods slowly, staring at Tucker. He doesn't look at me at any point, it's like I'm not even there. Like he's not allowed to look at anyone other than the tall, dark-haired guy who walks me through the door of the place.

I admit it, I am totally dying of curiosity. So, swallowing my big mouth, I let him lead me into the narrow corridor. The chapel is almost completely in ruins. When I follow him down an even narrower staircase, everything become clear to me. Music comes from below. A strange smoke is rising from this coveted basement. I don't know what they're smoking down there, but it's not just cigarettes.

"*Get out of here,*" the rational part of my brain orders me. Debauchery cannot be in my future.

But I don't have time to back down. We are entering a world of depravity.

I reach the last step and Tucker hasn't let go of my hand, as if he's afraid I'll run away. The basement is quite small. The walls are very old. Music pulses, from speakers hanging from the ceiling. Couches are spread around the center of the room…where students are literally having an orgy.

My mouth drops open as I slowly realize what is going on here. My eyes land on a chick sandwiched by two masked men. She's not wearing a wolf mask; she's barefaced, and her overexcited eyes make me realize what a state she's in. Some are watching them, others are also doing their little business.

A guy without a mask is lying on the floor. A girl wearing a mask leans over him and nips at his neck, pulling his hair. But what world have I landed in?

I should feel nothing but revulsion, and yet that is not entirely the case. A hint of arousal rises in me, and I try to stifle it. There are far fewer people here than outside. Only a privileged few have managed to get into the chapel. And I am one of them…

Who said that Denver was a quiet city? Shit, Portland looks pretty shabby by comparison.

"Does this scare you?" whispers Tucker in my ear.

I don't want to show him any weakness. I look into his eyes again and reply, unclasping my fingers from his, "I've seen a cock before, Tucker. To tell you the truth, I've seen pussies too. So no, I'm not afraid."

My answer seems to suit him. He nods. I point to the maskless girl who is getting taken by two guys. "She wants to be one of the wolves?"

"Correct."

"So this is some kind of test here? You have to give your body to the others to get to the second phase?"

Tucker smiles softly in the dimmed atmosphere of the place. "Once again, you've got it right. You give your body and your pleasure to others, and they will give theirs back to you."

So that's what I thought. The first step is to give your body and soul to the Pack, and what could be more symbolic than giving your body while taking others'? There is no awkwardness between them, only desire.

I'm getting hot under my mask.

"You think I want to join your 'Pack,'" I retort, mimicking quotation marks with my fingers. "So what, am I supposed to get through this first step by stripping down and getting banged by several guys, offering myself to them?"

Tucker suddenly squints his eyes. His jaw twitches but he simply shakes his head.

"I thought this was the first test," I say to test him.

I know for a fact that I'm not going to sleep with any of the guys or girls in this room, but his behavior intrigues me. I decide to torment him more. I place my hands on the back of my head, on the mask's clasp. Tucker is faster than I am.

"What the hell are you doing?" he exclaims, stopping me from removing the mask.

I stare at him, surprised. He doesn't want me to take it off. He wants me to do the steps to join his group, but he doesn't want me to take the mask off in this room and fuck anyone?

"I thought that—"

"We'll consider that this test has already been completed for you," he says curtly.

And therefore send me directly to the next one? I analyze silently.

"But I didn't sleep with any of the wolves for that."

Then I twist the knife.

"You don't want one of those cubs to end up between my legs, do you? Why is that?"

In fact, I think I understand the reason for his behavior, but I want to trap him in turn, back him into a corner like he tried to do with me. His breath hits my face, and he clenches his fists. The heat coming from his pores is almost unbearable.

He whispers, inches from my lips, "I told you, Iris, I'll be the only one to eat you."

I stare at him, totally disturbed by his proximity and by his words. The sexual connotation that emanates from them does not escape me. For a second, I imagine him between my thighs, in the middle of all these people. I shake my head to forget this…this fantasy that has come over me. I won't sleep with him. I won't let that bastard get what he wants like he seems to be used to.

"And how—"

He cuts me off again as he leans into me. As his hands grip my hips tightly, he whispers in my ear, "How do you want me to?"

A furious desire to stick to him assails me. This sucks. It's the atmosphere and the smell of sex around us! When his mouth lands on my ear and is about to nibble it, I push him away firmly, coming to my senses. "I'm curious but not stupid. Keep your tongue in your mouth."

My refusal and the way I push him away seem to make his eyes glow with intensity.

He brings his index finger and thumb to his mouth. A whistle sounds as all heads turn in our direction. The music stops. I see TJ, a little further away, taking off his mask and splitting the crowd towards us. OK, what the hell just happened?

"The first phase is over," Tucker says loudly, turning to his audience. "Let's see if our little lambs are ready to become cubs in the second."

The crowd practically roars. TJ bursts out laughing before doing the wolf cry, quickly followed by others. Tucker hurries up the steps of the chapel. My instincts and the adrenaline pumping through my body urge me to follow him.

As we arrive outside, I take off my mask. "What is that supposed to mean?!"

He turns to me, a charming smile stuck to his face. "Let's see if you can handle the second part. Are you ready to be hunted, beautiful?"

Then he walks away towards the fire and the students gradually join him.

10. TEMPTATION

IRIS

Like the others, I walk towards Tucker, and a shiver goes through me as a young man takes the spot next to him and TJ. He is shorter than them but more built. His head is shaved, his eyes black. A tattoo starts along his neck, continues its way under his T-shirt, and ends on his forearms. He presses TJ's shoulder before letting out a little laugh and then staring at the crowd that is gathering around them.

Who is he?

I can't help but notice the pained expression on his features behind his cheerful expression.

"If you ask me," says a girl behind me, "Tucker is definitely the hottest. But Dan…Dan is a pretty little flame that turns into a real blaze when it touches your skin."

I turn around and come face to face with Sarah, Yeleen's friend who seemed so possessive of Tucker. Her face is tilted towards me, her blue eyes contrasting with her tanned skin slightly crinkled as she analyzes me in turn. She is wearing tight jeans and a pink shirt with half the buttons open, revealing her white lace bra.

I don't let anything show on my face. Her voice seems rather friendly, but her look…a look does not deceive. A look is a direct reflection of the soul. It shows others what we would like to hide. And it tells me that Sarah doesn't like me.

I turn my attention back to the three guys standing side by side and linger once more on the guy with the shaved head. *A pretty flame that turns into a real blaze when it touches your skin.* So this is the famous Dan? The angular features of his face make him look rather austere, but Sarah is right: he exudes a raw beauty.

"I'm not interested in Dan," I say simply.

A small laugh comes out of Sarah's mouth as she leans a little closer to me. "Of course you're not interested in him. Can you tell me the same thing about Tucker?"

The fake innocence in her voice doesn't escape me. The brat seems displeased, and you know what? It makes me laugh. I don't move an inch, keeping a relaxed look on my face, while the other students gather around. A few guys are having fun imitating the wolf howl again, and one of them gets punched playfully in the shoulder.

Those who didn't make it to the first stage continue to party all over the property, glancing at us enviously at times.

My hazel eyes wander over to Tucker, and I find that he is staring at me as well. We stare each other down for long seconds. I remember his warmth next to me, his breath on my skin. His expression becomes slightly puzzled when he discovers who is standing next to me, but he doesn't make a move, simply watching us.

"You're right," I say to Sarah, keeping my attention on the tall, dark-haired man. "Tucker is definitely the hottest of the three."

The girl holds back an exclamation at my words.

"But," I say firmly, "I'm not interested in him."

"But he is interested in you," she finally admits after a few seconds.

"You don't need to be jealous," I say. "Nothing will happen between him and me."

Sarah moves to face me, and I have just enough time to see the angry look on Tucker's face before she blocks my view. "You silly girl," she scoffs. "If Tucker decides there's going to be something between you, then it will happen."

I purse my lips to keep from laughing and let her finish.

"And I'm not jealous," she continues. "I'm not a toy…he and I…it's much deeper than anything you can imagine. I saw you two earlier, it was ridiculous."

And what exactly did she see?

"Look, that was a nice chat, but I've got other things to do. I'm going to stop you before you try to make some stupid threat thinking it will terrify me, which isn't the case. You don't seem to care about me, either. To tell you the truth, I don't really give a shit, so I'm going to ask you to move your little ass and forget about me." I take a step in her direction. "Yes, you are jealous," I say, keeping my voice neutral. "Look how your muscles tense up. The thoughts and insults are spinning in your head, ready to be spilled. Your mouth wrinkles a little more, you hardly hold back your words, yet you're dying to get at me, aren't you?"

My analysis of her behavior doesn't seem to please her.

"Listen, if I were to give you advice…it's not by considering me as a pseudo-threat that you're going to get him," I continue by nodding to Tucker. "If you want the guy, tell him. Friendly advice, of course."

From the offended look on Sarah's face, the conversation isn't going the way she wanted it to. "I don't want your advice," she spits. "But I'll give you a little. Stay where you belong, which is away from us."

I can't help but let out a little laugh.

"I just told you I didn't want him. But hearing you threaten me…oowhoo," I breathe in deeply, "makes me want to piss you off even more. So don't make me want to do anything you wouldn't like."

I don't wait for her answer before walking away. She doesn't hold me back, but I can feel her eyes piercing my back. Who says I won't make enemies by coming here? Quiet town…yeah, my ass.

I weave in and out of the twenty or so students who are in front of me, watching as Dan leans over to Tucker and says something to him. The two smile knowingly at each other as TJ opens his mouth in shock.

I spot Yeleen a little further away. She looks busy, pressed up against the tall black man who has her pressed against his chest, hands on her hips. She gives me a small delighted smile when she discovers me here. She must have been expecting me to be here tonight as much as I was.

"So…ready for the second step?" shouts TJ, and the others around me shout back.

Am I really going to follow instead of running away? I am completely sick. At this point, everyone looks like savages.

"This year, we decided to make things a bit more intense than the previous two years," he continues, as "oowhoo!" is heard. "For centuries, the Bomley estate has been known for its huge deer hunts.

So we thought we'd carry on the tradition tonight…in our own way."

A girl in front of him asks a question I can't hear. TJ laughs softly and nods happily. He pulls a thick ribbon, about 6 inches long, from his pocket. A bright red ribbon. He waves it in the air for all to see.

"Of course, doll," he replies to the young woman. "There are many of you who want to enter the wolves' home tonight. A limited number of ribbons have been hidden in the forest,"—he points to the trees behind him—"four, to be exact. The rule is simple. You go, you find a ribbon, you come back. And above all, you don't go into the house. The hunt is only in the woods."

I raise an eyebrow. Wait, is this a joke?

"Your stupid hunt is a simple treasure hunt? All that's missing is the birthday cake…"

A guy next to me laughs at my mocking tone. TJ notices me and smiles, "My best friend," he says softly in my direction.

"Who said it would be simple?" Tucker yells.

Tucker doesn't seem at all amused by my question. His eyes are focused on me. His jaw is clenched. His arm muscles are still tense. Is the boss offended?

"The goal is for you to find a ribbon…without getting caught by the wolves that will be throwing themselves behind you," he tells the crowd, who seem to be hanging on his every word. "If you manage to find one of the four ribbons before a wolf finds you, you win your place on the next step."

"What if the wolves find us?"

"Then they will throw you out of the woods, and you will be eliminated."

He addresses everyone, but his gaze remains on me as he finishes, "Let's see how fast and smart you are or if they catch you."

A guy near me exclaims that he can't wait for a wolf to catch him. Laughter rings out.

I take a step back. This is ridiculous, this situation is ridiculous. I should be working on my classes. I should be warm under my comforter. I don't belong here. Yet, as I step back, my body doesn't seem to want to obey me. I meet Sarah's eyes, and she smiles triumphantly as she sees me giving up.

Be quick and smart.

I can do it.

As TJ continues to answer the few intrusive questions, Tucker is still focused on me and it makes me uncomfortable. Because I know full well that if I go into that forest, he's going to be the one to come after me. But I'm pretty sure he's going to let me win because deep down he wants me to be part of his group.

The real question is: do I want to win? I don't even know what the third phase will be. The only thing I do know is that as his steps get closer, I freeze.

Sarah says that Dan is the flame that turns into an inferno. But at this moment, I feel like Tucker is the more dangerous of the two. The more destructive.

He's only a few steps away from me now. His imposing stature allows him to pass between the students.

"You think you'll be fast, redhead?"

I am startled when a whistle sounds. I wake up from my lethargy. The other students rush toward the forest. Laughter and cries of excitement ring out as they reach the trees. My breathing quickens. I take a deep breath and glance behind me. I can see from here the cars parked a hundred yards away.

But I do nothing. Call me a stupid girl, I deserve it because I don't back down. I straighten my chin and walk straight ahead. It's just a stupid game. A stupid mask. No need to make a big deal about it.

Tucker stops as I walk by him, ignoring him. I feel his gaze on the back of my neck. I ignore it and continue towards the damn trees. I glance around and notice that the students who entered the forest have all disappeared from my view.

After about ten yards, as I walk away from the fire and the waiting students, Tucker's voice snaps at my back, "Go!"

We listen. As a joke, a boy screams bloody murder. His friends laugh. Finally, footsteps are heard. In turn, other students—the wolves—join the party. Great, a little Hunger Games atmosphere! If someone had told me that I would be racing through a forest in the middle of the night, I wouldn't have believed it. I don't waste a second before I start running, going deeper into the darkness.

A minute later, I hear scream close by. I jump and turn right. I don't see anyone. How many miles is this stupid forest? How can I find one of the four ribbons in the middle of this godforsaken hole?

I hold back my own scream when a spider web gets caught in my hair. I vigorously rub my red locks as my heart tightens. Bloody spider!

I walk forward while regaining my composure. I mustn't think about the fact that I'm alone in the middle of the woods, or I'll really freak out. I'm not usually a wimp, but right now, I don't know what's come over me. My mom would be screaming at me to get back to civilization and stop pretending to be someone I'm not.

Hanging out at eleven o'clock in the middle of gloomy trees is really not my thing.

I let out a curse as I nearly twist my ankle. My shoes are going to be ruined. Great, really great.

I hear male laughter on my right. I rush behind a tree and press myself against it. A guy I don't know walks right past me. From his quiet posture, I could swear he's one of the wolves. This is confirmed when I see his mask. He doesn't notice me. Once he passes me, I start to move away from the trunk, but an object nestled in the bush at my feet catches my attention.

A silly grin appears on my face as I crouch down. I push aside the leaves, and my fingers grasp one of the four ribbons.

I don't waste a second and put it in the back pocket of my shorts. A twig snags on the lace of my camisole, and I let out another cuss word. I have to get out of here. I've won. I won, you guys!

I can't wait to get in front of Tucker, to show him that I didn't need him to let me win to win.

The jubilation that invades me catches me off guard. I feel like I'm getting caught up in the game despite everything. I hear a cracking sound to my right. The guy who passed in front of me earlier is running east.

I discreetly hide behind a tree but tilt my head to observe him. A girl is leaning towards a bush and doesn't see him. The guy approaches her slowly. It's too late, he's found her before she could find a ribbon. So it's game over for her. I'm about to run away on my own, but I haven't taken a step when a palm presses on my mouth, and I'm pulled back.

My back is pressed against a male torso. I elbow my opponent in the ribs and try to shake my head to get out of the way. A light rumble answers me. A hand settles firmly on the back of my neck and grabs my hair before turning me around. I find myself stuck, my back against the trunk of the tree. My breathing stops, and my eyes meet a look I know well.

Tucker is pressed against me. One hand is still placed against my mouth. He lifts the other to tap his index finger on his lips, ordering me to remain silent. I slap his chest, furious.

"What's wrong with you?" I try to spit behind his palm.

He leans into me further, making a barrier between me and the rest of the forest. He keeps his index finger pressed on his lips, still warning me.

Over his shoulder, I see Yeleen and a guy walking past us, laughing.

"I think there's one over there," the guy says, dragging her a little further.

Tucker's hidden us in the shadows. They don't notice us as they walk by just a foot away from us.

I don't move. My chest heaves quickly as I catch my breath. Tucker is leaning towards me. His eyes scan every inch of my face. Neither he nor I speak. He finally lowers his hand and places it on the trunk behind me, right next to my head.

"Found you…I guess this 'simple treasure hunt' wasn't so simple…since you just lost."

Okay, I get the picture: he's getting back at me for all the times I've stood up to him, especially tonight. He wants to make me pay for it dearly…by eliminating me.

His intention wasn't to let me win, in fact. It was to prove his fucking superiority as a pack leader, to put me in my place as a little lamb.

But he doesn't know that the lamb is in possession of the precious ribbon…

"You wanted to make sure I wasn't just a little puppy…all right, you've got your answer now?" he continues in an arrogant tone.

I get it. He's not a puppy begging for attention. He's a wolf staring me down. A wolf looking for more than a few scratches behind the ears.

My breath hits his parted lips. I ignore his words, unable to concentrate. This isn't good; we're much too close. I should back off, punch him in the nuts and run away from here to declare my victory. But I am attracted to his magnetism.

His mouth is suddenly on mine. A growl resounds in his chest while all thought abandons me. His other hand, on the small of my back, pulls me into him.

My fingers wrap around his hair, and I pull him in even closer. My lips open to his. I don't think, because I can't or don't want to. It doesn't matter.

My tongue, conquering, tries to make its way between his lips. He refuses me access. I move my mouth back. Our breaths intermingle. His eyes seem as confused as mine. Then he falls against me again, impatient, and my back meets the solid tree trunk. I nibble his lower lip and my tongue begins a sensual dance with his.

It's as if we are cut off from the rest of the world. I can't hear anything. I only feel him. The tension between us keeps growing, ready to explode and shatter all our inhibitions in its path.

Then his lips move down my right ear to nibble it. It sends a jolt through my lower abdomen. I hold back a groan, not wanting to show him the effect he has on me. Of all the guys out there, my body decided to set its sights on him? Damn it.

We don't talk, we don't need to. It's not our brains, it's the tension between us that makes us weak and pushes us to our lowest instincts. When I feel his erection against my lower abdomen, I realize he's in as much of a hurry as I am, inhabited by a madness that doesn't have a name. I put my mouth on his neck and suck his skin between my teeth. He lets out a growl while crushing me harder against the tree.

"Damn," he growls against my ear.

His voice almost makes me shiver. It's hot, hotter than anything I've experienced in the last few months, and it's too good for me to resist.

"I want you," he whispers irrevocably.

The tiny part of my brain that is still lucid reminds me that this is nonsense, that we are in the middle of a gloomy forest, that people could arrive at any moment. The two wolves that were close by earlier are maybe still a few meters away!

And besides…

"Why did you want to hide me earlier, when they were

approaching?" I ask suddenly, trying to catch my breath.

He made it clear that it wasn't to let me win…

Tucker continues his way down my neck, and it's only when I put my hand on his chest to push him away slightly that he seems to come back to reality…and to my question. He seems annoyed by this interruption but ends up giving me a small smile while holding up a ribbon in front of me.

Instinctively, I reach into my jeans pocket, but the ribbon is still there. He didn't take it from me during our…moment of distraction. And suddenly, I understand.

"You never meant to get me out of the game, did you? You just wanted to put me in my place and teach me a little lesson by winning the hunt. But you still grabbed one of those ribbons to give to me and make sure I got to the next step anyway? And you didn't want your buddies to find you cheating instead of kicking me out of the woods?"

Tucker just nods, looking satisfied.

"So you didn't think I could win, did you?" It shouldn't bother me so much, and yet I just want to prove him wrong for underestimating me.

"And I was right, apparently," he continues, crowing triumphantly.

Well he's about to eat crow. He wanted to prove his superiority to me, but he's done the opposite. He couldn't bring himself to eliminate me. He was willing to cheat to keep me going, again. He just proved to me that he had a weakness.

And that weakness was me.

Wait, except that I don't want to be his weakness! And I don't want him to be mine. I can't be alone with him again like this.

I take the ribbon out of my pocket, under his surprised look, before grabbing the one he still has in his hand and tying it to a branch to put it back in play. "I told you I wasn't a helpless lamb. I won your stupid game. Now leave me alone!"

Then I leave him there as he silently stares at me, lost in thought.

11. MADNESS

TUCKER

The last car pulls out of the circular drive. All the others have already left the property. The headlights fade away and leave me alone out front.

No sound resounds in the night, except the usual song of the owls in the trees. My gaze is lost for a second on our extinguished fountain tonight.

The four ribbons have been found. TJ told me who the winners of this second stage were, but I couldn't concentrate on his words.

Iris won.

I thought I'd won the hunt by finding her before she could unearth a ribbon. I wanted her helpless in my arms.

Holy shit, I hate cheating but I was going to cheat for her. All because I wanted her to reach the next step.

But she didn't need me to get to that second step. She had found a ribbon. She won it on her own. She pulled it out of her back pocket, waving it in front of me like a trophy. I was fooled like a rookie tonight. She was faster and smarter than me.

Because I thought with my dick.

I hate to lose.

I'm still frustrated. Why is that? I don't fucking know. Everything went pretty much the way I wanted it to. She jumped right into my trap and got into the game without ever looking back. She passed the second step.

But I didn't want her to get there on her own.

And then there she was, hot under my fingers, and she stopped everything. That wasn't the plan.

I run a hand over my tired face and turn to the heavy front door. As I climb the four stone steps, my thoughts don't shift. My mind is completely consumed by this little slip of woman who should leave me indifferent.

Damn her.

She knew she had already won when I put my mouth against hers. And yet, she was still starting to give herself up to me by devouring me with her little tongue. Was she playing a game? Trying to turn me on, knowing we wouldn't go any further?

I should have let her go through the first phase alone.

I'm lying to myself.

Watching some random guy take her in the middle of the room when I hadn't had her myself yet? No way.

Also, despite her curious look, I could see that she wouldn't take the plunge with all those students. She looks much more conventional, and a pain in the ass. Definitely not my type.

So why have I had a hard-on for almost forty minutes? Damn witch!

Maybe she's right. Maybe she's not a helpless lamb. The real question is: will I now be able to leave her alone, as she wants?

I know deep down the answer is no.

I am about to push open the heavy wooden door when it opens by itself. "Mr. Bomley," Abraham greets me, looking as awake at three in the morning as if it were the middle of the afternoon. "Was the hunt good tonight?"

Was I really the hunter tonight?

I'm having my doubts.

I pause for a second on the doorstep and give him a small fake smile out of habit. Disregarding my surroundings, I walk through the darkness as he walks away down a small hallway.

I'm at the first step of the marble staircase when a tired voice calls out to me, "You're home early."

I sigh, closing my eyes. I finally walk to the large living room behind me and approach the velvet chair. Here again, no lamps are lit. A fire crackles in the huge fireplace, lighting the room somewhat.

I say nothing, waiting and praying that time will pass more quickly.

The sound of crystal tinkling once again as a frail hand tries to pour another glass of whiskey. It shakes, and I hold back a curse as I catch the glass before it explodes on the floor.

When I set it back down on the small wooden table by the chair, thin fingers circle my wrist. I hold back from recoiling but clench my jaw. The contact burns me so badly that a lump forms almost instantly in the hollow of my throat.

"My boy, my beautiful boy…"

I inhale and resign myself to raise my head. My eyes meet those of my mother, so similar to mine, but also so empty. She stares at me but doesn't really look at me.

Her attention is focused far away, in a place that only she has access to.

"You should stop drinking so much," I whisper firmly.

A small smile springs to her lips before fading away as her mind goes back to the shadows that cling to her. She is dead from the inside, completely eaten away by darkness. I notice the nightgown she's wearing is inside out, but she doesn't seem to care.

She leans towards me, trying to put her index finger on my arm. I gently shift to avoid her touch.

"You know, you remind me of your father sometimes. I see him in you."

"Stop talking about him," I command.

His memory is painful enough as it is. I loved him. He raised me in the middle of this jungle. But I don't want to talk about him anymore. I put both my hands on the armrests of the chair and stare her straight in the eye.

"He's dead. He's not coming back."

Her mouth trembles, so I don't finish my sentence but repeat it to myself mentally, over and over.

You killed him. You killed him and he's not coming back. Not ever.

I should scream these harsh words because they reflect reality. She took him away from me. But I can't say them.

"Damn it," I spit out, clenching my fists.

I have to get out of this room right now. I don't want to see her tears. I don't want to see the madness dancing in her eyes again.

Her voice starts again behind me as I walk away, "The music was too loud tonight."

Just leave me alone!

"I'll be careful next time," I murmur.

"I hope so, otherwise Debbie won't be able to study anymore. She works hard, you know? You mustn't distract your little sister from her studies, she needs peace and quiet to pass her year."

My breath stops as my heart misses a beat. I clench my jaw so hard I can almost hear my teeth grind. I rest my fingers against the door, almost slapping myself as I realize I need support.

She starts talking again as if her words aren't breaking my bones one by one. "Could you stop by her room and ask her to come say goodnight? She hasn't come downstairs, and I don't like it."

I hesitate for a second to turn to her and order her to shut up. I want to yell at her to wake up, to snap out of her madness and finally face the reality that this will never happen again. But I would only make her worse so I don't contradict her. I let her believe in something that no longer exists.

I don't wait for the rest of her sentence before leave the living room. I climb the stairs two by two while the anger invades me a little more.

As I reach the corridor that leads to my room, I stop in front of a door that is supposed to remain closed but is open tonight. Worry fills me for a second but disappears immediately when I discover Abraham in the room. It's only him.

Nothing has moved inside. For a year, it's always the same. The same beeping of the medical devices.

My gaze wanders to the frail figure of my little sister, Debbie, under the white blanket. Motionless. A porcelain doll.

Broken.

Abraham checks one last time that everything is in order before leaving the room. This is the same ritual he does several times a day.

Debbie's eyelids remain closed. I step into the room, my hand gripping the door handle. I stare at the screen showing her vitals. The various connections to her are keeping her alive, but her mind must be dead already after all this time. I inch closer. It's been days since I've been in this damn room. I hate seeing her like this and not being able to do anything to get her out, to make her wake up.

But I hate myself even more for knowing that it's partly my fault she's in this damn condition.

A creak, then footsteps in the hallway, interrupt my thoughts. I turn abruptly to the bedroom door and leave the room without waiting a second. My eyes search the corridor but there is nobody there.

Silent, I walk towards the double door of my room. I am both reassured and furious when I discover the intruder.

"What the hell are you doing here?" I growl as I close the door behind me. "I ordered you not to come."

Sarah stares at me with a teasing little smile on her lips.

"I've always had trouble with the rules."

I let her come to me, watching her walk sensually. She thinks she has some power over me. Bullshit. When she puts her right hand on my chest, I grab her wrist.

My behavior excites her, I can see it. It's not the goal. Yet I notice her pupils dilate a little as she nibbles her lower lip. But she has disobeyed me.

"My rules are not meant to be broken," I say firmly, pushing her away from me. "Get out of my way."

She opens her mouth but remains silent, as if she doesn't know how to take my sudden refusal. I turn my back on her and walk into the bathroom, taking off my shirt. I need a fucking shower after tonight.

The tall brunette chases after me disobeying yet again.

"I know I had no right...I'm sorry."

I ignore her and undress under her burning eyes. Sarah blows as if to give herself courage and then also starts to undress. What the...?

Once naked in front of me, she flinches slightly when she sees that I don't have a hard-on for her. I don't know why but my persistent erection has finally given up.

"Did I do something wrong?" she asks in a small voice. "Is everything okay?"

Is everything okay? No, damn it, nothing is okay!

"Get your stuff and get out," I repeat, turning on the shower faucet. I hate it when people don't obey a damn order. No one is going into my house!

She doesn't let go though, not understanding that I have no desire to fuck tonight. "Don't you want me? Just one more time," she asks me with a devilish smile starting her antics back up. What's wrong with her? We had fun together a few times, nothing more. At what point did she think she could walk in here and offer me her ass? With a serious look on my face, I tell her, "I've had you before. Why would I want you again?"

I point to the door with my chin. After a second, she nods, looking embarrassed. I barely have time to make out the furious expression on her face before she throws on her clothes and leaves.

I close my eyes and let the water fall on my shoulders, my forehead against the stone.

What a fucking night.

12. FORCED PARTNER

IRIS

"Move, you bastard! Do you have a stick stuck up your ass or what?"

It's no use, the idiot in front of me and his shitty car keep on driving at two miles an hour. Seriously, we're going fifteen miles an hour on a road limited to forty-five! I'm going to get out and beat the crap out of him.

Who said that Monday mornings were synonymous with good moods? No one did? That's what I thought.

I swear I'm not doing it on purpose, it's like I'm conditioned to miss half of Mrs. Richards' classes.

I put my hand down on my horn again and let out another curse.

Finally, after a half mile, the road widens, allowing me to pass the old van.

Like a kid, I raise my middle finger in the direction of the stunned driver and finally press the gas pedal.

A few minutes later, I run into the building. I blow on a strand of red hair that falls in front of my eyes while preventing my bag from tumbling off my shoulder. I almost bump into a student at the corner of a hallway. She stares at me with a bewildered look. What? I have a booger hanging out? Forgot to put on a bra?

No time to think, I pass her and go back to the amphitheater. I stop about fifty feet before the entrance and hurry to catch my breath. There's no way I'm going to go in there sweating like a pig and breathing as hard as a porn actress in full orgasm.

As I place my hands on my knees, the door opens and several students exit the lecture hall.

What? But it's not possible, I had a class here, right? I'm only twenty minutes late. I catch a guy on his way out.

"Hey," I call out, putting my hand on his shoulder, "isn't Mrs. Richards here?"

He quickly glances at my upper body before answering me with a little smile. "We finished early. She had an appointment."

I almost cry out in relief. At least I didn't miss much of her class!

"For the record, we have a group assignment due in three weeks, the pairs were formed this morning."

"But I…I wasn't there!"

He laughs softly at my panicked tone. He stares at my chest again with an interested look. I hold back from rolling my eyes. I'm definitely not ready for a laborious attempt at flirting.

"So I guess you can prepare yourself for a zero. I'm just kidding," he is quick to correct when he sees my eyes pop out of their sockets. "Just go to her."

I nod and walk away, mumbling a quick thank you.

"Hey!" he calls out to me again. "Is that—"

"No, I'm not interested. No, I won't sleep with you. Thanks for your proposal," I cut him off, absolutely not in the mood for this.

I hear him laughing frankly.

"I'm not asking you out. I just wanted to tell you that your T-shirt was backwards."

I close my eyes for a moment, breathing in calmly. Don't fucking tell me that…

Damn it, I growl inwardly as I notice my tag is on my upper chest instead of on my back. This is why he was looking at me weirdly. With no time to change, I avoid the students coming out of the lecture hall and rush in.

There are only a few people left. Without worrying about the image I must give off at this moment, I run down the steps and reach the dais. Professor Richards is putting her MacBook in a pouch when she sees me bursting in.

"Hello…I…excuse me, I think I have a little problem."

Very bad opening. She raises her piercing gaze to me and immediately notices the tag on my top, which I'm wearing backwards.

"I can see that."

"I...Yeah. I was absent earlier, but I heard you gave an assignment due in three weeks. I would just like to know if there is another person who is alone as well, so I can pair up with that person."

She doesn't seem to be listening to the words coming out of my mouth. She puts her manicured hand on her hip and tilts her head to the side:

"Why weren't you in my class?"

My lips open and then close again.

"You are Miss...?" she continues.

"Foster. Iris Foster. I'm so sorry, I..."

She sighs softly and pulls out several sheets of paper from her pocket. "Miss Foster," she begins, looking for my name on the sheets, "if you're not interested in my class, you simply shouldn't have enrolled. The least you can do is attend."

"I am interested in your class," I immediately say. "I was stuck on the road behind an unconscious motorist who was driving at fifteen miles an hour."

But why am I telling her about my life? She looks up at me for a few seconds and to my surprise, a small smile comes to her face. "Ah, Miss Foster," she finally says, finding my name in the list, before frowning. "You already have a partner, he has his name next to yours."

"What? No, I...that's impossible."

She hands me the sheet, before taking it back a few moments later.

"Don't waste my time again," she orders me, walking away as I stand still, my fists clenched.

You bastard.

That idiot Tucker wrote his name next to mine.

Part of me isn't even surprised. I should have expected it, I know he's not going to let me go. I got his damn ribbon, took it back to TJ and *basta*. I made it clear to him that even though I won the event, I was done and he should leave me alone. Which he didn't do.

Okay, my mouth almost swallowed Tucker's tongue this weekend, but I'm not stupid, I've realized that this game is not for me. I'm not ready to play by rules I know nothing about. So, despite the effect it had on my traitorous body, it's up to me to control my brain so that it's not attracted to that fool.

With a sudden determination, I step off the dais, and as I begin to walk up the steps out of the lecture hall from the top door, my foot stops on the first one.

Tucker is sitting on the very top row, right next to the exit. Both of his feet are resting casually on another seat as he watches me patiently, his eyes laughing.

I straighten my chin defiantly and climb the steps, ignoring his damn gaze as it scans my figure. He looks proud of his little trick. He's just stuck me with him for a damn assignment and seems to be delighted.

"So…partner?" he asks as he places his black cap backwards on his head.

I decide not to bother with him and walk by his seat without giving him a glance. I raise my middle finger in his direction as I walk away. A small male laugh answers me, way too close.

I walk out of the lecture hall and slam the door behind me. Hopefully, he took the door to his face.

A few students from my class are still standing in front of the entrance, talking to each other.

"Iris."

I hear his deep voice slamming into my back, but I ignore it again as an idea suddenly occurs to me. "In times of hardship you have to make the best of things," I repeat to myself as I walk towards two guys leaning against the wall next to me.

"Hi," I exclaim.

I feel Tucker's eyes burning into the back of my neck but I try to ignore them.

"Hi," one of them smiles back at me.

I decide that he will be the instrument of my revenge. "Would you do me a favor?" I ask him, biting my lower lip with an innocent look.

He nods cautiously.

"I'm paired with a big dummy for Professor Richards' group work, so would you mind if we swapped pairs?"

I hear footsteps right behind me. I can imagine Tucker rolling his eyes and holding back from killing me.

The student in front of me shrugs, almost agreeing with me.

"Who's the dead weight?" he asks me. "I can take care of him if you want."

The footsteps stop right next to me. The two guys look up at Tucker without understanding. His jaw clenched, he crossed his arms over his chest. "It's me, the dead weight," he announces in a hoarse voice.

Understanding who he is talking to, the student loses his confidence and stares at me, looking sorry. I understand that he is about to say no to me. I then call him out before he does.

"Is it okay?"

He stares at my face then at Tucker, who seems to be patiently waiting for the guy to open his mouth so he can pin him to the wall. "I…I don't know."

Tucker leans toward him. "Do you want to settle the score with me?"

The student shakes his head without answering as Tucker's muscles tense a little more. "I can't help you," he announces hastily as he and his buddy walk away.

"That's not cool, man!" I shout behind his back.

I turn angrily to Tucker, who seems to be slowly relaxing. "What's your problem? Why was he scared?"

Just because he's the king of the campus or even the world doesn't mean he has to come and mess with me!

He shrugs his shoulders with a falsely innocent look. "I don't know, maybe he was afraid of your T-shirt."

I glare at him a little more as he takes another step toward me. His chest is almost touching my chest. My breathing slows down, and I stare at him without flinching. His eyes land on the tag above my chest. He puts a finger on it and pulls it between his index finger and thumb. I don't move an inch. My brain commands my knee to rise up and hit his family jewels, but my body doesn't obey. At that moment, what I should do is the exact opposite of what I want to do.

"Unless…" Tucker gasps. "Unless it's you who's afraid to work with me?"

His fingers let go of my label but stay on my T-shirt. They slowly move down. I grab his wrist fiercely as his hand comes to rest over my right breast.

"Why should I be afraid?"

His gaze meets mine. and I know we are thinking the same thing. Namely, my body pressed against a rotting tree trunk as his rubs against me and I pull his hair.

"Because you want me between your legs," Tucker suggests in a husky voice.

I don't contradict him, because that wouldn't be believable. I'm pretty sure he can see what I'm feeling through my eyes, like an open book. But noticing his tense features, I whisper back, "I think you want this even more than I do."

And he doesn't contradict me either. Instead, he puts his mouth on mine. Firmly. Just for a second, before pulling away from my body without a glance. A furious kiss, just to punish me.

My lips are stiff, but I don't move away.

What the hell just happened?!

"Will we go to Rocky Mountain when I come to Denver?" Agnes asks me over the phone.

"If you want," I sigh as I head inside. I quickly get rid of my sandals and my bag, which falls to the ground, and throw my car keys on the hallway cabinet.

"And we'll go to Six Flags Elitch Gardens too?" she shouts in an excited voice.

I hastily pull my cell phone away to keep my eardrum from bursting while holding back a curse. I'm not going to insult a kid, especially not my little sister whom I love more than anything—except when I want to kill her.

"Yes, yes, whatever you want."

Agnes is coming here during her fall break, which won't be that long from now. She's already planning a huge program and seems to think I'll be able to survive it without ending up on the floor. I take a drink as an idea suddenly comes to me, a much simpler idea.

"We could go to Chatfield State Park, if you prefer, there are places to swim there."

At first, Agnes doesn't answer. But I can hear her breathing.

"No," she finally whispers in a small voice.

"Why, honey?"

I hear her walk to her room and close the door, probably so our aunt won't listen.

"I don't want anyone to look at my body…"

I can't think of anything to say. My breathing stops. A flash comes to me. My brain sends me back months.

I see that bastard hitting me in the face as I was trying to get to the bathroom with my little sister. I see myself collapse weakly on the floor. But mostly I see him undressing her with his eyes, then actually undressing her as I tried to stand up.

I hear his scream in my ears. I remember grabbing my scissors from the cabinet…

I close my eyelids tightly. I don't want to think about that. I feel hot, all of a sudden. I feel dirty. I need to take a shower. I quickly take off my pants, which I throw away, and my top, which suffers the same fate.

"Then we won't go," I say in a reassuring voice to Agnes. "We'll do what you want, my darling, okay?"

She then spouts stiffly, "I love you," in record time.

Still in my underwear, I walk over to my TV and turn it on to the music channel. I nod and shake my hips quickly as I throw the remote on the couch, making my way to the bathroom while listening to my little sister tell me about her day.

As I pass the entrance, two knocks against the door startle me. I don't move an inch as the banging starts again. I cautiously walk towards the entrance, the phone still against my ear.

"Iris?"

Frowning, I stick my eye to the peephole. What the hell is he doing here? How did he know where I live?

"Tucker?"

13. WELCOME TO MY HOME

IRIS

I keep staring at Tucker through the peephole. Seriously, how likely was it that he would show up at my house tonight?

My little sister calls me through the phone, but my half-opened mouth doesn't let out a word. I remain rooted to the spot, torn between several contradictory feelings. Exasperation finally wins out.

"Two minutes, sweetie, I'll call you back right away," I tell her while putting the phone on the front table.

A new knock, a little brisker, falls against my door. This idiot is getting impatient. While I look for the most suitable place to hide his body once I've killed him, I retort, "If you break my door, I swear I'll break what's between your legs!"

My threat seems to have the desired effect because a silence answers me. But then I hear a small laugh, and I hold back a curse.

"Open up."

This asshole is clearly laughing at me as he bangs against the door again, more gently this time. I take a deep breath and retort, "Why should I open the door for you? This is private property! And more importantly, how did you know where I live?"

He repeats my name a little louder. Damn it, I'm going to have trouble with my neighbors! I open my door but make sure to show only my face in the crack, hiding my half-naked body behind the door.

"Oh, are you deaf?! Stop knocking," I whisper angrily.

Tucker stands before me, arms crossed. Unperturbed by my angry tone, he raises his eyebrows. His hair is soaked. Shit, is it raining? My eyes follow a drop that traces its way down his neck just before being blocked by the black cotton fabric of his T-shirt, also wet.

I swallow my saliva with difficulty, staring at him openly.

What the hell is wrong with you? Stop it, I order myself internally, looking for his gaze to hold on to something more neutral. Big mistake. The two marbles staring at me have apparently not lost any of my "discreet" analysis of his body and even seem to be amused by it, if I believe the slight glow that shines in them.

"How do you know my address?" I repeat, trying to keep my voice distant.

Tucker brings his face close to mine, and I try not to look down. His unshaven jaw catches my attention, but I refuse to digress again. I raise an eyebrow as I wait for his response.

"Yeleen helped me," he whispers with a small smirk.

Yeleen? What?!

"What?!" I can't help but scream.

Traitor. Hey, wait…I never gave her my exact address.

"Is there a problem?"

My neighbor is standing in front of her door, looking at us warily. Damn it!

"Everything's fine!" I tell her so as not to alarm her.

"Why don't you open the door, then?" asks Tucker.

Why should I open the door first, huh? I'm not a dog that does exactly what you tell me to, buddy. But I feel that he's not going to let me go. I'm taking it on the chin. Well, I'm half naked, I have to find a way to get to my room without him seeing me.

"I'm going to walk away and you're going to wait ten seconds before opening the door, okay?"

Faced with my unusual request, Tucker frowns. "Why do I have to wait? Are you naked or what?"

I don't answer his question, but his look changes completely: he understands that he is in the right.

I squint and repeat, "Ten seconds or I'll slit your throat, got it?"

I don't wait for his answer. I slam the door and run out into the hallway. The ten seconds have barely passed when I hear him open the door as I rush to my closet.

"Are you hiding a body?" his deep voice echoes through the walls.

"If this keeps up, I'll be hiding yours!" I grab an old Portland Steel T-shirt and a pair of black gym shorts. At least he won't be able to imagine anything. Let's not give him the wrong idea.

As I head back down the hallway, I make a detour to the bathroom and grab a small white towel. It won't be long before Tucker is messing up my place with his soaked hair.

Tucker doesn't answer me. To tell the truth, everything is silent on the other side of my apartment. This instantly worries me, and I hurry back into the living room.

"Where did you go?" I grumble.

I freeze as I discover him in my doorway. His gaze is on me, but he seems disturbed. It is at this moment that I discover MY cell phone stuck to his ear.

I hear my little sister's voice bawling in his ears. It must be some kind of insult because of the shocked look on the big brown guy's face.

I run towards him, holding back my screams. I snatch my phone from his hands and throw the towel on his surprised face. I ignore him, turn my back and put my phone to my ear.

"I don't know who you are! But if you don't put my sister on the phone, I'm gonna come over there and hit you! I know how to hit people! I've been in a fight with Mindy. I can call my friends too and they'll help me!"

I hold back a smile at my little sister's threats, which are anything but believable, but adorable nonetheless. "It's me," I tell her.

Agnes is suddenly silent. I turn towards Tucker and discover his glance on my naked legs. Seriously? I snap my fingers at him to bring him back to reality, but he ignores me and walks into my living room, analyzing every detail of this carefully decorated room.

"Sorry," Agnes apologizes. "But when he told me you were coming back soon, I was afraid. Who is that?"

My attention is fixed on the tense shoulders of the man wandering around my home. He seems to be sucking all the energy out of the room as he invades.

"No one," I whisper into the phone. "No one. I'll call you back, honey."

I hang up and walk over to Tucker, arms crossed.

"What the hell are you doing here?" I almost growl defensively.

"You're a soccer fan," he remarks, ignoring my question. He's staring at my chest, so I tighten my arms a little more.

"You didn't come to my house to talk about sports, did you?"

Tucker is now facing me. He eagerly rubs my towel over his face and then tosses it onto my small two-seater sofa. "Why do you think I'm here?" he asks me with a particularly intense gleam in his eye.

His tone is teasing, and I know he's looking for me to push the boundaries, as if my anger is amusing him. I try to keep a calm tone as I say, "If you're hoping to get laid, you're in the wrong place. If you're hoping to come and tell me about your little psychopathic fraternity, ditto."

He seems to get the answer he was waiting for. He tilts his head to the side again. I can't help but notice that his hair is now sticking up on all sides, which makes him almost irresistible. Almost.

"Look, this isn't a shelter for stray dogs," I say in exasperation, "so talk or get out."

My annoyance brings a glint of amusement to his eyes.

God, give me a gun.

How can one be so attractive and so unbearable?

"As enticing as these two ideas of getting laid and talking about the next step are, I'm here for something else…partner."

And I finally understand. "Wait, you show up at my house to talk about our damn assignment?"

"I'm sure you're excited to work with me," he teases.

"I'd rather soak in a bath of bleach."

He lets out a hearty laugh. I ignore the effect that sound has on my body and turn my back on him. I walk into my small open kitchen, put my phone on the counter, and sit down on one of the two chairs at the bar.

He follows me, and his gaze is lost on my abandoned phone. "Was that your sister?" he asks.

I nod in response.

"She seems to have quite a temper," he says with a worried look on his face.

By automatism, I ask him in turn, "Do you have a sister too?"

I see his muscles tense up as he leans against my fridge. A dark, murky glint crosses his eyes. I have the impression that he is elsewhere as he runs his hand over his chin, as if by habit. He doesn't answer me and, I think he's not going to when he finally says, in a broken voice, "No. No, she's dead."

Shit. A heavy silence settles between us, and I don't know where to put myself anymore. I stare at him without blinking, but he doesn't look at me. What am I supposed to say or do? I've never been good at comforting people. I don't even know how to do it.

Tucker puts a neutral expression on his face, blocking out any emotion that might try to impose itself on his features. I can't help but wonder what happened to the poor girl.

As I'm about to offer my condolences, he suddenly turns his attention to the picture hanging on my fridge: me, at age 7, with a baseball bat in my hands.

"Hey, that's personal!" I exclaim as he laughs softly.

"Do you play baseball?"

Glad to change the subject, I answer him, "No, I…I just played when I was a kid."

With my father. My throat closes a little. I take a long breath to get out of my memories. I need to talk about something else, right now.

"Are you on the college baseball team?" I ask Tucker.

He raises an eyebrow at me, looking surprised.

I hold myself back from telling him that TJ mentioned a team that he himself is on. Tucker shrugs nonchalantly, though his face says otherwise.

"I got kicked off last year."

Oh…

His words are falsely casual, but the tension in his body is not escaping me. He purses his lips for a second, letting me know that this is a sensitive subject. His jaw contracts several times, and I can't help but analyze it: this habit is like a mannerism for him. I understand that he is very preoccupied, at this moment.

"Well," he says, bringing me out of my thoughts.

"Well…," I repeat as he takes my abandoned computer and puts it in front of me. "Make yourself at home," I exclaim with exasperation.

While his mouth is a few inches from my ear, he whispers to me, "That's what I plan to do."

I don't turn my head in his direction for fear of getting too close to him. Okay, I'm a coward. It's true, I admit it. His smell, mixed with the rain, invades my nostrils. I am unable to move away, but I refuse to give in. I slam my hand on the bar and gesture for him to sit in the other chair. "So," I start, opening my computer, "how do we proceed?"

My angry tone makes him laugh. After I type in my password to unlock the device, he takes it out of my hands again and slides it in front of him. I glare at him and lean in toward him, grabbing his wrist to stop him. "Don't. Touch. My stuff."

I realize that my face is now right in front of his. Why the fuck does his beautiful face disturb me so much?!

Maybe I just need to get laid.

Still leaning over him, I feel his hand on my waist. I flinch at the touch of his fingers under my shirt. His expression changes. He seems ready to jump on me.

I hold back a smile. Mister is aroused, now it's up to me to play. The ball is back in my court.

With an unruffled face, I move away from him and take back my computer. "So, let's start," I order, waiting for him to speak.

He stares at my mouth, then at my outfit. "I sent you an e-mail with our subject," he finally says.

I raise an eyebrow in his direction, my fingers tapping rhythmically on the counter.

"I guess asking you how you got my email address wouldn't do anything?"

"Well, actually, it was just written next to your name on the list."

I stop myself from slapping my forehead, remembering it. I ignore his mocking expression and open my e-mails. "What's the topic?"

"A trial in progress. I'll explain in more detail what she wants from us, but first I'll let you read the main facts."

I shrug. Knowing that it's an assignment for the criminology class, I can already imagine a sordid case. Maybe a woman who killed her husband because he cheated on her? Or a poisoning?

Only, as I read the first words of the file, my heart misses a beat.

Swallowing hard, I read through the investigation, as sordid as I had anticipated. I feel Tucker watching me as the details chill me.

A man killed his wife then his daughter after abusing her several times. He'd already abused her and raped her in the past without anyone knowing anything about it until this evening, when neighbors called the police after hearing noises. The police found the lifeless bodies of the woman and child, mutilated and sexually assaulted.

It's impossible not to think about what my little sister went through.

I'm breaking down little by little. Faced with my reaction, Tucker gets up from his chair to stand closer to me. He leans against the furniture and bends his head towards my face. His arm muscles tighten, and I try to focus on them. It doesn't work.

"Hey?"

My eyes are lost in the void. I find myself plunged months back in time. I see blood. Blood everywhere, and screams. Screams and tears. Those from my sister. My own.

Tucker grips my chin firmly between his forefinger and thumb, then lifts my head toward him. His other hand clings to the back of my neck, preventing me from moving. I can't get out of his grip. His posture is dominant, allowing no contradiction, but his gaze is worried.

"Look at me," he orders me firmly. "Look at me." *Are you okay?* I can read in his eyes.

My eyes get lost in his.

No, no, I'm not okay.

He seems to understand that. He seems to notice that I am totally disconnected from reality. I need a lifeline, immediately.

So, when he pulls me towards him, when he grabs the back of my legs roughly and pulls me up, when he unceremoniously puts me on the counter and presses himself against me, I let him.

I rush through the escape he offers me.

14. GAME MASTER

IRIS

His hand twists in my hair. It settles on the back of my neck again, refusing to let it go. He holds me in place, almost forcing me to accept him, but my body does not see Tucker's attitude as an intrusion. As my breath mingles with his, my fingers grip his hair.

A silent dominance battle then begins between us. I assert my grip, and he does the same. A dull growl escapes from his chest, then he presses himself a little more against me.

His strategy works. My mind is totally focused on the moment. A warm human shield presses against me from all sides, preventing the darkness from enveloping me.

Tucker shows no signs of letting go of me—if I believe his other hand, which presses down on my exposed thigh and squeezes it unmercifully. The mark of his fingers will remain on my skin, for sure. His lips slide over my ear. I feel his tongue along the earlobe just before it continues its descent and ends in the hollow of my neck.

The sensitivity I discover within my own body should send me warning signals. I tilt my head back as he presses himself a little closer to me, sucking my burning skin between his lips.

This is a really, really bad idea.

I have to back off. Just a second. Just a second, and I'll stop.

My mantra runs on a loop in my head as I abruptly tug at Tucker's hair. His eyes meet mine. He looks as lost as I do. But mostly crazy, crazy…with desire? And I'm pretty sure my face must reflect the same expression. I just have to listen to my stupid heart, which palpitates like I'm running a marathon.

Push him away, my conscience tells me. Yeah, I'll do it…

He doesn't give me a chance to think. His lips press against mine once again. A furious kiss where anger and frustration are mixed. The arousal is at its peak between us, forming a thin thread, ready to break. At any moment.

But I shouldn't.

I try to think. Believe me, it's hard enough when you have an insufferable—but sexy as hell—man making you consume yourself from the inside. My reason calls me to order once again.

I don't know him. I can't let him stick his tongue in my mouth. Okay, I want to, but who says we have to let our desires dictate our actions? We all know how it ends. Let pleasure drive you, and you will suffer in some way.

I've been through this before, and I have to admit that I'm not ready to go through it again. The pain is far too great when the desire is replaced by the loss of the loved one. Of course, it fades with time and remains only a shadow over our heads. But it never totally disappears…

I can't let another man have that power over me. Not again. What is happening right now must not go any further. Not under these conditions. I'm not opposed to a one-night stand once in a while. I like to enjoy the male body, the forgetfulness it gives me. It helps me not to think about all the shit that surrounds me and tries to ruin my life.

But when I look into this man's eyes, I feel like he could be much, much more than just a one-night stand. And that sucks.

My willpower returning to the gallop, I pull my head back. Tucker doesn't seem to think that way. He presses himself against me a little more, pressing his erection that stretches his jeans directly against my inner thighs. I need all my concentration to ignore it. Damn, this is way too hot.

While he doesn't seem intent on pulling away, I do the only thing I can think of. My mouth closes, my teeth trapping his lower lip, and I bite. Hard.

A growl comes out of his chest.

"Damn," he swears.

He glares at me. His so particular glance catches me and won't let me go. And I freak out, because I think I kind of like that. So I decide to play it tough. I frown and glare back at him.

My panting breath hits his lips, and my eyes rest on them. His lower lip is slightly open.

He runs his index finger over it, wiping away the single drop of blood.

I swallow my saliva with difficulty. I fidget, my burning thighs sticking to the kitchen counter on which I am still sitting. There is no way to escape. But do I really want to?

"You bit me," he accuses me in his deep voice.

With a small smile on my lips, I shrug my shoulders, trying to look relaxed.

Then his gaze turns dark and calculating.

What the…?

I don't have time to think. His eyes still fixed on mine, Tucker tilts his head toward me. As I rear back, I realize my lips weren't the target of his attack. His mouth reaches my right nipple, and my breath catches.

Is he going to…?

A small cry leaves my mouth as his teeth gently close on my flesh, tugging on it through the fabric of my top.

The muscles in my lower abdomen twitch in response. I barely hold back a moan…of pain? Of unfulfilled desire?

Tucker then runs his tongue over the fabric covering my flesh, hoping to soothe the pain.

Finally, my lips let out an incoherent sound, a sort of ridiculous complaint. Well, not so ridiculous if I believe the boiling body that answers me and the hand that grips my hip.

Then, almost immediately, Tucker steps back.

Is he trying to be reasonable, too?

His gaze wanders to my breast, then to my face. His fists clench, unclench, then clench again. A lock of dark hair falls on his forehead, which he pushes back. His bulging muscles are contracted, his shoulders tense a little more while I still don't move an inch.

The atmosphere is far too heavy. The pressure between us doesn't fade. And that's not a good sign, because too much pressure always ends up exploding.

So, trying to break out of my lethargy, I try a line of irony. "You have this annoying habit of kissing me. I'll end up believing that I really do have an effect on you."

The humor hardly pierces in my voice, and neither he nor I laugh at my teasing sentence. On the contrary, his expression becomes a little harder at my words, as if I meant that comment to be taken seriously.

"It's true," he finally grumbles.

I raise an eyebrow, not sure I follow. What's true? I can't even remember what I said specifically.

"You're having a fucking effect on me," he grumbles under his breath.

He seems to be in the grip of an inner dilemma, as if he hadn't planned to tell me this.

I am stunned by these words. I didn't expect this answer. Shock overwhelms me. Did he really just say that I had a "fucking effect" on him?

Okay, so I'm not the only one who feels that way.

"What the hell are we doing?" I whisper almost to myself.

But he understands my words perfectly. I look for an answer that I can't find on his face. His eyes crinkle a little more, and he nods curtly several times. He doesn't seem to know either.

Faced with this sudden tension, I jump off the counter and try to ignore his gaze on me. I turn my back to him. My palms are sweaty, my heart still beats madly. In a heavy silence, I go back to my computer and close it again. Finally, I tell him in a voice that I hope sounds normal, "I was a little distracted while reading the damn thing, I'll read it again and analyze the facts calmly later."

My sentence makes him understand that he is not welcome here anymore. Faced with the silence that answers me, I raise my head and find him a few steps away from me. He still hasn't moved and is staring at me.

Too disturbing. Turn your gaze away, you sexy bastard, or I won't answer to anything.

"We have three weeks to work the case properly. The trial is on Friday, October 20. We're supposed to go there and compare the jury's decision with the report we've written."

I nod awkwardly and can't help but interrupt him. "Where's the trial?"

I linger for a second on his sore lip, remembering my still sore nipple, and then turn away while waiting for his answer. But first

I have time to notice his expression. He's thinking about the same thing I am.

"Brighton isn't very far from here. So we can leave early, attend the trial, and come back the same day. Since it's a Friday, we'll have the whole weekend to work on our analysis and hand it into Mrs. Richards on Monday. She wants us to critique the jury's decision once it is given to us. What would we have done in their place? Anyway, you know what I mean. For two weeks, we have to immerse ourselves in the case to understand every element of the behavior of the man behind the suspect. She doesn't just want a legal analysis."

I nod again, silent now. Brighton. I know this city, by name at least. I'm looking forward to going there and back in a day. At least we won't be stuck together too long. Honestly, I don't think that would have been a good thing.

This trial better be wrapped up before the vacations at the end of October, before my little sister comes here. I don't want to upset her by being in a bad mood by constantly comparing our fucking past with this case. I don't want Agnes to go back to it against her will. I don't.

I put my computer away, my mind preoccupied.

"All right," I conclude. "I'll read the file as soon as I have some free time."

My tone clearly dismisses him. Yet, once again, Tucker doesn't move. His eyes scan me, and I feel like he's reading me like an open book. For a second, I'm afraid he'll notice my confusion, that he'll understand that this case affects me personally.

My sense of foreboding grows stronger as he approaches and places both hands flat on the furniture between us, the last barrier between our two bodies.

"Are you okay?" Tucker asks me gravely.

Why does he want to know that? I thought he just wanted my body. I try to look irritated. "Of course, why wouldn't I be okay?"

My attempt seems to be a pitiful failure. He understands that I am lying, so he resumes, "I don't know…just…you didn't look right when you found out about the case."

Oh no, I was pretty damn bad, but I'll get over it. I have to. I can't let the horror of my past dictate my future. For me, for my little sister. I smile softly, mockingly.

"So when you saw I was in trouble, you tried to save me by sticking your tongue deep into my mouth? Well done, you just saved a life."

Once again, my line of humor doesn't reach him. "Look, I don't know what's going on with you, but if this case is bothering you, we can—"

"I'm fine," I cut him off firmly, raising my hands in front of me. "I'm just tired. I'll study it later with a clear head."

My harsh words allow no argument. He raises an eyebrow and crosses his arms. I don't like his scrutinizing look. It's far too frank, analyzing me far too much for me to be comfortable. I'm a psych major. Normally it's my job to analyze people. I can see him coming miles away, him and his fucking eyes.

I don't want it to be like this. I lift my chin cheekily and walk towards the front door, silently inviting him to follow me.

I open it wide and put on a polite expression. "I'll text you once I've put together a summary of the facts on my end. We'll just have to combine our summaries afterwards." After all, I have his number since he texted me.

He walks up to me, stopping a few inches away. "We'll have to meet anyway, yes," he says enigmatically.

I raise an eyebrow, inviting him to continue. The expression on his face changes, his eyes are nothing but molten lava. He comes a little closer to me.

"Well, have you forgotten that you won the second game?"

How could I forget, seriously, when the leader of the Pack is coming to hunt me down at home?

"And what are the consequences of my victory? Did I win a star? Oh, maybe a sticker?"

At last, a little scoundrel smile appears on his face. "You've earned the right to continue the competition."

"A new race in the forest? Another orgy? What if I don't want to? I asked you to leave me alone."

"No… and no," he says, his voice getting stronger. "And about your desire…come on, redhead, I know you're dying to win again. In fact, we're going to test you a bit to see if you're worthy of joining our—what did you call it again?—our psychopathic fraternity."

"In other words, you want to see if I'm a chicken?"

He nods in agreement. "We're not interested in weak people. We want you to have guts."

Then I look solemn and announce.

"Honey, I've got more balls than any guy you know."

He bursts out laughing at my sudden declaration. But why did I say that? Why am I so anxious to prove to him that I'm a match for his psychopathic cult? Why does my fucking curiosity always silence my reason?

"Only your mentor will judge," he announces.

I almost choke. What's this new shit?! "My 'what?' Wait, are you serious? You're going to graft a mentor onto me who will have to tell me what to do to prove that I have balls? No kidding."

Tucker stares directly at my inner thighs. "Yeah, I'm not sure you actually have any."

My mouth hangs open in surprise as he finally steps out of my apartment. His broad shoulders cross the small hallway and move out of my sight.

"Wait!" I exclaim loudly.

He stops but doesn't turn around.

"Who is he, my mentor?"

He tilts his head back slightly but I can't see his eyes.

"Who do you think is it, redhead?"

15. SAVE HER

IRIS

Blood. Blood everywhere. I bend down and, with my trembling hand, pick up the broken frame from the floor. A drop of blood has splashed onto the picture of my parents, my little sister, and me smiling at the camera.

"I know you're hiding," a male voice rumbles a few feet away.

I stick against the wall of the hallway. My heart misses a beat. The stranger passes by me. He doesn't see me, the darkness hiding my silhouette. I don't glance into our living room, I know what scene I'll find there. Before I pushed open the front door, I heard from outside the house the screams. My parents were screaming. Then I heard gunshots. But I didn't hear Agnes, she must be hidden. And I must find her before that man does.

I tiptoe through the narrow hallway to the stairs. I don't hear any noise.

I try to ignore the panic that is growing in me. A part of me urges myself to go to the living room. But another part of me orders myself to save my little sister before it's too late.

The police are coming. I must get Agnes out of danger. I reach the last step of the wooden staircase. It creaks gently.

Shit, no!

I stand still, feeling sick. My limbs tremble. Please.

I hear footsteps at the bottom of the stairs. A voice slams into my back.

"I love this game," exclaims the man.

I turn towards him. He's a stranger. His face is covered in blood. His orange jumpsuit is torn in some places. A serial number is written on his pocket.

My eyes fall to his. They freeze my blood. He seems crazy, lost in a world that is not ours. A proud smile curls his lips as I turn and start running.

"It's no use," he laughs behind me.

"Agnes!" I shout.

No answer comes. I hear the man's footsteps on the stairs as I run towards my sister's room. But my intuition tells me not to stop at that door, but to go to my own.

I remember those stupid hide-and-seek games Agnes used to force me to play. Her favorite hiding place comes to mind.

The footsteps of the stranger come a little closer. As I reach my room, a hand grabs my shoulder.

"Let me go!" I shout.

His powerful fingers squeeze my skin. I scream and scratch his face. The man grunts while moving away. I don't lose a second and push him before slamming the door behind me. As I lock it, a fist slams hard against the wood of my door.

"You think you can hide?" he yells, knocking again.

The police will come. They're almost here, I repeat to myself in my mind.

"Agnes," I gasp, dropping down beside the bed to look underneath.

But my little sister isn't there.

"Agnes, it's me." My voice trembles with despair.

The door won't hold for long, the wood might break at any moment. But I know she's here.

"I…Iris?" whispers a tiny voice.

I stand up abruptly and run to my closet. I open it wide and discover my little sister, curled up. Her light brown eyes, so similar to mine, are filled with tears that she tries to contain bravely.

I pull her to me.

"It's okay," I whisper, grabbing her face.

Her lips are trembling. Seeing her pink pajamas torn at the neckline, my stomach twists.

"Mo…Mom…" she moans with difficulty. "He…he killed her."

I close my eyes and inhale deeply. I can't let it overwhelm me now. I have to save her. The police are coming. What the hell is taking them so long?!

I turn around, staring at my bathroom door, on the other side of my room. We have to lock ourselves in. I pull my little sister behind me, but at the same time, my bedroom door shatters.

The stranger enters the room, his eyes are staring at Agnes' body with an appreciative look.

"Found," he breathes, victorious.

I stand up in front of him to block him with my body. He hits me violently in the face. Out of breath, I collapse on the ground.

My head hits the floor, my vision becomes blurred. I close my eyes tightly and open them again, trying to fix my gaze on something. My fingers rest on my aching jaw.

A muffled scream wakes me from my torpor. Stifling a groan of pain, I pull myself up as best I can, on all fours.

My vision remains blurred, but I manage to understand the situation: the stranger is pinning my little sister on the ground.

Agnes hits his large chest with her small fists, which has no effect. The man laughs harshly and pulls her hair to immobilize her.

"No," I try to scream despite my sore mouth.

My little sister screams as he grabs her throat…so little…he'll kill her.

I try to draw on my last bit of strength…but I'm weak…no. I don't have the right to be weak, I have to protect her. I straighten up and almost flinch before jumping on the man's back with a raging scream.

"Let her go," I roar while pulling his hair with all my strength.

He sends his elbow in my ribs. The impact cuts my breath. I groan and kick him, but he throws me off to the side again. I roll on the carpet. Agnes is crying. Her cries resound in my ears, tirelessly. She begs him. She doesn't understand what's going on, but she begs him to let her go, she begs him not to kill me.

The man doesn't care. A lustful gleam appears in his eyes.

"I always preferred the children," he murmurs on a tone of confidence.

Then he passes to the higher level. His hand with the bitten nails settles on the belly of Agnes. I shake myself mentally. I look desperately in my room for something which could help me. I straighten up as best I can, leaning on my dresser, and my eyes rest on an object that glows softly in the semi-darkness.

Agnes screams louder. I must save her. I would do anything for her. Anything.

I grab the pair of scissors lying on the cabinet. My hands are shaking with fear, but also with pure hatred. I turn to them. Seeing my little sister lying on the ground, the man getting ready to undress her, I don't hesitate for a second.

I rush to his back, my hand in the air.

A scream resounds in my ears. This time, it is not my little sister's. The scissors dig into the man's shoulder blade. He swings wildly, trying to push me away, but I can't let him go. I pull the scissors out of his body and stick them back into his flesh, a few inches further.

A searing pain hits my thigh. My eyes go down as a red stain starts to grow on my clothes. And I understand why: he had a razor blade in his front pocket, and he just sliced me with it. But I don't care about the pain. Adrenaline is running through my veins. Agnes' cries help me to hold on.

Then with a last howl of rage, I take out the pair of scissors planted in the back of the stranger and push them with all my strength into his neck.

Blood splashes on me, an inarticulate sound comes out from the mouth of this sick man. He collapses to the ground. My trembling fingers are covered in blood. My vision is still blurred, but I can see his breathing weaken then stop completely a few seconds later.

My crying increases as I fall backwards. I am in shock, I can't see anything. I can't see my little sister, but I can feel her throwing herself at me, sobbing. Her little hands grab my cheeks as she says incomprehensible words.

I killed him. I just killed that man.

Does that make me a bad person? I saved my little sister. I will always save her. Always.

I wake up with a start, gasping for breath. Sitting up in bed, I feel sweat dripping down my back. I try to understand what's going on. It takes me a few seconds to reconnect with reality. I examine my room in the darkness.

The moon lights up the small room through my curtains. I rub my swollen eyelids and discover that some tears were shed.

I swallow a grunt as I massage my aching neck, then glance down at my tangled sheets. Papers are scattered all around me. That's when I remember. I fell asleep while I was studying the case I need to analyze with Tucker. An unpleasant chill runs through my body. This study is going to be difficult.

I can only imagine how the mother and daughter of this psychopath, who is going to trial in just over two weeks, must have suffered.

Ever since Tucker stopped by my house two days ago and things got…off track again between us, I've been trying to figure out the damn thing. I know he's going to get back to me soon to debrief, yet I can only scratch the surface. It's like my brain refuses to focus, refuses to dive into this case.

A part of me would almost urge me to drop it, to unenroll

from this course and take another. But I know that won't solve my problem. So I have to push myself and move my ass.

I have to move on and let my past heal, even though we all know that scars don't go away. We know that the most appalling wounds we suffer never close.

"Notice to the lambs who have become cubs!"

I startled and put my hand on my heart.

"You scared the shit out of me, asshole," I growl at TJ, without slowing my pace.

He laughs softly and walks beside me as I head out to my car. He puts his arm on my shoulders and matches my pace.

"Come on, I'm not the big bad wolf…not me."

I shake my shoulders to get out of his grip and sigh with a falsely defeated air.

"Come on, don't pout," TJ says in an almost pleading voice, grabbing my shoulder.

I stop and glare at him. "What do you want this time?"

He raises his eyebrows as if it were obvious, "Well, to talk to my best friend."

I resist with all my strength the smile that tries to show up on my face. This guy makes me desperate! He's a total freak, that's for sure. How can he be friends with Tucker? I feel like I'm seeing night and day. While one attracts others with his super douchebag magnetism, the other goes out of his way to charm hearts with his poor humor.

"I don't have time right now, TJ."

He smiles cheekily, revealing a row of white teeth. He tilts his head at me, raising his eyebrows.

"I know…your time is for someone else."

I ponder his words, lost. Then, realizing he's talking about Tucker, I throw my fist into his shoulder hard. "Stop talking shit, you little prick."

He pretends to be really hurt, then gives me a solemn look. "I'll be as quiet as a grave, Scout's honor."

"If you keep this up, you're really going to end up in a grave, Scout's honor," I repeat with a smile that is anything but innocent.

He laughs softly, as if he was really amused by the threat. "Well, having fun with you helps pass the time, but that's not why I came. I'm the messenger. The sexy messenger."

"Sexy, huh…not sure we have the same definition of the word," I tease him in turn. "Tucker sent you?"

"A girl, actually. But I can understand why you think Tucker is a girl."

I look at him, speechless. I…what the hell is this guy on, drugs?

"I'm here for Yeleen. She's inviting the Cub Scouts to join the party she helped organize in one of the student residences. Be there at 8 p.m. in the west wing of the campus, and just follow the screaming and the music that will be playing."

I shrug my shoulders and shake my head. "I'm working tonight, I can't go."

"Oh," sighs TJ, disappointed. "I thought I was going to surprise my cousin by taking you, but you just ruined my joy."

"Gee, I'm so sorry, honey," I exclaim wryly, finally walking away. However, as I replay his words in my head, I stop and turn around abruptly. "Wait, what did you say?"

TJ, who was already backing away, turns to me, one eyebrow raised.

"Your cousin?" I repeat, confused. "You and Tucker are cousins?"

He gives me a big smile and walks away without answering me.

"Fuck, does it run in the family to walk away without answering, or what?" I shout as only his laughter reaches me.

So, Tucker and TJ are cousins? Holy shit, why do I even care? It's not my problem.

I go on my way, determined to banish their stupid family from my thoughts.

A few hours later, I count the minutes until my shift is over.

The bar is pretty quiet tonight, so my colleague Buck was able to go home early. I stifle a yawn as I stare at the dial of my watch again. It's almost eleven p.m. A colleague will take over, and I can go home and collapse on my bed.

I am rinsing a glass when a male figure enters my field of vision.

"Good evening, what can I get you?" I ask politely, raising my head.

My heart misses a beat when I recognize the man standing in front of me.

I try not to let anything show as I try to remember his first name. Matt. The guy who had started to annoy me before Tucker intervened and ordered me to stay away from him.

"Hi," he says cheerfully, resting his elbows on the bar.

His smile is meant to be charming, but I ignore it completely. I throw a glance at the surroundings. He is not in the company of his stupid friends tonight. He runs his hand through his blond hair, tangling it in the process. He seems stressed.

"Good evening," I repeat, "what can I get you?"

A nervous twitch comes to him. He blinks strangely, as if he didn't like my tone.

"We can be on familiar terms, you know. After all, this is the second time we've met."

And I wish I'd never seen you again, asshole.

"So, what is your—"

"Do I look like I want to make friends?" I cut him off coldly.

I resume my task, no longer caring about him. I hardly know Tucker, yet my brain has heeded his warning. I become suspicious of the guy waiting right next door, as if I really should be warry of him. I replay Tucker's words to myself while glancing at Matt. What happened between them?

"I'll have a Busch," he finally says in a less than pleasant voice.

I nod and pour his beer as he hands me a twenty.

"You can keep the change," he says with a small smile.

Does he think he can get any power or right over me that way? No, thank you! I need the money, but I'm certainly not going to take his tip. I make a return trip to the register, collect the change and slam it next to his hand.

"High Peaks Bar wishes you a pleasant evening," I say coldly.

"Maybe you can make it better," he says in my direction.

"I'm not open for business, not at all. So let's calm down and you can pack up your stupid and heavy flirting. I made it clear the other day. Do you understand?"

I walk away without waiting for his answer. I don't like this guy, there's something strange about him.

I approach my colleague who has just arrived. "I'm done," I tell him as I head to the back of the bar, eager to get changed and go home.

This day has been way too long. As I walk out into the night and get to my car, I see Matt approaching from my left. I ignore him but the bastard is blocking my way.

"Move," I order him.

"So we're on familiar terms?" he laughs, refusing to let me pass.

I take a deep breath, trying to calm down…and not to panic. This glint in his eye reminds me of someone else, and I hate it.

"You don't act very nice," he continues, staring at my legs, "but you're hot."

Without me expecting it, he grabs my arm.

16. EXCITEMENT

IRIS

"Say that again and I swear I'll make you eat your balls," I reply, pulling my arm away from his.

"Calm down, redhead."

That nickname makes me cringe. Why do I hate it when he says it, but I'm okay with it when it comes from Tucker?

"Get out of my way," I order again.

Just as he is about to get a little closer, a figure appears in the night, just behind him. I don't recognize him at first, but I am sure I have seen him somewhere. I look at his dark eyes, his shaved head. He's not huge, but he's pretty beefy. Staring at the tattoo that runs along his neck, I remember.

He's that guy who stood next to Tucker at the party. Dan.

As Matt places a hand on my forearm, Dan stands up beside me. He puts his body in the way and roughly grabs the blond's shoulder.

"Didn't you understand what we said, Deels?" he spits in a powerful voice, pushing Matt away from us.

Speechless, I look at this stranger taking my defense.

"Dan," greets Matt coldly.

"We've already warned you, stay away from her," orders Dan.

I stare at his back, confused. Wait…what? What does he mean, they warned him?

"That's cool," laughs Matt, throwing his hands up in the air. "We were just talking, right, pretty?"

I glare at him a little more, holding back from spitting in his face. My voice snaps dryly, "I'm not your pretty girl."

Matt undresses me with his eyes while a smile remains on his mouth. He takes a step back when Dan seems to lose patience.

"I wasn't going to hurt her," the blond man continues with a calculating look.

"You break everything you touch, Deels," mumbles Dan, shoulders still tense.

Matt leans towards him, as if he's going to confide in him. "Come on, man, it's not my fault Debbie was fragile. You should have kept your lioness on a leash, man. Her claws loved digging into me."

I don't know who this Debbie is, or what happened between her and Matt, or between her and Dan. But what I do know is that Dan seems transformed when he hears her name.

A raging sound comes from his chest as he moves at breakneck speed and brings his fist down on Matt's face. The latter steps back, holding his jaw. His features are distorted with anger, but he doesn't take a step in our direction.

"Talk about her one more time, one more time, and I won't come to you. He'll find you and he'll break your legs before he blows your face off. Then I'll finish you off, and we'll leave your body to rot in a pile of shit."

He? Who is this *he* that will come to kill Matt?

Tucker?

I'm caught up in the middle of the fight and can't get away.

Matt walks away as Dan catches his breath. After a minute, the hatred hasn't left his features, but he tries to control himself by turning to me.

Neither he nor I say a word. I don't understand half the conversation, but I know Dan has come to rescue me, so I pull out the first thing that comes to mind, "I believe I should…thank you."

He seems surprised. His features soften slightly. He looks older than me by a few years, but he is still young. Yet he seems to carry a heavy burden on his shoulders, as if he had already seen too much for a lifetime, as if he had already gone through awful times that had marked him forever.

"It's nothing," he replies carelessly.

A question loops in my mind, and I can't hold my words. "Were you watching me?"

A small smile comes to him, as if this idea seems absurd to him. And it's absurd to me too. Why would he play babysitter when we don't know each other?

"Actually, TJ sent me to pick you up."

I finally understand. I hold back a growl as I roll my eyes. "He never fucking lets go," I grumble, crossing my arms. "You came for nothing, go tell your friend that I won't come. The cub refuses to join the cult of psychopaths tonight."

He clenches his jaw, looking at me intently.

"You shouldn't say that," he says in a calm voice.

I raise an eyebrow. So he can't stand me insulting their group? "And why not?"

His gaze is lost in the void.

"Because they're a family. Always there for you. When you're down, when you've just lost the only person you love and you don't want to do anything else, this family helps you get back up. Maybe it's not your blood, but it's the one you chose.

A family…a word that grips my heart. I used to have a close family, a family that loved me. And it was ripped away from me overnight without warning.

I can't disagree with Dan. Because I know how important family is.

"Come on," he orders me gently. "Come with me."

TUCKER

The Pack is more complex than it seems. There's the core group of ten or so members—My Family—and then there are the ten or so other members who are in the group but not totally part of it. They're basically there to help us throw the most insane parties ever and the first two stages of selection.

Tonight was supposed to be a small committee, just the core group. We were supposed to talk about potential newcomers. Two spots are available, and there are four candidates.

That's the rule this year. Only two spots because I don't want to go overboard. We need freshness, we need renewal, but most of all we need balance in our fraternity.

So, it was just supposed to be a couple of us, but obviously the plan changed, because when I arrive, the student house is packed.

Can we ever be at peace? It wasn't enough that my mom threw a fit trying to unplug my sister's breathing tube right before I left, I also had to have Yeleen and Sarah invite the whole campus?

I mutter a swear word when a guy nearly spills his fucking cup on me. He looks up and, when he recognizes me, apologizes several times as he moves out of my way.

That's right, man, move before I explode.

Because it's going to happen, it's inevitable. I've been under a lot of stress the last few days, and what happened tonight isn't exactly helping me contain myself.

I make it the rest of the way through the crowd without difficulty. I'm not seen as the tough guy in this room. No, it's much deeper than that. They respect me, my reputation precedes me.

I join Yeleen and her boyfriend, sitting on an old couch, and drop into the chair next to them, my head back.

"Tucker," Yeleen exclaims in surprise. "I thought you weren't coming."

I mumble a grunt but don't bother to answer her.

"Are you okay, man?" asks Trey as he leans over to me.

Are you okay? Damn it, what kind of question is that? Who cares if I'm okay? I don't answer him, my gaze settling on the small crowd gathered in the living room.

TJ is talking with a pretty brunette who is smiling at him far too much to be disinterested. I give her another five minutes before she gets caught up in his net.

Trey hands me a cigarette, I take a drag and give it back to him after a nod of thanks.

"You should stop smoking," Yeleen says reproachfully. "You'll die faster with that."

"Who cares," I say with a chuckle. "Where are the new guys?"

"Amelia is outside with Chase. Sanchez had to leave early. We couldn't have talked tonight anyway, considering the number of strangers who showed up."

"And the redhead?"

An image of Iris, all hot between my arms, imposes itself on my mind. While my cock hardens almost instantly at this memory, I try not to let anything show on my face.

But Yeleen seems to have picked up on it. Clinging to Trey a little more, she says to me, "Why are you asking me where Iris is when I'm sure you did your own research?"

I don't answer, but I glare at her because, damn it, she's right. TJ told me she was working tonight and wouldn't be coming in. And while he was telling me how much he liked her temper, I could only think of her bare skin under my fingers.

And I don't like that. I don't like that at all.

I'd better find another girl just as hot and get the redhead out of my head, and fast.

I intended to fuck her and leave her. But that's too dangerous now. I don't like the hold her body has had on me in such a short time. I don't like the way I react around her. My brain wants to be reasonable, but my cock…

A feminine scent invades my nostrils as a hand rests on my tense thigh, close to my erection. A heady scent, much too strong, as if my nose was dipped in a bag of candy.

Nothing to do with the light vanilla smell that stuck to me two days ago. My God, what am I saying? I'm being a total idiot.

I let Kacey's hand squeeze my thigh and move up slowly, brazenly. The freshman wants to make it here but screwed up the second test. She seems to think that being between my thighs will help her.

I rest my arms on the armrests, watching for her next move. Let's see what she does next. Her long black hair is scattered over her shoulders as she gives me a shy look.

Oh, no need to pretend, honey, I know exactly what you want.

Sarah stares at us strangely from across the room, but I ignore her. Eventually, I am able to focus on the moment.

Kacey brushes my erection with her fingertips, clearly not caring that we're being scrutinized by half the room.

"Am I the one who's making you feel good, Tucker?"

No.

I frown as the word almost leaves my mouth. I pull myself together, a smile on my lips. "What do you think?"

She laughs softly, biting her bottom lip and pressing her chest against my chest as her tongue goes for my neck. I close my eyes and struggle to focus on her tongue, not someone else's. But my cock is somewhere else.

Shit, I'm just confused by what just happened, nothing else, right?

"My best friend!" shouts TJ from across the room.

My eyelids open abruptly. I turn my head toward the living room entrance while Kacey is still licking my neck.

My fists clench, and I restrain myself from tossing the girl aside unceremoniously. I don't understand my reaction until I notice, a few feet away, a hazel gaze pointed at me. A look which wants to be neutral, but which is far from achieving that.

A furious look.

17. AN EYE FOR AN EYE, A TOOTH FOR A TOOTH

IRIS

My brain tells me to move, to turn my head, but I can't. Like a dummy, I stare at the scene. The brunette on Tucker's lap continues to stroke his cock while whispering something in his ear.

She moans and rubs her breasts against him.

Tucker watches me strangely. The look of surprise in his eyes disappears, his expression changes. His hands rest on the girl's shoulders, as if wondering what he should do.

My eyes analyze his body while he remains frozen. From here, I can see the erection stretching his pants. He's enjoying her attention. I bet he's already imagining fucking her.

I'm stupid.

This is what assholes like him do. I knew it, I have only myself to blame.

A few days ago, he was between my thighs. Okay, we were caught up in a moment, without thinking, and okay, we definitely didn't have sex. But damn, his tongue was in my mouth and he was moaning against me.

Maybe he realized that I wouldn't give him what he wanted, so he's getting his action elsewhere? After all, he doesn't have to answer to me, right? We keep pushing each other away, calling each other names. So…why do I feel this way? Damn it, am I jealous?

I take it on myself to not let anything show and then, with a haughty air, I smile widely at him. I know my expression is far from friendly, I know my eyes must be shooting lightning bolts. But I can't let him understand that he just touched me. I can't let him see that his behavior is doing something to me.

Don't let it show, Iris. Don't look at them anymore.

Hold back for a few more minutes.

Yet I can't help but give them a quick glance.

I stifle a grunt when I see him push the chick away unceremoniously. Shit, shit.

I take a step back, refusing to pay attention to this scene for another second. But I don't know where to go. Dan, who is standing next to me watching this all go down, shakes his head, eyebrows raised, at Tucker. TJ stares at me with an apologetic look on his face.

Dan puts his hand on my elbow and says, "Follow me."

His tone doesn't leave me any room to refuse. I let him lead me into the kitchen, which is a little less crowded than the other rooms. Out of sight, I finally let myself go. I pull away from Dan and run my hands through my hair.

"Shit," I whisper angrily. Fucking asshole. "Fucking ball-less asshole."

Dan laughs beside me. His serious face relaxes in front of me for the first time. He opens a beer from the fridge and hands it to me. I wave it away, still lost in my thoughts.

Why did Tucker push the girl away? He seemed to be enjoying himself. I'm sure he would have let her suck him off in front of everyone. A half-naked girl pleasuring him in front of other people's eyes, is that what gets him off? Like at the party in the old chapel? The intertwined bodies, the moans that come from all sides, that's his thing? Well, fuck him, it's not mine.

If he likes horny girls chasing him, good for him.

Dan asks me another question but I don't catch his words. I look at him, stunned.

"Look, I don't need anything," I tell him, determined to get out of this house.

What the hell am I doing here anyway?!

He ignores me, opens a bottle of vodka, and pours it into a glass that he hands me. I stare at the cup without seeing him. I shake my head again, and he finally takes the alcohol back. I will never let another drop of liquor enter my body. Fuck, the last time I did that, I…I try to slow my breathing, trying to control myself. I lean against the counter and run my hands through my hair again.

I want to block out the memories, but I can't. I see us pouring vodka glasses, ignoring the warnings. I remember him getting angry behind the wheel because he was a mean drunk. Then I remember the sound of the impact, the sound of the metal hitting the ground, the sound of the hood folding over itself. Then the smell of blood…

It's only after a second that I realize that Dan is standing beside me. He takes a sip of beer, looking at me. I swallow my pain and look away.

Among the crowd I see through the open kitchen, I see Tucker elbowing his way through the students. He doesn't seem to know where we went. His gaze wanders around the room, eyebrows furrowed. That's right, look for us, you poor jerk.

I squint a little more as I see the girl from earlier trying to hold him by the arm. I know I shouldn't care. I should look away, but I can't.

"Stop staring at him," says Dan. I raise an eyebrow in his direction, but he doesn't let me speak. "Believe me, that girl may have been rubbing against his dick, but he was imagining a completely different person in her place."

"What are you talking about? He does what he wants," I announce, shrugging my shoulders and taking a casual look.

"Of course, I'm going to pretend you don't look like an angry and probably jealous little redhead."

"I'm not jealous." I say as I approach him. "And stop playing devil's advocate. We don't know each other, you and I. And I don't know him either. He can rub up against whoever he wants, I don't care."

That's a lie.

Dan rolls his eyes and puts his beer on the counter next to me. "He's my buddy, but he can be a real jerk when he wants to be. "Make him struggle," he says before leaving the room.

Struggle? Why is Dan on my side? For that matter, are there really two sides?

"Make him struggle."

I repeat this sentence to myself mentally. Give him a hard time, that I can do.

Of course, I was jealous. And what better way to make him struggle than to return the blow he just gave me?

TUCKER

"Where is she?"

"Who?" asks Dan with a little smile as I reach him.

He might be my best friend, but at this very moment, I want to kill him. Because he's clearly fucking with me.

"Are you talking about Kacey?" continues Dan, raising his eyebrows. "She's probably waiting for you in a room, hot as hell. You should join her."

I swallow a growl while passing a hand over my neck. My eyes scan the surroundings and the words come out of my mouth without me being able to hold them back. "I don't want her."

Fuck, am I really trying to track down a chick who's going to reject me for sure now? What the hell am I doing? It's not my style, girls come to me, not the other way around!

"Not redheaded enough for you, maybe…?"

"Fuck you," I growl at Dan. "Help me to find her, now."

His eyes twinkle with amusement as he stares at something behind me.

"I think I just found her," he says, laughing under his breath. "Maybe you're interested in her, but right now, she really doesn't seem to be interested in you. Damn, that's hot…"

My jaw nearly drops as I turn toward the living room. My fists clench instantly, and I see red.

18. FUCKING AMAZING

TUCKER

"I have to admit, she puts on a pretty good show. Right?" says Dan to tease me.

A rumble comes from my chest. I try to put on a casual face, but I can't. "I don't care," I spit.

My eyes stare at Iris, that little bitch, as she approaches the guy lying shirtless on the table. My breath quickens as I move through the crowd.

"Hey," Dan calls out to me, "who cares what they do, right?"

I ignore him, continuing on my way. The guy laughs softly when Iris takes a pinch of salt from the palm of his hand and licks it off with her tongue. I know exactly what's going to happen.

Eyes glistening, she pays no attention to the cheering students and leans toward the student still lying down, his head close to hers.

The son of a bitch is holding a piece of lemon in his mouth between his lips. My breath quickens and my jaw contracts a little more as Iris lowers her head. Her mouth opens, and her teeth catch the part of the lemon that is sticking out. She puts her lips right on the end, sucking the juice.

"She's fucking amazing," laughs TJ, a few steps away.

I glare at him, but he doesn't even notice me.

"You, you're about to lose it," Yeleen whispers as she stands next to me.

With some difficulty, I shake my head, wanting to show her that I have everything under control.

"I know you, Tucker, I probably know you better than you know yourself. You want to get her back, like a jealous caveman. Is there something going on between you two?"

"Nothing," I say through my teeth.

But then Iris leans into the guy's belly button and prepares to suck down the tequila, and I can't hold out anymore. Without further thought, I walk towards them. Some of the others turn their heads towards me, probably not understanding the murderous look that clings to my features.

"Move," I order the guy lying down.

I don't wait for him to do it. I grab his shoulder firmly and pull him off the table. He almost falls and cusses as he looks around.

"Damn it," curses Dan, realizing that I'm not in control of anything anymore.

Iris stares at me, a smile forming on her lips, as if she had just won something, as if I've just reacted exactly as she expected.

"What's wrong with you?" the guy spits as he pushes me away.

He reeks of cheap beer, and his glassy eyes don't make him threatening at all. I absorb his shove, but as he tries to push my shoulder away again, I shift and grab him by the throat. I hate fighting with these assholes. This is my territory. I don't have to use my fists to get respect. Playing tough guy has never been my thing. But I can feel my fingers tightening a little more.

"Get out of my way or I'll break your knees," I say through clenched teeth.

I release him and push him away, sending him bumping into one of his buddies who was waiting at his back. He passes by me to get away, but I hear him mutter to himself, "All that for a little pussy."

Nobody seems to have heard his words, but I did. "Hey!" I call out to him.

He turns to me, looking annoyed. I send my fist into his right cheekbone. His head snaps back as several people scream. The student is too drunk to get up. He spits at my feet, grumbling that he is going to kill me. Dan pushes him back, blocking my view.

The music continues to echo between the four walls, yet no one dares to speak anymore.

"Is there a problem?" I ask the silent crowd.

Nobody answers, but someone lets out a little laugh. It's Iris, who seems to be laughing at me.

What is all this shit?

"OK, the show's over," says TJ in a friendly voice. "We came here to drink, so let's drink!"

People are slowly looking away, going back to drinking and finding hook-ups. As for me, I don't move. I continue to stare at Iris, who is standing on the other side of the table.

She leans towards me.

"An eye for an eye, a tooth for a tooth."

With furrowed brows, I analyze her words, and then I understand. She did this on purpose to provoke me. And, damn it, I jumped right into her trap. "You bitch," I spit in her direction.

"You jerk," she retorts, now with a dark look on her face.

My head gets closer to hers. Our bodies are still separated by this damn table.

"Shut up," I snap at her. I hate her behavior. It makes me want to…why the fuck is she turning me on when I'm so mad?

She lets out a throaty laugh. "I'm not a dog, I'm not going to shut up just because Tucker Bomley asks. You may be a king to them, but to me you're just a big asshole."

My jaw nearly drops as an unrivaled fury rises inside me. She stares at me with a disdainful look and then rolls away with her hips. Dan, who was watching the scene with his arms crossed, joins me.

"Well, it seems that this time you have found a playmate worthy of you…"

IRIS

I walk away from the living room without a backward glance. Yet I feel his eyes burning into the back of my neck. Oh, he's on edge. I'm pretty sure he's going to start a fight with someone else, just to let out his anger, or maybe he's going to grab a girl who's flirting with him and fuck her. I block out my thoughts, my feelings, wanting only one thing, to get out of here. I didn't think tonight, I acted on my instinct to push Tucker over the edge, like he had just done with me. He had to understand that I'm not a little thing that obeys him at his word.

And that fool finally dared to talk to me like a dog that should be begging at his feet.

As I cross the hallway toward the front door, I hear footsteps behind me. I don't need to turn around; I already know who is behind me. I pick up the pace, and instead of going straight ahead, I turn right into the hallway. When I feel a hand grab my upper arm, I give him a nudge with my elbow.

"Easy," Tucker growls as I hit him in the stomach.

I turn to him, refusing to let him reach me. "Don't touch me," I order him. Then I push him again. "Don't touch me again. Or next time I won't aim for your chest, I'll aim for your balls."

Everything comes out, my anger at his grumpy tone and the so-called jealousy I felt when I saw the chick touching him.

He doesn't answer me. His jaw is so contracted it looks like his teeth are going to break. His eyes are black, their color difference muted by the fury in them. Good, because I'm furious too.

"Do you get it? I'm not one of those—"

I let out a little scream as he grabs my wrists with one hand, my neck with the other and presses me against his body.

No, no, no, it's too easy!

But already, his mouth is crushing mine. A muffled noise comes out of his chest when his lips press on mine, conquering.

I release my wrists and hit his face with my right hand. I step back as he lets go of me, short of breath.

"What did you just do?" he asks, letting out an incredulous laugh.

I glare at him. I had decided to stay calm, but it's difficult in front of him. So, I explode too. "Who do you think you are, kissing me again? I'm not a bitch in heat. You can't kiss me and then have someone else blow you the next minute. And you can't forbid me from touching other guys, either."

Tucker moves closer to me, looking threatening. "You asked for it. You looked for a reaction from me, so you got it."

"And that confirms to me that you're an asshole. We don't know each other, and you acted towards that guy like you were… jealous."

He silently takes the hit and then retorts, "Like you were jealous of Kacey."

I'm pissed that he could read me so easily, so I lie, "No. I was disappointed when I realized you were just looking for some pussy."

The reasonable part of my brain wonders why I'm reacting so bluntly when I shouldn't care, but I guess I don't really know myself. Tucker brings out my beastly side, a side I had carefully buried. I hate that he gets to me so easily. The only comfort I get is that he seems as damaged and lost as I am. And by the angry look on his face, I can tell my words got to him. Good! You asshole!

He snaps, "Fuck you."

"Just so you know, if I do get fucked, it won't be by you."

He comes a little closer, and I find myself cornered against the wall. I am trapped, my back against the stone, yet I stare him down. My breathing quickens in spite of myself. I hate the effect he has on me. It's as if my body is laughing at his foolish behavior, as if he only wants one thing: his lips, again.

Tucker leans forward. He doesn't touch me. He places his hands and then his forearms against the wall behind my head. He locks me in a human cage without ever making contact with me.

"Why are you trying to drive me crazy?" he whispers to himself.

His breath slows down, hits my lips.

"Tell me I'm not the only one who is," he then orders me, almost desperate.

I say nothing. But when his gaze becomes calmer, as if the storm were receding deep inside him, I finally confess, "I was jealous."

He inhales deeply, nodding slowly. "And so was I," he replies.

We continue to stare at each other for a good minute. His arms tighten a little more around me, but he's still careful not to actually touch me.

"I don't want to be jealous of a guy I don't know," I continue. "I also don't want you to kiss me and act like you own me, which you don't. You don't want a girl who acts like that either, do you?"

He swallows hard. "No," he says simply.

The truth is, I'm constantly stirred by Tucker, and I have no right to be. I can't let him have such a hold on my body. No one will be able to reach me again, love me and then abandon me. I won't let anyone get close to me until I feel that way. So, I have to cut off everything that's messing with me, while there's still time.

I can't fucking do that to Rafael. I remember the sweetness of his arms, his fiercely protective air, his presence when I needed him. Then I see him again, his body frozen, half crushed under the metal of the destroyed car. I see him again, his breath fading as he whispered to me one last time that he loved me.

But what's wrong with me? No one will take the place he occupies in my head. No one will be able to stir me up like he did.

I won't let anyone get close to me and then hurt me and destroy me even more, not when I'm still not rebuilt.

"So, we're going to stop this bullshit between us. We're going to stop letting our damn bodies speak. You don't touch me anymore, you understand? We reacted stupidly tonight, and I don't want to react like that again for a boy, for you."

He doesn't answer me, but I guess he agrees with me. These barriers are necessary, especially knowing that we'll have to work together.

So, after endless seconds, Tucker steps back and releases me. "Okay." He walks away, but just before he turns the corner, he gives me one last look. "If you can fake it, then so can I," he adds.

And he disappears from my sight.

19. UNKNOWN TERRITORY

IRIS

It's time for me to suck it up and do what I said I'd do. I grab the file on the Mikael Larey case that Mrs. Richards gave us and start to flick through it. I have to get to work on this assignment.

According to the report, the police arrived at the crime scene at 1:53 a.m. after being called by the neighbors, who were alerted by screams coming from the house. When they entered the living room, they found the woman and the little girl lying in a pool of blood, right next to the father.

I break out into a cold sweat as flashes of memories try to impose themselves on me. I try to stay focused, but these damn images are burning my skin. I take a deep breath while rubbing my eyes.

This is different, Iris, your situation is completely different from this case. Pull yourself together, damn it!

I swallow hard and continue reading the report. The father is accused of abusing his daughter. There's evidence of rape, but no DNA was found inside her. A taste of vomit invades my mouth as I read the next sentences. The girl had been sexually penetrated by an object, the same object that her father was holding in his hand when the police entered the house.

I drop the paper and catch my breath. My God…my God… how can such an abomination take place?

What do I have to study here? I don't understand. The father's criminal behavior? Clearly he is guilty, and he was apparently not mentally ill or under the influence of any disorder or hallucinogenic substance that might have clouded his perception of right and wrong.

I just want to write "scumbag" on my notepad because I tell myself that he is an evil person who deserves to die in prison.

Nevertheless, I grab the other pages that make up the file provided by Mrs. Richards. I come across the testimony of a former co-worker of the defendant, Bob Harrison, who describes Mikael as the nicest and most patient man he knew. Both worked at a bank in their small town. Bob says that Mikael always smiled and talked about his daughter with a glint of pride in his eyes. He explains that his colleague acted like his daughter was the apple of his eye and that he is deeply shocked by the acts of which Mikael is accused.

This description of Mikael Larey doesn't fit. So he was two-faced? That's it…kind and patient, until the day he murders his own daughter! Just because he behaves normally in public doesn't mean he can't be a perverted and violent man in private!

Mikael Larey's lawyer has sent several messages proclaiming his innocence. Despite the way he was found, in the middle of his wife's blood and next to his daughter's body, she still believes in his innocence.

"What the fuck…" I sigh, running a hand through my hair, "what the fuck did you do, you lunatic?"

Immediately, I text Tucker, asking him to meet me on campus with his notes. I just want to get this fucking assignment done so I can leave all these psychos behind.

When I arrive on campus, still no answer from Tucker.

"You're such a pain in the ass," I mutter to myself as I stare at my screen, as if the tall, dark-haired man could hear me from where he is.

Besides, what could he be doing this early in the afternoon? Maybe he's just in class…or maybe…with…the chick who was glued to him the other night?

I mentally slap myself trying not to think about it anymore. It's none of my business, after all. I made it clear to him this weekend I'm not interested.

After a few minutes, Tucker still hasn't arrived. Still, I need to talk to him right away about the case. I'd like to know what he thinks about it. Why on earth do I have to have him as my partner?

I finally call him, unable to wait any longer.

"Yeah," he picks up the phone after just one ring. His voice is deep, much deeper than usual.

"Are you on campus?" I begin bluntly.

I hear him grunt something to someone, and then a cracking noise sounds in the background. "I was sleeping," he grumbles.

I'm pretty sure he's lying but I don't say anything. "Well, sorry, but we need to talk. About Larey," I continue when I'm met with silence. "I'd like to wrap this up quickly, just to get it out of the way."

"Have you finished taking notes and studying the file?" he then asks me.

"Yeah. And don't tell me you haven't done anything yet or I'll kill you."

A small laugh echoes in my ear. He replies, "I've been done studying the papers since last Friday, babe."

I don't like the little nickname he gives me at all. "I'm not your—"

"I can't leave my house right now," he says, cutting me off. "I have something more interesting to do. I'll see you later."

Then he hangs up without letting me reply.

"What a jerk," I sigh.

A sexy jerk, maybe, but a very big jerk nonetheless.

I arrive about twenty minutes later on the narrow road leading to the Bomley property.

Do you understand what I'm doing?

Am I in trouble? Yes, I am. Following my own damn instincts, I decided to go straight to Tucker's house. Sorry to bother him "if he has something more interesting to do" than to give me five minutes of his time.

I sent him a message a few minutes ago, asking him to meet me at least in front of his house so we could exchange notes. But again, no response.

You know what the worst part is? The damn messaging app tells me that he read my words but didn't deign to reply.

My wheels venture out onto the gravel and tar mix only to come to rest in front of the huge wrought iron gate. It is open, as if someone was waiting for me to come.

I pace and move along the path leading to the main property, through the trees. Memories of my evening here come back to me. The scavenger hunt, the red ribbons…and Tucker ruthlessly slamming me against a tree trunk.

What the hell am I doing here? I should have forced him to meet me at a coffee shop near campus, in a neutral place, instead of entering the devil's den. I'm going crazy, that's the only possible explanation.

I snap out of my thoughts when I see the circular driveway and the huge statue in the center, the naked woman looking straight ahead.

I park near the stairs leading to the house. I get out of the car and stand up in front of the Victorian style house with its huge white columns. After climbing the few steps leading up to the heavy wooden door, I glance at my cell phone but see no answer to my texts. Maybe I should have just sent him an e-mail, like a good classmate, right?

Stop thinking, my conscience orders me.

And so I do. I put my hand on the golden knocker and bang it on the door several times. A silence answers me. Finally, the door creaks softly as a head pops through the crack. I recoil at the sight of an elderly man in a black suit. He frowns at the sight of me and quickly analyzes the holey jeans and tank top I'm wearing. He purses his lips, then seems to pull himself together and opens the door a little more.

"Can I help you?" he asks me politely.

"Erm… hello, is Tucker there? I'm Iris, we have a paper to do together and—"

"Did Mr. Bomley invite you here?" he says, as if he doesn't believe it himself.

Why does it seem impossible? Tucker must have people over regularly. Given all the friends he seems to have, there's no way he only uses the garden and the chapel for his parties, right?

We stare at each other for a few seconds, each as skeptical as the other. I think back to his words. Was I invited? Erm…not really. I am about to admit it out loud, but the man regains his composure and says, "Forgive my rudeness. I am Abraham, at the service of the Bomleys and their guests."

Huh…okay? I'm not sure how to react to the little bow he gives me next.

His doubtful look disappears. He seems to think that I am a guest. Except I'm not…Tucker didn't ask me to come here, and now that I'm here, I understand that I should have stayed on campus and waited for his answer. The man in front of me seems benevolent, but his gestures are forced. I can't help but analyze his behavior, his methodical, almost automatic gestures. He steps back into the house and leaves the door open for me.

"I'll tell Mr. Bomley you're here," he says.

Then he moves away, leaving me alone on the threshold. I hesitate for a second, glance at the heavy door, at my Chevrolet parked a few feet away, and then step inside, holding my breath. A huge wooden and marble staircase rises before my eyes in the middle of the hall. I see Abraham disappear at the top. The tapestries look old, almost too old. The lights, on the other hand, are modern, in a contemporary style.

A delicate mix between the old and the new.

A huge room opens on my left, but I refrain from entering it; after all, I am not at home. I hear light music, like an old jazz piece. I quickly look around the room and discover on the other side a large record player that plays the soft melody. Large sofas are arranged around a huge stone fireplace in which a fire is crackling.

I feel guilty for being nosy, so I go back to the entrance and wait for Tucker without moving.

"Who are you?"

I stand still as a high-pitched voice rings out to my right.

When I turn my head, my gaze is met with lightning eyes, but it's not Tucker standing in front of me.

Someone from his family, no doubt. His mother?

She's in a silk robe, with slumped shoulders and long dark hair. She seems to see me, but I think her mind is elsewhere, disconnected from reality. Her posture is so hunched over that it looks like she's holding herself back from falling.

"Um…hello," I begin, not knowing what to say as I look around like I'm just admiring the house.

The woman's eyes widen as she stares at my face. "Debbie, is that you?" she exclaims.

What? I've heard that name before…the other night, in the conversation between Matt and Dan, outside the bar!

I don't have time to understand what's going on when she runs to me, arms outstretched.

20. DEMON

IRIS

I hold back a scream and raise my hands in front of me to stop her.

"You're mistaken!" I exclaim as I shift back.

Her body stops a few inches from mine. Her breathing is perfectly calm, as if she hadn't just tried to jump on me a second earlier. What the hell, am I in a madhouse or what?!

Okay, I'm about thirty feet from the front door. Iris, you shut your mouth and run away from this place! I'm about to bolt when the woman's peculiar eyes fill with tears, pinning me in place.

"Aren't you Debbie?" she asks me as her voice breaks with that name.

I put my hands down, realizing that she won't move again. I can't help but scrutinize her. She has absolutely no makeup on. Her features are mature, yet she keeps a youthful beauty. But what never ceases to disturb me is her eyes, exactly the same as Tucker's.

I take a step back as a precaution while continuing to observe her. Her silk robe hugs her long, slender figure. She tilts her head to the side, her piercing gaze on me, yet she doesn't seem to see me. Her body is present, but her mind is not, it seems plunged into madness. She tilts her head to the other side.

Okay, I'm really in trouble. I glance at the entrance to the huge living room, and when no one comes, I raise my hands again and tell her in a calm but firm tone, "I'm not Debbie. I'm Iris Foster."

I don't know what kind of madness she's in, what disease she has, but something is wrong.

She seems to come back to reality at the firmness of my words. A single tear escapes her eyelid and traces its way down her right cheek.

"But I…no. Where is Debbie?"

I don't know who Debbie is, but this woman is going to go berserk in a second. My lips open on their own. I remember my cognitive psychology class, mentally replay it. Calm her. We have to calm her down.

"She is right next to me," I lie with a polite smile, making sure to maintain eye contact so that she focuses on me.

"Who's next to you?" she asks me, as if I had just started a conversation.

My breath stops. Damn it. "Debbie," I continue in a reassuring tone, "she's next door."

The woman frowns then pinches her mouth.

"Of course, she is next door! Where could she be?"

Then she raises a hand to me. My breathing slows down, I don't move a muscle and keep my eyes in hers. She grazes my cheek with her index finger.

"Who are you?"

So she doesn't remember our conversation. Post-traumatic stress disorder? Did she experience something that made her retreat into the darkness?

"I'm Iris Foster," I introduce myself again, as if for the first time.

She comes a little closer. Her breath hits my face.

"I'm one of Tucker's friends," I add to fill the silence.

Her breath cuts off, her eyes look into mine, and her expression changes dramatically. Her eyes cloud over as a small cry comes from her mouth.

"That murderer! He took my Debbie!" she screams.

I step back hastily when her right hand grips my shoulder hard and squeezes it, then I push her away calmly, knowing that it would be useless to be violent.

"Let go of me," I command.

"He killed her!" she exclaims again.

Her nails dig into my skin. I curse and push her away again, but she tightens her grip.

"Mom!"

I recognize Tucker's husky tone and the anger in his voice. I can't see him, but I can hear his footsteps coming toward us quickly.

The woman screams, then tears begin to flood her face. I stand still, almost motionless, as Tucker steps behind her and wraps his arms tightly around her.

He locks her in his embrace, trying to calm her agitation. She finally lets go of me.

Staring, I let out a sigh of relief as I take a step back. Tucker ignores my presence. He continues to hold on tightly to his mother, who is still struggling. I can't take my eyes off the scene. Tucker's muscles tense up at the strength of this woman…his mother.

A mother who has just accused him of killing someone.

"Let go of me!" he mother shouts again.

Tucker ignores her. He tightens his grip, leans in, and talks in her ear. I can't hear his words but he talks without stopping. This goes on for a good minute, and then finally calm returns. His mother relaxes little by little. I look down at his hands and discover her nails digging into Tucker's skin, making him bleed. Yet he doesn't let go for a second.

Not for a second.

It's only then that I notice he's shirtless, dressed only in old gray sweats. My eyes land on the wolf's head tattooed on his pectoral.

The least we can say is that he takes this Pack story seriously.

His hair, as black as ink, is disheveled, his eyes veiled. So he was really sleeping…his beard is a bit longer now. He still doesn't look at me, keeping his attention entirely on his mother.

I suddenly realize that my stupid hands are shaking. I clench my fists and unclench them to get the blood flowing. No sound interrupts the heavy silence in this huge room except the crackling of the fireplace and the soft sobs of the woman. She closes her eyes, totally helpless.

It is at this moment that Tucker raises his head. His gaze plunges into mine, burying itself so deeply in me that I can only do one thing, let him analyze me without flinching.

I know that my concern is easily spotted, and the questions that torment me can surely be read on my features.

But he's sending me a message, too. His eyes reflect so much hatred, so much resentment. Are they directed against me? I swallow with difficulty as we face each other with our eyes. Neither he nor I make a move.

Suddenly, I notice another expression behind the anger. A feeling of embarrassment and awkwardness after all this. And I understand perfectly why. He's always seemed confident to me since we met, and now I just saw him in a moment of weakness. At school, he is seen by many as a kind of king, and here he is portraying a completely different image, one that he would surely prefer to keep to himself.

Then everything disappears, an impenetrable mask falls on his face, blocking out the rest of the world. He becomes a simple stranger with an imperturbable gaze.

I take another step back in front of this unbearable coldness which has just fallen on me. I am lost. I don't know what I have just lived, and a surge of panic swells in me. I try to repress it as best I can.

The old man from earlier enters the room, his eyes haunted. He stares at the half-collapsed woman, as if this were a normal scene, as if he were used to seeing Tucker imprison her in a human cage to keep her from spilling out.

"I'll help you," he whispers to Tucker.

The latter nods and hands over his mother, who slowly begins to sob again. As she and Abraham walk away, her words loop in my mind.

*He killed her, he took Debbie from me…*Tucker told me his sister was dead. Is there a connection between the two?

Did he kill his sister?

As the panic grows inside me, I almost stagger away another step. What the hell am I doing here?

Tucker watches me strangely. He sees me backing away, uncertain, with doubt in my eyes. His jaw clenches. He takes a step forward, and my breathing stops as I raise my hands in front of me.

"No," I command.

I need a second. I need a minute…just a minute, and I'll be fine. My brain needs to recover. Tucker turns to the fireplace, and before I have time to figure out what's going on, he grabs a crystal bottle and throws it into the fireplace. The glass explodes as a raging sound comes from his chest. I hear his breathing quicken as mine becomes scarce.

I don't know why I'm doing this, but I take one step closer.

Then two. Then three. I don't know what just happened, I don't know what will happen, but I can't not react.

"Are you okay?" I finally ask.

Damn, did I really just say something that lame? Seriously, does he look okay?

An incredulous laugh answers me. "Am I okay?" Tucker repeats under his breath, staring into the flames.

Suddenly, he turns to me and finds me closer than before. Resignation shows on his face.

"Ask what you really want to ask," he finally orders me.

When I understand what he is getting at, I keep my lips closed, feeling unable to speak at this moment. He is unsettled. I saw something he would have preferred to keep secret, I heard something I shouldn't have heard…and he knows it.

He approaches me, towering over me. But I don't flinch.

"Go ahead," he spits, "ask the damn question."

I shake my head. But in front of his piercing gaze, my lips open by themselves, without listening to my brain. I need to know, I can't help it.

"Did you kill…this girl Debbie?"

A tight smirk appears on his mouth, yet his eyes are far from happy. "Would you run away if that was the case?"

His breath falls on my face, his eyes probe mine.

"Maybe," I whisper.

The questions rush through me. I wonder if he is capable of taking the life of a family member. My own hand struck a blow that was fatal, but I…I was defending my sister. What happened with Tucker? I need to know who's in front of me.

"Did you kill her?" I repeat simply, my voice slightly shaky.

He doesn't speak, but he shakes his head gently. I release a breath that I didn't know was stuck in my throat, and my relief seems to irritate him a little more.

"What you just saw, you forget any of that happened," he says coldly as he walks away.

His words hit me like a storm uprooting a tree. I can see what he's doing; he's rejecting what's around him, protecting himself, burying himself in his own shell to try to keep control and manage things.

So that's why Abraham was surprised that I was there. I'm pretty sure that very few people know what goes on inside these high walls. I do now, at my own risk.

"I get what you're going through," I announce, ignoring his words.

He raises an eyebrow and crosses his arms. "Yeah? What you been through that you could understand any of this with your futile little problems?" he asks me in a falsely mocking voice.

Eight months ago, my parents were murdered by a man who tried to rape my little sister. And I killed him. A month later, I lost the only man I ever loved. He died inches from me as I begged for help to hurry. I could tell him all that, but he doesn't deserve it. He doesn't deserve to know me on that level.

"You know nothing about my life. You don't know anything AT ALL about my fucking life. I understood what you were doing. You don't have to act like an asshole, even though that role sticks to you. I'm not going to go around telling everyone what just happened," I spit back in his direction.

He takes the hit but moves on. "We'll meet later to talk about the case," he says in a voice so neutral that an uncomfortable chill runs down my back.

He stares at my knotted fingers as if he's holding back from touching them, from taking my hands and squeezing them in his.

"I think you already know where the door is."

I lift my chin, give him one last look, and walk out of the room, not looking back.

Be damned, Tucker Bomley.

21. SURPRISE GUEST

IRIS

I try not to worry about his absence, but I can't help it. Since the beginning of the class, my gaze keeps landing on the seat Tucker usually occupies in the B4 lecture hall. The mystery of Debbie has been tormenting me all weekend. Ever since I left his house on Friday night, ideas have been spinning around in my head, never leaving me alone. Okay, he's not a killer, he told me he didn't kill her. But what happened? What was he hiding behind that anger and discomfort? And why isn't he here today?

I know that I stepped into something that was none of my business. I came to a place I shouldn't have been and saw things I shouldn't have seen. But I can't stop thinking about it.

Professor Richards' loud voice pulls me out of my thoughts:

"And finally, don't forget your group assignments! I want to see reflection, I want you to try to understand, I want to see reasoning. Don't give me an all-black or all-white result, I want contradictions, opinions that clash."

Well, for that to happen, I'd have to get my hands on Tucker first!

I mentally replay Professor Richards' words as I leave the lecture hall. I think that life is sometimes all black and white, and that people are sometimes just psychopaths. And, to be honest, I don't see how I could have an opinion that would contradict Tucker's about Mikael Larey. Because he sounds like a fucking murderer to me.

"Iris!" a female voice snaps at my back as I walk down the hallway.

I find Yeleen leaning against a wall and Sarah standing next to her. As Yeleen smiles widely at me, Sarah purses her lips and squints at me. I barely have time to join them when Sarah moves away from Yeleen quickly, swaying her hips exaggeratedly.

Good riddance.

"How are you?" Yeleen begins cheerfully.

I nod with a small smile, wondering what she wants. She's a little too friendly, too excited. Something is wrong, but what? "Great," I answer anyway, "and you?"

She nods vigorously, a smile still stuck to her lips.

I can't take it anymore, so I lean towards her. "Okay, what's going on? You killed someone, and you need help hiding a body?"

Her expression changes. A real smile appears on her face as she drops her mask of fake enthusiasm. "Nope, but I know who to turn to if I need to murder Trey." She runs her tongue over her lips and glances around us. "Was…was Tucker in class?" she finally asks me.

Of course she wants to talk to me about him!

I shake my head and feign indifference. "I don't know, I didn't really pay attention."

Yeah, right.

"This is probably going to sound strange, but do you know where he is?" she continues in a slightly worried voice. "He hasn't answered me since Friday afternoon, and the little bastard probably wouldn't want me to go to his house."

I stumble on her last words. So she can't go to Tucker's without permission either? What the hell was I thinking, going overboard and barging in like that?!

The questions keep coming into my head. I still don't know what to think, what to deduce. So I confess to Yeleen, "I…I stopped by his house on Friday."

Her jaw nearly drops, and she widens her eyes. "You…what?" she asks me, unsure.

"Yeah," I breathe, running a hand through my short red hair. "Tucker didn't know about it. I came to talk to him about the case we have to work on together and…"

"And he lost it, right?"

I frown but nod anyway. Did the same thing happen to her?

"Look, he's got a few things on his mind," Yeleen starts.

She seems to be searching for words, probably because she

doesn't want to give away Tucker's secret, which she seems to know. I do too, but I don't tell her that.

"You should ask him next time," she says gently. "Tucker is… special, and the place where he lives…anyway, nobody would like to have people show up unexpectedly, right?" she tries with a little laugh to lighten the mood.

Yeah, I didn't like it when Tucker came to my house by surprise either.

I swear I said those words only in my head, but seeing Yeleen's expression? I think I spoke out loud. Shit. "It was you who gave him my address, right? How did you get it?"

She nods with an innocent look on her face. "I might know some people who have access to the students' files."

I'm about to ask her more questions, but Trey appears a few feet away. He waves at me, but then his focus goes to Yeleen.

"I promise I won't do it again. Look," Yeleen finishes, "if you hear from Tucker, let me know."

"If he's going to give news to someone, it's more likely to be you, right? I think he's just trying to ignore me." After all, they are friends. We're…nothing.

Yeleen smiles softly and looks at me conspiratorially. "Oh believe me, he won't stay away from you for long." Then she walks away, joining her boyfriend a few feet away.

Not staying away from me for long? My ass, I'm sure he has a picture of my head with a huge red cross on it.

"You can't do that, Agnes, you have to be good with our aunt," I explain to my sister as I push open the door to the little café on the east side of campus.

"I didn't mean to," she mumbles on the phone.

I quickly order a cappuccino, then sit down at a small table in the back to avoid being disturbed. "Oh…you didn't do it on purpose, did you?" I repeat, holding back a laugh. "You didn't pour the whole bottle of nail polish in her stuff on purpose?"

"Nope, it fell out by itself," my little sister justifies herself in an innocent voice.

"You have to be good," I continue as my drink arrives.

"Why can't I come and live with you?"

And, as always, I dodge her question. Because even if she knows that the judge gave her custody to our aunt, she doesn't know that it's because he found me too financially and emotionally unstable.

"You're already coming for the vacations, honey," I remind her.

"But…"

At her sad tone, my chest tightens. "Agnes," I begin, "I want you to continue your school years, at least for a while, with people you know."

When my situation gets better, I'll come back to Portland. But for now, Agnes needs stability. And as much as it pains me to admit it, living with my aunt in a place she knows and with people she knows is the best solution. Of course, I miss her every day. Part of me says I should have stayed in Portland with her. That I would have saved money there, hoping to get my little sister back one day. But I wouldn't have made it, emotionally. I tried for eight months, and it was a huge failure. I needed this fresh start in an unfamiliar city before I lost myself for good.

"Well, okay," she grumbles. "And the boy I talked to on the phone the other day, is he your boyfriend?"

I let out a little sarcastic laugh. "No, he's not my—"

My words are lost as a tanned, muscular hand rests on the back of the chair in front of me.

What the hell is he doing here?

"He's not my boyfriend," I repeat softly as Tucker sits down quietly.

I can't help detailing him quickly: he hasn't shaved, his beard is slightly longer, and the grey T-shirt he's wearing molds him like a second skin. My eyes finally meet his. I confront him with my gaze, and he does the same.

Oh, so it's like that?

When he reaches for my drink, I glare at him and slap his hand to stop him.

How dare he!

"I have to go," I say to my little sister. I hang up and lean towards Tucker, furious,

"What the hell are you doing here? And how did you find me? Are you following me or what?"

"You invited yourself into my house so I invited myself to your table," he says hoarsely.

My words choke in my throat as a murderous urge takes hold of me. What a real bastard.

Pray for him, I think there will be an assassination.

22. THE CALL OF THE WOLF

IRIS

"I think it's time to refresh your memory," I say, pursing my lips.

His amused gaze probes mine and I ignore the warm feeling that comes over me. Keep a cool head, Iris!

"You're the one who barged into my house first, with your oversized ego, in the middle of the evening, acting as if my apartment belonged to you," I retort.

My snarl seems to amuse him more than anything else, and once again, I get the impression that he likes to piss me off. He looks at me with a small smile and then raises his eyebrows but says nothing to defend his cause, as if his behavior was perfectly acceptable. Well, no, not okay, buddy.

"It seems to me that your little body was not against me coming that night."

"Nonsense," I almost growl.

He leans over and whispers, "Go tell that to your little pussy who was wet for me."

I jump back, my back hitting the back of the chair hard as arousal takes over his features. "Goddamn it, Tucker! You can't say things like that," I whisper angrily, looking around to make sure no one heard us.

"Why is that?" he asks me innocently after ordering an iced drink.

I glare at him instead of answering. Why does he have to act like that? Like nothing happened on Friday night, like his mom didn't jump on me and call me Debbie?

"Come on, we made a deal the other night," I reply. "No more dirty talk between us. We're classmates, nothing more."

He laughs a mirthless laugh just before crossing his arms over his broad chest. My eyes can't help but admire the play of his muscles.

Forget it, Iris, wake up!

"You decreed that we made a deal. But I don't have the same terms as you. I told you, if you're going to fake it, I will fake it too."

"I'm not faking anything, Tucker. Okay, I'm attracted to you, but I like a lot of guys, if you want to know everything," I lie.

His eyes darken. Oh, oh…he doesn't like my words. Well, too bad.

"Besides, I don't see why you insist when I've turned you down several times. Don't tell me your ego isn't hurt," I suggest in a teasing voice to try to lighten the mood.

He continues to stare at me without blinking.

I take a sip of my drink under his dark look. His jaw is tightened; he's holding back from telling me something. I sigh and cross my arms, taking the same position as him. "Okay, what's your problem? What words did I say to offend Tucker Bomley?"

He still doesn't answer. Come on! I'm dealing with a seven-year-old or what?!

"If only you would shut up like that all the time," I add.

Here he is coming from nowhere to ruin my little break in this coffee place when I thought he was trying to avoid me. And now he's upset because he thinks I talk to other guys. I suddenly think of Yeleen's words.

"Yeleen is looking for you," I tell him. "She's worried sick. You should send her a message to let her know that everything is okay."

"Right now, I don't give a damn," he retorts.

"Do you know that she cares about you, or does your caveman attitude prevent you from thinking straight too?"

He seems to regain his good mood despite my reproach, which amuses him more than anything else. He then nods as if he is making a mental note to contact her.

"What?" I ask him next, while he is still staring at me. "It's disturbing to be stared at, you know?"

"Look at you, always standing up to me. You're a demanding little thing, you know that?"

His eyes roam over my upper body as if he himself doesn't

understand my behavior, nor the fact that he accepts that I stand up to him and send him packing.

His words should perhaps offend me, yet I feel almost… flattered? As if, in his mouth, it was a compliment. So I let it go this time. But I can't help retorting, "You don't scare me. I've put a man heavier than you on the ground before."

A loud laugh comes from his throat as he throws his head back. Seeing my serious face, he calms down slightly but his eyes continue to shine. "Really?"

"I even killed him," I add sourly in my head. But I keep these words to myself. I take a deep breath to counteract these stupid thoughts.

Tucker nonchalantly takes a sip of his drink. After a minute, I crack up. I can't stand pretending the episode with his mother never happened.

"Listen, about Friday night…" I start.

"Iris," he replies sternly to shut me up.

I raise a finger in his direction, forcing him to listen to me, "I'm sorry for barging in. Well, not really, but I'm sorry I found out something you didn't want me to know."

"Shut up," he orders me as his voice deepens.

"It's none of my business," I finish without listening to him. "That woman, your mother, I, uh…it's none of my business. And know that I won't say anything or ask any questions about Debbie."

Even though I'm intrigued by the mystery surrounding her. How did she die? Who was she? Tucker, Dan, Matt…they all seem to have a connection to her.

Tucker doesn't answer me, but he doesn't need to. I know how he must feel. He doesn't want to talk about this, and I understand him. I'm the first one to protect my secret garden. I know he won't say anything more, but I have to get it off my chest.

"As I told you, I know about problems, in spite of what you may think," I retort a little bit dryly, thinking about his sentence of the other day about my *"little futile problems."*

Tucker's gaze becomes more intense. I have the impression that he is trying to analyze me. Shit, I don't like that! I'm the one who can read people's minds, not the other way around. Stop it!

"What happened?" he then asks me.

"Forget about it," I say to him curtly, I don't want to dwell on the subject.

But he doesn't. He leans towards me again. "Hey," he calls me.

I turn my head towards him, looking at him without flinching.

"I'm not stupid," he continues in a calm voice. "I remember very well your reaction the other day, when you read the Larey file. I understood that you had your own demons to fight. On Friday, I was…I was angry."

I swallow with difficulty, surprised by his words and his first step in my direction. So he understands that I had a painful past and seems ready to break down that barrier between us to find out more. But I'm not ready. His voice sounds like an apology as the atmosphere between us becomes too heavy. It feels like we're sharing something important, and I don't want that. I decide to break this connection that is making me slightly dizzy.

"Speaking of the Larey case," I announce as I open my bag, "here is my research. I made a summary of the hearing of Mikael Larey's colleague. He is described as a man who cared deeply for his daughter, but I still think he is the culprit in this case."

Tucker nods, presumably sharing my opinion.

"Yeah. I think so, too. Have you looked at the whole file?"

I shake my head, silently denying it. Since I started out on Mikael Larey's guilt, I admit I didn't look at all the pieces the other night. Tucker grabs the file from my hands and picks up one of the sheets I hadn't looked at yet.

"Here, it's the testimony of the Larey's neighbors. They say that the little girl was an angel, that she often played alone in the garden with her dolls. The neighbors also explain that Mikael was always smiling and friendly with them."

I curse as I read the following lines myself. Something catches my attention: the neighbors explain that Mikael's wife, Mrs. Larey, who was found dead, had a completely different behavior. She didn't say a word to them, as if she was always closed in on herself. How could I have not read everything?

Neighbors had seen the mother act harshly towards her daughter on several occasions, even insulting her in the middle of the garden a few months ago. They also stated that this must have been caused by the father's obnoxious behavior which would have been reflected in his wife's attitude.

I reread the last few sentences several times and, for the first time, I start to have doubts. I find it a bit strange.

I have a feeling, deep down, that something is wrong. His behavior doesn't match. I take another look at Bob Harrison's audition, painting a glowing picture of Mikael Larey. What if…what if my first impression was wrong?

"What?" asks Tucker as the questions start to race through my head.

"What do you think of the neighbors' questioning?"

He shrugs. "To me, it's just a mother talking bad to her child. I stand my ground, Mikael Larey is probably our culprit."

I don't answer anything and he raises an eyebrow at me.

"You don't agree with me anymore? What, you have doubts about the culprit, when we know in what position he was found?"

"I know, but…I feel like something is wrong. I wonder if we're making a mistake by declaring him guilty immediately. I don't know," I sigh, closing my eyes and rubbing my eyelids.

"He killed his wife and daughter. I don't think we're looking at an innocent man."

"That's what part of me thinks too. But maybe we need to dig a little deeper?"

My own words amaze me. Yet, as I say them out loud, I think maybe this isn't such a bad idea.

"I feel like something doesn't fit. I read the words of his co-worker, he describes him as an honest and decent man. And what you just showed me in the neighbors' report…"

"All parents are tough on their kids," Tucker tells me. "The cops came into the room, the mother was dead, the kid was dead, and her father had abused her. I don't know what more there is to understand."

"Do you really think that Professor Richards gave us this case so that we could just repeat the same scenario as the media?"

"So," Tucker resumes after a minute, "you are thinking there's a chance that the mother is guilty. And what? She stabbed herself after strangling her daughter?"

"That's not what I said," I reply calmly but firmly. "As far as I know, Mikael's DNA was not found on the knife that killed his wife. The girl was abused with a statuette, Tucker, no fluids from her father were found in her. And the fact that she was strangled…I don't know, I feel like something's wrong. Maybe he didn't kill his kid? Maybe the mother was the one who clutched the scarf and abused the kid. I don't know," I sigh, closing my eyes and letting my head go back. I think my brain is going crazy.

Look at me, I'm trying to find extenuating circumstances for a guy who probably killed his wife and daughter. But why won't my brain stay on the main trail we've been given?

Instinct.

"That could hold," Tucker finally tells me, after a few minutes. "But on what do you base this? Simple testimonies of neighbors and colleagues?"

When I open my eyes, I discover his so particular look on me. He observes each feature of my face as if he was trying to memorize them.

"You're right. Maybe we should try to contact his colleague Bob Harrison. But we don't even know where to find him…"

I yawn until my jaw drops as he grabs his phone and taps away.

"It's just a lead," I continue, shrugging my shoulders.

He doesn't even listen to me. But you never know. No lead is to be ignored. Talking with Harrison will surely not bring us anything new and our first impression, namely Mikael Larey's guilt, is probably the right one.

A silence answers me. The little bastard isn't listening to me anymore. I'm pretty sure he's talking to some buddies… or a girl?

"Tell me if I'm bothering you," I say, while he's still typing on his screen.

"Put your claws away, redhead," he retorts, holding his phone to my nose.

I frown, staring at the screen. What the…?

"Whose number is this?" I ask, unsure.

"Bob Harrison," he proudly announces. "You wanted to talk to him, now's your chance."

So he was just looking for his number?

"How did you get his number?" I ask him as my heart pounds in my chest.

"The net is our best ally in these things. Come on," he urges me, shaking the phone in my face. "Don't you want to call him and hear what Bob has to say about Mikael?"

"Of course, I do, but…hey, stop!" I order him as he dials the number. "You're crazy!" I exclaim. "Who says he's going to talk? He's going to screw us over! Come on, hang up."

He puts his index finger over his mouth, telling me to shut up. I can hear the ringing through the receiver.

But, my God, what are we doing?

After three rings, Bob picks up. "Hello?"

Tucker hands me his state-of-the-art cell phone, eyebrows raised. I glare at him and pick up the phone, racking my brains.

"Hello?" Bob repeats a little more loudly as I put the phone to my ear.

"Hello," I say after a few seconds.

"Who's this?" asks Mikael Larey's ex-colleague in a tired voice.

I consider hanging up, but the gleam in Tucker's eyes pushes me to go through with it. After all, I want answers. So I shove my way through the lie, determined to get them.

"I'm Sonia Dallson," I claim. "I work for the Brighton Independent newspaper, and I was wondering if you could answer some questions about Mikael Larey?"

A silence answers me. I hear a heavy sigh coming from Bob Harrison's mouth. "Listen…I would like to get this story out of my head once and for all. I'm as shocked as everyone else by his arrest and what he is accused of. I'm waiting for the trial."

"Look, it'll only take a few minutes, I just want to understand. Please."

A new sigh answers me. "I'm on break, you have five minutes."

Tucker seems to be as attentive as I am and comes closer, focused.

"Great! So," I begin, pulling out a pen to take notes, "the day Mikael Larey's wife and daughter were found dead…that afternoon, your colleague was at work. Did you notice anything strange about his behavior?"

"Are you a cop or something?" the guy asks me bluntly.

He's not supposed to know that I'm a student and that our professor has given us access to a complete file, including police statements. But I don't have time to deny it when he finally resumes on his own, "Mikael looked exhausted that day. He was slow in all his movements, as if he hadn't slept the night before. But he continued to work perfectly. You know, Mikael never allowed himself to be late for work. He liked everything to be in its place, every task to be completed on time. When I left the company that night, he was still working there."

I try to write everything down as quickly as I can. In order to listen to the conversation as well, the demon with the different colored eyes moves closer to me, his ear almost glued to the phone.

"Was Mikael a good colleague? I mean…could his behavior have been a sign that—"

"I know what you mean, miss," Bob cuts me off. "He's probably one of the best guys I've ever worked with. Helpful. He covered for me several times when I had to go home early to pick up my son. He was serious about his job, friendly, polite, respectful."

Exactly what his neighbors said, according to the newspapers.

The more he paints a glowing picture of Mikael, the more doubt begins to creep in. Is it possible that I was blinded by my hatred for my parents' killer and let it cloud my judgment, thinking straight away that Mikael was the culprit without even asking the right questions? What if he really is innocent? I need to think objectively, to see beyond my personal history, at least for the time of the investigation.

One last question comes to mind.

"Regarding his marriage, do you know if he and his wife had any problems?"

"You know, we didn't tell each other our lives. But I remember… one time, yeah…he and his wife had a fight in the morning. During the day, she harassed him. She would call him every two minutes and yell at him hysterically."

I slowly turn my face to Tucker's. His thoughts seem to match mine as he nods slightly. Then his gaze settles on my half-open mouth. I don't move an inch, as if hypnotized. His masculine smell invades me.

"My break is over," Bob says, "I wish you a good day."

"Have a good day too," I whisper as he hangs up.

Tucker continues to stare at me and I stare back, disturbed by his proximity.

"Are you finished?" the waitress asks, interrupting us.

I jump up and scramble back, a guilty look on my face as if we've been caught in the act. But it is not the case.

Who am I trying to convince, anyway?

Tucker is well aware of my confusion, and he seems to like it.

A few hours later, I arrive in front of my apartment building. I stretch as I get out of my car and get my bag just before I slam the door. It is nighttime now. The moon starts to trace its way in the starry sky, positioning itself as the master of the night.

It's 11:30 p.m. and I've spent most of my evening studying in the library about apraxia, a movement disorder, because I have a paper to do on it for one of my classes. As my eyes slid across the pages and I couldn't focus, I decided to go home and am eager to take a hot shower.

I take the stairs and quickly reach my floor, the hallway darkened. It's been two days since the light bulb burned out partially, leaving the place in a partial darkness. And you know what? The fucking building manager doesn't give a shit.

I walk to my door and unlock it with difficulty with my free hand. I don't know what's going on, but the little hairs on the back of my neck suddenly stand up.

There is a presence behind me.

I take a deep breath and throw my elbow back, then start to scream as one hand stops my blow and another rests firmly on my mouth. A male torso presses against my back as I struggle in vain.

My eyes fall on another guy standing in front of me, a cloth bag in his hands. I barely have time to catch a glimpse of the wolf mask he's wearing before he slips the bag over my face.

So these are guys from the Pack?

"What's going on?!" I yell again, totally disoriented.

The guy behind me holds me a little more tightly, his arm tightening around my waist. Then my feet leave the ground. I am lifted up. A perfectly recognizable male voice comes out of the mouth pressing against my ear.

"Ready for another trial?" Tucker whispers to me.

23. THIRD TRIAL

IRIS

I hear the other guy trotting behind us as Tucker strides across the hallway as if I weigh nothing. I don't say a word, trying to figure out what's going on. I can't see anything around me, but when I hear the sound of a car door, I realize that we are in the parking lot. Finally, I connect with reality. I pull on my wrists, which are held together by who knows what shit.

"Untie me," I order.

My voice is cold, sharp. I'm not hysterical because it wouldn't help. I have to be reasonable and make them understand that I'm not kidding.

I'm not laughing at all at this little game. I don't know what's going to happen to me, and I can feel the panic growing inside me little by little. But I have to calm down, nothing will happen to me. Tucker wouldn't hurt me, would he?

He doesn't respond to my command. My breath quickens as I am gently seated on a leather seat. My attempt to remain calm gradually fails. "Damn it, untie me!"

"Why is she winding herself up?" asks the second guy. "She's the one who wanted to be in the game, right?"

What?!

"Shut up and drive," Tucker commands.

His voice is close to me, inches away. I turn toward him and speak through the lightweight bag. "I didn't want to be part of this stupid game! You dragged me into it, Tucker! I swear to God, if you don't let me go, I will rip your balls off and make a necklace out of them."

My voice falters on those last words as I try to catch my breath.

"It's one thing to be in your third trial, but to be kidnapped?"

Tucker puts his hand on my waist. "Hey, it's okay," he whispers in my ear so only I can hear him.

"No, no, it's not okay. I have to…I have to breathe," I say, panting hard.

His forehead pressed against mine as my breathing barely slowed. "Stop panicking. This is what you were made for. You're made for danger. I want you to succeed, you have to succeed."

"But this is just a stupid game," I spit out as I try to move my shoulders to free my hands. "It's so creepy."

"Wait, she wasn't okay with this?" asks the guy at the front of the vehicle.

"Shut up," orders Tucker again.

"Why are you doing this?" I spit in his direction. "Just let me see where we're going."

The driver stifles a laugh. "Let you see? No way."

But already I can feel Tucker's hands on the back of my neck.

"Tucker! What are you doing?" the guy shouts.

But Tucker ignores him. He pulls the stupid cloth away from my face and I inhale deeply.

"You had no right to pull the bag off her!" exclaims the guy driving, wearing his wolf mask. "Tucker, those are the rules!"

"And I make the rules," growls Tucker. "So either you shut up or I'll shut you up."

The guy curses and his hands grip the steering wheel harder, but he keeps driving. The tension rises between us. I stare at Tucker, restraining myself from thanking him and then slapping him—not that I can anyway since my hands are tied. He returns my gaze without blinking. His behavior is totally different from when we are alone. He seems closed and almost distant. Impenetrable.

"Where are you taking me? In a forest? The one at your place?! Answer!" I shout while he keeps his lips closed.

I can see that he is angry at me for getting my face free. Yet it's as if he couldn't help himself. "I told you it was the third trial," he replies.

His posture is totally hostile. Both of his fists are clenched on his thighs, and his breath is rapid, as if he is forced to be here.

"Where are you taking me?" I ask again.

"We want to see if you have guts," retorts the guy behind the wheel without answering my question. "And if you're not just selfish cubs."

Selfish? Are we going to have to help each other?

Tucker plants his eyes on mine and gives me a small smile. It's as if he's trying to send me a reassuring message through his unfathomable gaze. "It's okay," he whispers, an inch from my mouth. "Nothing will happen to you."

"I hate you," I whisper back.

He straightens up, swallowing his saliva with difficulty while his gaze still catches mine. He nods as if he understands my words but refuses to get them into his fucking head.

"Why are you doing this?" I ask him a little louder.

He doesn't answer me.

The guy at the front of the car seems taken aback by our exchange. "Well, why wouldn't he? We train potential wolf cubs before we bring them into the Pack," the driver laughs. "Tucker came up with the idea last year, we're not going to give up on that now."

Tucker isn't laughing. His fists are clenched a little more tightly as he clenches his jaw. And suddenly, I understand. He doesn't want me to go either. He doesn't want to take me to this place I don't know where, but he has no choice. He's the one who had imposed these fucking lousy rules. He can't give them up in front of everyone without looking weak. Breaking them by removing the bag so I can breathe better is one thing, but outright cancelling a trial is another. He already broke the rules the first time in the chapel, and he can't do it again today.

But what's next for me? Why did I get that damn ribbon, why did I let myself get caught up in this whole absurd joke?

The worst part…the worst part is this little spark of excitement that lights up inside me. This unhealthy curiosity. Because, in spite of everything, I'm in a hurry to know what's going to happen.

I remain silent, lost in my thoughts. Cold anger grows inside me as I push away the exhilarating feeling that came over me moments before. I'm not allowed to feel an adrenaline rush when I'm stuck in a game I don't know the rules to, right?

I don't react when Tucker squeezes my hand once. I also don't react when the vehicle stops in the middle of nowhere. But when the guy who was driving hands the bag to Tucker to put on my head again, I panic. I back up against the back of my seat and glare at them.

"No," I say curtly.

Tucker picks up the bag but doesn't make another move. My reaction makes the other guy laugh, and he retorts with a mocking look, "Stop being afraid, you're not going to kill each other. It's just a little thing. I was scared last year too, but I managed to get out in two minutes with a sexy little blonde as a partner."

I don't listen to his words, but my brain analyzes them without my permission. "I won't get out of the car. I swear, if you force me, I will break your nose."

The guy stares at Tucker's hand, which is still holding the bag. He frowns.

"Hey, you have to put this on her. The other three are already ready, we're just waiting for the Brat."

As Tucker leans towards me, I back up against the door and send him a brutal blow in the shin. He pushes an expletive and says to the guy who observes us from the driving seat, "Get out."

The guy looks puzzled. He must know something is wrong. He looks at the bag again and then put it back over my head, with a closed face.

When the guy gets out of the car and I hear the door close, Tucker throws the bag on the floor as if it were burning his hand.

And I throw myself at him, furious. "You bastard," I yell. "Who do you think you are? You think you can kidnap me and take me somewhere and put a bag over my head? Untie my hands, damn it, untie them! You don't kidnap people like that! You don't play with them! You bunch of freaks! Couldn't you send me a text message?!"

He doesn't listen to me but grabs my shoulders hard to keep me still. "You have entered the game yourself," he announces calmly but firmly.

A voice inside me repeats his words. He is right. But I didn't know what it meant. I didn't know it would go this far.

"So I want to quit the game," I tell him. "I have the right to quit, right?" He doesn't answer me, so I continue. "You didn't get me through the first test. So take me somewhere else, and don't force me to pass this one."

"I can't," he blows in my face.

Why can't he? For his damn reputation or something?

I take a deep breath and let my head fall back against the seat. "You guys are a bunch of nutcases."

Tucker grabs my jaw in his hand and stares at me without blinking. I feel like he's probing my soul. I hate this. "You're excited," he points out.

I pull my face away from his grip. "Of course not," I spit out. "I'd have to be stupid to be excited!"

But we both know what it's like. Something inside me urges me to know more. What's happening to me?

"I don't know what to expect, but when this stage is over and my hands are free, you better not be in my way."

Tucker grabs my arm gently.

"You're going to put that bag over my face?!" I continue.

He shakes his head and runs his thumb over my lower lip unceremoniously.

"Close your eyes," he orders me just before opening the door.

I feel a cloth brush my eyelids, then he forces me to get out.

I hear several doors creaking, metal noises, and I soon realize that we are in a warehouse of some kind. Or maybe a closed-down area? With the blindfold on, I can't see anything. But it's still better than the bag…I hear some voices I don't know, and the guy who was driving asks Tucker why my face is uncovered, but Tucker doesn't answer and keeps going. A new door opens with a terrible creak. We turn in different directions several times in a row, as if we're walking through corridors. Finally, we enter a rather cold room. All I can hear are my footsteps and Tucker's. Are we alone?

He sits me down on a concrete floor before putting his hands on my still bound wrists and starts rubbing them gently, as if he is saddened by their state. That's right, all you had to do was not tie me up, you bastard.

"What's going to happen now? Did you just hand me over to the big bad wolf?"

My voice is sarcastic but my heart is pounding.

I hear a male laugh behind my back, and it's not Tucker's… who's in this room with us?

"*Idiota.*"

Idiot? Who just called me an idiot?!

Tucker leans toward me—I can feel his breath on my neck—and inhales deeply before whispering, "I'll see you out, baby."

He takes another breath as if soaking up my scent before straightening up and leaving me alone.

"You know the rules, Sanchez," Tucker begins, taking a few steps away. The door opens once more before he says, "Amelia and Chase are locked in at the other end. I want you to get out before they do. Don't be selfish, don't just think about yourself. The first two people out the door, whoever they are, will win."

This is the second time they've said selfish. Why?

Then he slams the door and locks it behind him.

My breath catches. I hear movement behind me. I feel like someone is trying to get out. Yet I can't make a move.

"Anybody there?" I ask stupidly.

I hear a curse and remember Tucker's words.

"Sanchez?" I gasp.

The guy doesn't answer me, but I hear him struggling.

"Hey, oh, I'm talking to you!" I exclaim, trying to get him to answer me.

"*Cállate!*" he finally says, still struggling.

I'm about to answer his insult when I hear the sound of something light being thrown on the ground.

"Of course, I get the pain in the ass with me," he grumbles with a Hispanic accent. His voice is no longer muffled. He must have succeeded in removing the bag from his face.

I think he's the only one who can help me in this situation, but I still try to free myself. I swallow a curse over my aching wrists.

"Help me," I command to the asshole next to me.

I hear footsteps at my back and stand still. An icy hand holds my wrists in place. I hear the young man inhale before pulling strongly on the two sides of the tie until it breaks with a snap. I move away hastily, relieved to be finally free, and tear off my blindfold before tossing it aside.

Sanchez stands with his back to me, staring at the door in front of us. His figure is quite small and stocky. I'm much thinner than he is, but he must be about my height. His dark, medium-length hair stops at his shoulders. He mumbles into his beard as he tries to open the door. I stop myself from rolling my eyes.

"It's locked, no need to force it."

"You're welcome," he announces, still with his back to me, referring to my broken ties.

I glance around, massaging my wrists. This place looks abandoned. "Thank you," I finally grumble.

There's nothing in the room except for some old, worn pieces of metal I can make out in the darkness and a skylight in the ceiling. It's too high to reach, even if we do a leg up.

Sanchez is still trying to break through the huge metal door, rusted in places. I hold back a mocking smile at this ridiculous sight.

"I don't think your little figure will be able to break through the door," I announce innocently.

He finally turns to me, making his hair fly as he does it. His dark look makes me swallow my smile. I frown. As he squints, I search my memory, but nothing comes to me. "Maybe you have a better idea?" he asks me.

The faint glow of the moon catches the piercing on his right arch. His face is closed, but I have to admit he's pretty cute. Okay, maybe even a little sexy.

I drop to the floor and stifle a yawn. "Nope," I sigh and cross my legs. "I suggest we just sit here and wait for these assholes to come and get us." I admit that part of me wants to fight but the other is too angry to play along.

Sanchez opens his mouth, stunned, but nothing comes out. Then he suddenly exclaims, "You think we're going to win sitting here like idiots? *Es estúpido!* You shouldn't have come if you were afraid to put in the effort."

I point my index finger in his direction as I stand up. "Listen to me, I'm stuck in this stupid thing with a stupid person after being kidnapped AGAINST my will! So, believe me, this is no time to mess with me."

"What do you mean 'against your will?' You mean you didn't want to be here?"

I roll my eyes. "Usually, when you're taken to a place by force, you don't want to, no."

"Why didn't you have a bag over your head?" he then asks me, stopping his movements.

"They didn't have any more in stock," I proclaim in a falsely unhappy voice.

He still doesn't move and insists, disconcerted, "Why didn't Tucker put a bag over your head?"

What the hell is wrong with him with his damn questions? I suddenly turn to him and notice that he is staring at me. I can see an ounce of excitement in his eyes. He's happy to be locked up here because he wants to win. Of course, he has accepted his role as a cub.

"Seriously," I say, "help me find a way out of here instead of asking me your questions."

"I thought you wanted to sit and wait for them."

I glare at him for an answer. Finally, at the far end of the room, I see another door, which seems worn. Much smaller, less massive.

"There!" I exclaim, heading toward it only to find that it's also locked.

"Knock it down," I tell Sanchez. "It seems less solid than the other one, maybe we have a chance?"

"I thought my little body couldn't do it?"

I ignore his words and knock on the door, which gives almost no result. I thrust my foot through it and yell, "Tucker, I'm going to kill you! Did you hear that?!"

I must look hysterical because Sanchez continues to stare at me strangely. I raise my eyebrows, silently warning him not to mess with me. He runs his tongue over his lips, and I see a piercing on it.

"Let me do it," he finally tells me.

With my arms crossed, I watch him try to break down the door. At the first knocks, it only shakes. It is only after several other attempts that the old worn door finally gives way.

But what I discover does not please me.

It is not the exit on the other side, but another part of the abandoned warehouse.

There are no windows, only an old, half-burned-out neon sign on the ceiling.

"This can't be true," I sigh.

I walk quickly to the right corridor but discover a dead end.

"So?" I ask Sanchez, who has turned left.

"Nothing," he says, shaking his head.

The only option left is to go into the dark and icy building. This place gives me the creeps. So why does a part of me keep getting excited about everything that's going on? Old wooden crates litter the floor. There are other hallways at the back of the room, but I'd rather look first to see if there's anything here.

"Do you think Amelia and Chase are out yet?" asks Sanchez after a minute.

His disappointed voice echoes through the deserted place. I glance at him, and my mouth opens by itself, "I think we'll win and get out before they do."

He raises his eyebrows in surprise. "You seem pretty excited for a girl who's here against her will."

I raise my middle finger in his direction as, in a corner, I discover a tiny window about six feet off the ground. Bingo.

"This way!" I call to him, smiling.

But he doesn't smile. He stares at the narrow window, and we come to the same conclusion: I might be able to slip through, with difficulty, but he will never get through.

"I'm going to get you out this way," he says. "I'll try to find another way out for myself afterwards."

"No," I tell him firmly.

"What do you mean 'no?' You want to get out of here, right? This is your chance."

I shake my head. "Tucker said, not to be selfish, and he's right. We're going out together. Move your ass," I order him as I run in the opposite direction to investigate another nook.

There's another window, a little bigger this time. But it's much too high and has no handle. I rack my brain. As I meet Sanchez's gaze, we exclaim at the same time, "The wooden crates!"

He runs to recover some and I do the same. We pile them up quickly against the wall, then he takes off his T-shirt to bandage his arm and break the old window, which gives way quickly.

"Come, I'm going to help you," he says to me.

I don't think for a second and reach out to him, but at the same time I hear a noise behind me. A tall blond man and a girl with brown hair are standing there, out of breath.

Sanchez looks annoyed, "Damn it. Chase, Amelia, how did you—"

He doesn't have time to finish his sentence when the guy jumps on him and hits him in the jaw.

"Sorry, buddy," he spits as he hits Sanchez, who is getting back up, "but I want to get out of here first."

The girl doesn't give me a look. With a tough look on her face— she doesn't care about the two guys either— she determinedly climbs on the crates and exits the sinister building.

I put my hand on the first crate, preparing to follow her. The first two win. So, if I get out now, I will have won. But Tucker said not to think only of yourself. Without thinking, I turn to Chase.

I could jump on his back, but that's exactly what I had done to try to stop Agnes' attacker, and it didn't work. Suddenly, I remember my coach's advice from self-defense class: always keep your opponent off balance.

I move quickly behind Chase, who is holding Sanchez against the wall, and give him a brutal kick behind the knee, knocking him forward. I see the surprise on Sanchez's face as he lets out a "Thank you" and regains the upper hand.

"Leave him!" I say to Sanchez as he continues to hit his opponent, looking grim.

Eventually he joins me, and I climb the wooden crates after him, fleeing the damn warehouse. I hold back a curse as I nearly cut myself with a piece of glass. As I look down, I realize that we are about six feet from the ground. Sanchez has already jumped, he's on the ground looking up to me.

"I'll catch you," he calls. "Come on," he repeats louder but with a reassuring air.

Chase straightens up at the bottom of the crates, looking furious. I inhale deeply then jump by the window. Sanchez almost falls under my weight as he catches me outside. He holds my waist firmly to stabilize me and sets me down on dry land.

"We lost," I say in his direction. "Amelia went first. There is only one place left."

Sanchez opens his mouth but no words come out as he bends slightly, still out of breath. That's when I notice other people, about thirty feet away. At the head of the small group is Tucker, who is waiting, arms at his sides. Head erect, fists closed, he looks implacably in our direction.

I see Amelia first, then I see TJ, all smiles, analyzing me from afar.

"Go ahead," I tell Sanchez, who hasn't moved an inch and is waiting for me to recover.

"What?" he asks me, not understanding.

"You wanted to win this trial. I'm here against my will, remember? Come on, go ahead, man."

He shakes his head as if I'm stupid and pulls me behind him, walking towards them.

"Hey? Did you hear what I just said?" I exclaim, trying to get out of the way.

"We came out together," he announces to the others while ignoring me.

TJ still has a smile up to his ears. I stare at them one by one and, when I notice Tucker's dark and possessive look focused on my wrist and Sanchez's grip on it, I hold back from laughing in his face. How dare he! Then I understand why Sanchez seems so confident and TJ thrilled.

"That's what you mean about the rules, isn't it?" I ask, breaking free of Sanchez's grip. "Don't be selfish, show that you don't just think about yourself. It's not what she did," I spit out, pointing at Amelia. "But we went out together. So we won."

TJ turns to Tucker. The latter swallows his saliva and nods with difficulty.

"Yeah, you won."

Whistles ring out as TJ claps enthusiastically for me. Tucker is still staring at me, and I know he's holding back from pulling me against him. I can tell by the look on his face. Yet, I'm not giving up on him. Yes, I'd be lying if I said I didn't like the last hour, but he brought me here by force as if I were just an object. And that doesn't fly. I move closer to him, my heart heavy but my hands free.

As his eyes shine brighter and brighter and as he moves towards me, I raise my fist and punch him.

24. JEALOUSY

IRIS

Tucker shifts at the last moment, and my fist meets his left shoulder violently.

"Asshole," I spit, furious.

Tucker lets himself be hit as I send my fist into his chest again. His breath catches slightly.

TJ bursts out laughing as the others stare, dumbfounded. I guess they don't often get to see their big but shitty pack leader gets hit. Tucker intercepts my fist and wraps his fingers around my wrist, trying to calm me down.

Sanchez stares at us from three feet away, as if trying to figure out the sudden closeness between Tucker and me.

"Stop it," Tucker orders me, his face serious but his voice steady. "You might hurt yourself."

I stand still, trying to catch my breath.

"Hurt myself?! Is that what you're thinking about now? Not when you kidnapped me, tied me up and left me in a frozen warehouse?"

"Come on, be happy," exclaims TJ with a big smile, "you are part of the Pack now. Congratulations, my cubs, that was the last test."

Sanchez seems thrilled with the news, but I feel like I'm overwhelmed by it all, and mostly wasting my breath. I stare at Tucker, ignoring his cousin, and retort through my teeth, "Fuck you all!"

Then I turn around and walk away, leaving them in the lurch. I hear footsteps at my back. A firm hand lands on my forearm and pulls me back.

"Iris," Tucker begins.

But I shake my arm to free myself.

I walk down the dark, winding path. I can't see my feet very well, and I don't even know where to go, knowing we're in the middle of nowhere, but I have to move away. Tucker's voice slams into my back. I inhale to try and calm myself and keep moving. Just as the trail gets narrower and starts to go downhill, my foot skids on a stupid rock.

My body follows suit. I close my eyes as I feel myself falling, but a firm grip grabs my waist and pulls me back.

"Damn it, are you okay?" asks Tucker, his face against my hair. His ragged breath hits my ear, proving to me that he ran to me.

I place my hands on his and pull them away from my body.

"Iris," he repeats firmly as I tuck a reddish lock of hair back.

"No, no Iris," I spit, turning to him. "Go ahead and have fun with your new recruit. It'll be without me."

The dryness of my voice disarms him. He stares at me blankly for a minute. His broad shoulders are tightened. His jaw is clenched behind his short black beard.

"I admit that I should have released you when I understood that you were really afraid and didn't want to play," he finally admits in a voice from beyond the grave.

I cross my arms over my chest. "Yeah, you should have, buddy. You're going to regret this."

"But you did it," Tucker whispers as he moves closer to me. "Are you going to tell me you didn't feel an ounce of excitement when you were in the warehouse? Liar."

I let out a mirthless laugh. So he really doesn't get it. "You don't get it, Tucker. That's not the point. I'm not a toy or a pawn on your chessboard that you can move around as you please." I make sure I have his full attention before I say, "You blow hot and cold, and just when I start to think our relationship is finally becoming friendly, you turn back into a real asshole. You want the truth? I liked winning that test. But I wasn't willing. You broke into the hallway of my building, then put a damn bag over my head. You took me to a car, leaving me panicking like a nobody. Then you put me in an icy room with a stranger. And all for what? To follow your stupid rules? You want me to say something? The only feeling I have is not excitement, it's disappointment."

I finish my tirade, catching my breath. Tucker clenches his fists, but it's not his place to be angry tonight.

"In that building, Chase jumped Sanchez, and I thought he was going to kill him. Is that what you're waiting for? A murder to satisfy your perverse need for adrenaline?"

I walk over to him, staring into his eyes. My breast touches his chest but I ignore the tingle that runs through me.

This traitorous body doesn't care about my anger. She wants a much more carnal connection.

"Life is too precious for some stupid people to play with," I continue. My voice starts to shake, and I hate it. "I almost lost my life once, Tucker. I refuse to try it again just to prove to a bunch of idiots that I'm a fighter."

I finally said everything that was on my mind and, my God, it felt good!

"Never mind," I sigh at his silence.

But Tucker doesn't let me take a step. He moves closer to me and tilts his face so it's level with mine. His fingers grasp my cheeks. "What happened to you?" he whispers softly.

I won't answer. I've said what I had to say. It's over.

Just as I think he's going to try again to find arguments to counter mine, he simply whispers, "I'm sorry I acted like a jerk. I followed the stupid rules I've imposed for the past two years, thinking I'd be okay seeing you locked up in there."

I stare at him, my mouth wide open.

"And I wasn't. I hated every second of it. I hated putting you in a team with Sanchez. I hated seeing you arrive hand in hand."

I feel his breath against my lips but I remain impassive, trying to hold steady.

"And I hate the way you look at me now," he whispers against me.

I get lost in his eyes for a moment.

"I know you're not like the others. I hate that, but it's the truth." Tucker puts his hand on my upper arm, gently.

"Is everything okay?" interrupts someone behind him.

Tucker mumbles a curse word as I pull away from him. Sanchez smiles casually, but I can see dozens of questions dancing in his eyes.

"Get the hell out," Tucker orders him.

Sanchez raises his eyebrows, his piercing shining in the moonlight. He stares at me, waiting for my own answer.

"It's all good," I say, trying to keep the situation from escalating further.

"Do you want a ride home?" Sanchez asks me politely.

"No," Tucker almost growls.

"Yes, I do," I reply.

Tucker is this close to freaking out, which is ridiculous. "Iris, don't go with him," he mutters through his teeth. "I'll walk you home myself."

Sanchez walks away just after telling me he's waiting for me a little further on.

A few feet away, TJ calls to Tucker to join him. He seems torn, as if he's wondering if he should go back with his cousin or stay with me. I decide to choose for him because, at this point, I'm tired of this situation.

"Join him," I say, pointing at TJ. "As for me, if I want to go with Sanchez, I go. I'm not going to obey your every word, Tucker."

And I move away without waiting for his answer.

The roar of the car softens as it comes to a stop in front of my building. Despite the anger I feel toward Tucker, his words keep spinning in my head. *"You're not like the others. I hate that, but it's the truth."* What did he mean by that? That I'm not like all the other cubs who obey his every word? Of course not, we already agree on that. Maybe it was deeper than that, that I'm not like the others, for him. That I am…special? No, my brain is tired and my mind is going crazy.

The silence that has reigned throughout the drive drags on as Sanchez cuts his engine. I stare at the outside of the car.

"So you really weren't happy to be in this trial, huh?" he begins calmly.

I shake my head, massaging my temples, a headache creeping up on me.

"And Tucker—"

"Tucker is getting on my nerves," I grumble.

Sanchez watches my profile blankly, and I finally turn my head in his direction. What's wrong with him?

"Are you guys…?"

I can guess his question perfectly well…and the answer is none of his business. He sees right away that I'm getting defensive and raises his hands as if to apologize.

"It's just that he was about to rip my head off when you followed me to my car. Making him jealous might not be the best thing to do."

"I wasn't making him jealous," I cut Sanchez off firmly.

That's true…isn't it?

He smiles gently at me. "Not at me, Iris. This guy is not just anyone. I just joined their group and I don't want to end up hanging by my balls."

"I wasn't making him jealous," I repeat a little louder.

But who am I trying to convince, really? I think about Tucker's words again, and this time I actually understand them. "*You're not like the others. I hate that, but it's the truth.*" He's used to girls falling into his arms just like that, and part of him hates that that doesn't happen with me. But another part takes me as a challenge, I can see that… well, he'll see!

"Thank you for driving me home," I finish simply by opening my car door.

Sanchez watches me get out, an enigmatic look stuck on his face. Such dark eyes. Damn, I swear I've seen that look before.

"See you soon, partner!" he shouts just before the door slams shut.

I walk down the corridor to my apartment, my things under my arm. Luckily the idiot who was with Tucker during the kidnapping grabbed my bag. My cell phone vibrates at the bottom of my bag. I pick it up, frowning. I discover five missed calls from Tucker, all from a few minutes ago.

The phone buzzes again, and I answer it with a sigh. "What now? Are you planning on annoying me all night, or am I allowed to get some sleep?"

I hear a jerky breathing through the phone, as if Tucker is running or just pissed off.

"Are you home?"

His question isn't really what I expected.

"What?"

"You're not with Sanchez anymore?" he continues as I get more and more confused.

"Well, no, but—"

"Good, good night."

And he hangs up as if this simple answer was enough.

A few minutes later, I fall back on my mattress, exhausted. Although my eyelids are heavy, I can't fall asleep. I can't help but replay the course of the evening. Now that I have passed this third trial, what will change?

I try to push away the growing curiosity that is taking over. I pull myself together and shake my head. I don't care! They've already kidnapped me, they're not going to force me to make friends with them on a daily basis, are they? So I'm going to go on living my life as before, and I don't care if they have a problem with it!

25. ACCEPT THE OBVIOUS

IRIS

Something quite strange happens when I arrive at the campus parking lot the next morning. The first thing I notice is the look on the faces of the few students who are present in the west hallway leading to my first class of the day. They stare at me strangely and smile at me with respect and envy, some as if they are almost… afraid of my reaction. I stare at my shirt, wondering if I've put it on backwards again or if something is wrong with my face. But nothing is wrong. And then the light goes on in my mind. Is it because I've joined the most elite group in school? As I walk down the hallway, I realize that yes, it is. A guy I've never seen before waves at me from a distance, and I remember his face. He was part of the small group waiting near Tucker and TJ outside the warehouse. I return his gesture, hesitantly.

The worst part is when I walk into the lecture hall. Two chicks are whispering while staring at me and I swear I'm the subject of their conversation. This situation is really ridiculous! Is this what it means to be part of the pack, to be a freak? No, thank you!

Tamells, my cognitive psychology professor, continues wasting his breath in front of the many students who are already rushing out of the lecture hall. And I am one of them.

"Iris?" someone shouts behind my back.

A Hispanic accent…I don't believe it! I don't need to turn around to know that Sanchez is behind me. What the hell is he doing here anyway?

I ignore him. I'm sure he'll think I'm just a mirage, not really there. Yeah, that's a great idea. At least that's what I keep telling myself until I see him trot alongside me and stop in front of me, blocking my way.

"Oh, hi," I mumble, "I didn't hear you."

"Sure, it's so crowded."

His dark look becomes mocking. He and I both know the truth.

"And the hallways are so wide," I add with a real smile this time.

His medium-length hair curls slightly. He casually holds a backpack over his shoulder and looks at me without answering.

"And so…? You were looking for me?"

Be civilized. He gave me a ride home on Monday night. I can't turn him down when he's been nice to me. Be polite. Yes, I can do that.

"Well, actually, I was in that class. But I didn't know you were too. I think I was too focused on Tamells."

I keep myself from rolling my eyes. Why does he have to take the same class? Seriously, I've already got Tucker in Criminology. I don't want to have to deal with every member of the Pack! People stare at me strangely enough like that. I'm not trying to draw attention to myself, quite the opposite.

"What fascinating news," I continue, smiling. "I'm in a hurry, excuse me."

He raises his eyebrows, walking at the same pace as me.

"I thought you were a pain in the ass the other night because you didn't want to be there, but actually, you just have a shitty temper."

Affirmative.

I shrug innocently, which makes him laugh, and go on my way, giving him a sidelong glance. "What, now? Are you going to follow me?"

"I'm heading to the cafeteria. Actually, I feel more like you're following me."

"I was here first," I mumble like an eight-year-old.

"I don't care," he says as he continues to walk.

Neither he nor I speak for a few minutes, although we walk

side by side. We look ridiculous. Finally, I go ahead of him by a few feet and push open the door of the cafeteria. I'm about to let it slam behind my back, but I hold it open for him to enter. I notice a small delighted smile on his face.

"I'm just being altruistic," I tell him.

He raises both hands in the air. "Of course you are."

A few minutes later, I find myself with a plate of fries in my hands. I'm almost drooling with anticipation. I have a weakness for anything caloric and unhealthy. I'm pretty sure my blood is slowly turning into a mixture of sugar and salt. A large free table catches my eye, and I rush to it, delighted to have all this space to myself. I didn't count on Sanchez, who decides to piss me off a little more by sitting there too.

"Listen," I begin as I wipe my mouth with my napkin, "I don't know what you think you see in me. But I'm bad company, okay?"

He starts eating his sandwich and then answers me. "I find you funny. You seem to be a pain in the ass and unbearable. Yet you didn't hesitate to help me on Monday night and refused to leave me behind. I think you're actually hiding your sympathy behind a bad temper. But I'm okay with that. Or maybe you're just really boring."

How does he get me so easily?

"I'm not hiding behind anything. And anyway, I don't have to justify myself."

He nods again and continues to eat. "Besides, I hope that all the problems between you and Tucker have been solved."

I go still, raising an eyebrow.

"Are we interrupting something?" exclaims a female voice, a foot away.

"Not at all," I reply as Yeleen and Sarah pick their seats. On the contrary, I'm happy to cut short this so-called conversation with Sanchez.

The two girls settle down next to us as if it were natural. I can't ignore the looks of most of the students, who stare at us with envy, as if we were the new attraction.

"I was just making sure not to interrupt a little something between you two," Yeleen whispers, staring at us.

Damn, that's all I needed. Sarah, on the other hand, seems thrilled at the idea that there might be something going on between

Sanchez and me. She couldn't be further from the truth. Sanchez stares openly at her, practically drooling on her plunging neckline.

"I wanted to congratulate you," Yeleen continues. "I heard you acted like pros."

"All the credit goes to her," Sanchez announces while pointing me with the chin.

"Don't be ridiculous. We did it together," I correct him, unable to help myself.

"You're our two new cubs," she continues in a motherly way, and I refrain from laughing at her.

"And what are we supposed to do now? Become your minions?"

She shakes her manicured finger.

"You don't get it. Okay, there's a core group with people I'm closer to and other members who are a little further away from us. But at the end of the day, we're all one big family, Iris."

This is the second person who's referred to their group as a family. Those are the same words that Tucker's best buddy Dan used the other day.

"What I mean," Yeleen continues, "is that from now on, if you have a concern, it will be the concern of the whole Pack. If you screw up, we're all responsible. If you need help, we all act to save your ass. I can see your skepticism—you're probably wondering what I'm talking about—but this is very serious. You're new, so you may not understand, but it's very important to us. With the boys, when we created the Pack, at the beginning, it was just a joke. We were best buds and we wanted to throw big parties…and then the group started to grow, and it took a little bit of a different turn, more focused on cohesion and helping each other."

She stares at Sarah as she says this, and I understand that their bonds are much deeper than I thought, much stronger than the simple "party bonds" that bind members of college groups.

"Just know one thing: you are bonded to us now, you are in our family, and that is a sacred thing that is going to have to come first."

"I think there is a mistake," I cut her off. "I already have a sister, and yes, for her, I'm ready to do anything. I don't need a second family."

"You won the third trial, it's a little too late," Sarah mutters reluctantly.

Damn Tucker and his screwed-up plans. I don't want to be tied to people I don't know, supporting them and doing everything for them. I'd rather play it solo, like I've been doing for the past few months. I once relied on someone, but that person was taken away from me. And when I lost him, I was even more broken. I'm not ready to do that again. It's too painful to rely on someone, to give them the power to destroy me.

Unfortunately, I have a feeling I won't be able to escape Tucker's gang.

"How many of you are there?" I ask anyway.

Purely out of curiosity.

"There are really nine of us," Yeleen answers, while Sanchez is hanging onto every words. "Among the nine, you have Dan, whom you've already met—although he's not in school anymore this year—Tucker, of course, TJ, Sarah, me, the two of you now, Sam—I think you saw him because he was the one who was taking you to the third trial—and Anya, who's currently traveling."

So that asshole's name was Sam. Such a jerk.

"What about Trey, isn't he one of them?"

Sarah looks disdainful, as if she's hiding some kind of resentment.

"Trey doesn't get along with everyone. We're buddies, but he never wanted to join us."

Her answer reminds me that I don't want to be one of them either! So why am I here asking them questions about their damn pack? I stand up and take out the first thing that comes to my mind, "I'm going to get mayonnaise."

Sarah looks outraged just hearing words coming out of my mouth, but I ignore her and go to the counter on our right. I take a deep breath, grab some packets of mayo, and turn back to the table, praying that only my stuff is left and the others are gone.

However, the situation is even worse because, walking towards them, I discover that two more heads have been added.

A blond with green eyes…and a tall dark-haired guy.

I walk towards them, noticing that Sanchez is no longer sitting in front of me but at the other end of the table. And the one who has taken his place…it's Tucker. I try to ignore his different colored eyes but it's complicated.

"My best friend!" exclaims TJ, noticing me.

He isn't even paying attention to me, instead leering at my fries. I stop behind my chair, and my gaze finally meets Tucker's. He locks me in, refusing to let go. I take a deep breath. Should I grab my stuff again and move in front of Sanchez? No, that would mean Tucker won.

"It's amazing how much you've changed in a few minutes, Sanchez," I reply, sitting down across from Tucker.

He crosses his arms but says nothing. He doesn't seem at all embarrassed. Did he just ask Sanchez to get off his ass and take his place? That would be just like him.

"I think someone is having her period," TJ suggests, poking me with a fry.

I slap his hand away, furious.

"Someone is angry because a lot of people are very stupid," I growl.

"Ooh la la," he laughs as he gets up. "The nerves are too tense here. I'm going to go and have a look at the first years who are waiting to lose their virginity. Shall we go?" he asks Yeleen and Sarah, who hasten to follow him.

Yeleen winks at me as she collects her things, as if trying to send me strength. That leaves Tucker and me, who stare at each other without flinching, and Sanchez, who watches us silently from the end of the table.

"Move," Tucker orders through his teeth.

I decide to ignore what his voice causes in my stupid body and turn to Sanchez, who is swallowing his food with difficulty.

"You were here before, you don't have to go," I say, smiling softly at him.

He looks at Tucker, then at me. "Uh…Iris," he finally says. "I…I don't want to be involved in this." Then he straightens up and moves away under my dark look.

Finally, I cross my arms over my chest and settle back in my seat, right in front of Tucker, who hasn't taken his eyes off me.

A few of the other students around are silent, as if trying to hear our verbal joust.

"Why are you defending him?" he finally says in a voice from beyond the grave, his dark eyebrows furrowed. "Do you like him?"

I should either tell him to fuck off or get up, give him the finger, and walk away. But a part of me urges me to stay right here, smile enigmatically, and simply shrug for any answer. Tucker runs a hand over his unshaven jaw. He seems to be grumpy today, in a bad mood.

"He's a piece of shit," he spits, seething inwardly.

I chew a French fry. Why am I secretly thrilled to see him react like this? Stupid girl.

"He's part of the group now," I tell him in a sweet voice. "So you'll have to like him because he's family, right?"

I continue to eat silently in front of his closed face. His right hand rests on the table and squeezes a few times.

"I don't want you to like him," he finally says.

I close my eyes, trying to ignore his words. "Look, Tucker—"

"I don't want you to like him," he cuts me off, "because I like YOU."

He leans in, towering over me. I stare into his exotic eyes, trying not to let anything show on my face, although his words warm my body in a way that should not be allowed.

"I know you're still mad at me about Monday night," he continues in a breath, "but you can't ignore what's between us."

"And what's between us?" I growl as my heart pounds in my chest.

"Don't act like you don't know. I can't be the only one who feels this way."

He's right. Of course I'm still attracted to him. And I blame my body for it. Why can't we control the chemistry?

"You and me, it's going to happen, Iris. You know it as well as I do. Even if we hate each other, even if we're both this moody with each other, even if I act like a jerk and you act like a little bitch. It's gonna happen, and it's gonna be good."

I can't think of anything to say. I don't like his condescending tone, and I don't like this heat that's born in my lower belly without even asking me. But he is right. I think fate decided to play me by putting him in my way.

"So, I ask you again…" he murmurs while leaning a little more, ignoring all the looks turned towards us, "do you like Sanchez?"

I should tell him yes, even if it's not true, just to make him eat his self-confidence. But damn it, I feel like he's pulling me close and slowly destroying my determination.

"No, I don't."

"Do you like me as much as I like you, despite all the shit that's happened between us? Despite my stupid behavior the other night?"

It's almost like another apology from him. I stare him straight in the eyes. It's whoever dominates the other pulls them into the darkness first.

I will never confide in Tucker. I will never love him. I will never give him my heart like I did with Raf. There will be nothing sentimental between us. But I feel something else rising. Something uncontrollable, while his eyes keep mine prisoner. Something bestial.

"Yeah," I whisper, letting my breath hit his lips.

He steps back, satisfied. I come back to reality, mentally praying I didn't say that stupid word. But I did. I'm in deep shit.

26. A HISTORY OF HAIR

IRIS

The customers at High Peaks Bar are completely overexcited, tonight I think there was a college football game. Shame on me, I don't even know who is on the team among the students.

Talk to me about baseball and then we can have a serious discussion. I've always been into this sport because of my father. A sad smile takes place on my lips as I let my many memories flood in. How many nights we spent watching a game, stuffing ourselves with chips and pizza? I miss him terribly. I miss my mom too. But my dad…I don't know a better man than him. He was always by my side, supporting me in every choice I made. My throat knots, and I blink, trying to reconnect with my surroundings. Thinking about baseball again makes me realize that I haven't watched a game since he died. It's as if, when he left, he took my passion for the damn sport with him. With that thought, I remember Tucker telling me that he was kicked off the baseball team last year. Again, I can't help but wonder why.

"Coming through," Buck yells with two trays on his arms.

I shift at the last moment to avoid him bumping into me, grab my notepad and walk over to the table that has just filled up.

The little smile that appears on my face as I discover Yeleen and her boyfriend disappears very quickly. Trey seems nervous, almost… angry.

"Hi," I began hesitantly, a little embarrassed to interrupt their discussion.

"Hey, hello, Iris," he greets me between his teeth.

Yeelen tries to regain composure when she sees me, but I can tell she's holding back tears. I raise an eyebrow in her direction, silently asking her if she is well. She nods discreetly, and a fake smile takes place on her face.

"Hi," she breathes just before repeating it in a louder voice. "You're working today?"

"As you can see," I say, pointing to my notepad. "What can I get you?"

"A Busch," Trey mumbles.

"The same," Yeleen says, looking everywhere but in his direction.

I nod and start to walk away, but I can't help but let my ears drag. I know it's none of my business, and I have no desire to get involved in their drama, but still…

"Are you sure you want to drink alcohol? You never know, you might say something hurtful, right?"

Ouch…was Yeleen mean to Trey while she was drunk? And that's why he's going berserk?

I continue my way to the bar, forcing myself not to look back. I prepare their order quickly, still preoccupied, and when I head back to their table, I see that Trey has left. All that's left is Yeleen with her head buried in her hands. Not good at all. I can't just pretend I don't see anything, damn it. I call out to Buck as he walks by.

"I'm taking my break," I tell him, keeping the two beers, under his questioning look.

I ignore him and sit down in front of Yeleen, who doesn't look up for a second. I don't know what to say, I don't even know what's wrong with her, but she's crushed. I would be the worst bitch if I ignored her. I slide her beer in her direction. The noise seems to intrigue Yeleen because she finally looks up and sniffs.

"I…what are you doing?" she asks, obviously shocked to see me sitting there.

"I'm bringing you your beer," I answer, not knowing what else to say.

She stares at the glass bottle with a confused look on her face and then nods several times, her lower lip trembling.

"Thank you. But you can have it back, I'll…I'll pay. Yes, I'll do that."

She's completely lost. I stare at my hand holding the second glass bottle. I only listen to my instincts and take a sip of the beer that was meant for Trey, getting more comfortable in the seat. This is the first time I've tasted this in months. I promised myself I would stop drinking strong alcohol. Not another drop will enter my body. But beer, I can control.

"It's on the house."

She nods again, tries a small smile, and then wipes her tears with an angry gesture.

"You must find me pitiful," she murmurs after a minute of silence. "We hardly know each other, and I'm crying like an idiot in front of you."

"I think the real idiots are the ones who hold back their tears indefinitely. Sometimes you just need to let go, let it out. That's why we look pathetic."

She doesn't say anything but seems to think about my words. She really looks like she's at the end of her rope, overwhelmed. I should probably comfort her for a second and then get up and go back to my job, but I don't move an inch. I take another sip and whisper, "You know, your family or your Pack, well, honestly, I don't believe in it that much. But I do believe in friendship. So, I can stand there and make sure you don't do anything stupid, and you can stay quiet. Or you can talk, and I won't judge you."

I'll put my loner personality aside. After all, I can play the role of a friend for a few minutes. Not because we're in the same pack now, no, but just because she seems like a pretty cool girl.

"We all judge each other at some point," she articulates with difficulty, taking a sip.

"Believe me, I know something about it, I'm the first one to be tempted to judge people before I know them. But I'm trying to fix it. Look, I'm trying not to insult Tucker every time he opens his mouth."

My pretend confession finally brings a smile to her face.

"He really likes you, you know?" she replies in a breath. "Usually, when he wants to have fun with a girl, he tells TJ and me everything. But he refuses to tell us about you. It's like you're a little secret he wants to keep."

Of course, these words make me feel something, but I don't answer anything.

A silent minute passes. A new tear runs down her cheek.

"Trey is leaving me," she finally articulates.

Here's the crux of the matter. I don't say anything, not wanting to interrupt her. I'm not usually a good listener, but I feel like she needs one right now.

"Wednesday night he came to my house. He told me he was considering transferring to Columbia next semester. He's been offered a crazy opportunity that he can't refuse. He…he asked me to go with him. I didn't know what to say because I don't want to leave Denver. I have my life here. My family, my friends. He freaked out when he saw that I was hesitating. He wants to leave me if I refuse. What do you think I should do?"

What an asshole!

Yeleen empties her bottle in one gulp and takes mine without even asking me.

On the one hand, I want to tell her that it's really disgusting of Trey to blackmail her and that she should send him packing. But, on the other hand, I know what it's like to have to live without the man you love. And I wouldn't wish that on anyone.

"Well, it's not cool of him to give you an ultimatum, and you should damn well yell at him for it. But…"

I should keep quiet, I don't want to say anything too personal, but I can't stop myself. My tongue loosens as I'm deep in thought.

"But if you love him and think you'll feel good with him, then maybe you should take the plunge. I didn't get the chance, and I regret it every day. Life didn't give me a choice, it just…took the man I loved. You have the opportunity to follow your heart, so…that's my advice to you, follow your damn heart," I finish with difficulty.

I raise my head and find her staring at me.

"I…I didn't know you had lost the man you loved," she murmurs.

"No matter," I answer in a louder voice than I would have liked.

"What…what was his name?"

My breathing stops. My throat becomes knotted. I want to run away. Yeleen leans over to me, gently probing my eyes, a kindly look on her face.

"Rafael," I say in a weak voice, suddenly straightening up.

Yeleen holds me by the hand. I stare at her fingers. I don't want to talk about this, damn it! She must read it on my face because she lets go of me and nods silently.

For the next half hour, I continue my shift and run from right to left to the four corners of the bar, the customers flocking more and more. I don't have time to breathe when a new table fills up. When I come back near Yeleen a little later, I notice with horror that one of my colleagues must have served her too many drinks because she is completely drunk. Damn it.

Yeleen waddles her head and sings at the top of her lungs to the music playing in the bar. When she starts to sing a little louder, Buck glances at me.

"Go ahead," he says. "You're almost done with your shift anyway."

I nod and don't ask for more. I walk up to Yeleen and a huge smile comes over her face when she sees me.

"Iris! I can't…I can't believe it! What are you doing here?"

I hold back a laugh and try to help her up, but she refuses and sits back down a little more comfortably in her seat.

"I work here, remember?"

"You'll never guess," she continues, ignoring my remark. "I saw a redhead who works here and who looks like you like two peas in a pod, but I promise you she has an ass bigger than yours."

I purse my lips, knowing full well that she's talking about one and the same person. Me. "Come on," I continue, trying to help her up. "Let's go, you've enjoyed the evening enough."

"Noooo," she whines, resisting with all her weight. "I won't go."

Out of breath, I stand up and look around. Buck is waiting behind the counter, silently asking if I need help. I shake my head and pick up Yeleen's cell phone.

"Look, I'll call Trey."

Yeleen wraps her hand around my wrist and now looks at me with a panicked look on her face. "No, no, no. He's going to see I'm a mess. You can't."

Her pleading tone stops me. I curse and grab my own cell phone.

"Don't call Trey," she begs me again, rocking dangerously in her seat.

"I'm not doing that, silly," I articulate softly. I bring my cell phone to my ear. A ring, then a second. Maybe I shouldn't have called him. He's probably busy or at a party. I'm about to hang up, but then a deep voice rings in my ear.

"Iris? Is there a problem?"

Hearing the concern in Tucker's voice warms my chest for some reason. I don't answer, my mouth half-open.

"Or maybe you missed me?" he says in a charming voice.

"Don't take your desires for reality," I joke.

His deep laughter reaches me. Everything is silent around him. There is only his voice. Maybe he was working on our report about the Mikael Larey case? His trial is in about ten days, after all.

"Listen, I'm at High Peaks Bar with Yeleen. I need you to pick her up."

His laughter stops immediately. I'm about to explain the situation, to answer his questions, but only one sentence comes to me before he hangs up. "I'm on my way."

This guy is really an enigma. He's got a heavy attitude sometimes, but he doesn't hesitate for a second to come pick up his friend in the middle of the night. Who are you, Tucker Bomley?

I wait for the next fifteen minutes next to Yeleen, who half-stands up trying to grab one of my red hair strands off my shoulder.

"Are you really a redhead or is it a wig?"

I raise an eyebrow, wondering if she is serious.

"I have another question," she continues. "Is your pubic hair red or blond? I think I heard it was blonde but…"

I'm about to burst out laughing, but I stop when I see Tucker standing three feet away, watching us.

I stand up hurriedly but can't help but glance at him. I hold back a smile when I notice the pillow mark on his cheek. He looks back at me, his eyes locked on mine for a few seconds. I swallow my saliva with difficulty and let my eyes continue their way to his large torso molded in a simple gray T-shirt. He runs a hand over his short black beard and walks over to Yeleen, breaking our connection.

"And here's my calamity," he murmurs as he leans toward her.

"Tuckeeer," Yeleen squeals as he pulls her up from the seat, looping his arm under hers to straighten her out in a smooth motion.

He quickly understands that she has indeed drunk too much and drags her towards the exit while I get her purse and follow them. Tucker's pick-up truck takes up two parking spaces because it was parked so hastily.

"I notice that your ability to park is still not improving," I laugh behind his back.

I hear a grunt in response. He struggles to get Yeleen into the vehicle. She clings to the door and focuses on me.

"I'm being kidnapped, help me," she yells with another burst of laughter.

I don't move an inch, already imagining the hangover she's going to have when she wakes up.

"You know what," she continues, "I'm going to listen to my heart. I'm going to follow Trey."

Tucker frowns, looking confused, and forces her into the passenger seat. Her arms are contracted, and I can't help but watch the dance of her knotted muscles.

"Come on, you little drunk, get in there," he mumbles through his teeth.

Yeleen leans over to the open door to talk to me.

"I'm not going to let him go. You're right, I love him, just like you loved your Rafael," she lets go before leaning back against her seat.

I take the hit and hold back a flinch. Damn Yeleen!

Tucker slams the car door and his eyes meet mine.

I pray inwardly that he hasn't heard his best friend's words, but I know very well that isn't the case. But he has the sense not to ask me any questions. He just keeps staring at me, a stern look on his face.

He takes a step closer, lips parted, and runs a hand over his neck. "Thank you for calling me," he finally says.

I nod silently. His gaze is burning, and I'm pretty sure the one I'm giving him back is similar. He's literally eating me up in his thoughts. Shit, none of this is normal.

But it feels so good.

For fear of doing something stupid, I start to back away but he calls out to me, "I have a question."

I freeze in place, crossing my arms over my chest. I swear I won't answer anything else if he asks me about what Yeleen just said. But his question will be quite different, I can tell by his mischievous look. He approaches me, brushing me.

"What color?" he whispers against my lips with a little smile.

I frown, confused. "What do you mean, what color?"

He licks his lower lip gently, but from the way he stares at me longingly, I bet he'd like to run his tongue somewhere else, but neither he nor I give in. It's much better to play with fire. To be ready to get burned.

"Your hair, blond or red?"

Realizing he's talking about my pubic hair, I let out a grunt and slam my fist into his shoulder. "Asshole," I mumble, raising my eyes to the sky.

But already, he goes to his car with a laugh.

"Good night, babe!"

I can feel that he's still staring at me with such intensity as I walk to my own car. I feel his gaze burning my back and mentally undressing me.

And I think I like it.

27. A POSSESSIVE MAN

TUCKER

I let the hot jet of the shower relax my tired muscles. Head tilted forward, both hands pressed to the tiled wall, I close my eyes. I hate this fucking insomnia. I can't sleep tonight. Bad memories keep coming back to me. Images that I want to forget and that seemingly won't let go of me.

One, in particular. My father, lying on the ground. Dead.

I hear my cell phone ringing by the sink.

"Oh, my God," I grunt as I step out of the shower.

I grab a towel and quickly wrap it around my waist, grabbing my phone with my soaked fingers. I feel the strands of my hair dripping down the back of my neck, the drops of water tracing their way down my back.

"Yeah," I answer as I make my way to my room.

"I got on campus early," TJ begins bluntly. "Look, I talked to the coach."

I clench my fists, restraining myself from throwing my damn phone against the wall. I turn on the speaker and put on a white T-shirt, not bothering to dry off completely.

I cut my cousin off with, "Don't waste your time. I don't give a shit."

I can almost picture TJ rolling his eyes and holding back a grunt. "He's agreed to let you back on the baseball team. Your suspension can be lifted. He thinks we all need to put a little water in the wine, or something like that."

I let out a little sarcastic laugh. Screw that damn Coach Small.

"I'm not coming back to the team," I mumble as I pull on a pair of jeans, eager to end this conversation.

"Look, last year you two went off the rails. He couldn't keep a player who half-smashed another student. And then you insulted the coach when he yelled at you about it. If you would just apologize, then—"

"I don't regret a word that came out of my mouth, or any of my actions. I should have finished Matt off. I should have let Dan break his legs and let him rot in a hole."

As I finish my sentence, I realize I'm practically screaming. TJ doesn't answer me right away. I know he's trying to find the right words to help me, to get me to go along with him, but he won't. I stick to my guns.

"Debbie is your sister, but she's also my cousin," TJ sighs after a minute.

Was. She was.

"I understand your reaction towards Matt," he continues. "I understand that you still want to kill him today for what he did to her. But damn, Tucker, you were so good."

"I'll see you later," I cut him off, ending the call with trembling fingers.

I take a deep breath, trying to calm myself down. A new week is starting, and I can't wait for it to end.

As I pass my sister's room, I slow down and check to make sure the door is locked.

But it's not. It's supposed to remain perpetually closed, except for when the nurses and doctors come in, or Abraham. He knows this. And I know that he respects this rule, which is only meant to protect my sister from my mother's madness. If that door is no longer locked, it means only one thing: that my mother has been there. A silent anger rumbles inside me.

I push open the door, my eyes adjusting to the semi-darkness in the room, and sigh with relief at the screen showing Debbie's vitals. Finally, my gaze settles despite myself on the little doll lying on the bed, motionless on the sheets.

I leave the room, trying to measure my movements, trying not to send the door swinging against the wall. I walk quickly down the stairs, hearing the sound of dishes in the distance. I hurry to get to Abraham and get an explanation.

I reach the last step, and my eyes meet his as he carries a tray with various plates containing breakfast.

"Did my mom go into Debbie's room last night?" I ask.

He nods, uncomfortable. "She wanted to tell her a story. She was very insistent. I was there, making sure everything went well.

"The last time she was alone with her, she tried to unplug her fucking pipes. I don't want that to happen again," I articulate through clenched teeth. "And make sure her doctor comes in today."

Abraham stares at me blankly, knowing exactly what I'm getting at. Then he nods, and I walk toward the large living room on our right.

I almost stop when I discover my mother sitting at the end of the table. She raises her head and smiles weakly at me, but I can see that, once again, I am dealing with a stranger.

I keep it cool, not wanting her to have a fit first thing in the morning. I don't need that right now. I don't want to make her feel worse, even though part of me wishes I could. She is my mother, after all. The situation is so, so complicated. I walk over to my chair at the other end of the table, put my things down, and sit back down, my jaw clenched.

"Hello," she finally whispers, seeming to come back to reality.

A heavy silence invades the room. The atmosphere is strange but so usual. The sound of dishes crunching reaches me when she can't cut her damn pancake. She stares at her plate without really seeing it. Her doctor is coming by today, and he better gives her some new medication. The ones she's on now seem to be making her even more confused. When I can't take it anymore, I pull my chair back with a muffled sound and stand up.

I ignore her and walk over to her plate, picking up her fork and knife to cut her pancake into several pieces, still without a word.

I'm about to return to my seat but I stare at the clear glass right in front of her plate. I close my eyes, feeling my patience slipping away. I bend down, pick up the glass and bring it to my nostrils. Vodka.

"You drink at eight in the morning? Damn, your doctor forbids it!" I spit between my tight lips, annoyed.

"I'm at home, and this is my health. You can't tell me anything, boy."

I step back and let out a forced laugh at her light tone. "About your health? It's not just about you, goddamn it." I take another deep breath. I take a deep breath once, twice, and resume in a calmer voice, "Mom, alcohol is no longer compatible with your medication, and especially not at this hour."

She doesn't answer anything, stares at her plate and purses her lips. A bad feeling comes over me.

"Because you're still taking them, right?"

I approach her and bend over, dominating her with my height.

"Did you take your pills?"

"No," she growls as her eyes cloud over again.

You've got to be kidding me! I want to scream, to hit something. She's off her meds, and she's a walking menace during her episodes, and she keeps drinking on the sly. "I don't want you to go into Debbie's room anymore when you've been drinking. I don't want you to go into that damn room!"

She suddenly starts to hold back her tears, but I can't be fooled. Not after everything that's happened. I've always refused to have her institutionalized, and she refused it too. But the deal was clear: she has to get better.

"You are a danger, you understand?"

She stands up suddenly, and I pull my face back just before she can hit it with her right hand. And now she's getting violent…

"The real danger is you! You destroyed this family. You are a filthy piece of shit!"

"You're wrong," I say again in an implacable voice. "You destroyed it. You killed our family the day you let Dad die without lifting a finger."

I can't stay here anymore. I collect my things and walk towards the huge front door without a backward glance. I open the door but freeze when I hear her talking to Abraham.

"Don't forget to wake Debbie up," she tells him gently, "I think she's going to be late for class."

My engine hums loudly as I reach the campus center parking lot. My fingers are still tight on the steering wheel. I can't even think straight. I thought I'd calm down for the twenty-minute drive, but

I'm even more grumpy, my patience having been tested to the limit.

I curse when I discover that my usual seat is taken by the only Chevrolet convertible around. A used car, which seems to tell a story.

Iris' car.

Strangely, knowing I'll be meeting her in a few minutes calms me. I know what she's going to be like: acid, reckless, and ready to show her fangs. Exactly what I need right now. I need to…to see her, damn it!

I park a little further away, slam my car door and ignore everyone who tries to talk to me on my way, in a hurry to get to my criminology class. I take the upper door and enter the huge lecture hall where hundreds of students are waiting for Mrs. Richards.

Since I came in from the top, I have a view of all the rows below. I should be sitting in one of the two seats usually reserved for me, but I am only looking for one person: my redhead. I walk down a few steps, analyzing the students with my eyes. A hand rests on my bicep, and long fingernails graze my skin.

"Tucker," Sophie says as she appears at my side, "it's been a long time."

Not long enough. I stare at the little brunette for a second, wondering what she's after. Noticing her eyes resting on my mouth, I hold back from sending her packing.

"I heard there's going to be a party at your place Friday night."

Fuck politeness. I abruptly get out of her grip and walk away.

"I don't have time," I mumble as I run down the stairs, having finally spotted my little redhead.

There's nobody sitting next to her, and seeing her grumbling in her corner, I understand that she is also in a bad mood and probably a bad company. I don't hesitate for a second and join her row.

"Why do I always have to lose everything?" she mumbles, rummaging in her bag without having noticed me.

A smile, surely stupid, appears on my face. I swallow it and let myself fall into the seat on her right. She continues to search through her things, cursing softly.

"You put something in one place and it magically disappears," she grumbles again.

I can't help but laugh at how stern she sounds. It's as if all my bad moods have vanished, as if I'm ready to make her go crazy again, just for my own pleasure. Just to see a spark of defiance light up in her eyes. The one that makes me want to fuck her so bad. Long and hard.

Finally, she lifts her head and purses her lips when she sees me. I cross my arms on my chest and plunge my glance in hers with calmness. I'm ready to throw a little pique at her, just to shake her up a bit. I love it so much when she talks back to me, like she's not afraid to blow me off. It's so new to me. I like that.

But she beats me to it by dropping her bag on the floor after retrieving a hair band and her computer.

"This is really, really not the day to mess with me," she warns me. "In fact, it's not even the right week, so either shut up during class or get your little ass out of here, and go sit in your seat."

I struggle to keep my damn smile from coming back, without success. My lips stretch on their own as I raise my eyebrows. Here we go. I lean toward her, inhale the faint scent of her shampoo.

"Bad night, babe? Are you sexually frustrated, by any chance?"

She mumbles something I don't understand and ignores me, turning on her laptop without a glance in my direction. "For your information," she answers without being able to help herself, "my fingers do the job very well. You know what they say, you're never better served than by yourself."

I inhale deeply, imagining her giving herself pleasure alone. I see her, sprawled out in the center of my bed, thighs spread for me, masturbating while looking me straight in the eyes. Fuck.

Why does she have such a strong effect on me? Why does my body and mind refuse to move on until I finally get her? Just once.

"It's because I haven't served you yet," I murmur after a minute.

She lets out a little laugh. Mrs. Richards finally enters the lecture hall, her heels clicking quietly on the floor. I pretend to focus on her, but Iris leans toward me, one eyebrow raised.

"The great Tucker Bomley, the leader of the Pack, is offering me his services? What a priceless offer," she quips.

"I'd say it's an invaluable offer. And an exclusive one," I specify by putting my hand on her thigh.

Iris stares at me, but I keep my eyes on the stage in front of us. Her breathing accelerates slightly, exactly what I hoped would happen. She dives into my trap, pull me in it and we both get stuck, one more time.

"And what does this offer include?" she finally whispers.

Hummmmm…oh yes, she really wants me. Maybe even as much as I want her.

I click my pen, once, twice, with my free hand. With my other hand, I squeeze her thigh a little more.

"You'll find out soon enough. Until then, I'll let you imagine us devouring each other."

"This is not what I am doing at all," she retorts, slapping my hand hard.

I let out a little laugh in response.

Right, babe.

Almost two hours later, I'm looking for the little redhead after having a quick lunch with TJ who tries once again to change my mind about the baseball team. But it's a lost cause. I go to lecture hall C4, where Iris's cognitive psychology class was held.

How do I know that? I could say that it's a fucking coincidence that I'm passing by, but the truth is that I've just asked Yeleen about it, like a fucking jerk in need. Officially, I have to work on the Mikael Larey case with Iris. Unofficially, I wanted to see her.

I think that until we have sex, the attraction will keep growing. We have to fall for it to go back to the way it was. Or maybe not. Maybe I'll want her again, and again.

The students leave the class that just ended. I wait, leaning casually against the wall, as if I wasn't expecting her. A small smile comes to me when I see her overtaking everyone else to get out faster, but it disappears quickly when I see a guy trotting behind her.

With a seductive look permanently plastered on his tanned face, his dark eyes, and his hair of the same color that is brushing the collar of his polo shirt, Sanchez tries to catch up with Iris without her even knowing it.

I tilt my head to the side, watching from a distance. Sanchez is a good guy. Since the beginning of the year, he's shown his desire to join our group. I've had the opportunity to talk to him several times. He has the answer for everything, and he's cool.

But there is no way he is going to get close to my girl.

What am I thinking?

I sweep this thought aside and try to stay still. He passed the tests, and he's part of the gang now. But as I see him put his fucking hand on Iris when he catches up to her, as I see his fingers wrap around her bicep, I tense up. And when she smiles at him and seems to mock him with a defiant look—the same defiant look she gave me earlier—I see red.

Iris is probably going to tell me to fuck off, to call me names, but I don't think about it anymore and move away from the wall, heading in their direction.

28. LET'S OPEN UP

IRIS

Sanchez removes his fingers from my shoulder as he notices my questioning and far from friendly look. I hate people who get touchy-feely too quickly.

"Do you understand anything about creating false memories? I admit I fell asleep in the middle of class," he begins.

His smile seems fake. He's seemed nice since we met, well, at least sort of. So why is my instinct to walk away from him? To run away from him?

I roll my eyes then finally answer him, trying to piece together what I've figured out on my end, "Loftus showed that memory could be…manipulated. We showed one hundred students a movie that showed a traffic accident. Then the group was split into three and each new group was asked a question about the impact between the vehicles, but worded differently. When the question mentioned violence, one-third of the students recalled seeing broken glass, except that there was none in the video. It's a false memory that's implanted in their minds. Get it?"

"Did you really just give me a super clear summary in a few sentences?" Sanchez seems almost stunned, as if he thought a few minutes ago that I was stupid.

I don't know if I should be thrilled to look smart or offended. I open my mouth to tell him that I have actually been interested in memory manipulation for years, but I am stopped in my tracks.

Behind Sanchez, I see Tucker rushing toward us, shoving a few people in his path.

Oh, oh. I think we have a problem.

He looks really mad.

What the hell is wrong with that jerk?

Sanchez doesn't see him. He says something to me, but I don't listen to him. My attention is focused on the lion who seems ready to roar. He comes close to us and gives a small shoulder blow to Sanchez, who moves away a few inches. He doesn't know it, but Tucker just did it on purpose. I know it. But what is the problem, again?

"Sorry," says Sanchez with a small contrite smile.

"A problem?" I ask the tall, dark-haired man, wondering if there is indeed a problem. Maybe something happened between Trey and Yeleen. I swear, if that idiot hurt her again, I'll punch him in the face. He doesn't even realize that this completely clueless girl who loves him is suffering.

Tucker clenches his fists. He stares at Sanchez, then at me.

"We have work to do," he spits.

I raise my eyebrows at his pitiful excuse. His tone and attitude let me know something is wrong.

"Oh, sorry, man," Sanchez apologizes, "I was just asking about the class."

"No worries, *man*," Tucker continues through his teeth. "Now that you got it, you can leave. We're in a hurry."

"You do seem to be in a hurry. But it doesn't look like Iris is," Sanchez says brazenly.

Tucker squints a little more, and I hold back a smile. Oh, oh…maybe the lamb isn't so weak, is he, my beautiful wolf?

Tucker continues to stare at him, with a mad look in his eyes. His jaw is clenched, and he looks like he's on the verge of exploding. He bows his chest and says, "You should not play with me, Sanchez."

The latter seems divided between the urge to get out of here and the desire to continue teasing him.

"I'll see you later," I tell Sanchez, signaling for him to leave.

He moves back waving goodbye. I ignore him and stand in front of Tucker.

"Did something happen to make you act like a lunatic?" I ask him, trying to get his attention, but it's no use, he keeps staring at Sanchez's back.

An idea germinates in me. A dirty idea which makes me furious. "Tell me it's not what I think." I ask.

He raises his eyebrows and crosses his arms.

I take a step towards him, brushing his chest. "Tell me that you have not come like a madman, with your dark look, just because Sanchez was with me?"

"Or what?" he growls between his lips.

"Or I'll headbutt you, man."

He shrugs his shoulders for any answer, not worried and not embarrassed by his caveman attitude.

"But what's wrong with you? You don't have to come like that, with your…macho attitude, just to keep me away from Sanchez," I explode, shaking my index finger in front of his face.

"I just came to get you because we have to work on the Larey case," says Tucker innocently.

I drop my head back, letting out a sarcastic, almost demonic laugh. I must look like a crazy person. Good, because he's driving me crazy. "Right, and I'm the Queen of England. To others, Tucker. Let's set the record straight, you and I. We've established the fact that we like each other. But you're going to stop right here and now with your little…jealousy attack."

"I wasn't jealous," he mumbles, but he can't stick to his guns. "Actually, I was, damn it. I didn't like him holding you like that, like you were longtime buddies, damn it."

"You put me in a room with Sanchez in the middle of the night and ordered us to escape together. So let me tell you something: it's obviously creating a bond. And if you're not happy, you have no one to blame but yourself. Maybe you should have thought a little harder before you kidnapped me and put me with him in your fucking warehouse. Maybe some chicks would be happy that you're possessive, but not me."

My words hit the target. I know he's pissed, too. He doesn't seem to know what to say, just glaring at me. Maybe some people run away from his domineering and dangerous look, but I don't. We both stand our ground, not wanting to give an inch to the other. It's not because the attraction between us is eating me up inside and that the tension is almost unbearable that I'm going to let him act like he just did.

I finally sigh and add, "And then there's nothing with Sanchez, so on top of that, you're ridiculous."

I understand jealousy to a certain extent, but that's pushing it.

"I…damn it, stop making me out to be the bad guy. I didn't like his reaction, period."

"But there are no bad guys or good guys, Tucker. I'm just asking you to be reasonable because your behavior is pissing me off. I told you I didn't like him. I told you that I like you. If you want that last sentence to be wrong, keep acting like you did in the last five minutes. I'm not Jane and you're not Tarzan who has to beat his chest while reacting like an animal."

He leans toward me, eyebrows furrowed, his different colored eyes locked in mine. I can see he wants to scream, to curse, but something is holding him back. His breath hits my face.

"I admit I was ready to jump on him if he hadn't taken his damn fingers off you. Okay, you don't want him. But I know the look of a man who wants to fuck a woman, and that's the look he had when he stared at you."

That's bullshit. Hey, but wait…"You recognize that look because you've given it to a lot of girls who are ready to drop their panties, right?" I ask him, unable to stop myself.

He raises an eyebrow as he moves his head back. "Who seems jealous now?"

I open my mouth and suddenly close it again, before saying, "But not at all! Well, not really…"

I don't have time to react, his lips press hard on mine, just for a second, then they move away just as quickly. His taste imposes itself on me, his print engraves itself on my mouth, as if he had needed this contact as much as me.

I stare at him, not really knowing what to do. Do I hit him? Or pull him to me so that he kisses me again?

I lean over him and bump into him while pressing my lips against his once more. This is good. It's way too good. It shouldn't be.

His tongue slips between my lips, searching for mine. It caresses my bottom lip, ready to conquer my mouth. His hand rests just above my buttocks, holding me close. But already I move away, short of breath.

I don't want him to see that I'm torn, I don't want him to notice my confusion. I should stay mad and not feel like rubbing myself against him while digging my nails into his skin.

"You're impossible," I mumble as I start to walk away to the outside tables so we can work.

He pisses me off, but I want him even more, as if this kiss has just warmed me up once again. Go find the logic in that.

"I know," he breathes behind my back. I'm betting he has a stupid smile on his face.

"Move your ass."

"I'd rather keep looking at yours."

I finish reading the draft of his report on the Mikael Larey case. I put his papers on the table and notice that he is watching me carefully.

"So you stand by our first idea? You think Mikael Larey killed his wife and daughter and raped her with the statue?" I ask.

Tucker puts my own papers down, shaking his head. I can't help but notice the way his powerful arm muscles move.

"It's not your case anymore," he says, bringing me back to reality.

I notice the small smile on his lips, he knows I was openly checking him out. I clear my throat and rest my elbows on the table.

"I've been thinking about this. I think Mikael came home, and his wife had killed and raped their little girl. In a fit of anger, he did kill his wife."

The words are hard for me to say. They stick in my throat because this case reminds me of my past and I am repulsed. Tucker is about to say something else, his mouth opens, but my cell phone starts ringing. I pick it up, a smile instantly spreading across my face when I see my little sister's name on the screen. I silently excuse myself and half turn away so I can't see Tucker anymore.

"Sweetie, tell me you haven't tried to mess with Aunt Emma yet."

Agnes laughs through the phone, with her childish laugh, and I fear the worst.

"No! I've been good! In fact, she bought me new clothes for when I come to your house for the vacations."

You bet, my aunt can't wait to have her here for a few days. But I keep these words to myself.

"Did you thank her?" I ask.

"Yep," my little sister mumbles.

Tucker keeps looking at his phone screen, his mood darkening once again. He seems preoccupied with something, but asking him about it would definitely be indelicate of me. "Was it the 'adorable' little girl who threatened to kill me the other day?" he resumes when I hang up.

I stop myself from laughing, nodding my head. My cell phone rings again, and it's my sister again, who seems determined to buttonhole me. Tucker lets out a theatrical sigh and whispers, "Can't she annoy your parents for a second?"

I stop breathing for a moment but try not to let it show. "No… she can't." My voice is drier than I intended.

Tucker crosses his arms over his chest, confused. "Why? Because she can't live without you for two minutes?" he then asks with a small smile.

I am determined not to answer, but my body disobeys me.

"Because they're dead."

I close my eyes, realizing that I said those stupid words out loud. Oh my God, when will I learn to shut up?!

I shouldn't have said that. Tucker already knows too much about me.

I look at him, unsure, but he doesn't show anything, he just keeps staring at me without a word. I don't want any. I'm sorry, that must be awful, poor thing, blah blah blah. I hate people who pity me, as if I were a fragile little thing.

But his reaction is quite different, simply "I didn't know."

I shrug, not knowing what to say. At least he didn't apologize, that's something. I pick up my paper again, determined to change the subject, but I stop when he opens his mouth again.

"My father is also dead."

My gaze locks on his. Neither he nor I speak. We communicate through our thoughts. I understand his loss, and he understands my pain. No fuss, no words we don't mean. Just a look.

A real connection.

His father is dead. His sister is dead. Did they have an accident?

Is that why we are attracted to each other? Because we are damaged? Because life has been hard on us?

Because it tried to make us warriors, at the risk of making us lose the fight?

29. SEDUCE ME

IRIS

I dip my hand into the popcorn bowl as I stare at the screen of my TV.

"But don't go downstairs alone, you idiot," I mutter.

The little blonde behind the screen doesn't hear me, separates from the group of survivors and takes another path, which leads her directly into a half-lit basement. But what an idiot! Never split up! Why do they always do that in horror movies? They have to learn the rules.

"Is anyone there?" the little blonde asks as she walks down the wooden steps.

"Because you think that if this person is there, he'll tell you?" I yell from my sofa. "Hi, yes I'm here and I plan to cut you into little pieces."

I take another handful of popcorn and let myself lean against the backrest. I roll my eyes when a guy comes up behind her and stabs her. There it is, what did I say…

Ring. Ring.

I swallow my saliva with difficulty while wiping my fingers on my pajama bottoms. I stand up, eyebrows furrowed, and glance at the clock above the fridge. 10:16. My front doorbell rings again. Who the hell is that?

Maybe Tucker?

But I don't think so. We've been kind of avoiding each other all week, playing cat and mouse. So I'd be surprised if he suddenly showed up tonight simpering. The truth is, I feel like our so-called relationship is taking a turn that we can't quite control, after the few revelations that have been made. And that scares me.

"I'm coming!" I exclaim at the next round of knocks on my door.

I look through the peephole before opening it.

"Yeleen? What are you doing here?"

She smiles at me with a knowing look. Instead of answering me, she pushes me slightly to enter my apartment.

"Please, make yourself at home," I continue in a gentle voice.

"Oh, that's nice, thank you!"

She stops in the middle of the living room, casually tossing her bag on the bar. "Why does it look like you're getting ready for bed?" she asks, pouting, her eyes fixed on my pajamas.

"Well, maybe because I am?" I suggest.

Which doesn't seem to be her case. The pretty little red close-fitting dress she's wearing matches perfectly with the pair of pumps on her feet. Oh, oh, that's not a good sign.

"Not anymore," she exclaims with a big smile. "I'm taking you with me. To the Bomley estate, dear."

I let out a small laugh before realizing that she is serious. "I don't think so. I'm off tonight, and it's not so I can end up in the middle of a debauchery at Tucker's, you understand?"

She makes a little pout that's meant to be adorable but doesn't work on me at all. "Don't you want to clear your head, ease off the pressure after this week of classes, with a glass of beer in your hand?"

"Um…Yeleen, I think you should avoid talking about alcohol, if you know what I mean."

I walk over to my couch and sit on the armrest. A guilty look appears on her face. She bites her lower lip as she tries to figure out what to say.

She and I both know what I'm talking about, which is that she gave Rafael's name to Tucker half-drunk while he was trying to get her into his damn car.

"I'm sorry," she whispers, before saying more loudly. "You're so secretive, so closed off to others. You finally decided to open up to me the other day, and like a fool, I ruined it. But I swear Tucker didn't even pay attention to what I said, otherwise he would have asked me questions, and he didn't."

She's wrong, I know very well that Tucker heard what she said. The information is written down in a corner of his head, I have no doubt. I sigh exaggeratedly, staring at Yeleen, who begs me with her eyes. I hesitate for a second to tell her to go away, but I can't. She takes her first step towards me, and I can see that she is genuinely sorry and blames herself. In reality, she couldn't really control the words that came out of her mouth.

After a second, I casually wave my fingers in her direction. "It's okay, stop giving me that mopey face."

She claps her hands, overexcited. Her eyes become sharper, more calculating. "Perfect, so get ready."

I let out another laugh, mocking this time. "I forgive you, but I'm not going with you, Yeleen."

"But you are part of the Pack, my dear. If you refuse to come to it, it will come to you."

She doesn't look like a fragile little thing anymore, so I glare at her. "You'd bring your friends to my house? Let me tell you, I'd kick their asses."

"You facing dozens of excited students, I'm not sure your tough-guy look will last forever."

I stand my ground, folding my arms across my chest. There's no way I'm giving in.

A few minutes later, I let out an expletive as Yeleen opens the closet across from my bed. I fall backwards onto the mattress, wondering what the hell I'm doing.

I stare at the ceiling, leaving her to search by herself.

"But why do you have so many sweatpants?" she sighs defeatedly.

I don't bother to answer her, immersed in my thoughts. A question is running in a loop in my head. I try to ignore it, while thinking that Yeleen would be the ideal person to answer it. My mouth opens by itself.

"Hey, what exactly happened between Sarah and Tucker?" I try to make my words sound casual, my voice relaxed.

A silence answers me.

I sit up on my elbows and find that Yeleen is watching me, a little smile on her face. "What?" I grumble. "It's a question like any other."

She raises her eyebrows and sits down gently in front of my closet. "I knew it! He likes you, that's a fact. But you like him too. No need to frown like that, I can see it," she continues, pointing her index finger at me.

I roll my eyes and try to look natural. It doesn't work. "It's just that Sarah won't admit it, but I don't think her interest in him is mutual. Am I wrong?"

She runs her fingers over my carpet, her mouth pursed. "I see. So I guess Sarah did her little act on you? Look, first of all, let me just say that she's basically cool, even though she's bitchy most of the time. But, her and Tucker…well…"

I sit down on the bed and sigh.

"It's okay, forget it."

"They didn't date," she continues, ignoring me. "She and Tucker had some fun for a while, nothing serious. But she eventually got attached, while he was looking for nothing more than friends with benefits. They cut it off quickly last year and moved on."

Tucker has definitely moved on, well, I think he has, but I don't think that's really the case for Sarah.

Quite the opposite.

With Drake to the max in the car, Yeleen presses hard on the gas pedal while singing out of tune. I find myself laughing as I listen to the abominable sound that comes out of her mouth. But what surprises me even more is that I also start singing like a fool.

What is happening to me?

"'God's plan, ooooh God's plannnnnnn,'" she shouts while pressing her horn without reason.

The car that we have just passed must not understand what is going on.

"'I hold back, sometimes I won't, yuhhhhh,'" I resume, singing as loudly as she is. With my hand out the window, I let the wind hit my skin.

I glance at Yeleen as she drives down the path to the Bomley property, then at my cropped white T-shirt that I've paired with low-rise jeans. Yeleen couldn't get me to put on a dress, but I think what I'm wearing might still hit the mark…

She honks again many times when we pass the gate of the property. We pass in front of the mansion, but the road doesn't stop there.

"What the hell are you doing?" I exclaim with big eyes as she leaves the road and her Jeep speeds across the lawn.

"I'm taking a shortcut," she replies with a wink.

"Tucker is going to kill you."

"Of course not, I'll say it was you who was driving. Like that I'm saved!"

The rest of the cars are parked along the road, but Yeleen continues to drive without a worry in mind. She crosses the lawn, leading us directly to the eastern edge of the property before finally stopping. She seems so carefree, enjoying the moment. What if, for once, I do the same as her?

Lights are planted in the ground, illuminating the dozens of students who are partying in the middle of nowhere. Indeed, it's a good thing they didn't come to my place…

They shout, howl with laughter, dance in close embrace without worrying about the rest of the world. I get out of the vehicle and slam the door. Yeleen does the same, greeting many people. I turn around, not really knowing what to do. It is at this moment that I see the chapel about thirty feet away. Deafening music is coming out of it. Kids are coming and going from it. The chapel seems so narrow from the outside, abandoned, half-ruined, but I know perfectly well that they are all in the basement.

"No mask this time?" I ask Yeleen as we walk towards the chapel.

"Nope. Now that we've got our two little recruits, you and Sanchez, we don't need all that. Tonight, it's just the members of the Pack and a few other hand-picked buddies of ours."

I follow her up the stairs on our right, letting the chaotic sound of the bass, the many screams that come to me and the smell of sweat and cigarettes guide me.

When I reach the last step, I look around the room. The old leather sofas are still there, placed all around. They frame an improvised dance floor. This time, the kids are not copulating but dancing with each other. I take a look at the sofa on my right. A chick is undressing on top of a guy while straddling him.

OK, I think I spoke too soon.

The ceiling and walls are in bad shape, and I fear the worst. But I must be the only one who cares about that.

"Oh, here is Sam!" exclaims Yeleen at my side.

I squint to see the young dark-haired man walking towards us, a small smile stuck on his face. A member of the Pack, but not just any member. This idiot is the one who was driving the car when Tucker kidnapped me the other day and he's the same one who was telling him that he couldn't take the bag off my face, that I should panic silently. He kisses Yeleen's cheek.

"Hi, beautiful."

Then he turns to me. I absolutely do not return his smile. I'm kind of part of their group—and I don't really want to be!—but I'm not going to hug him when I'd rather punch him in the face.

"Hi," he begins with an almost regretful look. "Sorry about the other day. Well, now you've passed the tests, so—"

I turn my back on him and walk into the room, ignoring him, leaving him in the lurch without any regrets.

Yeleen bursts out laughing and joins me. "Don't ignore every person you meet… Ohhh, here comes TJ!" she says.

I follow her gaze to TJ, having fun picking out a straw stuck between a girl's breasts. Yeleen whistles loudly and he raises his head, seeing us a few feet away. His mischievous look and his scoundrel smile do not look good to me.

"Hey, hey, my little chicks," he yells. "I ask you to put away your genitals for a few minutes and listen to me."

The music magically stops. Oh, no, please don't. He walks over to me, mischievous. All eyes turn to him, and therefore to me as well. I glare at him. I hate being the center of attention. He waves his hand behind my back, and Sanchez comes up to us, as uncomfortable as I am.

"Meet our two new recruits! Our charming sex machine straight from Montana!"

He points to Sanchez who waves to the crowd with a smile. So, he's from Idaho? That's news to me. That's one of the neighboring states to where I lived until a few weeks ago.

"And our fiery redhead, incidentally my new best friend. Yes, she is beautiful. But don't try to flirt with her, she hits easily. Behavioral disorder, I think."

I roll my eyes, holding back a laugh at his stupid warning.

I'm surprised to see all the people shouting and cheering for us as if they're really happy to see us. It's…strange, this welcome. And strangely, a shy smile appears on my face. I, who have always been unnoticed, always stayed in my corner, this whole situation is beyond me, but it doesn't bother me as much as I thought it would.

The music starts again quickly but Yeleen has disappeared from my side. I finally see her, in the distance, sticking to Trey. Well, I think things are getting better between the two of them…

All start to take part again in this debauched environment. Two girls, both half-naked, approach Sanchez, who doesn't seem disturbed by this. He lets himself be dragged to a corner of the room. I cross my arms on my chest, preferring to remain a wallflower.

"Boo!" exclaims TJ, jumping up in front of me.

I raise my eyebrows. "Was I supposed to be scared?"

He curses and puts his arm on my shoulders. "Stop being stubborn. Let's look for your male."

"What? No way…stop it with Tucker," I grumble.

He bursts out laughing, releasing me. "But who said I was talking about him, young lady? Well, no worries, let's look for another cock that will do the trick."

My jaw nearly drops. And he's laughing, this jerk. He's so unbelievable, it's crazy.

"So this is what it's like to be part of the Pack? Sex parties around the clock?"

"Of course not, tonight we're just having a little fun with all our friends. Come on, let's go."

"No…I'll just…hang around."

But already he's ignoring me, joining the improvised dance floor, following a gorgeous black woman.

More or less discreet, I can't help but searching the room, plunged in a semi-darkness, for Tucker. I take a few steps forward, nearly getting jostled at least three times—but I must be the only one who realizes it.

"You coming to move against me?" a tall guy with brown hair asks as he comes up to me.

"Move against you?" I laugh and stop when I realize he's serious. "Wait, was that a real invitation?" I ask.

He doesn't seem to know what to say, instead running a hand over the back of his neck. No doubt he expected me to willingly accept rubbing against his legs like a horny little pussy.

I'm about to walk away from the guy but my gaze suddenly dips to Tucker's.

He's across the room, sitting on a black leather couch. A chick next to him is smoking I don't know what. I keep my gaze on the dark-haired man, on his legs slightly parted, both arms casually resting, one hand on the armrest next to him, the other hand on his right thigh. Even at this distance, he manages to hold me prisoner. He stares at me without flinching. He watches me like a predator watching his prey.

Unless he is mine?

A delicious challenge to take up.

His air is serious, his eyes dark. He doesn't seem to appreciate a guy being half-glued to me, and I think seeing his tense muscles pleases me somehow.

He's immersed in gloom and his hair is inky black, but I can see exactly what's going on. The chick next to him puts her fucking manicured hand on his thigh, bringing her dizzying cleavage almost under his nose.

It's my turn to boil inside. I glare at him, then look away. I mustn't show that I don't like it. I inhale deeply and ignore him with difficulty, then stare at the guy who is still waiting next to me.

"Actually, I do want to dance." I say.

I don't wait for him and walk towards the small dance floor. He follows me, and I feel a completely different gaze on us. I take a deep breath and try to get into the music, to match the rhythm of my hips to the bass beat. The guy stands in front of me, also undulating in a peculiar way. When he gets a little closer, I mumble, "Don't touch me."

He frowns for a second and then resumes his dance, probably wondering if I'm a little crazy. I don't know why I'm doing this. I know for a fact that I'm driving Tucker crazy, and I know for a fact that he's watching me.

I think I want him on the edge of blowing up, as close to the brink as I am.

So, while undulating my hips, I bring my hands down my body to my waist and glance at him. And I'm right.

The explosion.

The girl who was at his side has disappeared to who knows where. Tucker is now leaning forward, elbows resting on his knees. His piercing gaze crosses the entire room to land solely on me. His mouth is pinched, his jaw contracted, but his eyes…desire is mixed with anger. I turn to him, continuing to dance.

We are both letting our attraction consume us. I think I'm tired of fighting it tonight. I think I want to give in to it.

Our eyes are lost in each other, holding each other, refusing to let go. Sweat beads on the back of my neck, a drop gently runs down my skin, tracing its way down my back. I inhale deeply as I see him stand up from afar. Both his fists are clenched at his sides.

He still doesn't come to me, unsure. Should he fall into my trap?

The guy from earlier comes closer to my back despite my warning. I feel his boiling body against mine. Tucker squints his eyes and moves toward us. My heart races as I watch him move in my direction.

"Get out of here," I whisper to the guy at my back.

He ignores me and sticks one of his sweaty arms against my shoulder.

Tucker comes up beside us, a crazed look on his face. "Get the hell out of here, man," he orders the guy who's been sticking to me. The tone of his voice sends shivers down my spine but I ignore them.

The stranger finally walks away, looking sorry. Tucker continues to stare at me, unmoving. I undulate my hips again, tilting my head to the side.

"Is something bothering you?" I ask.

He moves his arm towards me to pull me to him, and I let him. I don't run away, I don't back away, I just press myself against his burning body. Both my hands wrap around the back of his neck, and his press down on my lower back. In one go, he pins my belly to his pelvis. He lets me know that he wants me as much as I want him.

I reach up slowly, bringing my mouth to his ear. "Mmmm," I purr while pressing myself a little more against his erection. And just with that little sound, I know he understands that tonight, I don't feel like playing, either. Tonight, I'm all about instinct. I silence the reasonable part of my brain, and he seems to like it.

I feel his fingers tightening a little more against me, digging into my skin.

"You were jealous," he whispers in my ear in a warm voice.

I nod, digging my nails into his skin in turn. His breath quickens, hitting my hair.

"You too," I can't help but point out to him.

His lips press the tender skin of my neck. His light beard grazes my skin in a delicious touch.

"He wanted to fuck you," he growls.

His tongue licks the drop of sweat that beads just above my breasts. A single stroke of his tongue that makes me understand that he knows perfectly how to use it. My nipples stiffen, and I ask for more. I don't even hear what he's saying, as focused as I am on the pink flesh licking my skin.

"But I'll be the only one to slide into that pretty little body," he then whispers as his hands move down to my buttocks.

His lips then brush against mine.

I want more. I need more. I let out an over-aroused little growl, which surprises me. I've never reacted like this when I want someone, as if I were ready…for anything. With Rafael, however, it was good, he was the man I loved, my first love. So how can my body want Tucker so badly, at this moment? I refuse to dwell on this question because tonight I don't want to think.

Tucker must be thinking the same thing I am. His lips press mine a little harder. He straightens my chin with his thumb, immobilizing my face in the process. He kisses me hard. His tongue meets mine, ready to conquer my mouth. I'm pushing right back. My own tongue tries to dominate his in turn, and this game seems to please him more. A sound echoes in his chest as my teeth nibble his bottom lip and I gently pull on it. We undulate against each other, his hand remaining on my butt pressing me against him.

It's hot, but fuck, it's too good.

I kiss him a little more wildly, my fingers tangling in his hair. But just as I'm thinking that this is perfect, that this is exactly what I need, a muffled noise sounds outside.

Someone screams hysterically where the rest of the party is going on. I pull my head back, looking into Tucker's eyes.

What's going on?

"Tucker!" yells TJ at the stairs. "Move your ass!"

He waits a second, eyebrows furrowed, and I'm the first to pull away from him. Other noises reach us. Seriously, what is going on?

"Go ahead," I order him, but he's already rushing away.

I don't waste a second and follow him. Others do the same. The first thing I notice as I leave the chapel is a small group that has gathered about thirty feet away. In the center of the circle, I hear noises, a cracking sound.

"Fuck," shouts Tucker, running toward the circle.

The students move aside but keep their eyes on the fight that has just broken out. I struggle to make out what's going on, but words fail me when I finally do. I know the two guys who are fighting each other.

Dan…and Matt. The last time I saw them together, they were ready to go for each other's throats. And that's what they just did.

Dan's fist slams into Matt's face just as Tucker steps in. He tries to control Dan, putting himself between the two guys. Matt gasps as he tries to stand right behind them. He carelessly wipes his bloody nose.

"Go calm down," Tucker commands to Dan, a hand on his shaved head as if trying to control him.

The latter steps back, spits on the ground and walks away. "Fuck all of you," he exclaims to the students who are watching him.

TJ comes up beside me, his mouth wide open.

Tucker then turns to Matt. "What are you doing here, you little shit? Get the hell out of here now."

Matt laughs at the insults. Tucker looks around for Dan to make sure he has walked away.

"Got a chick you can get me, Tucker? One who spreads her legs as easily as your sister?"

Oh, fuck. He just signed his own death warrant.

Matt had implied that he'd had a sexual relationship with this Debbie during his fight with Dan outside the bar. Now I have confirmation, no more doubts.

Several things are happening simultaneously. I yell Tucker's name as he throws himself on Matt, who falls to the ground and drags Tucker with him.

"Damn it, Tucker, you're going to kill him!" I cry.

I think I'm dreaming as I notice that some people are filming the scene instead of trying to separate them. What kind of world do we live in, for fuck's sake!

Tucker restrains Matt on the ground and brings his fists down on Matt's face several times. I see blood and hear a crack. He's completely out of control. TJ grabs him and tries to pull him away, but to no avail. Yeleen comes running up to us, looking distraught.

"Trey!" she yells.

Trey runs over and tries to pull Tucker away from Matt. Between them, they succeed. Tucker struggles, screams, and spits curse after curse. When he stands up, he looks grim, a dark look in his eyes.

"I'll kill you," he promises Matt.

TJ and Trey drag him away from the scene. Kneeling on the ground, Matt sniffs hard, his face smeared with blood.

What did that bastard do to Debbie? I want to smack him too. Yeleen clings to me, her eyes glistening with tears. How the hell did this night get so out of hand?

We don't speak, looking at each other with a blank stare. It's TJ's voice that brings us out of our lethargy, a few minutes later. He comes back alone, without Tucker, Trey, or Dan. He yells to everyone that the party is over. His face is panicked. I walk over to where Tucker has disappeared, but Yeleen holds me back.

"Let him calm down, trust me, he needs it."

I hesitate for a second, then let her lead me to her car, my eyes still lost in the darkness.

Lying in the middle of my bed, I stare at the ceiling, motionless. The open window lets in a light breeze that blows on my skin, covered only by my shorts and my cotton tank top. An awful silence invades the room. Sleep keeps refusing me its arms. I turn and throw a glance at the alarm clock. One-forty in the morning.

I turn again and continue to observe the ceiling. Then I almost jump when I hear a slight noise. A single knock against my door. Who is it, at this hour?

But my instinct knows the answer to this question. It makes me forget my doubts and my sudden fear. I jump up and leave my bed. I hurry to the entrance, knowing full well who is there. A new knock against the door echoes in rhythm with the sound of my heart.

I put my hand on the handle, quickly glancing at the peephole to see who it is.

And I catch a glimpse of a large wolf who broke his cage tonight, roaring at another with the urge to break his bones.

Tucker.

30. SUCCUMB TO ME

IRIS

A creaking sound resounds when I gently open the door. It's the only sound that disturbs the quiet of the night. I stare at Tucker in front of me, and the danger that emanates from his pores sends a shiver down my spine.

He says nothing as he stares back at me. He doesn't move, arms at his sides. My eyes linger on the blood stains on his bottom shirt and at the neckline. But what really catches my eye are the scrapes on his knuckles.

He frowns as if he's just realized who's facing him, and where he is.

As if he hadn't thought about it, as if his instinct had pushed him to come here. Near me.

"I don't know what I'm doing here," he mumbles in a broken voice. "I…I think I needed to come here."

I swallow with difficulty, think a second, then shift.

"Come in," I murmur.

He walks past me, and I try to ignore his smell. A mixture of sweat, ground, and musk.

"Sit down," I order him as I walk to the bathroom.

He doesn't answer me, but I know he's obeying me. I can hear the springs of my sofa squeaking under his weight. I retrieve the small first aid kit from under the sink, realizing only now that Tucker is in my house.

I straighten up, clear my throat, and head for the living room.

"All this so that I take care of you," I tease him, trying to lighten the mood.

He doesn't answer me, his look lost in the void. Shit. I don't know what to do. He lets me sit right in front of him. He spreads his legs so that I can sit on the coffee table, in front of the sofa. I try to ignore his closeness, the warmth that comes from him.

It's difficult because it causes my skin to rub against his. Even though my brain is focused on his injuries, my body is not at all.

That traitor.

I open the small kit and take out a compress and disinfectant. Both of his hands are on his thighs. I hold mine out and wait for him to hold one out to me. After a second, he does.

With furrowed brows, I sanitize his knuckles. He observes my gesture attentively, looking surprised by the gentleness with which I do it, a gentleness that contrasts with my usual character. I don't know where it comes from. But I can't send him packing now, I'm not inhuman either.

I then let go of his hand. He rests on his thigh, and I'm about to ask for the other one, but I don't have time to before he notices the blood stain on his T-shirt. He grabs the shirt by the back of the collar and removes it with a sharp movement before dropping it beside him.

I stumble for a few seconds at the sight of his naked torso.

Stop being horny, Iris!

I force myself to look away but end up resting my gaze on him. I observe his large uncovered chest discreetly, his leader of the pack tattoo, the strong muscles of his shoulders. My glance goes along the few hairs of his chest, then the trace of darker hairs down his lower abdomen, their path ending under his jeans. I swallow again and notice that he stares at me, too, with intensity.

We don't speak, we simply continue to observe each other. He doesn't throw me any digs and I don't insult him. A great first for us. This evening and that fight disturbed us both. I believe we are a little confused, plunged in our thoughts without really knowing how to act.

He holds out his other hand.

"Stop thinking," he whispers softly, as if he could read my mind.

I frown and resume my task without answering him. That's not true, I don't think too much. Right?

Shit, he's getting on my nerves, that stupid telepath. I press a scrape a little too hard but don't say anything.

"I didn't know if you were asleep. I wasn't thinking when I came here," he finally admits after a minute.

I set down his hand, now sanitized, and put mine on my bare thighs before shrugging. "I was awake."

I don't move, seeing that he's about to speak. It feels like something is stuck in his throat and forcing its way out.

"Sometimes your fiery temper, the way you talk, reminds me of my little sister, Debbie."

So Debbie was indeed his sister…I freeze, looking into his eyes. He's going to confide in me, damn it.

What should I do?

"I'm not sure that's a compliment," I say in a light voice to keep him talking. I need to know. I need some answers to my many questions.

"You two were close?" I continue after a few seconds.

He stares at the ceiling, swallows hard, and answers me. "We were two years apart. I was always the protective but annoying big brother. And she was the little rebel of the family. From a very young age, she did exactly the opposite of what my parents ordered her to do. She told me to let her do what she wanted to do, that their orders were meant to be contradicted. But she never really got away with it. She always got caught. And she always found refuge in me, knowing full well that I would always stand up for her."

"I do that too with Agnes, my little sister," I say again with a small smile of understanding. Agnes is the specialist in doing stupid things and then coming to nestle in my arms with an adorable little pout.

"When she came to college," Tucker continues, "I had just entered my second year. Dan and TJ and I were the kings of the campus. We had the best parties, no limits. We'd act tough in front of everyone else and impress the girls at the same time. People started to worship us and sometimes even fear us."

He taps his index finger on his knee, like a nervous tic. I can't help but analyze his posture. Nerves must be eating away at him. He is undoubtedly reliving the memory he is about to tell me, and it's painful for him.

"She was enjoying telling everyone that I was her big brother, she…she was proud."

He takes a deep breath, probably wondering if he should continue. I look for his gaze but he avoids mine. I'm not thinking and place my fingers on his knee and gently squeeze it, wanting to draw him back in. He does so with a surprised frown, then resumes. "She didn't quite know that at the time I was a dirty prick who only thought of getting into every possible excess with his gang. She saw me as a nice guy. And then, that year, we decided once again to expand our group. There were challenges, and Matt won them."

So Matt was friends with Tucker and his gang? Was he part of their group?

"Months went by, and something strange happened. Dan… he started hanging out with my little sister."

I'm not sure if this is really strange, but I'm holding back my words.

"At the time, I went slightly mad. My sister, damn. And then she wanted to get closer to us. She wanted to mingle with my buddies. I didn't want her to be immersed in a world filled with booze, sex, and drugs of all kinds. She wanted to mingle with everyone. You can imagine that I refused. Damn it," he sighs, almost pulling his hair out.

I understand. I probably would have done the same thing in her place. The orgies, the fights, the decadence. I can see why Tucker didn't want his little sister to fall in.

"I'd forbidden her from going near all that," Tucker mutters. "But I told you, she was stubborn, she liked to disobey the rules. There was a party at TJ's. Everything we liked. Everything that gradually disgusted me. She snuck in. Fuck, she was smoking up while I was in the next room, unaware."

His breathing is getting faster and faster, his fingers are clenching, and I understand that his story is going to get complicated quickly.

"She ran into that son of a bitch Matt, who took her upstairs. And she, she was too high to realize anything. He took advantage of her. He slept with her, and neither I nor Dan knew about it."

He runs a hand over the back of his neck and stares me straight in the eye:

"When I was in the living room, I saw Matt, in the distance, coming into the room, a satisfied smile stuck on his face. He was joining his buddies, showing them something on his phone. One of them stared at me from across the room, then another. Matt then noticed me and lost his smile."

He lets out a joyless laugh and my heart misses a beat. I think I understood.

"I could feel that something was wrong. I stood up, and as I heard the voice coming out of the phone, I knew something was fucked up. I realized it was my sister, damn it. This motherfucker was showing his buddies a video of my little sister that he had just fucked. You could see her laughing while he was…"

"I get it," I whisper softly.

"I went berserk. I beat Matt until he passed out, until his blood covered my shirt, my hands. Yeleen was screaming behind my back. And after a few minutes, I remembered that…well, I…I tried to reach my little sister upstairs. But she wasn't there anymore, Iris. Dan couldn't find her either. We were devastated. And then we realized that she had run away. She had run away, ashamed, lost. She drove away, alone, in a terrible state. And she hit a tree."

I remember my discussion with two students in front of the posters promoting the tests to join the Pack, a few weeks ago. The girls were whispering about how another one had ended up in the morgue at a party. So they were talking about Debbie.

I close my eyes, her words bringing back awful memories. I can only put myself in her shoes, I can only feel the fucking pain.

The man I loved died in a car accident because I let him get behind the wheel.

I feel like Tucker thinks he's guilty, but he's not. The only guilty person is Matt, and his own sister who thought she was okay to drive.

Just like Rafael was partly guilty that night. And me too. Because I had let him drink and drive. Unlike me, Tucker didn't knowingly let his sister drive, because he didn't see her leave the scene. He has no reason to blame himself for her death.

I stare at him with wide eyes and his pain jumps to my face. I can't find the right words to comfort him.

"She's just a vegetable in the middle of a fucking bed, a broken doll. In the days that followed, I punched Matt again and got kicked off the baseball team. Tonight…what he said…I tried to pull her away from the debauchery in my life only to throw her into the lion's den. And, partly because of me, my stupid rules, she has been immobile for months in bed, hooked up to devices that keep her alive artificially."

I hang on to his first sentence. So Debbie is not dead, but in a coma…and Tucker blames himself. His situation breaks my heart. I try to strengthen my barriers, but to no avail. His distress hits me hard.

"It wasn't your fault, Tucker. It was only Matt's fault."

"Your sister decided to go to that party on her own and drive home when she was high," I hold back from adding so as not to hurt his feelings.

"Don't try any of the psychology techniques you see in class on me," he orders me dryly. "I don't need that. I just…needed, I guess, to say it."

"Why wasn't Matt convicted? Could what he did to Debbie have been rape?"

Tucker shakes his head. "The cops got Matt's phone and that damn video back afterwards. According to them, all they could see is my little sister having fun and laughing at the situation while both of them were drunk."

I let go of his knee. He's off in his thoughts now, reliving that awful memory. I think for a second. My brain orders me to be quiet, reminding me that I barely know him. But a part of my mind urges me to open up to him in turn.

Maybe it would do me good to put my past into words? To talk to someone who has suffered as much as I have?

"My parents were murdered last year," I begin with difficulty. "That's why I came to this city."

Back to reality. He suddenly turns his head towards me, his lips half-open. All his attention is focused on me, and I resume before I am unable to.

"I told myself that life had played with me enough, that it wasn't cruel enough to play another bad trick on me. But a month later, I lost another person who was dear to me."

I frown, my eyes resting on my fingers, which I am currently fiddling with. He doesn't know I'm talking about Rafael, but I can't tell him everything. I can't.

"About my parents…I…one night I came home and found them murdered in the middle of the living room. There was so much blood," I murmur.

He moves closer to the edge of the couch, leans over me, and places both hands on either side of my body. His thumbs graze the tender skin of my hips, but he says nothing, waiting silently.

I don't tell him everything. I don't tell him that I killed their killer, I don't tell him that I was completely messed up by this situation and that everything turned into an even bigger nightmare afterwards.

"Which explains your reaction the other day to the Larey case and to my being an asshole when I kidnapped you for the third trial."

I simply nod. "My little sister survived because I arrived in time."

I raise my eyes to him, hardly holding back my tears. I pray to swallow them, I pray not to look weak.

"The other day, you were wondering about the little problems I had…we've all been through awful things. We deal with our worries in our own way. And I would never judge someone who has gone through and overcome whatever this damn life has decided to put in their way."

I rest my index finger against his cheek, brushing it gently.

"I'm not going to judge you," I whisper. "You've opened up to me, and I won't ask you any questions."

He tilts his head at my touch and closes his eyes. "And I won't either."

We nod at the same time. He stares at my bare thighs, my breasts almost visible under my little pajama top, then rubs his face. He leaps to his feet, leaving me confused.

"I'll let you sleep" he declares as he retrieves his T-shirt and walks to the front door.

I look at him for a second. I can't let him go. "Tucker!" I exclaim as I straighten up as well.

Still with his back to me, he stops. His shoulders are tense, his body impatient. I can see that he is still on the edge of the abyss. But he forces himself to calm down.

"Tucker," I call him again.

After an interminable minute, he turns to me.

"I'm not in a good state right now," he breathes with difficulty. "I'm on the verge of exploding. All this, it's…"

He doesn't have time to justify himself again before I approach him, moving towards him until my body presses against his. He says a curse as I furiously press my lips against his. A dull roar echoes through him, rekindling my desire. We both need it, to let ourselves go after this shitty evening, to obey our bodies, to give in to this tension that has been choking us for weeks.

He drops his T-shirt and grabs my ass with both hands, pressing me against him. I wrap my legs around his waist, my fingers grasp his hair, my tongue caresses his. His breath mixes with mine. I tighten my grip.

"Your room," he whispers against my lips.

"At the end of the hallway, on the right," I gasp.

He carries me across my small apartment, and the bedroom feels miles away. He pushes with his shoulder my bedroom door, and it bangs against the wall. I bite his lip and he bites me harder in return, fighting back.

He then drops me bluntly on my bed. I don't wait for a second and hurry to undress myself. He stares at me for a moment, motionless, as if he thinks he's in a dream. When I get to my shorts, he decides to take care of them himself, bends over me, and nearly tears the cotton fabric as he abruptly pulls it off.

I am not ashamed of my body, I'm proud of it. But under his burning gaze, which proves to me that he is going to devour me, I have to refrain from hiding.

When I try to straighten up to undress him in turn, he stops me by putting his hands on my naked thighs. He spreads them with a certain control, but I understand that he is on the verge of explosion. His gaze openly stares at my uncovered crotch, and he runs his tongue over his lower lip.

"Look at that," he murmurs, stroking my hairless sex with his index finger, "how could I have stayed away from that little wonder for so long?"

I stop myself from laughing when I see that his question is really serious and let him analyze me while trying to relax. But when his glance becomes burning, my body burns, too, and the desire to touch him becomes more urgent. Not holding back any more, I reach again for his fly, but he blocks my fingers in his grip.

He climbs on the mattress and his breath comes to strike my crotch.

When his tongue starts to tease me slowly, I struggle to hold back a small cry which gets stuck in my throat. He discovers me, savors me with a slowness which surprises me. My clit pulses in his mouth, and I swear I'm going to faint. After all this waiting, I thought he would put his pleasure first, but he already seems delighted just by titillating me with his tongue.

"I like the way you taste," he growls.

I run my fingers through his hair but can't help saying, "Don't get addicted to it. It's a limited edition."

He lets out a little laugh and bites the skin of my thigh.

He draws out my orgasm little by little but refuses me at the last moment.

"Don't be a jerk," I sigh as he steps back.

He smiles mischievously and puts his mouth against mine again. It is the first time I discover my taste. A first time that makes me a little more aroused. It's different, and I think I like it.

"It's all about frustration, babe," he murmurs.

Then he hurriedly takes off his jeans, and I understand that despite what he shows, he is even more aroused than me.

"Top drawer," I whisper.

He seems delighted that I have condoms but also a little perplexed. After a minute, he spreads my thighs hard, positioning himself between them. His torso is pressed against my chest and he crushes my breasts while lying on top of me. For a simple "fuck," this is too much…too good, too intimate. But I can't react otherwise, I can only join him in the pleasure that consumes us little by little. His gaze is plunged in mine, our breaths merge, set us on fire.

Do I have the same expression on my face as he does? That mixture of intensity and desire ready to be satisfied? I raise my hips, hitting his eagerly. His arms land on either side of my head, trapping me in a burning human cage.

Again, I can only realize that this is too…intense. I don't know what's going on. So, to reassure myself, I seek his gaze and state, "Just tonight."

He frowns then kisses me again to shut me up. "Just one night," he finally confirms.

My fingers plunge into his hair, and as the pleasure penetrates every pore of my skin, Tucker simultaneously penetrates my pussy. Slowly but powerfully.

"It feels so good," he whispers in my ear.

What else can I say? That's exactly what I think. He slowly invades me, showing me how much he can fill me. He takes every inch of my body, owns it in its entirety.

"I've been waiting for this," he continues, nibbling on my ear. "Do you know that?"

I dig my nails into his shoulders and contract around him. "Then shut up and do it."

He speeds up with a smile, obeying me without a word. The pleasure rises even higher and reaches new heights, setting everything in its path on fire.

"Tucker," I moan as he slows down his thrusts to drive me crazy.

I dig my nails into his skin, wanting more. One of his hands settles on my neck and immobilizes my head. His gaze latches onto mine, and I can't escape it, can't close my eyes. We communicate silently.

There is nothing more but the contact of our bodies, the sound of our flesh as we slide against each other.

"You're almost there," he whispers against my mouth. His tongue caresses my lips, teases them.

But I want it to last longer. I push his shoulder back, and he lets himself move, rolling onto his back the next second. I follow suit and place myself on top of him, my taking him within me again. As I slide gently down him, I hold back a moan.

His right hand pulls my hips toward him, and he penetrates me completely. A small cry comes from my mouth at the sudden thrusting. I sway over him, my gaze wandering over his slick skin. He is boiling under me, ready to explode at any moment. As his teeth nibble on my right nipple, an unparalleled hunger grows inside me.

I want to come. I need it.

Tucker straightens against the headboard but still holds me tight around him. He continues to thrust into me while taking hold of my head again, his hand firmly holding my neck. My face is right in front of his, his eyes in mine. His grip is firm. He waits for only one thing, that I contract around him. When our breaths mix and he brings down once again his mouth against mine, I orgasm.

His hand runs along the back of my neck to rest on my throat and squeeze lightly. My breath catches for a second, and in response, my cunt tightens around his cock.

"Oh yes," he groans in my ear as I contract a little more. "Are you hungry for me, babe?" he asks me bluntly.

At that moment, I can't think of anything else. No restraint. This is our most primary instincts being expressed. The need to possess the other. Roughly. Bestially.

For the first time in many months, I let another man take me. And for the first time in forever, I feel like I'm totally possessed.

The sex with Rafael was good. He was careful to control his actions. He was always considerate. But with Tucker…it's something else. He stirs up a deep desire in me that I can't fight. Guilt slowly begins to work its way into my mind.

"Answer me," Tucker orders me, bringing me back to the present moment.

"I'm hungry, but not as hungry as you," I reply with the courage to challenge him a second time.

No more games. Tucker takes full control, and I feel like I'm losing this power struggle. The next second, I'm back on the mattress and Tucker's thrusts accelerate, sending a wave of pleasure through me. The teasing is over. Our hunger is too overwhelming. It demands to be satiated.

Finally, I explode. I clench around him and let a deep well-being invade me. With a cry, he joins me in this carnal bubble and collapses on top of me, his breath burning against my ear.

Amazing.

31. BAD TEMPER

IRIS

Rafael pulls me behind him. He crosses the long corridor leading to my room and throws me a complicit glance, his hazel eyes staring at mine for a moment. The threshold of my room is hardly crossed that he kisses me intensely, his numerous piercings to the lips leaving me a metallic aftertaste.

"We have to hurry," I laugh. "If my dad comes home early, you're dead."

"I'm ready to take on Mr. Foster for you," he jokes back.

He doesn't believe me. My parents are against our relationship. After all, Rafael is a few years older. He doesn't go to college and he doesn't hang out with the right people. He's far from an angel, but I care about him. And I know he loves me. That's the most important thing.

I let out a small laugh as his fingers brush my ribs. I hear the front door slam. I suddenly freeze, but he doesn't.

"Did you hear that?" I whisper, half panicked.

He straightens a little, keeping his fingers on me. His pale eyebrows furrow and he purses his lips. "No, nothing," he whispers.

"I think my parents are home," I whisper against him.

I quickly forget them when he kisses me again. His hands lift my T-shirt. I close my eyes as he pulls the fabric over my head. Keeping my eyes closed, I let him kiss the tender skin of my neck. But something suddenly catches my eye.

A beard rubs against my skin.

"What is…?" I stammer, opening my eyes.

This time, it's not a brown gaze that confronts me…but a different colored gaze. A blue eye and another stained with brown. No more piercings.

"What's the matter, babe?" Tucker blows me with a cheeky smile.

No! Rafael!

I wake up with a jolt, short of breath, my head buried in a pillow. I raise it and discover that I am lying flat on my stomach across my bed. I am in my room, on campus, and not years behind. I let my head fall back onto the pillow and inhale the masculine scent that emanates from it.

Damn it.

I turn onto my side and lie on my back before glancing down at my naked body. No doubt about it, I did sleep with Tucker last night. I sit down on the mattress, my gaze falling on the scratched skin of my thighs, exactly where Tucker rubbed his beard. I inhale deeply, listening to every sound coming from my small apartment, but nothing reaches me. I am alone, Tucker is gone.

I run a hand over my tired face. Why did I have this dream? Can Rafael see me from up there? Is he disappointed in me?

I don't know, but another thought keeps nagging at me. I don't know why I'm upset about realizing that Tucker has left during the night.

It's silly, after all, it was clear between us. Just this one night, to finally put out the fire that was burning inside us, then we'd move on.

That's what I want, of course. I mean, I think. Does that mean he's going to leave me alone now? That we're going to pretend we don't know each other, him and me, even though we're in the same pack? We both got what we really wanted, so now we just forget about it?

Maybe he'll move on, go for another chick he hasn't tried yet.

Shit, I have to stop torturing my mind! After all, the whole point of having a one-night stand is to not wonder about it afterwards. I don't know why I feel this discomfort inside me. It's unpleasant and I don't like it.

During the night, I felt his arms around me. He was holding me tightly to his body, without even realizing it. Or maybe I imagined this contact between us?

I straighten up and get out of bed. Not caring about my nudity, I go to my living room in search of my laptop and notice the small sheet folded in four on the couch. I grab it, knowing full well who left it there. I find some rather crude but masculine handwriting.

Quite frustrated that I didn't get the answer
to my question about your hair ;)

I frown and then smile slightly as I understand what question Tucker is referring to. I don't know why that little note makes me feel better inside, but it does, as if he wanted to leave something out to make sure there was no discomfort between us.

I block out all my thoughts, making sure I get back to being realistic and thoughtful. We both got what we wanted. It was…it was great, but it was temporary. I won't let anyone break down the defenses and barriers I've struggled to put up.

I walk toward my bathroom, resolute. In the end, it's better that he left while I was sleeping, it saves us a long and awkward discussion.

I park in the parking lot of High Peaks Bar and notice that there is a crazy crowd tonight. There must have been a college game in the afternoon. It promises to be an evening without a moment's respite. I take a deep breath and go to the crowded entrance. I elbow my way into the room and…cheers ring in my ears. There's definitely been a game. The customers look overexcited. A few girls are dancing near a crowded table where some of the players are apparently gathered.

Buck waves to me in the distance, looking overwhelmed. I quickly go to the locker room to put my things down then meet him behind the counter.

"Hi, doll," he says hurriedly.

"It's crazy tonight," I begin, helping him serve two beers. "Game?"

He nods but seems delighted.

"A few players from both teams and some fans have made this place their home for tonight. You were supposed to help me behind the counter, but considering the crowd, you're going to take care of the room exclusively. Tony will serve in the left wing and you take the other side. It's going to be tough tonight, are you ready?"

I nod and quickly get to work. I go back and forth for almost half an hour, feeling my little black shirt getting wet around my arms.

Super glamorous.

The service is going well, but it's getting more and more crowded and, more concerningly, tempers are starting to flare. I nearly bump into a guy who must be twice my size when another one shoves him, drunk.

Fuck, I have a bad feeling about this.

I look around for Buck to let him know that things are going to get ugly in a few minutes.

"You're the one who was playing like shit!" shouts the guy who almost ran into me. "Don't complain about losing."

"You're the one who's talking? You can't even run without getting your feet tangled up, you fucking asshole."

The first guy grabs the other by the top of his T-shirt while the latter hits him in the shoulder to get him off. Other guys stand up, some pissed off, some cheering. And that damn Buck is nowhere to be found. I elbow my way to the two guys who are about to fight, bursting with testosterone.

"OKAY, OKAY. Gentlemen, there are places to fight," I say curtly, placing a hand on each of their forearms. "And this bar is not one of them."

They turn their heads towards me in the same motion, which freaks me out slightly.

"Give us some beers," yells another guy behind them.

"A light ale for me," shouts yet another as he shoves me to get to his seat.

I take a deep breath, holding back from calling them names.

"I'll get your beers if you calm down. I don't need to know who has the biggest balls," I continue firmly.

The two guys open their mouths wide but don't answer anything, surprised by my reply. One of the guys behind them bursts out laughing and retorts loudly, "Just so you know, it's me, if you want to come and check, honey."

I roll my eyes and turn my back to them to reach the bar. Phew, we avoided the worst. At least, that's what I tell myself before I hear a big crash behind my back…I turn and have the reflex to jump on the side to avoid the two guys who have finally come to blows.

Damn it, I can't believe it.

"Buck," I shout, seeing him in the distance.

"Tony, it's an emergency!" he exclaims as he runs towards the fight.

Tony arrives and together they manage to separate the two drunken players. But not for long, judging by their tense muscles.

I've got to figure out how to stop this before the situation explodes.

In the distance, on the right side of the room, towards the pool tables, two other guys are getting angry too. I'm racking my brains, looking for a plan.

"This is going to be a real mess," I mutter to Buck.

He walks over to the other group of guys and gives me a look.

"If you have a way to calm them down, please do. Every game day it's like this."

Then he walks away with a few shouts. I can see the bar counter about 30 feet away.

Find a solution. Distract them. Make them want to party instead of killing each other…I think I have an idea.

I don't wait a second and head for the counter. As soon as I get behind the bar, I turn up the music to full volume, pick up two full bottles of vodka and put them on a corner of the counter.

"*Don't do it, Iris,*" my conscience orders me.

Of course, I'm going to do it. With the strength of my arms, I pull myself up onto the counter. Buck watches me from a distance, with a questioning look on his face. I wink at him and stand on the bar.

Let's get this show on the road.

TUCKER

My car runs along the narrow tree-lined driveway. I park in front of the huge modern house and leave the engine running. The passenger door opens immediately and slams shut. I stare at my cousin, who sits down and drops his head on the headrest.

"Are you okay?" I ask him.

TJ opens his mouth, angrily wipes away the tear that runs down his cheek, and finally lets out a joyless laugh.

"I hate him. I fucking hate him so deeply it's embedded in my skin."

I don't say anything, simply driving back to the road. I leave the property while letting my cousin relax beside me. I hate seeing him like this, and knowing that his father is the one putting him in such a state pisses me off even more. My dad was a great man, damn it. He supported me in every choice I made before he died. That's not the case with the scumbag that is TJ's father.

"My mom wouldn't tell me, but I saw the bruises on her arms, Tucker. Damn, he hit her again, and she shuts her mouth. I'm going to beat the shit out of him, I swear, I want to so bad."

"I know, man," I say through my clenched teeth.

This isn't the first time his father has laid a hand on my aunt, my father's sister. TJ has come to blows with him before for this reason. But then his mother always sides with her husband, preferring to save appearances rather than her own skin.

I hear TJ sniffle quietly and glance at him while clutching my steering wheel in my hands.

"Stop holding back, damn it," I mutter. "You've seen me messed up enough times. We've got each other's backs."

He mumbles a curse, lets it go for a minute, then leans over and pokes me in the shoulder.

"Thank you, pretty girl," he says.

I laugh, delighted to find him back. He's the best definition of a good mood, and I wouldn't have it any other way. "So, where do you want to go? Delta is having a party on campus tonight."

He shakes his head. "I told Dan to meet us at High Peaks Bar. He's already on his way."

I don't answer, swallowing hard. Iris will be there, I'm sure. That means I'll have to see her again. How will she react? Insult me because I snuck out like a jerk? Or laugh with me because she's moved on?

I don't know why I've had this fucking knot in my stomach since I left her apartment. I usually do that, leave just before dawn. But I knew I had a problem when I woke up in the middle of the night and was holding her close.

Fuck, my nose was buried in her hair.

And I liked it.

It's never happened to me before. So I got scared and ran away, scribbling a little note before I left, as if I couldn't quite get away like a thief.

We both got what we wanted, finally releasing the tension that had been building up inside us the past few weeks. It's cool. Now we can…stop thinking about it and move on to the next problem. I'm laughing inwardly because all I can think about is her little pussy since I left her arms. We're moving on to the next problem…

In my defense, I didn't expect to enjoy this night so much. She's as much of a tigress in bed as she is out, so yeah, it was more than good.

But now that I've had her, I need to get her out of my head, move on to another girl.

Yeah, that's exactly what I'm going to do. And maybe she'll do the same. A thought I don't like at all.

"Are you okay?" TJ asks me, quietly observing me.

That's when I notice that I'm gripping the steering wheel like crazy. I loosen my grip and try to relax my muscles. "Yeah, yeah, I'm fine." I pull into the parking lot and notice that the place is completely packed. I'm in no mood to meet a lot of familiar faces. I park and turn off the car.

"Try not to piss off Iris, tonight, I really like her," says TJ while taking off his sweater.

I glance at him without answering. I've noticed he likes her. He likes hot-blooded people.

"I'm not going to piss her off," I retort more curtly than I would have liked.

"Come on, man, stop making that face. I know she doesn't want to give it up to you, so try to find another girl tonight. You're pissed she's refusing you, but you've got others waiting for their turn."

I open my mouth but don't say anything. I don't want to admit to him that we fucked all night. I don't want to tell him that she came on my cock and I felt like I was seeing fucking stars.

So I let him think I didn't get her, much good may it do him.

"Wait, what's that look?" my cousin asks, a little too perceptively, as he leans in toward me.

"Nothing," I mumble, opening my car door.

"Was there something I don't know?" he asks, following me. "Did you fuck her?"

I stop abruptly and turn towards him, glaring at him. I dominate him with my height, shoulders tensed, jaw tightened.

"Mind your own business," I order him forcefully.

He nods slowly, confused. I don't wait a second and enter the bar, letting the door slam behind me.

My bad mood resurfaces.

But what's happening to me?

I search the room, looking for the sort of girl that I like. I am absolutely not looking for a certain little redhead…

I tell myself that's what I'm doing, but I tense up a bit when I can't find her.

I do, however, notice a few groups ready to fight. The quarterback of the college team greets me from afar, a chick on his lap. I stop by the pool tables.

"Oh fuck," exclaims TJ as he comes up to me. "Is that Iris?"

I follow his gaze, my eyebrows furrowed. My jaw nearly drops when I see Iris standing on the wide wooden bar. Heads turn to her, to her tight little ass that is displayed in front of us, covered by her black jeans. I'm not liking what's happening. I think there's something wrong with me, damn it.

She gets on the bar with the bottles of vodka and whistles for everyone's attention.

A few people approach the bar when they see that she is holding a bottle of vodka in each hand.

"It seems to me that you guys are hot tonight, who wants to get wet?"

Helpless, I watch them crowd around her feet. Iris bends down, unscrews the cap of one of the bottles, and pours a glassful directly into a guy's mouth. Cheers erupt from all sides. Those who were practically fighting join the bar as well. Standing on the counter, Iris pours alcohol into mouths. I notice bills raining down at her feet. TJ explodes with laughter next to me, and a small smile breaks out on my face. She really seems to be enjoying herself.

But I don't like to see her like that, like a free chick wiggling her little ass…even though she is?

"She's going to be the bar's mascot. I bet the guys in town will be rushing here to get her to fill their mouths."

My smile fades immediately. I don't think so!

Iris stares at the waiter who is watching her, two thumbs up, a foot away, then she plunges her gaze into mine. Then another problem arises because when I see her slowly running her tongue over her bottom lip, I instantly feel myself hardening.

I still want her.

IRIS

I walk down the bar to the applause of Buck, who whistles at me.

"Where the hell have you been hiding that?"

I shove him with a little smile and grab a notebook to go back to taking orders.

"You asked me to find a way to calm things down, and I think I did a pretty good job."

"Damn you succeeded, you were damn hot!"

I glare at him and raise my pen in his direction. "Don't even think about it."

He raises his eyes to the sky and pretends to wipe my face. "Go on, get out of here, you naughty girl, before I jump on you."

I mumble to myself and walk away, ignoring his mocking laugh. I try not to look at the two pool tables at the back of the bar, but unfortunately, they are on the side of the room where I am serving tonight. Luckily for me, two guys and a girl call me. I walk towards them with a little smile on my face.

"What can I get you?" I ask.

"Light Ale!" they exclaim at the same time.

"I'll get that for you."

I walk away and look straight ahead as I pass by the pool tables.

"Iris!" shouts TJ as he notices me.

Damn it…I freeze and slowly turn in his direction. I keep my gaze on him, trying to forget about Tucker who is staring intently at me behind him, leaning against one of the pool tables. I walk over to them, noticing two other guys who have joined them in passing.

"Hi."

TJ stares at me, a big smile on his face, stars in his eyes.

"Would you do a personal show for me again?" he jokes, grinning wickedly.

"If you want to end up with your family jewels pinned to the wall, we can try."

He bursts out laughing and puts his arm on my shoulders as if we were old friends. "This is Quinn and Cam." continues TJ.

They both greet me quickly, focusing on their game. Dan is also there. He nods when he sees me. I am forced to turn my gaze to Tucker next. A distinctive warmth invades my body as it remembers the delicious bite of his penetration. Think of something else…

"Hi," I gasp, trying to look calm.

He nods his head. "Good evening, Iris."

His voice almost sends a shiver down my spine. "Some beers? Shall I get you some beers?" I say loudly as I walk away.

TJ stares at us in turn, a stupid smile plastered on his face, then nods.

Tucker still doesn't take his eyes off me. Did he tell his cousin we slept together? Did they both talk about it? I don't want people to…shit, I don't want people to know.

I walk over to the bar, questions running through my head. I give the order for the first table to Buck and go straight to putting out the beers for TJ, Tucker, and the others. I slam the bottle down a little hard after opening it, then bend down to get some more from the fridge under the counter. When I straighten up, I almost jump when I see that Tucker is standing right in front of me, on the other side of the bar.

"Here are your beers," I say, handing him the four bottles.

"Thanks."

He pulls out a twenty-dollar bill and places it on the counter. I feel like he's waiting for me to say something as an awkward silence falls. Finally, he grabs the beers as I stare at his arm muscles, remembering their movements when he lay on top of me last night. I inhale deeply, but he doesn't seem at all disturbed. Perfect, he's moved on, and I'm stupid. He starts to walk away, but I call out to him.

"Wait!"

He freezes, turns to me, eyebrows furrowed, then puts the beers down. His eyes stare at my half-opened mouth.

"Did you tell TJ what happened?"

"And what happened?" he asks.

I roll my eyes.

"The two of us, last night, Tucker. We—"

"Fucked like animals?" he continues.

I stare at him blankly. "I don't want you talking about me and what we did to TJ or Dan or your buddies."

He glares at me. "You really think I was going to do that?"

"Well, I really don't know. You and I needed to relax, and that's our business."

He wrinkles his mouth, glaring. "'We needed to relax,'" he repeats.

"Erm…" I murmur, disconcerted. "Well, that was it, wasn't it? A night to clear this tension between us…no?"

I'm not so sure myself anymore.

"Yeah, that was it. And now that the tension is gone, we can move on. I know."

He slams his hand on the bar and then takes the beers back.

"Don't worry. I'm not going to tell them about your fucking need to relax," he mumbles just before walking away.

I stare at his tense shoulders. What's his problem now? I purposely made light of what happened yesterday, and yet he doesn't seem to like it. But what would he have wanted, this prick?

I go back to my shift and try not to think about it anymore.

A few minutes later, I'm serving customers while glancing discreetly at the pool tables and nearly let out a curse when I notice the tall blonde bending over right next to Tucker. The tiny skirt she's wearing leaves no room for imagination. She looks at him with a seductive air while talking with him.

He doesn't seem to give in to her advances, but the girl suddenly starts laughing and moves a little closer to him. I should go back to the bar but I can't take my eyes off this stupid scene. I'm waiting for the moment when he's going to look at her breasts, practically uncovered, but he keeps his jaw clenched, immersed in his thoughts. The girl leans in a little more, a teasing smile on her lips. I walk towards them, not really knowing what the hell I'm doing. The chick is talking to TJ now, but she's shaking her boobs in Tucker's direction.

I want to kill her.

Tucker suddenly raises his head and notices me a few feet away from them. He looks as if he was waiting for me to come to him. As if he was waiting for me to tell the girl to fuck off just to mark my territory. But I can't do that… That would be… insane! Shit! The whole point of spending one night together was that we wouldn't let it get to our heads afterwards. No strings attached, just good times through sex!

So why do I want to throw my fist in this girl's face?

She laughs exaggeratedly and then runs a hand through her long locks of hair, biting her lower lip. Tucker continues to stare at me, arms crossed over his chest. I feel like he's really waiting for me to walk up to him, to take another step I don't know about. His apparent anger is mixed with something else, something more intense, something darker.

But what does he want? He himself made it clear that he didn't expect anything from last night, that he didn't want anything but to spend a night with me. Just one time, without complications. So what is this hot and cold behavior? I'm confused.

I take a step towards him but finally stop. I can't. I can't make my life more difficult. I ignore his gaze and return to the bar, deciding not to worry about the pool tables for the rest of the night.

While I am wiping glasses and yawning as discreetly as possible, Dan and TJ stop in front of me.

"Bye," Dan says with a small nod, which I return.

I remember Tucker's words. Dan had a relationship with Debbie, which explains a lot. He's practically lost her, which explains the shadows dancing permanently in his eyes that sometimes give me the creeps.

"Are you leaving?" I ask.

"Yep," TJ replies. "When are you done?"

I glance at the clock behind my back.

"Twenty minutes."

Dan pulls a pack of cigarettes from his back pocket. "I'll wait for you outside," he tells TJ. "Good night, Iris."

I wave at him, watching TJ as he leans against the bar, a small smile glued to his face. Usually when he looks like that, it's not a good sign. I glance towards the back tables, realizing that Tucker is still sitting there, alone.

But what is he doing? Isn't he going with his cousin and his best friend? TJ seems to read my mind as he announces in a mischievous voice, "Tucker was supposed to drive me home, but now he's making Dan drive me. Can you believe it?"

"Why is he staying here?" I ask, more to myself than to him.

Tucker stares at the beer bottle in his hands, not really paying attention to us. "He says he's staying a little longer. I think he's watching someone. With all the creepy guys in this bar…"

I turn to TJ again. "Wait, what? He's watching me? But I don't need a babysitter."

TJ raises both hands in innocence. "Officially, he's just finishing his beer, but I know him. Honestly, when he's in a mood like this, I avoid asking him too many questions, you know?" He straightens up. "Good night, Iris."

And Tucker sits at his damn table for the next twenty minutes, not giving me a single glance, just sitting there. He sips his beer, ignoring my scrutinizing, half-irritated, half-questioning look. I don't know what game he's playing, but I'm not going to go see him. I finally make it to the locker room, eager to get home so I can fall into bed. When I emerge from the locker room through the bar, he is no longer sitting at his table but walking towards the exit.

Just before he reaches the door, the chick from earlier, the tall blonde with the exceptional cleavage, joins him by undressing him with her eyes, her stupid seductive smile on her lips.

I stop again, ignoring my heart which beats at full speed. The blonde leans towards Tucker and whispers something to him.

Why do I want him to send her packing so badly? We don't owe each other anything, he and I. We slept together once and only once, the way he wanted, the way I wanted. He can do what he wants from now on, I know that. But it hurts me to see him pull the door open and walk out, the blonde following him.

I know exactly what they are going to do.

I try to suppress this stupid feeling.

He's just a guy, Iris. It was good between you. Now get over it.

No complications, we said. Shit, I think this is going to be harder than I thought.

I finally walk over to Buck to ask him if he needs backup, my throat tight and unable to leave the place right away for fear of seeing Tucker and his chick of the day.

TUCKER

I sit behind the wheel of my car, my mind filled with dark thoughts. Brenda—I think that's her name—joins me in the passenger seat, looking very happy.

"Wow, your car is so cool!" she says, laughing.

The same fake laugh that has rung in my ears a dozen times tonight. I hate people who force themselves to laugh. Still I let her stick to me, thinking my dick would wake up sooner or later. After all, blondes like her are my usual thing.

Failure. My dick was limp all evening. No desire to fuck this chick.

Well, I did have an erection, but it was for another girl. A girl who made it clear that we weren't going to have sex a second time.

I can handle that, but my ego took a hit. So I agreed on the way out to let Brenda join me. We'll go to her place, I'll fuck her a couple of times, and my life will go back to the way it was before, as if Iris had never disturbed it. I repeat this phrase to myself several times as I put the car in reverse to get out of my parking spot.

"I love watching guys drive," Brenda says, laughing again.

When she leans in close to me and flutters her eyes, a horrible sweet scent invades my nostrils. Nothing like the faint fruity scent wafting from Iris' hair last night.

Brenda places a manicured forefinger on my thigh, and I nearly gasp. I take a deep breath and turn off the car in the middle of the parking lot.

"Okay, get down," I order her.

She opens her mouth wide, looking discomfited.

"But...what?"

"Brenda," I start seriously.

"My name is Briana!" she replies with a pinched mouth. "Come on, stop taking this so serious, I just want to have some fun."

She tries once again to touch my thigh, but I catch her wrist and tighten it strongly.

"You're hard," she murmurs to me with lust. "I can see it."

I throw a glance at the erection which stretches my jeans. "It's not for you," I spit.

I let go of her as if her touch burns me. What the hell am I doing? I should let her do it, let her take me to her place. But I can't.

"Get out," I order her a little more firmly.

After a few seconds, she opens the door, furious. "Loser!"

I mentally count to ten to calm myself, in vain. My fist slams down hard on the steering wheel.

Iris, get out of my head!

32. ARM WRESTLING WITH A DEMON

IRIS

I take a seat in the center of the lecture room as it starts to fill up little by little.

I pull my computer out of my bag and let out a curse as my laptop falls on the floor in the process. There are days like this when you know nothing is going to go right. Well today, this is one of them.

I bend down to pick it up, and when I look up, I see that Tucker is coming down the stairs. He hasn't seen me yet. I place my bag on the seat beside me. I hope this will discourage anyone from sitting here.

Of course, I'm not targeting anyone.

Actually, I am.

Since Saturday night, bad thoughts have been running around in my head. The fact that I saw him leave with his blond girlfriend haunts me. I stopped looking for the reason for my annoyance. I didn't like it, and that's it.

I know, he does what he wants and blah blah blah. But I kept imagining the two of them fucking. It's stupid, but that's how it is. My brain is tormented and apparently doesn't want to move on.

Maybe I should do what he did to make everything better? Find another guy and get laid quick? Except that's not like me at all. I let myself go with Tucker, forgetting all my rules, but it's not likely to happen again with another guy.

I keep my gaze pointed in front of me, towards the dais, so that I watch him take his seat right in front of me, without a word. I squint my eyes as I stare at the back of his head. So, what, now this is it? We ignore each other while staying close to each other? Can't he sit in one of his damn special seats?!

Let's not forget that we have a case to do, and for that we have to go to the trial in Brighton on Friday. So we're going to have to cooperate despite our shitty tempers.

The class has barely ended when Tucker is already running down the stairs. I take it on the chin and step in behind him.

"Tucker!" I shout as he walks through the door.

He doesn't seem too thrilled that I'm calling him. I have the answer to my question: now that we've actually slept together, he just doesn't give a shit.

I thought everyone was buddies in his stupid pack?

I breathe in to calm myself and walk over to him, a mask of indifference stuck on my face. "We need to talk about Friday." I say.

He frowns a little more, and I realize he doesn't know what I'm referring to.

"About this Friday, not…not last Friday. Um, I have a class that starts at eleven and ends at one. Since the trial is at four o'clock, shall we leave directly after my class?"

He just nods.

"Shall we take two cars and meet there, or just one car? I don't know where we're going."

"I do. I can pick you up," he says a second later.

The irritation is apparent in his voice. His jaw is clenched.

"Are you sure? I don't mind…"

"I'm sure, Iris. We leave here at 1 p.m. Anything else?"

I stare at him and feel my own anger rising in me. "Yes, something else. Can I ask why you're being such an asshole?"

He raises his eyebrows and lets out a joyless laugh. "I'm sorry?"

"Yeah. We slept together and you left me a damn note. I thought we were cool, but I see you show up Saturday night with a six-foot head. What's the deal, you fucked me so you ignore me?"

He didn't say anything for almost a minute, just glares at me. "Do you expect me to follow you like a puppy? You're the one who wanted a single night to avoid complications, right? So don't come and ask me for an explanation afterwards."

Isn't that what we both wanted? Just one night?

"I'm not asking you for an explanation," I sigh, trying not to roll my eyes. "But the fact that you're totally cold and grouchy makes me wonder. Anyway, you know what, forget it. Go back to having fun with other girls like we agreed. Like the little blonde from Saturday night, I'm sure she was perfect."

His shoulders tense a little more. He looks like he wants to kill me.

"Oh, yes, she was delicious." His bitter tone doesn't escape me.

"Great," I say in a neutral voice.

"Great," he repeats loudly, like a kid.

I give him the finger, and he turns his back on me abruptly and walks away. I stare at him, my mouth half open. God, why do his stupid words hurt me? I should laugh and tell him I don't care but I do. Right now, I'm imagining them giving each other pleasure. And it hurts me.

When he's already several feet away, Tucker suddenly turns around and comes at me quickly. I almost feel like he's going to run into me, but he freezes a few inches away. I watch him silently, holding back from backing up under his dark gaze.

"No, not 'great,'" he barks at me.

I cross my arms over my chest like a little girl. I don't even know why we're fighting. He's just being ridiculous, and so am I. Yet I stand my ground, waiting for him to speak.

"I didn't fuck her," he spits between his teeth.

My mouth opens in surprise.

What? Did I hear that right? But why?

"I was in my damn car, she had her hand on my cock, and I was getting a hard-on, as I had been for hours. But you want to know something funny? It wasn't for her."

I swallow with difficulty. I know perfectly well what these words mean, but I turn a deaf ear and ask again piteously, "What?"

He gives a slight grunt and leans in so close our faces nearly touch.

"One night, no complications, just one fuck. I get that. But my body refuses it and gives me a hard time. I still fucking want you. Satisfied?"

He doesn't wait for my answer and walks away again, furious.

He didn't sleep with the other blonde? He imagined himself sleeping with me again? And he wants to. Tucker, what are you doing…what are you doing to us?

I ask myself this question while ignoring the fact that deep down, my body also refuses to let us have just one night. Did I imagine another night between us? It would be a lie to say otherwise.

Do I still want him? Hell yes, of course I do.

But I can't. Because I feel guilty about Rafael. Because I don't want to be attached anymore, to let someone else have the power to destroy me. And because if, after just one time, Tucker and I are in such a pitiful state, then what will it be next time? We can't do this. I just…I have to move on and ignore the attraction that was supposed to be diminishing between us but keeps getting stronger. This was the plan, after all. He'll do the same, I know it.

And everything will go back to the way it was before.

I am walking towards the library of the central campus when I feel my cell phone vibrating in the back pocket of my jeans. Lost in my thoughts, my head elsewhere, I pick up without looking at who is calling me.

"Yeah?" I ask as I walk along one of the stone paths.

Nobody answers me. I look at the screen to see who's calling.

Blocked number.

Is it Agnes playing a prank on me? She already pulled this stunt last month, because she was bored.

"Agnes, that's not funny," I mumble.

Still nothing. Actually, something. A murmur. Then the caller hangs up. What's that?

A dark thought invades me, but I push it away. It can't be the one who attacked my family. He…he's dead. This whole thing is over. I have to make him stop haunting me, stop ruining my life. I run a hand over my tired face and rub my foggy eyes.

This is a shitty day.

The next morning, my psychology professor, Mr. Tamells, arrives twenty minutes late in the small lecture hall. From the look of his messy hair and the trace of the pillow on his cheek, it looks like he slept through his alarm clock. The last students are taking their seats, and for once, he doesn't reprimand them for being so late.

I lose my smile when I see Sanchez sitting next to me.

Do I have to remind him that I am bad company in the morning? Certainly. I slowly turn to him, my mouth pursed.

"You don't—"

"Let me guess, you're going to tell me to piss off, give me a hard time because it's morning and you're in a bad mood? Me too," he grumbles.

I part my lips, not knowing what to say. I wasn't going to tell him to piss off…well, not exactly.

His long locks hide his face from me. I give him one last sideways glance and then turn once more to Tamells, who is scattering his papers on the desk in the middle of the stage. He picks up a white chalk and walks over to the huge board.

"Hey," I whisper to Sanchez, "are you okay?"

He mumbles something unintelligible, in Spanish, but still doesn't move. When a light snore reaches me, I realize he's fallen asleep. I can't believe it!

"Go sleep somewhere else," I whisper harshly, leaning towards him. "I don't want you snoring and drooling near me."

He responds with a louder snore. A student in the front row turns to us, both eyebrows raised as if to let us know to go have fun elsewhere. I glare back at her, not really knowing what to do.

"So, young people," Tamells begins, "did you have a good time studying in the library this weekend?"

Few people answer him in the affirmative. Sanchez rumbles in his dream, and I roll my eyes when he starts snoring again without discretion.

Just have to make the best of things.

I retrieve the small water bottle from my bag and unscrew the blue cap.

"Today we're going to talk about the Stroop test, its theory, and execution."

The students drink in his words, attentive. I listen only with a distracted ear, leaning toward Sanchez to place the small water bottle over his head.

"Any volunteers to talk about it?" the teacher continues with a big smile on his face.

When a small trickle of water falls on Sanchez, he wakes up with a start, lets out a little scream and jumps to his feet.

I almost burst out laughing when his knees hit the wood of the table. He glares at me, and a few people turn towards us, noticing that he is standing in the middle of the row, looking half crazy, half asleep.

"You?" the teacher says, catching sight of Sanchez. "Please remind me of your name, young man."

Sanchez turns to me, silently cursing.

"Next time, snore in someone else's ear," I murmur with an innocent air, with a small smile.

He sticks his tongue out childishly, letting me see the piercing that goes through it, then he turns to Tamells.

"Sanchez," he answers boldly. "I, um…"

"Well, please tell me about the John Stroop test."

"So, um, John Stroop was…an important man?"

A few laughs erupt, my teacher grumbles something.

"Sit back down, you little clown, and try to open both your ears."

Sanchez sits and throws me a glare.

"The Stroop effect," my teacher continues, writing those two words in large letters on the board, "also known as the Jaensch effect, is the disruption of a cognitive task caused by extraneous information."

The teacher starts spouting a steady stream of information at us while writing on the board.

"You're so uncool," Sanchez grumbles, leaning toward me. "My hair is all wet now."

"Oh, you poor dear. I'm so sorry. What do you say we go get a blow-out together after class?"

He settles back against the backrest without answering, arms crossed.

"This effect is traditionally attributed to the interference of one cognitive process on another. In this test, the reading of the word interferes with the naming of its color," says Tamells.

I glance at Sanchez, realizing that he is really offended. When he leaves the lecture hall half an hour later, his jaw still clenched, I give in.

"Oh, come on, Sleeping Beauty," I exclaim as I walk beside him, "stop pouting."

He grumbles and finally holds the door for me so we can get out. "I'm not pouting," he mumbles as we walk onto the lawn of the west wing of campus. "I'm just in a bad mood. You might know that."

I'm about to answer him but I hear exclamations from about thirty feet away.

"What's all this noise?"

Sanchez shrugs his shoulders, throws his backpack over one, and walks towards the small gathering. "I don't know. Let's go and see."

My curiosity pushes me to follow him, and I discover a small white sign with a fluorescent orange inscription in the center:

"$3 to come and face one of the arms of the hells!"

This puzzles me. I elbow my way through the waiting students. The first thing I see in the middle of the crowd is TJ collecting dollar bills and writing names on a notepad. His baseball cap partially conceals his blond hair.

Is this an activity organized by the Pack?

"Hey, TJ!" I call out to him in the distance.

He turns to me, a big smile on his face. "How are my little cubs doing?" he asks as he approaches us.

"We're fine. What's going on?" I ask.

"Well, in addition to being a beautiful face, an exceptional man, kind, funny?"

"Humble?" I resume by raising my eyebrows.

"And humble, you're right," he continues, "I am also involved in various associations that the university sponsors. Today, we're fundraising for an organization that helps battered women get the financial and psychological support they need to get away from their violent partners."

He stiffens on those last words, and I can't help but stare at his tense shoulders. He seems to know the subject personally, or maybe my instincts are wrong. Either way, I think it's an honorable fight. I know how many women are beaten to death every year. Men too, but the majority are still women.

I open my bag wide and take out three dollars. I hand them to him without a word. A frank smile spreads across his features, making him look much younger.

"Thank you, Iris, that means a lot to me."

I don't know what to say, so I just nod. At my gesture, Sanchez also gives money to TJ.

"Perfect," he continues, "so Sanchez, I'll put you on list number two, and Iris on list number three."

He is already starting to walk away, but I call out to him in surprise. "Wait, what list?"

"Well, each participant who donates three dollars can then try to face one of the hell hands," he continues with a smirk. "I'll let you go ahead and find out what it is."

"Don't you think the arm wrestling will cool off some people?" I continue, puzzled.

"Are you kidding? Succeed in beating one of the kings of the campus, and it's eternal glory! They'll all be fighting to prove their worth."

I glare at him, already feeling the bullshit coming. Don't you?

I elbow my way through again and finally reach the center of the circle. I see three tables on the lawn. I quickly understand. Behind each table stands a guy. At table number one, a tall, muscular, blond guy is arm wrestling a skinny college girl. I saw him at Tucker's the other day. At number two, Sam, a guy from the Pack, is doing the same thing with a guy. He quickly folds his arm and yells:

"Win again! So, who's coming to fight me, darlings?!"

I swallow hard and turn my head to the last table. Tucker is arm wrestling with another student. The two stare each other down, and within seconds, Tucker puts his opponent's arm down, winning the round. I check the table number. Number three. Is this the list TJ put me on a minute ago?

I look around for him, murderous urges rising in me. I find him a few feet away.

"I'm going to kill you," I articulate silently in his direction.

He raises his hands in the air with an innocent look and winks at me. Next to me, Sanchez is like a madman. He walks over to table two, a fighter's look on his face.

As for me, I start to back away, wanting to run away. I turn on my heels just as TJ's voice slams into my back.

"Come on, Iris, it's your turn."

I freeze on the spot, knowing full well that the others—and therefore Tucker—have heard his words. If I leave, I'll look like a wimp. I don't care what they think and I know I don't stand a chance against Tucker. However, I risk a glance behind my back. A good portion of the students are watching me with big smiles, and a few girls are cheering me on.

I turn to the three tables, and the gaze I've been trying to avoid all this time finally hits mine. I hear Sanchez and Sam clashing and cursing, but I still don't move. Tucker frowns as he notices me and slowly straightens up behind his table.

The words he spoke yesterday come back to me. Joining him now is definitely not a good idea.

"I think she's forfeiting," laughs Sarah next to TJ, a petty look on her face. "Not very brave."

Tucker continues to watch me silently, his different colored gaze far too intense to bear. So I decide to stare at his shoulders, but that's not a good thing either. They're hugged by the sleeves of his red shirt, and it reminds me of the way Tucker was tensing his muscles as he entered me this weekend…

Mayday! Mayday! We have a problem.

Sarah laughs a little louder, and I don't want to give her an opportunity to think I'm weak.

"I don't give up," I announce with a fake tough guy look, "I was just warming up my wrist."

I spin my wrist as I walk toward to table number three. Tucker opens his mouth, and his voice finally snaps, "What the hell are you doing?"

He turns to TJ, looking furious.

"I'm going to beat the shit out of you," I say, but inside I'm not so sure.

Tucker raises his eyebrows defiantly. He's bigger than I am, way bigger. His gaze is now similar to a predator's. And I am his prey.

"You know I'm going to eat you up," he says with a smirk.

No doubt, but at least I didn't run away with my tail between my legs. I walk past Sarah with a big smile, letting her glare at me, stop in front of the table and lean against it.

TJ approaches, his eyes gleaming. Oh yes, he's proud of himself, this idiot.

"Well, you guys know the rules."

I keep my gaze on Tucker's. He slowly analyzes my figure before observing my mouth. I know exactly what he's thinking, because I'm thinking the same thing.

"Oh," TJ replies, snapping his fingers," we're fighting here, we don't fantasize about our opponent."

I come out of my lethargy and glare at him. "Your lack of sex is making you see things," I spit in TJ's direction.

Tucker laughs softly at my jab, and his cousin mumbles something in his beard.

"Come on!" he exclaims before taking a step away, his and the others' attention focused on us.

I get into position, thinking fast. Okay, Tucker is probably a hundred pounds heavier than I am, and his arm is twice mine. Let's play it smart. We need to break his concentration. But how do I do that when he's distracting me?

Tucker leans over the table, resting his arm on it and getting into position as well. His hand hooks mine, and I try to ignore the heat it gives off. I knew it was a bad idea to agree to their stupid game, but there's no way I'm giving up now.

"The game is on!" shouts TJ from beside us.

Tucker doesn't move an inch, leaving me to try to flatten his hand with difficulty. He laughs, and I want to headbutt him.

"Come on," I order him. "Don't be a wimp."

"I can put your hand down in two seconds, babe," he whispers so only I can hear him.

I lean in a little closer to him, staring at his mouth. Playing it sneaky, clever. I can do it. I feel his gaze dive into my cleavage. He frowns and clenches his jaw.

"Damn," he mumbles.

He sees me ogling his mouth. His hand slowly starts to force itself on mine. My God, he's got quite a grip.

"Stop imagining your mouth on mine," he orders me with a smile.

I inhale slowly, deeply, and stare him straight in the eye.

"You're wrong, babe," I whisper, "I imagine my mouth around your cock."

I take advantage of his surprise to bring down his arm on the table.

"Fuck," he yells, jumping back. "That's cheating!"

I explode with laughter and start a ridiculous dance to celebrate my victory.

TJ walks towards us, looking surprised but happy.

"Well, I didn't see any cheating. You just lost, buddy." TJ exclaims.

Tucker mumbles something as he stares at me from across the table.

"See, the beating of your life."

I wink at him and walk away as he swears loudly behind my back.

33. RAFAEL

IRIS

"I'm in my pajamas, and I don't feel like partying right now," I bark out as I pick up the phone. If Yeleen calls me, it can only mean one thing: she'll insist on dragging me to a party again!

But it's tears that answer me at the other end of the phone.

"Yeleen?" I say again, suddenly sitting up. "What's going on?"

"I'm at a party on Eighteenth Street. It's…it's Trey," she hiccups with difficulty. "We had a fight…a big one."

I take a deep breath. It's not as bad as I thought it would be. I know she's a mess, but at least she's not physically hurt.

"I'm sorry about that," I answer her honestly. "Look, I—"

"I love him," she continues, crying more.

"Listen, beautiful," I say softly. "Why don't you call Tucker?" I've never been good at breaking up with lovers.

"If I call Tucker, he'll come over and beat the crap out of Trey."

It's actually not a bad idea.

"Besides, he had to do something tonight. I…never mind, I…I shouldn't have called you. I'm sorry, I…"

She apologizes again and hangs up suddenly. I glare at my damn phone. I go back to the paper I was working on, but I can't concentrate on the black swan theory anymore.

Yeleen sounded so bad, in the middle of a party, crying.

I can't help but wonder why she hasn't called Sarah or another member of the Pack. Probably because I saw her in a bad way the other day at the bar, and she had explained the situation with Trey? Maybe the others don't know about it.

Damn it!

I get up from my chair, not caring about the ridiculous black shorts and Bart Simpson T-shirt I'm wearing, and walk to the kitchen to get my car keys.

"Yeleen, I'm going to kill you," I mumble as I leave my apartment.

I arrive twenty minutes later on Eighteenth. I don't need to look up the exact address because I can see a bunch of students in front of a three-story house in the distance. Music blares from the windows. I park along the sidewalk and notice that red cups are already littering the ground. A girl is throwing up in the corner while another girl films her, laughing.

Bitch.

I scan the property for Yeleen while walking towards the entrance.

"Retro t-shirt," exclaims a guy as he passes me.

I answer him with a small smile before noticing the penis drawn with a marker all over his face and the inscription "I suck" on his forehead.

He doesn't seem to mind and walks out of the house with a carefree air. I walk into absolute chaos. Music resounds in all the rooms. I don't see Yeleen anywhere. I don't recognize anyone, in fact. Two guys near me who are snorting lines of cocaine. Where the hell did I end up?

I hear a high-pitched laugh on my right and recognize it immediately. I follow it and find Yeleen dancing in the middle of the improvised dance floor, a red cup in each hand. She drinks and then continues to sing off key, not caring about anything. I look around for Trey. I want to punch him in the face.

At the same time, a guy approaches Yeleen and tries to touch her butt. She laughs, not even realizing the situation. I walk towards them, a murderous look on my face.

"Get out of my way," I order the guy, pulling Yeleen towards me.

The latter opens her eyes wide. Sweat is dripping down her forehead, and her dark skin is burning.

"Iris? Oh, my God, I'm sooooo glad to see you," she exclaims as she pulls me close, both arms around my neck.

I hold back an expletive as cheap beer splashes down my back and abruptly removes the cups from her hands.

"No," she complains in a small, childish voice, "I'm thirsty."

"If you want to drink, drink water," I mutter, pulling her behind me toward the exit. "Let's go home. I'll take you home."

She lets go of my hand, managing to break free of my grip. I don't have time to think about it before she disappears from my sight.

"You're a pain in the ass," I shout at her back as I follow after her.

I look for her for a two good minutes before a man runs into me.

"Oh, excuse me," a hoarse voice says in my ear.

I turn towards the man to see who it is. He has a big smile on his face, but his look is evil. Matt. That bastard. I walk by him to get away, but his hand wraps around my right bicep, holding me back.

"Where are you going, little cub?" he whispers as his boozy breath hits my face.

"Wherever you're not," I say, pulling on my arm. I stare him straight in the eye. "Get off me before I crush the tiny pair of balls that hang between your legs."

He laughs softly, and his eyes get a little darker. He's having fun.

"You have a big mouth, I like that. You like to act tough."

"Just like you like to take advantage of drunk girls. To each his own," I growl, freeing myself from his grip.

This idiot hurt me, but there's no way I'm going to show my pain. I keep my fingers from running over the skin on my arm.

"Oh, so you know," he smiles before running his tongue over his lips.

Tucker sometimes does this gesture when he's focused, but seeing Matt do it makes me want to throw up.

He stands in front of me for a second. "But you don't really know who I am." His hand goes up to my face as if he's about to caress it. "And I think I like you. A word of advice—"

I slap his hand away abruptly, pulling it away like a bug circling around me. "You disgust me," I cut him off. "Try to touch me again and you'll regret it. I'm not a shy virgin who's going to tremble before you. Believe me, it's not a threat, it's a promise."

I don't wait for his answer before walking away. I can hear him laughing behind my back as if he liked my answer.

You sick bastard.

Frustrated that I can't find Yeleen in the kitchen, I step outside to find her staggering toward her car a few feet away, her keys spinning in her hands. An unpleasant memory takes possession of me without asking my permission.

It imposes itself, and I relive it, powerless.

I'm doing something wrong. And if my parents are watching me from up there, they're probably disappointed. But I don't care. I just need to forget this shit, their murder. Just for a moment. This last month has been beyond difficult. I tried not to sink, but I failed. The people most important to me have been taken from me. My heart was taken, trampled on, and then given back to me to deal with it. I wasn't strong enough to be okay. And that's when my downward spiral began.

I started to drink. At first just a few drinks, just to relax. And then…things got a little bit worse. I ended up hanging out at a lot of disreputable parties. Rafael, who was a regular at these parties, let me go with him every time. I could see that little glint of concern in his eye, but he knew I needed to relax. So he let me. I discovered another world over which I had no control. I stepped into quicksand, and the only way out was to drink more to forget. Tonight he took me to some of his friends' houses.

Sitting on a crappy old couch, I watch him chaining shots of vodka while retrieving a bill from his pocket. I don't know anyone here, but I don't care. I don't need to know any faces to relax. The alcohol is working. It flows through my veins and helps me forget all those horrible memories that cling to my skin.

Rafael winks at me from afar and raises his next shot in my direction before letting the liquid burn down his throat. Normally he holds his alcohol remarkably well, but that doesn't seem to be the case tonight.

He comes to me a minute later, his hazel eyes locked in mine.

He staggers as he leans toward me.

"Hi, honey. How are you?"

His breath is alcoholic. Much more than usual.

A guy walks by and hands him a new bottle of beer. Rafael takes it back with a little laugh. I don't know why, but it's like a shock to me. A warning.

"Maybe you should stop drinking tonight. You're bad enough as it is."

He laughs and takes a sip. "Who cares? You're as bad as I am."

I try to focus on his lips to understand his words, but it's hard. He's right, I've had way too much alcohol.

Fuck…my parents would be really disappointed in my behavior. Instead of taking care of my little sister, all I can think about is clearing my head by emptying bottles, unable to face reality. They are dead. They won't come back.

And I am weak. A fucking weak person with a destroyed heart.

I now have no desire to drink alcohol at all. I put my beer bottle on the table next to us, as if the glass was burning my hand.

"Can we go home?" I ask.

He mumbles something unintelligible and shakes his head.

Before I'm really knocked out for the next few hours, I grab my cell phone and try to call a cab. I have to try three times to type in the right number, my head is so dizzy. I feel like I'm going to throw up.

Rafael starts a conversation with one of his buddies, not worrying about me, then it starts to get out of hand. Things get heated, and Rafael grabs the guy by the throat.

"Hey!" I yell, running to him. "Stop it!"

He doesn't even see me. His look seems crazy. I pull his arm so that he releases his grip. I've seen him fight before but never get violent with me. Yet, the next second, he pushes me hard on the shoulder to throw me off of him so he can keep fighting.

"Let me go, and don't tell me what to do," he spits in my direction.

I stand still, half-drunk and shocked by his gesture.

I know he's a bad drunk, but this is a side of him I've never seen before. He drops the guy and picks up his jacket, then walks towards me with a heavy step. I move back, unable to stop myself.

"Let's go," he grumbles.

I frown and try to find my cell phone that I dropped while approaching him.

"Wait!" I shout at his back while following him towards the door. "I'll call a cab, it will be here in a few minutes. We can't drive like this."

He stops so suddenly that I bump into him. "Hang up the phone," he orders me harshly.

I refuse, and he reaches over and snatches my phone out of my hand before hanging up. I stand still as he leans in toward me with an angry look on his face.

"Don't you trust me?"

"That has nothing to do with it," I whisper, unsettled by his unusually calm demeanor. "We drank too much to—"

"Answer my question," he asks me dryly, squeezing my right elbow in his left hand.

I nod slowly, pulling on my arm. He's hurting me.

"So if you trust me, it's all good, honey. Let's go," he tells me as he walks to his car.

I take a deep breath, not knowing what to do. All the people around me are completely drunk, too.

"Rafael, wait!" I yell again behind his back. "Let me drive!"

I say anything to try to stop him. I've been drinking too, but much less than him.

I run to the driver's side but already he is sitting behind the wheel.

I lean towards his window, feeling my tears welling up because I'm so frustrated and don't understand his attitude. I know he's drunk, he can't take the wheel. Usually, we take a cab, we stay overnight, or he drives home when he hasn't had so much to drink. But there…his eyes are glassy, and I begin to understand that he's not just drunk.

He glares at me, with his mouth wrinkled.

"Get in the car, Iris. I'll take you home."

I look around again.

"Now!" he yells, slamming his steering wheel.

His shout makes me shake in my boots. I'm afraid of his

reaction because I don't recognize him tonight. But I can't leave him, so I get into the passenger side of the car, as silent as a grave. A headache starts to invade me and I regret the drinks I had. Fuck, I'll never touch another drop of alcohol.

The first minutes pass with the sound of the engine as the only background noise. When he misses a stop sign in the middle of town, I grab my door.

"Slow down," I whisper to him.

He lets out a little laugh and speeds up a little more. He brushes my thigh with his free hand. "It's all right, I'm in control."

No, that's not true, but I don't want to make him angry. Not when we're going a hundred miles an hour in the middle of town. Yes, this road is deserted, but I don't feel it. When he misses another light, my mouth opens by itself.

"Stop acting stupid," I almost beg him.

"You said you trusted me," he spits, looking at me instead of the road.

"Not when you've been drinking like this! Turn your head towards the road, please."

"I love you from the bottom of my soul," he says. "Do you think I would let anything happen to you?"

I take a deep breath, holding on to his words. With his head still turned towards me, he doesn't notice that the light in front of us is turning red.

"The light!" I exclaim.

But it's already too late, the car is running at full speed. The city was deserted until then. Not anymore.

A van—also speeding—comes up on our left and hits us full force.

I feel as if my life has come to an end, and it probably has. A howl of agony echoes in my ears, mine. The shock is awful. My head is turned upside down, the blood rushes to my head. My seatbelt prevents me from collapsing on myself.

I blink several times in shock. I don't really know what's going on. My vision is blurry.

I'm still tied up, and I'm sore all over. I try to turn my face slowly and notice a spot of blood on my right arm.

What's going on?

Did we just have an accident? I move carefully to try to see Rafael ,but my breathing becomes wheezy. My breath is shallow.

"Rafael," I whisper to him.

I hear him move limply near me. Finally my head turns to him. My limbs do not respond. It's as if I'm disconnected from reality. But I can see his face smeared with blood. He too was tied up, thank God. But his nose is full of blood. And his mouth too.

"Rafael," I whisper again.

I want to cry, but no tears come. I don't even feel the pain, I only see him. He doesn't open his eyes.

"I called for help, don't move!" someone yells outside the car.

I can't move anyway. I try to lift my hand, but I can't.

"Rafael," I repeat in a voice that is now panicked.

Finally, his eyes open weakly. Finally, only his right eye opens, the left one is drowned in blood.

"Iris," he articulates with difficulty. "It hurts."

"Someone will come and help us," I say with a groan. "Stay with me."

He moves his hand slowly and touches my arm with a grunt. It's almost like I can feel his forces leaving him.

"Don't move," I beg him. "They'll be here soon."

"I'm sorry, Iris."

He's crying. I see tears running down the roof of the flipped car. My lips are trembling. I try to move my arms, but it's hard. I try to touch my seatbelt. I have to unbuckle myself. Or maybe I shouldn't move?

But he looks so bad.

"I love you. I love you so much," he repeats as he touches my arm one last time with difficulty.

I have to…I have to help him. I hear sounds outside the vehicle. A siren.

"Help is coming," I whisper. "It's going to be okay."

I notice he's not moving, and I start to panic, repeating his name several times. Suddenly, I feel a tiredness invade me. I bleed, I hurt, and then, all of a sudden, I feel nothing.

Then I close my eyelids, just for a moment…

A few hours later, I wake up alone in the hospital, while his eyes remain closed for eternity.

My mouth trembles slowly. I almost feel myself losing my balance, but I can't. Yeleen has just reached her car and is trying to unlock it. I run to her and snatch her keys from her hands.

"Leave me alone," she orders me, her words slurred, her eyes blankly staring at nothing.

"No, I won't. You're going to get in my car before I get mad for good."

She grumbles like a little girl and crosses her arms over her chest. "I can drive just fine."

"You'll kill yourself if you drive," I spit in her face. "GET IN MY CAR."

My tone startles her. She glares at me but finally goes to my car.

I let out a sigh, my heart beating wildly in my chest. I'm about to follow her, but I see Trey walking like a madman through the doorway. He scans the area, worried.

A little too late, mister.

"Iris!" he exclaims as he gets close to me. "Have you seen Yeleen?"

I glare at him. "She was about to take her car, drunk," I begin bitterly.

"Damn it, she always has to do the opposite of what we ask her to do. You should have let her do it, let her learn from her mistakes."

I raise an eyebrow and put an index finger in his direction. "Aren't you tired of being a big, reckless, selfish jerk? Would you have let her drive? What if she had died?!"

I can see that he is shocked by my insults, but I don't give a damn.

"That's the second time she's gotten wasted because you make her feel bad. I don't know what's going on between you two, and I'm not going to interfere with your bullshit ultimatums. But you better get your head out of your ass, man, because you're going to lose her forever."

I don't wait for his answer and walk to my car, discovering Yeleen sound asleep in the passenger seat, a little saliva dripping from her half-opened mouth.

34. GUILTY?

IRIS

I can see Tucker's pickup truck waiting for me in the distance, parked in the lot in front of my building. To say I'm dreading the next few hours would be an understatement. After our…talk on Monday, and then our confrontation on Wednesday, we've been kind of avoiding each other all week. We haven't talked, not even during lunch with TJ and the rest of the gang yesterday. I didn't really have a choice but to join their table when Yeleen called out to me in the distance. Her eyes silently thanked me for bringing her back, but we didn't exchange any words about the events. As I imagined, no one must really know about her troubles with Trey.

Well, actually, I could have had lunch somewhere else. But…I didn't want to be alone in my corner. I swore to myself that I was a new person when I came here, and I'm starting to realize that human contact is essential to my reconstruction. So, once again, I settled in with their Pack, even laughing at TJ's dumb jokes. Damn, I felt like I was surrounded by buddies. And I wasn't afraid of how others would look at me. Even though I tried to ignore the few glances Tucker gave me on the sly.

What could I possibly say to him? *I admit, I want you too, Tucker, so bad, even. But I can't, because sleeping together again would bring new complications, and that scares me. Because I mustn't get attached?* Yeah, definitely not a good thing.

I reach his car and open the door silently. He glances at me a little more kindly. I think he's calmed down in the last few days. Or maybe he's planning revenge for my victory on Wednesday.

"Hi," I say with a little smile.

He takes a deep breath, starts the engine and finally answers me. "Hi."

A minute passes silently. And to think we have an hour's drive to kill…it might get awkward quickly.

"So, your class?" he finally asks me.

Surprised that he starts the conversation, I decide to answer him. "Well, not bad, actually. It was about behaviorism. And you, sociology?"

He just nods and clenches his fingers on the wheel. So cordial. Damn, that doesn't sound like us.

"Did you finish writing your report?"

"Yeah, I sent it to the teacher this morning. Did you?"

I nod while digging through my bag to find my copy of it. "I printed it out too."

I stare at the outside of the car and slowly sink into my thoughts.

The trip promises to be long…

Brighton is completely different from Denver. The courthouse is quite small and fits in well with the charm of the city. It doesn't feel like a totally austere place where a lot of trials are held. Tucker pulls up a few feet away, and I pick up my bag before noticing he's not moving, still sitting behind the wheel. He's watching me intently, looking worried.

"What?" I whisper.

"Is this going to be okay?" he asks, leaning towards me. He moves back almost immediately, as if he had just realized what he had done. "I know you've been through a lot of shit, and you told me your parents were murdered. So…"

I put a fake smile on my face. "Of course, I'll be okay."

I'm strong. At least I try to be. And I've been working on this for a long time.

I'll be fine. I just need to focus on the case, not my own life.

I look to his eyes, but he's staring at something else: my body.

Shit, did a button on my shirt pop off or something? But when

I follow his gaze, I see that he's analyzing the small bruise on the inside of my arm.

Thanks, Matt. Remind me to send him a nice card sprinkled with cyanide.

"What's this?" Tucker asks me in a voice from beyond the grave.

Telling him who did this to me is probably not a good idea. Let's avoid another war between Tucker and that bastard Matt.

"Who?" he growls harshly.

I shrug my shoulders in a relaxed manner.

"I bruised it on the corner of a table, it's nothing."

"And you hit the inside of your arm? Do you think I'm stupid?" He tilts his head to the side, eyebrows raised.

He knows perfectly well that I'm lying. I open my mouth, trying to sound insulted by his implication. "If I answer 'yes,' are you going to start roaring and pounding your fist?"

"Why does it look like a fingerprint?" he insists gravely, holding back from touching my skin.

I let out a mocking laugh.

"You should see an eye doctor, Tuck-Tuck."

I get out of the car, praying that he will let go. Tucker mumbles something and walks down the sidewalk without waiting for me, looking dark and closed.

The distinctive sound of thunder interrupts my thoughts. I look up at the gray, stormy sky.

Let's go.

The courtroom is silent although many people are getting settled. I take a seat on the far right of the wooden benches, Tucker right next to me. I pull out a notepad, and he raises an eyebrow at me.

"Aren't you writing anything down?" I ask him spontaneously.

Catching me off guard, he leans over and taps my forehead with his index finger.

"I'm writing in here."

Then he steps back, a little smile stuck to his face at my confusion. I'm about to ask him a question, but the serious stuff starts. It's not the first time I've been so close to a trial. The last one was the one that cleared me after I pleaded self-defense against my parents' killer.

I glance over at Tucker. How would he react if he found out I killed someone myself? Would he see me as a monster?

The judge comes into the courtroom in a heavy silence. To the right, a small door opens to reveal two policemen holding a man: Mikael Larey. I can see from here his haunted eyes, his face completely destroyed. Maybe he is really guilty. I don't know.

The facts are quickly recalled to the assembly and the jury on the right.

As stated in the documents provided to us by Mrs. Richards, Helena Larey and her daughter Meredith were found dead, murdered in the middle of their living room. The police, upon arriving at the scene in the middle of the night, found Mikael Larey amidst his wife's blood.

The judge calls Mikael to the stand. He walks in slow motion, his eyes blank.

The prosecutor stands up and begins the indictment.

"Mikael Larey, you are accused of the murder of your wife and the rape and murder of your child."

Mikael doesn't answer anything. It's almost as if he's not listening to the words of the authoritarian old man.

"Can you tell us what happened from the moment you left work until the police arrived at your home?"

Mikael doesn't answer anything, again. He remains perfectly still, silent.

"Why isn't he fighting back?" I whisper to Tucker, surprised. "He doesn't say anything."

Tucker shrugs his shoulders, as confused as I am.

"Please answer the question," the judge orders.

Mikael blinks several times but still says nothing. He seems to be disconnected from reality.

"Did you abuse your daughter Meredith?"

Mikael stares at him. His frail shoulders tense and his jaw tightens. But again, he says nothing.

"Mikael, do you understand my question?"

The latter swallows his saliva with difficulty and finally answers with a broken voice. "I never hurt my daughter."

"I want an exact answer. Did you or did you not abuse your daughter that night?"

"No," Mikael sighs.

Other questions follow, but once again, Mikael refuses to answer them. He's stupid, he's going to get into trouble on his own. He has to plead his innocence, damn it! Or is he really guilty? Damn! I want to know. I lean over and rest my elbows on my knees, completely forgetting to take notes. After a few minutes, it's his lawyer's turn to get up and join him. She is a woman in her fifties who doesn't seem to understand her client's silence either.

"Mr. Larey," she begins, "you are accused of the murder of Helena Larey, your wife. Can you describe your relationship with her?"

He shrugs his shoulders. His lawyer glares at him as if to force him to answer. In fact, he doesn't seem to want to fight, as if he accepts the fate that was reserved for him.

"Our relationship was complicated," he finally admits.

"Why was that?" asks his lawyer.

"Because…because Helena was so…extreme. About everything."

"What kind of mother was she to your child?"

Mikael takes a deep breath as if it were difficult to answer. "I thought she loved her," he finally confesses.

"You said you didn't touch your daughter. Can you tell us what happened when you got home that night? What did you see?"

He leans forward. His lips are trembling. And I can almost feel mine doing the same. What the hell is he doing? Plead your case! Defend yourself! He has to prove his innocence, he has to show the jury that he's not guilty. Staying silent will have the opposite effect. He'll ruin everything, destroy his life by keeping his lips sealed.

"I came home late that night…I…when I came home, I heard screams. And I saw my baby on the floor. Blood. A scarf. Helena was there…"

The prosecutor mumbles something I can't hear from my seat. Mikael raises his head, looking crazy. "Go to hell," he shouts.

Basic technique, subtly destabilizing the defendant.

"You entered the living room and discovered your little girl on the floor?" his lawyer resumes, trying to remain calm in the face of his stubbornness. "And then you saw your wife? Is she the one who assaulted your child?"

Mikael doesn't answer, his eyes moist. He is certainly reliving this nightmare and doesn't know how to get out of it.

His story reminds me of another one. My body boil and my breath tightens. I need air, but I also need to know what happened that night. I need Mikael to talk!

My first instinct was against him. From what happened in my life and the few clues I had discovered at first, I immediately believed he was guilty. I would have dreamed of seeing him rot behind bars. But once I dug into the case, I managed to overcome the hatred that had been present in me since the murder of my parents. I managed to not let it blind me. And today, after all that, and discovering him in front of me, broken inside…I really believe in his innocence.

I blink, ignoring Tucker, who is focusing his attention exclusively on me. He must have noticed that I'm sweating profusely, unable to hold back everything that haunts me. I feel his fingers brush my shoulder, which makes me jump.

"Are you okay? Do you want to get some air?" he whispers, leaning towards me.

I shake my head vigorously. I'll be fine. I have to stop being weak.

"Did you kill your wife? How do you explain the knife that caused her death? Lodged in her chest?"

Mikael shakes his head to deny it, but it's the words that matter. "Don't call her my 'wife!'" he yells as he stands up.

He's getting angry, now, and that's not a good sign.

"If she was in front of me today, I would make her suffer. I would rape her without any doubt, I would destroy her slowly. I would break her just as she broke me."

"Calm down," the judge orders him with an impassive air.

This is not the answer his lawyer was expecting, and she was about to swear. The trial is not going as well as it should.

Did he mean it? I didn't think he would but maybe I was wrong?

"Helena Larey was seeing a psychologist," the woman continues, turning to the jury. "She had behavioral problems. My client's neighbors—who will also be called to testify—witnessed this woman raise her hand to her daughter several times."

This reinforces even more what I thought. The lawyer walks slowly toward the jury, her hands intertwined.

"My client is described by everyone close to him as a loving father. A good man. We found no trace of his DNA on his daughter's body, no fluids belonging to him. Only his fingerprints on the object that was used to rape her because he grabbed it when he discovered the scene, not knowing what it was used for. There were no prints belonging to him on the weapon that killed his wife.

She walks up to her client again, looking serious. She tries to lighten the mood, but it isn't working.

"Did you abuse your daughter?" she asks again.

Tucker tenses up next to me. His face shows no expression, but I know his brain is racing.

"I would never do such a thing," Mikael says between his pursed lips.

Many must see the madness in his face. Deep inside me…I see the truth.

The jury is attentive to every piece of information given. The lawyer stands in front of them again, trying to catch the eyes of each of them.

"Mikael Larey is not a criminal. He's a man whose life has taken everything from him. His wife shattered his future with a snap of her fingers. I appeal to your common sense, to your humanity. Should an innocent man pay for crimes he did not commit?"

The following minutes are more and more intense. The cage closes little by little. And the more I hear from neighbors and colleagues, the more I am convinced: Mikael is innocent. After a while—I don't know exactly how long the testimonies lasted—the twelve members of the jury leave to deliberate.

"He didn't kill them," I tell Tucker. "Please, Goddamn it, tell me they're going to see that."

He doesn't say anything to me, but I know deep down he doesn't entirely agree with me.

"On the charges of first-degree murder and rape of Meredith Larey, the jury finds Mikael Larey…"

Please, please…I bite my thumbnail inwardly praying.

"Guilty."

I sit there in shock. Tucker gets up beside me.

"On the charge of first-degree murder against Helena Larey, the jury finds Mikael Larey…"

"Guilty," says the jury spokesman.

My heart misses a beat. My hands are sweaty. I lean forward with tears in my eyes. This can't be true. It can't be true! I am positive that he did not kill them! That he didn't rape anyone!

I hear crying in the distance, I open my eyes to see Mikael collapsing. His relatives who attended the trial are in a similar state. I observe, powerless, the scene that unfolds before my eyes. This man is going to be locked up for the rest of his life even though I know deep down that he shouldn't be.

"Come on, let's go," says Tucker.

The jury has made its decision, and there's no way to argue with it. It's over. But I can't move. Powerless in the face of justice's injustice.

The return drive takes place in a heavy silence. The only sound in the car is that of the windshield wipers trying to cope with the rain that is pouring down on the windshield.

It's raining hard and thundering too. I feel as if it is echoing in my heart. I stand there, staring at the landscape, my skin tingling with fear. After many minutes, Tucker's pickup truck pulls into the parking lot in front of my house. He keeps the engine running, and I can see his index finger tapping the steering wheel out of the corner of my eye. I keep my gaze focused on the outside.

Bad memories haven't stopped tormenting me for an hour. Neither he nor I speak, but I feel his gaze on my profile. He lets himself go against the headrest, his dark face turned towards me. I hear his breathing, long and deep, and his masculine scent invades my nostrils. It's almost reassuring. This heady smell helps me focus on the present.

"The world isn't fair," I whisper, letting myself sink back into the seat. "What should be fair isn't," I say, turning my head toward him. "But that's the law, right?"

He runs his tongue over his lips, thinking about what I just said. "Sometimes it's better to have an injustice happen than to live in a world without any law."

I know deep down he thinks Mikael killed his wife.

And there is no evidence to the contrary. Mikael just got mad and explained the abuse he would do to her if she were still alive. All those hours of work for nothing, to finally attend a lousy trial and discover a defendant who, haunted by his demons, couldn't express himself, couldn't find the words that would prove his innocence. If only he had spoken…I'm sure there's something else. We must have forgotten something.

Mikael will end up behind bars when he may not be a murderer. But I, who really killed a man, am free as a bird. I should have ended up behind bars too, shouldn't I? Yes, the monster who killed my parents was terrible, but that doesn't excuse what I did. Murder is murder. I am a murderer, no matter what anyone says. No matter why I did it, my hand killed.

I thought I had moved on, but I haven't.

My eyes begin to water, and I can feel the tears pooling at the edges of my lids. This isn't true. I abruptly close my eyes and take a deep breath. I feel like everything is going out of control.

"Are you okay?" Tucker whispers to me in a worried voice.

"No," I grumble and furiously open my eyes again. "Nothing is right!"

"The Jury has decided, Iris. Mikael was pronounced guilty. I know you thought he wasn't, but—"

"You don't understand," I whisper.

"Then explain it to me, babe," he continues, leaning towards me worried. "What's going on?"

My gaze plunged in his, I want to confide in him. To release the words that hurt me inside. But I can't get them out…

And then, suddenly, my shell cracks a little more. How does he reach me so much? To make my mouth open by itself without obeying my brain?

"I should have ended up behind bars too."

He frowns, bewildered. "What?"

"I'm a monster too. I have…I have…"

35. SECOND ROUND

IRIS

I jump back, realizing what I was about to say. I was going to tell him everything. Something is really wrong in my head. I ignore my trembling lips and pick up my bag. I open the door hastily and mumble between my teeth, without turning to him, "I'll see you later."

I don't have time to get up from the seat when a firm hand grabs my wrist and turns me the other way. My body faces Tucker, still in his seat.

"What—"

I don't have time to ask my question, Tucker leans in and brings his mouth to mine.

It takes me a good ten seconds to react. I pull back with difficulty, my breath on his lips. "What the hell are you doing, you idiot?"

He puts his other hand on the back of my head.

"I'm giving us what we need," he growls just before kissing me again.

What we need. Not what we want. Do I need it, deep down? I can't need his touch, I don't want to be addicted to a man's body again. I don't want to be destroyed again.

The physical need leads to the emotional need.

There's no way I'm going to hold on to someone else the way I held on to Rafael. I can't let another man invade my life when the first one to do so is probably watching over me from above. I don't have the right to do that to him.

When I try to pull back again, Tucker's fingers twist in my hair. I bite on his bottom lip. He pulls away, looking furious. He breathes hard and fast, as if this simple act is difficult for him.

"Why do you say that you're a monster?" he finally asks me with a serious face.

His look follows my every move, analyzes my every reaction. I swallow with difficulty, not knowing what to answer. My big mouth opened too much again, and here I am in the poop up to my neck. "I…" I start with difficulty. "We said no questions, Tucker."

His hand moves from my hair to the back of my neck, his warm grip refusing to let go. It keeps me trapped, making me want things I shouldn't want.

"No questions asked," he reluctantly agrees.

His other hand, however, lets go of my wrist. I sit in my seat, leaning toward him and he toward me. I lower my gaze to his tightened arm holding me, to his tense muscles, to his…his erection straining the fly of his jeans.

I should just walk away and run—my shell is cracking and I really don't need this—but I also feel an intense heat in my lower abdomen. I remember the sensations that came over me when he was on top of me, penetrating me deeply.

He must remember it too, because a little roar sound echoes in his chest, making it vibrate gently.

He places another kiss on my lips just before he pulls his face away. He wants me to follow through, I see it. I have a choice: leave this car and return to my residence or join him in the abyss of pleasure.

"We'll go back to playing assholes who hate each other in a few minutes," Tucker murmurs in a barely controlled voice. "Until then, shut up and enjoy."

My lips open on their own as I stay leaning into him, his hand against the back of my neck. "I thought you only wanted me once? We said just one night."

A laugh comes out of his mouth. He stares for a second at the rain falling on the windshield. His fingers tighten their grip on my neck in an involuntary contraction. He is on the verge of explosion, I feel it.

My wolf wants to bite me.

"Technically, it's not night yet," he mumbles.

I raise an eyebrow and hold back a laugh at his lame justification. I glance at the door of my residence. Anyone can walk out of the building and see us.

"I told you not to get addicted to my taste."

He runs his tongue over his lower lip.

"I want you again tonight. I don't know why, maybe my body will finally be satiated after this. Dare to tell me that you don't?"

It's not reasonable. He doesn't understand that…I need to protect myself.

I meet his gaze, which makes me question everything. His desire provokes mine.

I lean out…and close the door on us.

It's only for a few minutes, just enough time to…succumb.

My breath mingles with his again, and a small cry escapes my lips as he places his hands on my waist and sits me on top of him.

Damn, that's hot.

He moves his seat back, and I get more comfortable, straddling his thighs. The steering wheel is jammed against my lower back, but the pain is nothing compared to the explosion I feel throughout my body.

Why can't I fight it? Why is he breaking down my barriers? Why does he make me feel like I'm alive again in his arms?

His hands go down on my butt, pressing them hard on his tense cock. My fingers twist in his hair, and I pull on his strands, making him lean his head back. My mouth travels down his neck and then back up, and my teeth bite into his earlobe. And I want so much more…

Look at me, I was ready to get out of that car, and here I am a few minutes later swaying on top of him, my body calling to his. It's like I don't have the will to fight anymore when Tucker touches me. It's so…strange. I undulate against his thighs, unable to hold on any longer.

He straightens up a bit against his seat, and his right hand reaches under my blouse, his hot fingers caressing my belly, tracing my belly button, before reaching my bra to access my breasts.

"Oh, babe…"

My nails dig into his skin, and he tugs on one of my nipples with an awful slowness. Then he moves his hands away and pulls off my blouse. I see a button pop, but I don't care. I am completely focused on what is happening, and I bite my lip. The only sound that fills the car is the rubbing of my hand on his jeans. My fingers land on his erection and squeeze it through the rough fabric.

"Fuck," he swears through his teeth, suddenly closing his eyes.

Again, his desire stirs mine. I squeeze him a little harder, and a thud is muffled in his chest. His fingers move down the cups of my bra, not bothering to remove it. His tongue runs tirelessly over my hardened nubs. It's far too good to stop now. My head falls back, and my hands grab the strands of his hair, on his neck. I pull his face to me, silently indicating what I want. And he gives it to me, pressing his lips to the vein that pulses madly in my neck. His tongue follows it until it reaches my breasts again. My ass slides on his cock. I can't wait any longer. I release his hair and undo his belt. The sound of his fly going down mixes with our gasps.

Then a thought comes to me. Damn it! I look up to find Tucker's eyes following the movement of my fingers.

"Tucker," I whisper, but he doesn't listen to me. "Tucker! Condom."

His left hand squeezes my hip, and a naughty smile comes over his face.

He leans over, taking me with him, and opens the glove compartment in front of the passenger seat.

"Look what I found," he says, waving a silver wrapper in front of my eyes.

I sit down a little more comfortably. "I don't know if I'm happy about the fact that you have one on hand or not. Did you think we were going to have sex?"

Actually, I'm more concerned about which bitch he was going to use it with.

"Ask your real question, Iris," he whispers.

I purse my mouth, trying to look detached. "I don't know what you're talking about."

"I'm sure you're wondering if it was meant for another girl."

1-0 for Tucker Bomley, ladies and gentlemen.

I part my lips, glaring at him.

He laughs softly and kisses the tip of my nose before frowning. His gesture shocks both of us. What was that?

I don't feel like thinking and rip the condom out of his hands. "Of course it wasn't for another girl," I affirm, "you want me too much to go find relief elsewhere."

He doesn't respond.

1-1.

He kisses me again instead and unhooks my belt. I sit up straight to give him room. "Ouch," I grumble when my head hits the ceiling of the car.

He can hardly restrain himself from laughing and resumes his task. He seems so good with his hands, as if this isn't the first time he's had sex with someone in his pickup. Has he? With Sarah, maybe?

What the hell is wrong with me?! I don't care about that! I hate to have these thoughts, but the question is still running through my head. I ignore him and hand him the condom. He gently lifts me up again, and this time a moan escapes both of us as he gently penetrates me.

It's not very convenient, and people are probably watching us, but at no time do I want to stop. We are launched, determined to reach ecstasy. Our tongues dance together to the rhythm of our movements. His fingers tighten on my hips, mine on his neck. And he lets me lead this time. I undulate on top of him, rise and fall quickly before starting again with a deliberate slowness.

"Iris," he mumbles while pressing me against him so that I can speed up.

My gaze meets his, and I come down on him even more gently. My teasing does not please him. He squints his eyes and raises his hips suddenly. My breath stops at his gesture. The pain mixes with pleasure. It's much too good.

It's dangerous.

But how to stop? How do I hold back from diving off the cliff to join this ocean of lust?

In spite of my inner warnings, in spite of our personalities and our headaches, our desire to kill each other every five minutes…

I follow his rhythm, I accelerate, and after interminable minutes, I let myself go to the pleasure. I contract myself and cling to his body desperately. It seems to please him. I watch his face break down, his mask melt away, and his features relax little by little.

He joins me a second later, closing his eyes, pulsing inside me. His heat spreads, even through the latex, to warm me from the inside.

The car is heating up. The only sounds we hear are those of the rain and our breaths. I am immersed in my thoughts. His index finger traces an arabesque on the bare skin of my back, and I can't stop the shiver that runs through me. The windows are covered with mist, we can't see the outside anymore. We have succumbed once again. And I don't regret it, come to think of it.

I stare at Tucker, and he stares back. We push each other away. We hurt each other. Then we attract each other and succumb. I feel like a real bond is forming between us. A bond that I will have a hard time breaking. A bond that I don't understand yet.

"So," I say, struggling to find the words, "are you satisfied now?"

I feel his cock hardening once again inside me as though in response.

I'm screwed…

He smiles at me softly, but he looks gloomy.

That's when there's a knock against the window. I hold back a startle, and Tucker lets out an expletive through his beard.

"I can't believe it," he mumbles as I struggle to put on my blouse.

Indeed, two buttons are missing. The panic is felt when a flashlight illuminates the interior of the car. We can hardly see anything with the fog but enough to guess what we were doing.

"Is anyone in there?" asks an older male voice.

I exchange glances with Tucker and finally get back in my seat. I hold back a smile as I watch him struggle to zipper up his fly over his semi-erection. I barely have time to reach my seat when he is forced to roll down his window.

A man in uniform bends his head down to the window, shining his flashlight in our eyes. It's one of the campus guards, damn it.

"You're on a college campus," he begins, running his free hand through his gray mustache. "What the hell are you doing?"

I'm racking my brain but Tucker is faster. "It's cold out there, we're just trying to keep warm naturally, sir. The ecology, all that…"

"Keeping warm, huh?" the old man chuckles. "Do you live here?"

"Yes, sir," I answer. "I live in the residence across the street."

"Zip up your jeans properly, young man, and you, get back to your residence before I call the cops for disturbing the peace."

I do not wait one second, dead of shame. I pick up my bag, and before I can move, Tucker leans over to me, perfectly serene and calm.

"Good night…dream of me."

I give him the finger in reply and hurry out of the car, praying to the gods that this is all just a big joke. Well, at least the last five minutes…

36. ACHIEVING YOUR GOALS

UNKNOWN

I pull a cigarette from my back pocket and light it, letting the wind lull me. The rain makes it difficult. I lean against one of the streetlights, the only one that doesn't work, and continue to stare at the pickup truck parked about fifty feet away.

I can hardly be seen, which helps me to observe in peace what is happening in front of me.

The security guard I warned earlier in a falsely friendly voice is leaning towards Tucker.

I see the little redhead get out of the vehicle, and my hatred for her grows. I could easily follow her back to her apartment, but that would be too easy.

That bastard Tucker puts the car in reverse and drives out of the parking lot. I can't make out his face, but I know he's got a little smile plastered on his face. I've seen them, they've slept together. I know it's not the first time.

The security guard returns to his watch. He walks across the parking lot and nods as he passes me.

"Thanks for the heads up, this isn't the first time students have had a little fun in the parking lot."

I give him a friendly smile. "No worries."

I start to walk away as he calls out to me, "Eh? Do you live on campus?"

I don't answer him and walk into the darkness behind a building.

No, I don't live on campus. But I don't need it to achieve my goals.

37. FIGHTING ON ALL FRONTS

IRIS

The first thing I see as I enter the lecture hall is Mrs. Richards taking her place at the podium at the bottom of the stairs. She is leaning over her MacBook, a crease of concentration between her eyebrows. I stare for a second at the seats left unoccupied among the students, but I'm not ready to sit yet.

Two things haunted me this weekend. The first: I kept waking up in the middle of the night after dreaming about a certain person. Tucker seems to have bewitched my dreams, making my thoughts of him all about lust. As a result, I held back from texting him yesterday to suggest we do this again.

I decided to stop thinking about it because it was so overwhelming. The moments we shared in the car were looping in my mind. This is not good at all.

The second thing that haunted me during these last two days? Mikael Larey. I kept seeing his defeated face as the cops took him away. I kept replaying the trial in my mind. Something was wrong. So instead of finishing my psychology essay, I spent my time immersed in the notes I had taken during the trial and in the theories and analyses I had formulated in the days before.

I can't peacefully get to my seat without thinking of this man who should be free too.

I see Tucker staring at me from his usual place. His eyes look tired and his beard is a little longer. Seeing me standing still on the steps, he frowns, probably wondering what my problem is. I look at his arm muscles molded by his black polo shirt for a second, and other, more intimate memories flood in.

Mrs. Richards pulls some papers out of her leather bag, and I stop thinking about him. I run down the stairs toward her, my heart beating rapidly.

"Hello," I begin.

She looks up at me, seeming to recognize me after a few seconds.

"Miss Foster," she begins, "so how did the trial go on Friday? Did you learn anything? Analyzed the different roles and occupations of the people in a courtroom?"

"That's what I'd like to talk to you about," I say, fiddling with the handle of my backpack. "Mikael Larey has been declared guilty."

She taps her manicured nails on the wood of the desk before straightening up. "I know that for a fact. I'm following this case closely since one of my colleagues is in charge of Larey. What is your question? The class starts in five minutes."

I shake my head silently. I don't actually have a question. "I think he is not guilty and has been wrongly accused."

She crosses her arms over her chest, and I stare for a second at the Rolex on her wrist. "I didn't ask you to determine whether he was guilty or not. In your report, you were to explain to me the elements to be used in defense and accusation and your analysis of every detail of the case. I wasn't looking for a guilty and an innocent, miss."

"And that's what I did in the work I sent you," I correct her, losing patience. "But now I'm not talking about my work, but about yours. I am convinced that he is not guilty. And today he is behind bars and—"

"And these are things that happen. Look, we'll get into that another day. I'm going to start my lecture now, so please take your seat."

I swallow hard. How can she be so calm? As if one man's life doesn't matter. I can't seem to react the way she does. Maybe I should, but it's not in my nature.

"These things happen?" I reply, holding back a grimace. "You have to help this man. Your colleague needs to appeal and—"

Mrs. Richards sighs as she loses patience and retrieves a document from her belongings, silently dismissing me.

"The jury has reached its decision, Ms. Foster. The defense

doesn't agree with it, but an appeal might be perilous. Stop hanging on to this case."

I'm not hanging on to a case, I'm hanging on to a man, damn it! We're talking about his future.

"I don't agree," I finally continue.

My teacher squints, annoyed. "I'm asking you to sit down immediately."

"Mikael Larey wasn't even defending himself! That's not what your colleague had planned, is it? They didn't find his fingerprints on the gun that killed his wife, nor on his daughter, but he was discredited because what he said was misunderstood. I'm sure there's something missing, something in the investigation that was missed! It's not right."

My voice is louder than I wanted it to be. Most eyes are on us. I almost regret getting carried away, but there it is. Mrs. Richards stares at me with her ravenous gaze, as if she is about to cut me into little pieces. I swallow hard but don't flinch.

"Get out of the classroom," she orders me harshly.

I don't look down. I've probably just screwed up my semester by yelling at her instead of sitting down like a nice student. My instincts, however, tell me that I did the right thing. I nod silently then add, "Perfect. Have a good day."

Tucker sits up straight in his seat, his eyebrows furrowed. He'll soon realize I just screwed up. Maybe she'll penalize us in the grades because of me. I shake my head to order him to stay seated.

I'm in the middle of the steps when someone calls my name. "Miss Foster?"

I freeze and turn toward the podium once more. Mrs. Richards purses her mouth as she looks at me. "I'll see what I can do. Now sit down."

I close my eyes for a second, holding back a sigh of satisfaction. Thank you, Mrs. Richards.

TUCKER

I glance over at Iris, who is sitting a few rows in front of me. She seemed to have been in the middle of a confrontation with Mrs. Richards before she kicked her out of class and then changed her mind. We all know how this teacher doesn't back down from her decisions. Yet, it sure looks like she did for Iris.

What earthquake has this little piece of work created again?

When class ends, I hurry to follow her. I reach the lobby of A-Wing and look around for her. Why does she always have to disappear like that? I see her about twenty yards away, at the entrance of a corridor, slipping a bill into the vending machine. I walk towards her. My attention is entirely taken by this redhead, as if I can't see anything but her hot little body.

Pull yourself together, man, shit.

She slips a can of coke into her bag and then lifts her head before turning to the glass door that has just opened. Her eyes suddenly cloud over, and I stand still, curious. Matt enters the room. He puts away a pack of cigarettes with one hand while consulting his cell phone with the other. Feeling a glance on him, he raises his eyes and sees Iris.

I don't want that little shit looking at her. I don't even want him to breathe the same air as her. She's mine.

I'm seized with a murderous urge when he winks at her with a mocking pout as he walks by. My breath catches.

Matt walks towards me without noticing me. I shift a few steps as he continues ahead, eyes on his screen, toward the bathroom on my right. Iris still hasn't seen me either. She stares at his back, looking glum, and absentmindedly rubs her arm with a glare, as if she's thinking back to a bad memory.

My blood runs cold. I know exactly what her fingers are on. The bruise I saw in my car on Friday. What the hell is this?

She and Matt? Or am I going crazy and making connections between things that have nothing to do with each other?

And as if my anger still needed to be fed, I feel a new wave of hatred surge through me.

I turn around and walk to the bathroom, a little evil smile plastered on my face as I think about what I'm going to do to this fucker.

I push the door open. A guy is washing his hands. The second person in the room is faced away from me, but I know it's Matt. He's standing at the urinal, humming a Drake song.

I walk past the guy washing his hands and mutter to him, "No one comes in." I say.

He opens his eyes wide but quickly recognizes me. He nods sharply and hurries out of the room as if he's on fire.

I lean against the wall opposite the urinal and cross my arms over my chest.

Matt straightens up and looks back at me. His mouth closes, and he loses his proud look for a moment before trying to look relaxed. But I can see the contraction of his muscles and his tense shoulders. He isn't relaxed at all. If, by chance, my doubts are confirmed and I learn that he tried to hurt her…

"What a lovely surprise," he begins in a calm voice.

Falsely calm. We both know how much trouble he's in. I tilt my head to the side and move away from the wall. It's the only movement I allow myself.

In reality, I want to do something else, but I wait a few more moments.

He'd better shut up, but Matt is one of those stupid people who don't think before acting. When he passes by me, I hear him whispering, "Did your little whore send you?"

I take a deep breath, trying to stay calm. I fail.

I put my hand on his shoulder and pull him back, sending him hard against the tiled wall. His back hits it, and he holds back a grimace.

I lean toward him. "Don't play dumb with me."

His jaw clenches. He hates being in a weak position.

"What? You don't want me to insult your bitch?" he asks, pushing me away. "Try not to damage her too much, so that I can enjoy her afterwards."

I press my forearm against his throat, sticking his head to the wall. "I'm beginning to think you're suicidal."

I tighten my grip. He tries to pull away but I press him a little more. I feel his Adam's apple under my skin, slowly being crushed. Matt has hated me for so long.

"Don't look at her, don't think about her, don't talk about her. Fuck, if you cross her path one more time, I'll break both your knees," I hiss coldly.

A laugh comes out of his mouth roughly.

"She was the one who crossed my path Wednesday night. She looked like a deer caught between the headlights of a car. She came right to me."

Last Wednesday? What the hell is this shit? When did Iris run into Matt? At a party? Connections are forming in my brain, I understand a lot of things, and I don't like the conclusions I draw at all.

"Did you hurt her?"

I'm talking about her arm, but he doesn't really seem to understand what I'm referring to. Maybe I've got the wrong idea about Iris's bruise, but I can't seem to calm down. The only thing I want to do is keep her away from that jerk and protect her.

What I couldn't do with my little sister.

"I don't—" he starts with difficulty.

I pull him towards me to slam him hard against the wall again. The back of his head bounces against the tile and his teeth clatter.

"Shut up," I order him. "Stay away from her."

I suddenly release him, turn around and start walking towards the door.

"The problem with you," he spits behind my back, "is that you don't have the balls to go all the way."

I turn around when I hear fast footsteps and just avoid his fist. I then send mine, not at his face, but to his ribs. He lets out an expletive, and his elbow ends up in my lower jaw.

Damn it.

I push his head towards the ground and raise my knee, which strikes his chest violently.

"Your problem is that you never knew how to shut your big mouth," I say.

I'm boiling inside, and all my anger is directed towards him. He tries to get up and hit me in turn, but I move away and take advantage of the fact that he is still bent over to pull his hair back. His nose cracks loudly, and a stream of blood escapes from his nostrils as I slam his head down on the sink.

All my hatred for him comes out in that moment. All my hatred towards him for what he did to my little sister and what he would probably like to do to Iris comes out. He falls to the ground, holding his nose.

"You broke my nose!" he screams. Blood drips onto the collar of his T-shirt.

I stand up and move my jaw from right to left. "I've been too nice to you all this time," I say, walking towards him. I squat down in front of him and smile softly. "Look at you, consumed with hatred and jealousy. You never had the balls or honor to join our group. You're trying to destroy me, but you just look like a loser. Next time I'll be a lot less nice, dude."

I straighten up and turn on my heels without worrying about him anymore. I feel him glare at me. Oh, yes, he hates me, but he's also scared.

The door slams behind me. The guy who was on watch stares at me, his mouth wide open. I smile at him and at the few guys who were waiting to get in.

"The bathroom is free," I say simply.

And I walk down the hallway, searching for a little redhead.

IRIS

What's with the crowd in the parking lot all of a sudden?

I've barely taken a few steps toward the crowd when Tucker's voice slams into my back.

"Iris!"

With a can of Coke already at my lips, I turn in his direction. He walks toward me, a dark, intense gleam in his eyes. I almost expect him to jump on me. Would I be willing to push him away?

Sarah is sitting in the grass a little further away, glaring at me. A pretty blonde is talking to her, but she doesn't care. She continues to stare at me, an enigmatic smile on her face, pulling from time to time on her cigarette.

May she choke on her smoke…

Tucker suddenly turns his attention back to the parking lot, and as I follow his gaze, I am speechless.

Two uniformed cops walk up to TJ, who was leaning against his car. I hardly have time to understand when they bend over him and handcuff him.

Someone jostles me as he runs past me. It's Tucker running towards them. He yells something as panic shows on his cousin's face. But the two cops don't care. They pull TJ towards the entrance of the parking lot, towards their car.

What the hell happened?

38. TEACH A LESSON

IRIS

I haven't seen Tucker or TJ in class since Monday. They seem to have disappeared from school. On Tuesday night, I gave in and texted Tucker, but he didn't respond to me.

This situation is driving me crazy. Why did cops come and arrest TJ? What did he do? His cheerfulness and good humor immediately made me believe that he wasn't a guy looking for trouble, but maybe I was wrong.

Yeleen didn't respond to my text either. Okay, I should probably mind my own business, but I'm worried. I think I really like TJ, so I need to know what's going on. We're in the same pack, after all…

And even though the idea seemed totally crazy at first, I'm slowly getting used to it.

Tucker looked as distraught as I felt as he rushed up to the cops, and worried, too, so I don't think he knows what his cousin might have done. Why doesn't he answer me, that idiot? Doesn't he realize that I'm worried sick about him?

I hate to admit it, but I feel a twinge of sadness at their silence.

I chew on the end of my pen, not being able to concentrate on the lectures I'm rereading. I look around and notice that the rows are silent. A student looks at me with a look of disgust when she sees what I am chewing on. Good for her.

I'm about to reread the same sentence for the umpteenth time when, through the library windows, I see Yeleen walking briskly. I immediately grab my things, and my psychology book falls to the floor with a thud.

"Shh," mumbles a small blonde with glasses sitting a foot away from me.

I grab my book and shove it carelessly in my bag. "You're making more noise than I am by saying that," I sigh.

She purses her lips, outraged that I would speak out loud in this place. I wink at her and leave the library, praying that Yeleen is still around.

"Yeleen!" I shout, running toward her when I spot her in the distance.

She flinches and turns to me, her eyebrows furrowed. Her eyes look tired, her face worried. "Oh, hi, Iris. I'm sorry, I meant to call you tonight."

"What's going on?" I cut her off bluntly.

She opens her mouth, but no sound comes out. She puts a hand on the back of her neck and sighs. Can you meet us at Tucker's tonight?"

What's all the fucking mystery about?!

"Where's TJ? Is he…okay?"

She shrugs with a contrite look on her face and I understand that she won't tell me anything right now. "I have an exam in five minutes, I'm sorry, I…come, tonight, if you want to understand."

And she turns away without waiting for my answer.

A few hours later, my car stops in front of the huge gate of the Bomley property. I don't think for a second and drive through it to the chapel. This must be the meeting place, since Tucker doesn't want us to go into the house where his crazy mother lives…

In front of the door, Dan is leaning against one of the ruined walls. He takes a drag on a cigarette, letting the smoke create a halo around his head.

In fact, it's not a cigarette at all, but a joint. He stares at his feet. He still hasn't noticed me. If he's there, then so are the others. I begin to understand, this is a meeting of the Pack. An unfamiliar feeling comes over me, like I feel strangely out of place.

"You should stop smoking that shit or you'll die young," I tease him as I approach.

He raises his eyebrows and runs a hand over his shaved head. "Thanks, doc, you can tell me how much I owe you for the consultation," he replies with a little smile.

"Are they inside?"

He nods and invites me in, crushing his joint under his foot.

"What happened, exactly?" I ask as I descend the steps leading to the basement.

He doesn't have time to answer. I find Yeleen sitting next to Sam on a couch. Sarah and Sanchez are sitting on a different one. The room is lit by a small light hanging from the ceiling. The place looks so different from the other night, when it was filled with half-drunk students.

Tucker stands between the two couches, arms crossed over his chest. Oh, oh, I think Mr. Grumpy-is-my-second-name was waiting for me.

I quickly look around for TJ, but he's not there.

Everyone has a serious look on their faces except for Sanchez, who is probably wondering what the hell we're doing here. Just like me.

"This looks like an AA meeting," I whisper to Dan as he walks by.

His shoulders twitch gently as he holds back a laugh. I cautiously walk over to the couch on the right, my attention focused on Tucker. So the grumpy has decided to react now? I hope he has a good excuse. Sarah gives me a nasty look, shifting slightly so I don't brush against her.

Stupid.

"So what the hell are we doing here?" asks Sanchez, rolling his eyes.

Tucker glares at him, and his jaw contracts a little more. He looks tired, at the edge of his nerves. His black eyebrows are furrowed and his eyes are bloodshot. Mostly he looks pissed off, ready to explode at any moment. His arms tense against the sleeves of his shirt as he contracts his biceps, looking for an answer.

"The Pack is a family," Yeleen says in his place.

I watch her on the sly.

"And when one member of the family is in need, the others help him," she continues, tapping her lower lip with her index finger.

And tonight, it's TJ who is in need. I understood that.

"The cops came for him, what happened?" I ask, not wanting to wait any longer.

Tucker's gaze suddenly focuses on my face and doesn't let go. I don't flinch, raising my eyebrows in his direction.

"On Sunday night, TJ's father, Mark, punched his wife in the face. He had no idea TJ saw him do it, but he did."

I close my eyes for a second. No way. Now I understand why TJ seemed so committed to the cause of battered women…

"It wasn't the first time?" I ask him.

I have the impression that Sanchez and I are the only ones who didn't know about it. It's logical, considering that we are the two newcomers.

In any case, even if I joined this group against my will at the beginning, I want to help TJ as much as any of them.

"No," Yeleen answers me with a mean look, but I understand that anger isn't meant for me.

"TJ intervened and beat his father up pretty bad," Tucker continues. "He then left his house. The reason the cops came for him on Monday was because that son of a bitch Mark made a complaint against him."

I sit on the edge of the couch, resting my elbows on my knees.

This sucks. "We need his mother to testify against Mark, to argue that her son helped her!" I exclaim.

Sarah lets out a mirthless laugh. "No kidding, Miss Know-it-all, do you think we hadn't already thought of that?" she retorts sarcastically.

"Being a bitch won't make you any prettier or smarter, Sarah," I say with a small smile. "In fact, it makes you uglier."

Sanchez laughs softly next to me before clearing his throat.

"We had already thought of that," Tucker continues, ignoring our verbal joust. "His mother, however, is afraid. She told the cops she fell and hit the corner of a piece of furniture. She's afraid of her husband, so she decided to give her son up."

So, if she said that she was injured by accident, nothing accuses her husband. Then TJ would have hit him for no reason, and he would look like the attacker. However, I can't totally blame his mother. Battered women are often under the control of their husbands, and the road out of an abusive relationship is usually long and perilous…

"Where is TJ right now? He can't still be in detention," I continue concern.

"He was released Wednesday night," Yeleen sighs, "but his father is still pursuing his complaint. It's going to ruin his future."

"The guy's an asshole, but what can we do?" mumbles Sanchez as he straightens up.

Tucker and Dan exchange a look. A look that brothers share. They understand each other in a second, as if they were thinking the same thing.

"We're going to go pay his dad a little visit," Dan announces with a mischievous grin.

Oh, oh. Big danger. I know in my heart that Dan remains the most elusive and unstable of them all. It's as if he's dead inside and no longer thinks about his actions.

"What do you mean, visit?" I ask, unsure.

"Every Friday night," Tucker explains, "Mark meets his secretary at a motel north of town. It's been years now. That's where we're going."

Dan taps his fists together, Sam next to him. Sarah and Yeleen exchange a knowing look. Only Sanchez and I seem lost.

"I'm in," announces Sanchez, rising from the couch.

Oh no, apparently, I'm the only one who's lost… "Go there and do what?" I ask. "Are you crazy or what?"

Dan and Sam are not listening to me anymore. They walk out of the chapel, Sanchez on their heels, excited to follow the Pack. Sarah and Yeleen are the next to leave. Only Tucker and I are left in the room.

"What are we going to do?" I gasp weakly. "I don't do all… that stuff."

He raises an eyebrow and takes a step towards me. I now understand the purpose of the little visit. They want to give TJ's father a hard time. They are completely nuts!

"Are you going to fight him?"

Tucker shakes his head.

"No, I'm not."

"No?" I repeat, surprised. "No one will get hurt?"

"We'll blow up his car," he replies. "It's a warning. So that he understands that TJ is not alone, without finding out who did this."

They're just going to smash up his car? I don't know why, but my instinct is to believe Tucker. I decide to be part of his evil plan.

"And what's my part? I won't let TJ down, but I don't want to break anything."

"Do you have your car keys?"

I nod and shake them.

"Then this will do."

And here I am, just past ten pm, driving through the deserted streets of the northern part of the city. A red Dodge follows closely behind us—Dan—and another car with Sarah, Yeleen, and Sam in it. Sanchez is sitting behind me with stars in his eyes. He's excited about what's about to happen. Next to me, Tucker opens a bag. I look down and think I see a baseball bat.

"Oh, my God," I mutter. "We're going to get pulled over by the cops. What about the cameras, did you think about that?"

"Where you're going to park, there aren't any. There are some around his car, but..." he pauses while taking out wolf masks, "I have everything I need."

Sanchez hurries to get his. Mine remains at the bottom of the bag because I will wait in my car. I'll drive them, but there is no way I'm going to participate. Although, of course, I want TJ's father to pay. He is a coward and a scumbag.

When we reach the motel, we all park behind the bushes in front. I cut my engine, Tucker puts the mask on his face, and the others do the same. Only his distinctive eyes remain visible. He puts them on me and extends his hand in my direction without worrying about Sanchez, who is waiting behind us. His index finger gently brushes my cheek.

"How are you?"

"I should be packing because I'm flying out early tomorrow

to pick up my little sister in Portland. I should turn around and leave you two alone," I gasp in response.

A small, husky sound comes from his chest as he leans toward me.

"But you won't. What do you feel? An adrenaline rush, right? Even though you know we're doing something bad, you want to teach Mark a lesson, too."

I frown but don't back down in my seat. How can he know that? He's right. That's exactly how I feel, damn it.

Sanchez gets out of the vehicle and hands the others a mask. It's weird to see precious Sarah and Yeleen ready to smash cars. They look like warriors, not just ordinary college girls.

"We'll be back in five minutes," Tucker tells me as he walks away. "Just enough time to redo his rearview mirrors."

"Tucker," I whisper before he closes the door. "Be…careful."

He winks at me.

"Sure thing, honey."

"And stop with the stupid nicknames!"

He slams the door, laughing, and walks towards the motel. I can't see the parking lot because of the bushes surrounding my car. I look at my watch every thirty seconds and hear some metal clanking. What the fuck am I doing?

Rebuilding my life peacefully, we said. I failed miserably.

In another five minutes, I glance out the window but they still don't come back. I tap the steering wheel with my index finger, but I can't stay put. Something is happening.

Suddenly, a woman's scream rings out.

I lean over to the passenger seat, grab a mask, and place it over my face. Then I get out of the car and run toward the parking lot. Dan and Tucker are breaking the back window of a shiny Mercedes. They stop when they hear another scream. We all turn our heads toward one of the motel doors. All the rooms face directly onto the parking lot, and one of the doors is open. Sanchez waits on the threshold, holding the baseball bat along his body. His mouth is open in surprise. He stands still, as if paralyzed.

"What the hell is this?" screams Sarah at my side.

Tucker spots me, but he doesn't understand what's going on either. He seems to be making sure I'm okay before he starts moving.

Only the car had to be hit.

"Where the hell is Sam?" yells Tucker as he runs to the room.

We've been seen. We're hidden under our masks, but Mark and his mistress will see us. I run back to the room, realizing that Sam didn't stick to the plan. He entered their hotel room. I hardly arrive near them when Tucker ejects Sam from the room. He's out of breath and there's blood on his baseball bat.

"He had to pay!" he yells at Tucker.

"Let's get out of here," exclaims Yeleen.

They all leave, but I can't move. Tucker is still in the room, figuring out what just happened. I step forward, my hands shaking. The mistress is against a wall but has no injuries. However, Mark is kneeling on the floor, holding his lips. He doesn't seem to have any serious injuries, but it looks like Sam hit him in the face.

Tucker stays in the room for another second and then turns on his heels. He frowns when he sees that I'm still standing in the doorway.

"Get out of here," he silently orders me.

Oh, yes, he's furious. Sam has disobeyed him, and we're definitely all in trouble. Tucker grabs me by the wrist, and we run to get away from the motel.

"I'll find out who you are, and I'll destroy you!" yells Mark behind our backs.

Of course he will find us, he will undoubtedly understand the link between his aggression and what happened between TJ and him on Sunday. Only, he wasn't supposed to see us in the first place. Sam is a fucking asshole.

"So remember one thing," Tucker tells him in a sharp voice, "if you mess with any of us, we'll kill you. Touch your wife or your son, and you won't have a dick to fuck your secretary with."

I don't have time to think as Tucker drags me toward my car. When he realizes I'm petrified, he gets my keys and helps me into the vehicle.

Tell me I'm in a nightmare and I'm going to wake up.

Unfortunately, this is reality. And this reality sucks.

39. WANTING MORE

IRIS

My heart continues to beat wildly as I observe my surroundings blankly. We've all returned to the chapel at the back of the Bomley property.

Tucker, furious, paces around like a caged lion, eyes locked on the ground, fists clenched along his body. Sam, sitting on a couch next to me, stands up, scratching the back of his neck.

"At least he'll understand that we're bonded to each other."

Tucker freezes at his words and slowly turns to him, glaring. A chill runs up my spine. As if my body, instead of being frightened by his dangerous attitude, finds his behavior attractive. You fool!

"For everyone's sake," says Dan, trying to lighten the mood, "shut the fuck up."

"What? It's not a big deal," says Sam with a chuckle.

He's giving himself a tough-guy look that doesn't suit him at all. In an instant, Tucker crosses the room and wraps his fingers around Sam's throat.

What the hell.

"No big deal?" he retorts with a joyless laugh. "You just got TJ into deeper shit."

Sam doesn't really try to free himself, as if silently submitting to the leader of the Pack. Seeing the hold that Tucker has on the others is impressive, a little creepy, too.

Dan must be thinking the same thing I am. He gets up from the old chair on my right, creaking it, and walks over to Tucker, looking puzzled.

"Give him a break, man. He acted stupidly, but I'm sure everything will be fine."

Tucker doesn't listen to him. Instead, he tightens his grip a little more. What the hell is he doing?! I feel like I'm looking at a new person. And I don't like it. I should keep quiet, sit quietly like the others, but I can't. I straighten up, analyzing Tucker's tense shoulders under his T-shirt. His back is contracted, knotted from the tension that doesn't leave his body.

"You should listen to Dan," I begin softly.

The only response I get is a muffled curse. A low sound echoes in his chest.

"You know what, fuck you," I retort.

I know he didn't really insult me, but I insulted him. At least his attention is now on me. I cross my arms over my chest. Tucker seems surprised for a second. I get it, he's not used to people opening their mouths. Well, with me, he's going to need to get over it…

"You had to know that something was going to go wrong," I point out. "Yeah, Sam acted stupidly, but smashing a car wasn't a great idea either."

"Shut up," he orders me, squinting.

His gaze and his tone admit no contradiction.

I raise my eyebrows and tilt my head to the side. "I'm not some little thing that will break under your gaze, Tucker. In fact, at this moment, I just want to fuck with you."

He squints his eyes a little more. Yeleen stands up behind him. She has a weird look on her face, like she's telling me to shut up.

"You're not going to fix this by threatening or choking Sam," I continue.

A silent minute passes.

All eyes are on me, but mine are still on Tucker. He doesn't appreciate me putting him in his place in front of everyone. He purses his lips, but no sound comes out. Finally, he looks at Sam before reluctantly letting go.

"Get out of here," he mumbles through his teeth.

He runs his hand through his brown beard and, dropping into the couch on my left, says to the Pack, "Get out of here, all of you."

Sam doesn't say a word before dashing out, Yeleen and Sarah leave quickly too. Contrary to what I would have thought, Dan also leaves.

"He needs to be alone," Dan whispers to me as he walks by.

I start to follow Sanchez then glance at my back. Tucker is leaning forward, elbows resting on his knees, head pressed against his palms.

His body is as tense as ever. I know that thoughts are swirling in his skull and that he is angry. I know he wanted to take care of TJ, to protect his cousin, and things got out of hand. He couldn't control the situation the way he wanted to. Giving him time to calm down would be the best thing to do.

But he also seems weary, downcast. I can't leave him like this.

"You coming?" Sanchez asks me, waiting at the bottom of the old stone staircase.

I stare at him for a second, my gaze meeting his. He looks exhausted with his long, tangled locks of black hair. I take a step in his direction then finally shake my head.

He frowns, glances at Tucker, and then nods silently as if he totally understands the situation. How could he when I don't understand it myself?

I turn and slowly walk over to Tucker. He doesn't hear me, his head still pressed into his palms. I stop a foot away from him, not really knowing what to do.

"Are you okay?" I whisper stupidly.

He slowly raises his head and plants his different color eyes directly on me. He wrinkles his lips.

"I asked you to leave. I want you to leave."

"And I want to be rich and famous, but we can't always have what we want," I retort, rolling my eyes.

He jumps up, walks quickly towards me, and stops just before bumping into me. "It's not a joke, I don't want to play, so stop provoking me."

I don't know why, but even with him acting like a jerk, I can't seem to leave. "I know that—"

"You don't know anything," he cuts me off coldly.

Exasperation begins to overwhelm me. I cross my arms on my chest and straighten my chin before saying, "I know that, behind your tough look, you are worried about your cousin. You're angry, you don't understand how the situation could have gone so wrong when everything was planned."

For a second, he looks shocked. "Spare me your bullshit psychology techniques, I don't care."

I need to push him over the edge. Maybe to get him to release the tension inside him. Or maybe I need to release mine. "Denying everything is typical for a man who doesn't know—"

My teeth clatter as his hands come to rest on my shoulders and he shakes me roughly. "Instead of trying to deal with my problems, deal with your own," he exclaims. "Are you trying to analyze my behavior? Let's see what I see when I look at you: an irritating chick who lost her fucking parents and—"

"Let go of me," I reply, but he doesn't.

Instead, he squeezes me a little more, his breath hitting my face directly.

"Do you want me to continue?" he threatens, ignoring me. "Then let me ask you a question. Why did you say you were a monster the other day? What did you do to think you are a monster? Oh…and now who seems angry?"

I hate it when he reads me. I hate it. I keep my mouth shut as I try in vain to pull away because, at this moment, I want to hit him as much as I want to hug him. I know there is more to his anger than that.

He laughs coldly as he leans towards me before saying, "Why should you have ended up behind bars? Is this related to their murder?"

A slapping sound resounds in the room when my right hand comes down against his cheek. I take advantage of his surprise to get out of the way, stepping back quickly. My fingers burn. He passes a hand over his cheek, his mouth half-opened. The surprise mixes with fury in him.

"I told you to let go of me! Unless you want to be like TJ's father and start beating me up? And don't talk about my parents and their murder when you don't know anything! I'm not talking about your crazy mother or your sister! How can you think for a moment that I will ever answer your questions when you're being an asshole?"

My words are harsh, I know that. But it seems to make him come out of his lethargy. He stares at me for a second, confused, then lets his head fall backwards while closing his eyes. He swears several times through his teeth.

My bottom lip trembles, and it pisses me off. I hate looking weak, I've fought too hard for people to think I'm strong and that nothing can get to me. But he destroys all my barriers with a snap of his fingers.

I run my hand through my hair. "Forget it," I sigh roughly. "I'll see you later."

"I'm sorry."

I freeze at his words. A part of me orders me to leave while the other urges me to stop and turn to him to hear what he has to say.

"I acted like a big jerk."

I don't say anything back but I agree.

"I was angry, furious, and I took it all out on you. I…shit, I don't know what to do!" he mumbles, running a hand over his jaw. "Tonight should have ended differently. I'm responsible, too. I should have known that Sam was too keyed up, that he would lose it."

He walks towards me, unsure. "You hit me. Again."

"And you shook me like a shaker, I think we're even."

His nose brushes mine. "You're still here, telling me to fuck off in front of everyone, challenging me. Why are you doing this?"

His face leans toward mine, but he doesn't touch me.

"Someone has to stop you when you go crazy."

His gaze softens as he looks into mine and leans closer to get to my height. He nods silently, deep in thought, as if he's just realized something important. "You're not afraid of me. I get angry, and yet you stand there. I insult your parents, and instead of running away, you insult my mother. You take my anger and turn it into desire. What the hell is going on?"

"I don't know," I whisper in response, arms along my body.

"Every time, I tell myself that this desire will go away. I've had you once, twice, and I'm not satisfied. I burn for you even though you annoy me. I can't get enough."

He's in the middle of a confession, which makes me want to do the same.

"Neither can I, Tucker."

My answer is simple and seems to satisfy him. The mood has totally changed in just a few minutes. I don't know why it's always like this between us. We want to kill each other, then our bodies disobey us and seek contact, pleasure, the satisfaction of our needs.

Then our consciences don't have a say anymore. They sit back and observe, spectators to the fire which burns between us, to the hurricane which prepares itself. The spark turns into a blaze, a heat that warms my skin and makes me want to dive in.

Yet, we both know that succumbing to it again would be foolish.

"I'm tired of this bullshit," he sighs without moving away.

I frown. "What do you mean?"

"I can see the look in your eyes that clearly tells me you want to fuck. And I know for a fact that the look in mine tells you that I do too. What's next, Iris?"

I bite my lower lip. I don't understand what he's getting at.

"This whole thing is bullshit. Sleeping together and promising each other it will be the last time."

I nod, not knowing what else to do. Okay, so he wants to stop. "You're probably right," I reply, hiding my disappointment. "We need to stop sleeping together and saying that it will be the last. Yeah, you're right, that was a load of crap. It's better that…that we stop now."

I nod my head a few times. After all, that's what I wanted too, right? That we stop jumping each other to avoid complications. So why does my heart clench painfully?

He laughs softly as he places his right hand on my cheek. His palm is hot on my icy skin. A delicious shiver runs through me, but I try to ignore it.

"You don't get it at all," he whispers.

"What do you mean, then?" I say again in the same tone.

An unknown feeling rises in me because my body understands.

"For a junior, you can be slow on the uptake," he says with a smile. "When I say it's bullshit, I'm talking about the promise to never do it again, not about sleeping together. It's the opposite. I want more."

"What exactly do you want?"

"I want to be able to touch you, to taste you, to fuck you without telling myself every time that it will be the last time."

An awful thought comes to me, and I decide to clear things up right away. "I don't want to be in a relationship, Tucker."

He obediently licks his bottom lip. "I don't want to be in a relationship either. No attachments, no feelings, I get it. But I do want us to be exclusive, to not hide from the fact that we're seeing each other for benefits."

"Exclusive?" I say again, swallowing with difficulty. "That sounds very serious to me, Tucker."

He moves his hand away, and I instantly miss his touch. "What?" he retorts. "If we do this, you don't want it to be exclusive? So you'd be okay with me going to find a girl right now and fucking her?"

He takes a step backwards, and my hand reflexively reaches for him. My fingers wrap around his right bicep. "No! No, I don't want you to sleep with another girl."

"And I don't want another guy to touch you. If that were to happen, I'd bust his nose, and I mean it. So we just…don't share ourselves with others, that's it. We just have to enjoy it, accept the attraction that exists between us, satisfy it without telling ourselves it's just for once."

"Exclusive," I repeat thoughtfully. "A relationship based entirely on sex. Only sex. And what will the—"

"I don't care what others will think."

I think for a few moments. His proposal challenges all my principles. We would sleep together, and we'd be open about it, but not a couple, I repeat to myself several times.

I observe him for long seconds. His broad chest rises quickly as he waits for my answer. He is right, I have to stop lying to myself. We have to stop sleeping together if we're going to lie that it will be the last time.

I like to feel him inside me, I like to feel him above me. I have the right to accept the pleasure I feel in his arms, right? This is by no means a couple with commitments. He wants something without headaches. He offers me pleasure and sex without feelings.

And that's what I want too, despite the pinch of guilt I feel when I think about Rafael. But after all, I'm not agreeing to anything serious.

Something is titillating me. Deep inside me, a small voice whispers that this will be the beginning of something else. It tells me that Tucker and I need something else, something deeper. But I can't listen to it.

"So?" he pushes.

I raise my head, staring for a second at his full lips, his straight nose, his eyes so peculiar, surrounded by black lashes, his eyebrows of the same color. I can't reject him, I wouldn't be able to. I inhale deeply, tightening my fingers on his biceps.

"I accept."

An adorable little smile forms on his mouth. Her eyes sparkle with amusement…contentment? Probably both. I don't have time to figure out what's going on before both of his hands wrap around my waist and squeeze.

"Great, let's have sex."

I burst out laughing at his demanding tone. He was really looking forward to it. "What? No! No! Not like that! Not right now! We just had a fight."

"And then we made a deal. Besides, anger sharpens the pleasure, you know?"

His fingers press a little more against my skin, tightening around me. His mouth slams roughly against mine. Before his tongue conquers mine, I pull my face back with difficulty, letting his breath hit my wet lips.

"I can't. When I get back, okay? I have my early flight tomorrow and—"

"And I'm sure you're already all wet for me. If it's not the case, I'll leave you alone this time."

"What?" I squeak.

I pull on his hair, but he drops to his knees in front of me.

"What are you doing?" I exclaim, praying for him to get up while pushing back the flush of desire that invades me.

He almost purrs and stays on his knees in front of my hips, like a predator. How could the situation have changed so much in fifteen minutes? It's as if the acceptance he heard in my voice, mixed with my desire, completely fulfilled him.

He quickly unbuttons my pants, and a cool draft passes over my buttocks as he pulls them down.

"Tucker," I grumble. "Someone might see us. Maybe they haven't even left yet and are waiting for you to calm down before coming back in."

The end of my sentence is lost in my moan as he pulls the lace of my thong aside with his fingertips. As his tongue delicately lands on my flesh and wraps around my clit, I pull his hair again. This time, it is to bring him closer to me. His index finger moves up the back of my thigh. I feel like I'm going to fall apart, but he keeps me upright with his other hand. His finger gently enters me to test my reaction. He titillates me relentlessly, making me pant with desire, before pulling out his index finger and bringing it to his mouth with a naughty look. He licks it while staring straight into my eyes.

"Hmmm…soaking wet. Who was right?"

He kisses me one last time, his fingers twisting over the fabric of my underwear. I hear a loud ripping sound as he tears it between his fingers. Without missing a beat, Tucker stands up, pulling his shirt over his head.

"I don't think you really want me to walk away."

The tips of my breasts harden as he shamelessly undresses in front of me. I nod my head before shedding my shirt. He leans gently towards me, and my arms go around his neck as my legs hook onto his hips.

"It's true," I whisper in his ear before nibbling on it. "I really want you to take me. Hard."

He purrs again. I hear the sound of a package tearing. A few seconds later, he's still standing and controlling my descent so I can impale myself gently on him.

"I'll see what I can do," he whispers against my lips.

I lick his mouth, his throat, his Adam's apple pulsing against my tongue. His hairs irritate the bottom of my chin.

"Harder," I order him without thinking.

When my flesh contracts around him to take him deeper, he obeys me. He takes me ferociously, as impatient to reach the paroxysm of his pleasure as I am.

"Ladies and gentlemen, we have just landed at Portland Airport, it is currently 10:13 a.m, and the outside temperature is sixty-two degrees—"

I'm already not listening to the captain's words. I squirm gently in my seat, my inner thighs still sore from the night before. A silly smile comes to my face as I think about what happened. I accepted Tucker's proposal, and I know we'll have sex many more times. But not today. Today, I'm in the city that saw me grow up. I'm picking up my little sister, then we're heading back to Denver this afternoon. I'll have her with me for a week on this vacation. To say I'm happy is an understatement. I have missed her little face so much. I want to feel her against me, I want her to tell me about all of her crushes, about the latest dirty tricks she played on our aunt.

I need to know she's okay.

After another security check, I finally arrive in the space where the passengers' families are waiting. I stand up on my tiptoes, my only bag slung over my right shoulder.

Finally, I spot her. Agnes looks in all directions, going through all the faces until she finds mine. Beside her, perched on a pair of cherry red pumps, my Aunt Emma is waiting. Eyes glued to her cell phone, she doesn't notice me. She frowns and runs a hand over her black sheath skirt, removing a few imaginary folds.

I turn my attention back to my 9-year-old sister, who stifles a yawn. It's Saturday, I'm sure she stayed up late last night, excited about coming to my house for a week. But before that, the three of us have to have lunch and get her things before our afternoon flight.

When she spots me, her tired little eyes widen.

"Iriiiiiis!" she shouts, running towards me.

My heart tightens, happiness filling me. My eyes shine, but I push back my tears. I bend down and pick her up, and she wraps herself around me. She has gained weight, that's a good thing. Just not for my muscles that are threatening to give out.

Her crystalline laughter echoes in my ears. I hold her close to me.

I hear the sound of heels walking towards us. I gently release my little sister, dipping my gaze to my aunt's as she purses her carmine lips.

"Your flight was late. If I had known, I could have left the house later and finished the urgent file waiting on my desk."

I put a fake smile on my face. She's the one who has to raise my little sister until I get the judge's permission to take her under my wing. I must remain cordial with her, even though I know that these next three hours will be hard to live with.

"It's her flight that was late, you have to complain to the pilot, auntie," replies my little sister, her fists on her hips.

Emma raises her chin and looks at me.

"Nice to see you," I say with a falsely friendly look.

Oh yes, the next few hours will be long…very long.

40. FAMILY CONFLICT

IRIS

Agnes throws herself into my arms once again, wrapping both her legs around my waist. I hold back an expletive as I catch her before she falls.

"Did you only eat protein bars or what?" I tease her gently. "You look like you're 12, not 9."

She laughs, pressing her forehead against my neck. "No, but I ate a bunch of candy behind Aunt Emma's back."

I can't hold back a smile. Seeing that my aunt is already starting to walk away, I hold my sister while praying that my bag doesn't fall off my shoulder.

When Agnes finally unhooks from my arms, I run my hand through her hair, making her wince.

"But Iriiiis, my hair was done."

"Really?" I say, pretending to think and starting to touch her long hair again. "Well, I hadn't noticed."

We are both exact duplicates of our mother. Our father, meanwhile, was a tall, dark-eyed man, like my aunt. Like him, she has that little something in her eyes that attracts. When my father or my aunt would walk into a room, I remember that everyone would turn to them, as if struck by the aura they gave off. But while my father was a sunny person, smiling kindly at everyone he met, my aunt never smiled. She never smiles.

She's not a bad person—my little sister would never have been left with her otherwise—but her behavior is cold.

Thinking about my parents squeezes my heart, as it always does, and I close my eyes tightly for a few seconds to calm myself down. This is no time to cry.

"You didn't take your car?" I finally ask Emma after two minutes of waiting on the sidewalk.

She sighs defeatedly.

"That piece of junk is in the garage. We'll take an Uber," says my aunt.

Sitting next to me, Agnes has stars in her eyes. "The Uber drivers always have candy for us," she exclaims with a scoundrel's look.

Incorrigible, that one.

My aunt pouts next to me. "We'll eat when we get home. Don't stuff yourself with all kinds of candy, Agnes."

My little sister turns to me in the hope that I will intervene to plead her case. Unfortunately for her, I agree with our aunt this time.

The trip to my aunt's house is a pleasant one. Agnes never stops telling me about her adventures at school. She is a real chatterbox. My God, I missed this!

When the driver pulls up to the small gravel driveway a half-hour later, I immediately notice the pink bike with pompoms on the handles lying in the middle of the lawn. A small smile comes to my face as I imagine my little sister on it, threatening to crush everyone in her path.

I don't really know this house, even though I've been there many times before…before my parents died. Our old family home, the one my parents rented, was on the north side of town. I don't think I'll ever be able to drive by it again without breaking out in a cold sweat. Just thinking about the different rooms brings back bad memories. I remember the blood, my parents' blood, on the living room floor. I swallow several times and get out of the car, welcoming the cool Portland breeze that pulls me out of my dark thoughts.

I quickly visit the house with my aunt, exploring the rooms as if it were my first time here.

"I had the whole living room redone," she explains, "I wanted something more…refined."

I look around the living room, almost wincing. Everything is white and gray. I laugh softly when I discover a doodle made with a marker at the bottom of the white wall.

"Your sister couldn't think of anything better to do than write on it last week."

I put on a stern face and turn to Agnes. "So you're going to use your two little hands and paint the wall yourself, young lady."

I don't sound very credible with this authoritarian voice, but I have to. My aunt has a lot of faults, but she is the one who keeps my sister in school and allows her to continue her piano lessons. Despite her desire to live with me, I know that my sister wouldn't want to leave this town for anything, so she has to put in the work too. She needs stability, something I can't offer her at the moment.

Agnes puts an angelic look on her face. "But I can't paint."

I cross my arms over my chest.

"If you can write on a wall, believe me, you can paint on it. And correctly," I say, emphasizing the word.

She mumbles something unintelligible and goes to sit at the table that is already set. My aunt is watching me, looking pensive. I raise an eyebrow in her direction.

"I...you sounded like your father...I, sorry," she sighs before moving to the table.

I pause at the mention of my father. Every time someone tells me that my behavior matches my father's or my mother's, it warms my heart. I miss them so damn much.

I wish they were standing in front of me so I could tell them one last time that I love them, that Agnes is safe, that I saved her despite everything. I would like to tell them that they can rest in peace.

I walk over to the table in front of me and sit down on the chair.

"What time is your flight this afternoon?" my aunt asks as she opens a bottle of water.

I glance at the wall clock before answering, "In about in four hours."

"Perfect, Agnes' suitcase is already packed. I'll be waiting for you at the airport when you bring her back next week. How long is your vacation?"

"Ten days," I answer quickly. "But I work in the meantime."

"In a bar, you said?" my aunt asks. She says the word as if it repulses her.

"Yeah. In a bar," I answer.

"Have you planned a schedule for this week?" Agnes interrupts us by stuffing a piece of bread ten times too big for her little mouth. "I have! For example, tonight, when we arrive—"

I don't doubt it for a moment. I pour her a glass.

"You're going to be completely exhausted after the flight," I warn her gently. "We can explore Denver starting tomorrow."

She makes a small pout but nods nevertheless. "And the people, are they nice or are they mean?" Agnes asks.

"They're nice, you'll see."

Aunt Emma serves herself a portion of chicken with satay sauce before handing me the dish. My stomach gurgles at the smell, and my mouth salivates. I could eat a whole boxer by myself. As I dip the spoon into the dish, my sister leans towards me.

"And am I going to meet your boyfriend?" ask Agnes.

I almost choke as I suspend my action.

"Come on, Agnes," my aunt gently lectures her, "don't ask such questions."

"What? You don't have a boyfriend?" Agnes whispers in a sad little voice.

I can see that my aunt is also waiting for an answer. My first instinct would be to yell that I don't. That's probably what I would have said a few days ago, but the situation has changed. Last night, Tucker and I agreed to be exclusive. He's not literally my boyfriend as my little sister might think, but there's something.

No matter how many times I lie to myself, I know I feel something for him. I just don't have the courage to let that feeling grow inside me. I prefer to convince myself that it's just sex. I'm hiding behind that pretext.

"I…I'm seeing someone," I finally admit, softly.

"What's his name?" shouts Agnes. "Is it the one I talked to on the phone the other day?"

"Yes, that's him."

My aunt also leans towards me, her dark eyes thoughtful. "That's a surprise. I hope he's not a bad boy."

I twitch at her words. I can't help but defend Tucker when he's not even here. "He's exactly how he should be."

Aunt Emma taps her manicured index finger on the table.

"I just want to make sure he's good to you. You're a beautiful young girl new in town, so maybe he—"

"No," I cut her off firmly. "In fact, it's me who's taking advantage of his…body," I whisper to her so that Agnes doesn't hear.

She jolts at my candor and opens her lips, shocked by my answer. She grabs her fork to continue eating, saying nothing more, but one detail catches my eye. I see the rose gold bracelet on her wrist and immediately reach for it. The last time I saw this bracelet, it wasn't on her wrist.

"What the hell?" I shout.

"Iris! No curse words in front of your sister, please."

I get up from my chair, put both my hands on the table and lean towards her. "What's that shit on your wrist? This bracelet is not yours."

She quickly touches the jewel, a guilty look on her face. "Oh, I…um…I don't understand."

No way I'm going to play her game. "It belonged to my mother. My father had given it to her many years ago. I remember it very well. I put this in her jewelry box myself when we packed everything. Why is this on your wrist?! Did you take anything else?"

"'Take'? Like I stole something?! I remind you that their boxes are in my garage, so I—"

"Give it back."

She raises her eyebrows. My little sister stares at us, distraught. She chews on a piece of potato, her eyes round.

"I just borrowed it," Aunt Emma justifies herself, straightening up in her chair. "I was going to put it back in the box right after."

"I'll save you the trouble because I'm taking it with me," I say, reaching for her hand.

I won't let her have it. My mother was very fond of this bracelet. My parents were not rich financially, but they were rich at heart. This bracelet represented my father's love for my mother. When I placed it in a box, I didn't feel like I could take it with me. The wound was too fresh. But today, seeing it on my aunt…no!

Seeing that I'm not giving in, she finally takes it off her wrist and drops it into my open hand. I keep quiet about many things and often keep my opinion to myself in order to avoid conflict with my aunt—especially lately, because I needed her permission for Agnes to come to my house for a few days—but I won't let her do whatever she wants.

And I know she's realized that she's gone too far. She looks at me apologetically, but I beat her to it by turning to my little sister.

"So, in a hurry to see my little apartment?" I ask.

And the discussion starts again slowly.

A few hours later, while in the boarding area, I'm about to turn off my phone when I realize I have an unread message from this morning.

I blush at the picture of Tucker, or rather his torso, with sweat sensually running down his pecs.

Tucker

I sent you a picture of my body so you can fantasize about me while sleeping on the plane.

I reply with a smiley face and a wink.

Iris

Thank you, but with the hottie who was sitting next to me, I didn't need to think about you.

In reality, this is totally untrue. For the outbound flight, my neighbor was a paunchy guy in his 80s, but Tucker doesn't need to know that. Yes, I've accepted that we're officially dating, that we're using each other's bodies for our own pleasure, but I'm not going to let him get too confident either.

Within ten seconds, he calls me. A mocking smile stuck to my face, I pick up. Agnes is playing with her Nintendo Switch at my side, her red hair falling in front of her face.

"Is this a fucking joke?" Tucker asks without preamble.

"What?" I ask innocently.

"This…this fucking 'hottie.'"

"Oh…that," I tease him.

He mumbles an expletive through the phone, but his breathing is calm and deep. What was he doing? I imagine him lying in bed, naked…no, don't think about it, damn! There are too many people around for me to think about a hot fuck scene.

"This is not fun at all," he then spits out. "Last night you agreed to be mine."

I roll my eyes even though he can't see me. "Uh, excuse me? Earth to Tucker, asking him to get his ass off the moon and back into the real world. I've agreed, I'll give you that, that we're exclusive. That's all."

"That's true," Tucker mutters. "But you want me to tell you something? The truth is, you were mine from the moment I first laid eyes on you."

He hangs up after dropping that bomb.

What? What exactly just happened? Did he really just say that to me? I stare at my cell phone, arms flailing, mouth wide open like I'm going to swallow flies. He thinks I've been his since he first laid eyes on me?

My feminist side should come out, I should call him names via text, to tell him that I will never be his. I don't want to belong to any man. I was Rafael's and he was mine, but that's it. Yes, I should send Tucker packing. So why is a damn smile spreading on my face? Because deep down, his words make me happy. He really cares about me…and I think…I think I'm really starting to care about him.

"Noooo!" shouts Agnes.

I jump and turn to her, reconnecting to reality.

"I lost at Mario Kart," she mumbles through her teeth. "They're all cheaters anyway!"

After another long flight and half an hour stuck in the traffic, it's early evening when we reach my small university residence. Agnes doesn't wait a second, she gets out of the cab like a rocket, practically jumping on the spot.

"It is really big! Do you have a lot of neighbors? Can we run in the hallways? I'm not allowed at Aunt Emma's…"

Seeing my little sister smile is worth all the money in the world.

I laugh softly, pay the driver, and grab her little suitcase with big pink flowers on it.

"Hey, calm down," I exclaim as she runs to the entrance.

A student coming out holds the door for us, and I thank her through clenched teeth.

"It looks like you're moving in here with that huge suitcase," I mumble to Agnes, "not that you're coming on vacation."

We hurry up to floor. I didn't die under the weight of the suitcase. Hallelujah! The students who rent the two apartments next to mine have gone home over break. We'll be quiet for a week.

"Why is there no light in the hallway?"

"Because the landlord is a jack—a bad guy," I correct myself.

Agnes laughs. I pull the suitcase behind me, my head buried in my bag, trying to find my keys. My cell phone starts ringing at that moment. I pull out my key ring, almost dropping it, and pick it up without looking to see who's calling.

"What?" I grumble.

"TJ's father has dropped his charges against his son," Tucker tells me, a hint of relief in his voice.

My heart almost leaps in my chest. So…it worked? What they did to his father and his secretary? Or maybe TJ's dad is planning something worse to get revenge…I'm about to warn Tucker but I'm cut off by Agnes, who abruptly stops in front of me.

"Hey, why is this open?"

I hurriedly raise my head, discovering the door of my apartment ajar by a few inches. Which should be impossible since I had locked it this morning when I left for the airport. My first reflex is to pull Agnes behind me.

"Get away from the door!" I shout to my little sister.

My heart is beating fast, my breathing is quickening. I don't know what happened, but I have a bad feeling.

I hear Tucker yell my name through the phone.

"I'll call you back," I answer in a shaky voice.

I hang up and lean toward Agnes. "I want you to go to the end of the hallway, near the stairs. If you hear a noise, you go down the stairs and press the little button by the door to go outside, understand?"

"But Iris…"

I put a hand on her shoulder and look her straight in the eye. "Do you understand?"

After a few seconds, she goes to the end of the hall, her little eyes on me. I put my bag on the ground near the suitcase, slipping my cell phone in my back pocket. I have nothing to defend myself with. Okay, maybe I'm imagining the worst, but you never know. I've been through enough shit to understand that danger lurks everywhere, especially when you least expect it.

I slowly push the door of my apartment which is pitch black. It's dark outside, which doesn't help me. I stop on the threshold, listening to the silence, before sliding my fingers on the wall next to the door to look for the light switch.

When the hall light comes on, my jaw nearly drops. The vase that was sitting on the kitchen bar to my left is exploded on the floor. OK, don't think about the furniture. I want to make sure that whoever came in here is gone. I walk to the kitchen as quietly as possible and retrieve a long knife. My cell phone vibrates in my back pocket, but I ignore it, instead surveying the damage. In the living room, several books from the small library are on the floor. In my room, a drawer has been opened and broken, clothes are scattered everywhere. But there is nobody there.

I calm down slightly as I realize that whoever tried to break in has left. Who was it? A student looking to steal valuables? I haven't checked yet, but it doesn't look like much is missing. Nothing valuable, at least.

I walk towards the hallway and then stop abruptly. On the wall of the living room, the one I couldn't see from the entrance, is written something big, in bright red.

Killer

My breath stops. This has nothing to do with a student, it has everything to do with my past. The person who came into my house and wrote that note knows exactly what I did. He or she knows that I killed Joe Nelson.

41. CONFESSION

IRIS

With my arms folded tightly across my chest, I watch the police officer write something down in his white notebook. He and his colleague arrived just five minutes ago. While one of them goes around the rooms, the other is with my little sister on the living room couch. I called them after I went to get Agnes in the badly lit hallway. I thought that their presence would reassure me, but the truth is that I am still afraid. For myself and for my sister.

"The front door was not forced open. None of your stuff was stolen," the police officer repeats, giving me a stern look. "So apparently it's not a robbery."

I clench my arms a little tighter, as if to protect myself, swallowing my saliva with difficulty. Of course it's not a robbery. And knowing that the door wasn't forced open gives me the creeps even more. The lock has definitely been picked. My brain imagines a thousand and one theories that don't reassure me at all. I let myself go for a few moments, knowing that I should look serene when I meet Agnes in the living room.

I should put her on the first plane. But I had barely suggested this idea a few minutes earlier when she was already bursting into tears and clinging to my waist. I…I don't know what to do. I probably won't be able to protect her properly.

"We need to talk about the word that was written on the wall of your apartment," the cop says, approaching me with a reassuring look.

I stare into his blue eyes, his little gray mustache. I can see that he would like to do something for me, to help me.

"Killer." The word loops around in my mind.

I sit down at the end of my bed, take a deep breath, and begin to explain to him what happened last year, from the escaped prisoner's break-in at my parents' house to the dropping of the charges against me for self-defense. As the minutes pass, the cop's expression becomes more serious. He listens to my monologue, jotting down information in his notebook. When I'm done, I fiddle with my fingers and raise my face to him.

"This person who came in tonight…it wasn't a mistake. It's not a coincidence. This person managed to get on campus and he knew Joe Nelson."

"Could it be a prank that students play on each other?" The cop asks me.

"No, of course not."

He looks skeptical. I know for a fact that once we get to the police station, he'll check the information I just gave him, just in case I'm a common liar.

"Maybe the person who broke into my house is someone close to Joe Nelson," I say. "Someone who would like to avenge his death."

I thought that all this was behind me. My little sister calls me, and I know she must have dozens of questions.

"We'll investigate," the agent continues. "I'll probably call you back and ask you to come to the police station. Tonight, a patrol will be on duty. You don't have to worry, everything will be fine. Is there anything else you can think of that might be important?"

I rack my brains for a few minutes. "A few weeks ago, I received a call from an unknown number. There was no one on the other end, just breathing. Maybe it was just a prank call but…I can't think of anything else."

"I'm writing this down," the cop tells me.

"Iris!" a male voice shouts through the walls.

I almost jump as I recognize the husky tone. Damn it, Tucker.

The cop suddenly stands up, looking around.

"It's all right," I hurriedly say as I walk to the entrance of my apartment.

Agnes is standing by the couch, her eyes squinting at the front door, the second cop beside her. I follow their gaze and fall on Tucker's. He looks crazed, a vein pulsing on his forehead. His eyes quickly scan my body before his jaw clenches a little more.

"What are you doing here?" I begin, approaching him.

His shoulders tense a little more when he sees the two cops. He clenches his fists but, instead of answering me, almost throws himself on me and kisses me hard, his fingers plunging into my hair. His breath mixes with mine before he abruptly backs away. I don't know why I want to feel him against me again, as if his presence reassured me, as if he was a kind of impenetrable cocoon that would protect me.

"What's going on here?" Tucker asks.

"This isn't a good time," I sigh, putting a hand on his forearm to calm him down.

He ignores me and look around. His gaze falls on my little sister, who is looking back at him.

The second cop approaches me and asks me something, but I remain focused on Tucker. I catch the exact moment he notices the word spray-painted in red on my wall. His body tenses up a little more. I can't see his face because his back is to me, but I can imagine exactly how he must look.

This can't be true, damn it. Maybe he'll think it's a stupid mistake?

He suddenly turns to me, nostrils flaring. The cops tell me they're leaving, reminding me they'll be in touch as soon as they have anything, but I don't move an inch. Neither does Tucker. He stands still, like a statue—a dangerous statue.

"Iris," he whispers in a voice from beyond the grave as he takes a step toward me.

His posture could frighten many people. But I can read beyond that, and in the depths of his eyes, behind his apparent rage, I detect worry.

Agnes, who doesn't know him at all, must be afraid. But no, she rushes in front of me as if to protect me with her small body. She plants herself between Tucker and me and raises her fist in his direction.

"Don't touch!" she orders him sternly.

He seems upset. He stops suddenly, his eyes lost in the one of the little redheaded girl who is knee-high to a grasshopper standing in front of him. He seems to regain some awareness, and I see that he makes an effort to relax his facial muscles.

"You must be Agnes. Hi," he begins awkwardly.

My little sister doesn't move an inch. My heart clenches painfully at the love I feel for her. I put a hand on her shoulder and squeeze it.

"It's okay, Agnes, this is Tucker. He's my friend," I say to her.

She slowly lowers her fist but still doesn't move.

"I'm the guy you talked to on the phone the other day," Tucker continues. "You know, the one you called names."

Catching me completely off guard, I see this six-foot-tall mountain of muscle kneeling in front of a nine-year-old girl, a mischievous grin on his face. A black lock of hair falls on his forehead.

My little sister tilts her head toward him, and I gently shift to observe their exchange.

"Are you her boyfriend?" she asks.

Please tell me she didn't say that. I close my eyes for a second, and when I open them again, Tucker has his full attention focused on me. Kneeling on the floor, he stares at me without flinching then turns to my little sister.

"Yeah, that's me."

My mouth opens slowly, but no sound comes out. My heart misses a beat. I don't know what to do. Run and hide? Pretend that this simple statement doesn't shake me up more than that? Yes, that's a good solution. I clear my throat and then say, "I want you to go take a shower, Agnes."

My little sister turns to me, faking a doe-eyed look to try to change my mind. "But…"

"Agnes."

She crosses her arms, and I feel like I'm in the same position a few minutes earlier.

"Are you sure there's nobody here?" she whispers.

I inhale deeply, anger building inside me. I wanted her arrival to be perfect, and whoever came into my apartment ruined it. My sister is scared, and so am I. But I'm the adult in the story, the one who has to take care of her. I put on a calm face. "There's no one here. I'm here to protect you."

"You promise?"

"I promise."

Agnes slowly backs into the hallway, but she stops for a

moment and stares at Tucker with a serious expression. "And you, will you protect my sister?" she asks him.

This question sounds like a request for an oath.

"Agnes," I say.

"Yes," Tucker says solemnly.

I turn to him, my eyebrows furrowed, as my little sister goes into the bathroom. We stare at each other for a minute, in silence. Neither he nor I speak. I still feel the violence of his kiss, the wild contact of his lips on mine.

"You shouldn't have come," I sigh as I walk to the kitchen. I rub my eyelids hard against my palms, suddenly exhausted. I hear the sound of his footsteps at my back.

"You were screaming on the phone in a panicked voice. What should I have done? Ignore that you might have been in danger and go on with my life?!"

I turn toward him and then back away a little as I notice the proximity of our two bodies. I lean against the kitchen bar and cross my arms over my chest. Worry doesn't leave his features, nor does anger. He's seen things he shouldn't have, and I know it's too late to back out now.

"I'm sorry," I simply answer, not knowing what to say.

He takes another step towards me but holds back. He opens his mouth several times and then closes it again without saying anything. I should tell him to go away, but I can't. Because his presence helps me to feel better. Because his presence helps me to relax, reassures me, gives me the stupid impression that nothing can happen to me.

"What happened?" he finally asks.

"Someone broke into my place," I confess. "The door wasn't forced open, so the cops think someone picked my lock."

"Did the son of a bitch steal things? Break stuff?"

"No, just a vase."

His breathing quickens, and I can see he's losing his patience. He points to the wall with his index finger and asks me, "What the hell is this?"

I swallow my saliva. He asks me the, question but I know perfectly well that he has understood. Tucker is far from being stupid, I'm sure he made the connection between my confession of the other day and what happened tonight. The other night, in his car,

I confessed to him that I was a monster. Tonight, he sees the word "killer" painted on my wall. It doesn't take a PhD to understand.

"It's just a word," I try piteously.

He squints his eyes a little more.

"Just a word? They wrote 'killer' on your wall, Iris."

"I know!" I exclaim in turn. "Look, I…I need to think. I need you to leave."

He lets out a joyless laugh. I'm well aware that I'm acting stupidly. He's worried, jumped in his car to come here, and rather than explain to him what he already half understands, I dismiss it. But I can't speak, the words get stuck in my throat. My instinct is to confide in him, while a part of me urges me to say nothing. So I choose the right option. The less he knows, the less power he has to destroy me, right?

"No," Tucker retorts, standing his ground. "No way."

I frown.

"What do you mean 'no?' You're in my house, and I order you out of MY apartment!"

"So what, we're going to pretend this never happened? Like I didn't see that word sprayed on your wall? I shouldn't draw any conclusions?"

"Draw whatever conclusions you want, Tucker. I'm exhausted. I don't want to talk right now."

The truth is, I'm a coward, I can't do it. So I reject him in the hope of postponing the moment. Because I know for sure that my confession will come sooner or later.

"Later," I almost beg him.

He analyzes me during long seconds. His look doesn't tell me anything good. All of a sudden, he turns around and heads to the door furiously. It slams behind his back as he disappears from my sight. A feeling of loss comes over me. The feeling I had of being protected has evaporated.

What the hell did you do, you idiot?

Thirty minutes later, I look at Agnes, deeply asleep under the sheets. I don't know if she really realized all that happened. I don't think she has made the connection between what happened tonight and what happened years ago. And that's good, otherwise she would be even more worried. Sitting next to her, I run the tip of my index finger over the bridge of her freckled nose. She's made me promise three times to keep her this week and not bring her back now, but I still don't know what to do.

Just as I pull my hand away, there is a knock on my front door. My heart misses a beat. Anxiety gnaws at me at once. A bad feeling comes over me.

I get up slowly and leave the room, taking care to close the door behind me. It's all right, Iris, the cops said they'd make their rounds, everything's fine. There's a little more knocking. If it was someone who wanted to hurt me, they wouldn't bother knocking, right? If it was the same person as before, they'd pick the handle again. Looking through the peephole, I am deeply surprised to discover Tucker standing in the doorway. He was angry when I asked him to leave, so what the hell is he doing here?!

I am confused as I unlock and open the door for him.

"Why are you still here?" I ask.

He passes by me without waiting a second, pushing me slightly. The smell of his cologne invades me again but I ignore it.

"You're getting on my nerves. I don't think I've ever been so angry," he starts, standing in the middle of my living room.

I lean against the door, arms crossed over my chest.

"Tucker…" I sigh.

He points his index finger at me.

"Damn it, I'm worried about you."

His sentence leaves me stunned. I had noticed the concern on his face, but hearing him tell me is something else.

He walks towards me again, unable to stay in place. "Don't push me out. Don't push me out because I'm not going anywhere."

"You can't—"

He places his hand against my mouth, pressing his body against mine. "I get it, you don't want to talk. It drives me crazy but I understand. But I don't want to leave."

I pull his hand away from my mouth. "You…wait, what? You can't stay tonight."

"I can and I will," he announces firmly as he suddenly walks away to my couch.

Stunned, I watch him fall back against the cushions, head back, staring at the ceiling. I must be dreaming. I told him to piss off half an hour ago, he left in a rage, and now he's back on my sofa? He doesn't want to talk, he just…wants to be here.

"So what, you're just going to sleep on my couch?" I ask him as I walk away from the door.

A growl comes from his chest but he doesn't answer me and closes his eyes.

"Tucker, seriously," I say louder to him.

Indeed, he seems perfectly serious. My heart is moved by his determination. He doesn't know how to put it into words, but I understand what he is doing. He's showing me that I'm not alone. He's just in this room, a few feet away from me, and I feel…safe. It's like he's figured out that deep down I need him. As if he understood that I was too stubborn to admit to myself that I needed his presence tonight.

I walk towards him.

"You don't have to," I whisper.

He keeps his eyes closed. "Good night, Iris."

He dismisses me firmly. I watch him for a few seconds and go back to my room. All these events are overwhelming me. I am used to rely only on myself, to be accountable to no one, and I have the impression that everything is changing.

I lie down next to Agnes, who is fast asleep, and stare into the void. I saw the gleam in Tucker's eyes. I hurt him. I shut him out like I always do and rejected him again, and hurt him. I shouldn't care, but I can't. I didn't mean to hurt him. Shit, I care about him. I'm realizing that more and more. He. Means. A lot. To. Me.

He rushed to my apartment, crazed eyes, body tense. When he placed his lips against mine when he entered my apartment earlier, his gestures were clumsy. He was trembling. He had been afraid for me and, because I was afraid myself, I sent him away. And yet, despite his anger, he came back, and is now lying on my damn couch. Because he cares about me too.

I toss and turn a few times but can't get to sleep.

I can easily imagine Tucker's body on my couch. I feel a sudden urge and sit up on the mattress.

Do it, my conscience orders me.

I wait a second, then stand up and leave my bed. My breathing is calm and deep, but my heart is in my throat. I stare for a moment at the pile of clothes on the floor that I didn't have the energy to put away after the cops left. A slight creak sounds as I gently open the door to my room.

The only light still on is the lamp next to the television, which is turned off. No sound comes from the living room. Yet I know in my heart that Tucker is not asleep. I enter the room and find him lying on his back on the sofa.

I stare for a moment at the word scratched on my wall, promising myself to go buy paint first thing tomorrow to cover the stupid thing.

I take another step forward, silently. One arm cradled behind his head, the other resting on his stomach, his eyes closed. I stop near the couch, not moving an inch.

I stare at his bare skin and the black cotton boxers he is wearing. His chest rises slowly, to the rhythm of his breathing. I move forward a little more, as if hypnotized by the air escaping from his mouth.

A hand lands on the back of my thigh, making me jump. His eyes open wide as he looks into mine. I can't see any sign of fatigue.

We don't move other than his fingers gently pressing my tender skin. I am still standing, and he is still lying on the couch. His thumb circles my skin lightly as my gaze gazes again at his body. The hunger is growing in the pit of my stomach, but there is also something else. I just want to…feel his skin against mine.

Taking him by surprise, I sit down astride of him. His hand hasn't left my body, it has followed my movement and is now on the front of my thigh. I feel his erection beneath me. It gradually hardens but neither he nor I move. His other arm is still lodged behind his head, and his gaze doesn't leave me for a moment, avidly analyzing my actions.

His breathing quickens slightly as I lean towards him. I press my lips against his once, twice, then I lie down on his body. I press my skin against his, make myself more comfortable and press my cheek against his burning chest.

I feel his heartbeat against my face. It rocks me, it helps me to forget everything, except this moment. I'm not thinking about who broke into my apartment anymore. I let go and close my eyes. Tucker doesn't reject me, his free hand rests on the back of my head and brushes the strands of my hair. His breath hits the top of my head.

I feel…safe, in his arms.

A part of me needed this. Tomorrow…tomorrow, reality will return. The anxiety will be back inside me. Do I want to be alone tomorrow? Or should I let my heart open, let my guard down?

"I killed my parents' killer," I whisper.

His body tenses under me. He doesn't answer me. I expect him to push me away or burst out laughing thinking I am joking, but he doesn't. He moves slightly, and his lips press against the top of my head.

"I kind of figured that out already," he murmurs softly.

I swallow hard. Of course he was going to make the connection between my parents, my half-confession the other day, and that note left on my wall.

"One night I came home late. There was…blood… everywhere. My parents were lying on the living room floor, dead. Someone was in my house, and I couldn't find my little sister. I went up the stairs as quietly as I could to find Agnes. We used to play hide and seek when she was little, and she always hid in my closet. I knew she was there. When I reached the last step, a voice rang out behind my back. It was the monster that had come into my house and killed my parents. I ran up the stairs, trying to escape him, and locked myself in my room just before he could hurt me."

Tucker's arm wraps around my body as he holds me a little tighter against him. His embrace is possessive but I enjoy it.

"You don't have to," he whispers in my ear.

My voice trembles softly but I continue. "I called my little sister several times and, thank God, she was hiding where I thought. I held her close, praying that the police would arrive soon. That's when the guy broke down the door. He was wearing a prison uniform. I later learned that he was a prisoner on the run."

I closed my eyelids hard to keep my stupid tears from flowing.

"He came into the room and hit me."

"What a son of a bitch," Tucker whispers.

I can feel the tension seeping out of his pores, and I know that if Joe was standing in front of him right now, Tucker would be going at him.

"Then he…started touching Agnes. He laid her down on the floor and tried to…to…" Shit, I can't say it. "That monster was going to abuse her. So I tried to stop him, but he was heavier than me. I saw some scissors sitting on the cabinet, and I didn't think. I killed him. I drove the scissors into his body several times, praying that he would die with each blow. The cops came soon after. I was proven innocent."

"My angel," whispers Tucker, pressing his lips to my ear again.

"So, yes, I'm a killer," I continue, "but I killed a monster who was going to kill my sister and who had killed my parents. A part of me will never accept that fact, but I…I don't regret what I did, even if some people think that nothing can give us the right to take someone's life."

"You're not a monster, damn it." His index finger rests on my chin, and he makes me raise my head in his direction. "You saved your sister. You saved yourself. You are not a monster. You reacted like anyone else would have, and anyone who doesn't understand what you did is a moron. Me, I understand it."

I nod, not knowing what to say to him. His arm is still tight around me, his burning skin pressed against me, my breasts pressed against his chest.

"I left Portland and came here hoping to leave my past behind forever. And then this all happened tonight. I'm scared, Tucker. Because maybe it's a friend of his coming to avenge him, how should I know?"

"Nothing will happen to you," Tucker says as though it's an indisputable fact, but he doesn't know that and I don't know that either. Yet, as I let myself sink into his arms, I feel a strange sense of release. I feel soothed, relieved of a weight after talking to him.

"Thank you," he whispers to me.

I don't know if I was right to confide in him, but at that moment I feel good.

42. IT'S HER

IRIS

A kid's laugh.

A deep and masculine laugh.

These two stupid sounds pierce my ears when I wake up. Lying flat on my stomach across the sofa, my face pressed against a cushion, I yawn until my jaw drops. The first thing I see is the clock in front of me. Nine thirty-four. But who gets up that early on a Sunday morning?

I turn my head and my eyes instantly land on the word painted in red. "Killer."

And then it all comes back to me like a big slap in the face. I pass a hand over my tired eyes. The details invade my mind. The stranger who entered my apartment and wrote that note on the wall. The cops who came. Agnes terrified. Tucker who showed up…Tucker!

Something was definitely born between us last night. Or maybe that something was there before, but has developed over the last few hours. I felt good against him, and I know he felt the same way.

It's like a part of me is telling me that I deserve to be happy again, to leave Rafael in one corner of my heart and open the other half to Tucker.

A childish laugh comes to me again. I sit down on the couch, my short locks in all directions, and turn to the kitchen.

The scent of sugar comes to me instantly, combined with a smell of…God, do I smell something burnt?

Tucker has his back to me, mumbling something unintelligible. He stayed and slept next to me. And now he's in my kitchen, barefoot, perfectly at ease. I should tell him to leave, but right now I don't want to.

On the other side of the kitchen island, perched on a chair, my sister is leaning towards the kitchen counter. A little bit of tongue is sticking out of her mouth, her eyebrows are furrowed. I know this ridiculous expression perfectly well because we both have the same expression when we are focused. My confusion increases when I see her mixing a strange mixture in a bowl.

Tucker cusses, and my little sister bursts out laughing.

"If you keep saying bad words, Iris will kill you," she warns him.

For the first time in a long time, my little sister looks happy. Like…really happy.

"Then it's a good thing she's sleeping like a rock," Tucker retorts gruffly, leaning towards something I can't see.

"She's going to kill us when she sees this," Agnes continues, not noticing that I'm wide awake.

Oh, what the hell have they done?

I get up, and the sofa creaks gently. My little sister suddenly turns her head towards me, a falsely innocent look on her face. Tucker leans in a little closer to her.

"The ogress is awake, right?"

I squint my eyes and retrieve a pillow from beside me. "Screw you," I grumble, throwing the pillow at his back.

He turns to me and I can see the little mocking smile he's holding back. He has put on his T-shirt from yesterday, the fabric crumpled in places, which does not prevent me from noticing the profile of his muscles. My gaze travels down to his jeans and bare feet. I inhale sharply as I feel my body warm up. The traitor…

And Tucker knows exactly what effect he has on me. He looks at me with an appreciative look on his face, like he's going to devour me in the next few seconds.

He stares at me so intensely that I feel like I'm on the breakfast menu. And speaking of breakfast…what the hell is this shit?!

I notice an eggshell on the floor. But that's not all. There's dough all over the kitchen island. My little sister is leaning over a bowl, and I see her pulling a big piece of eggshell out of the bowl, looking extremely focused. That's when I see batter in her hair.

"What the hell did you do?" I sigh as I walk over to them to see the extent of the damage.

I discover what Tucker was hiding, which is a pan with what looks like a burned pancake. I bring a piece of the pancake to my mouth and nearly choke on its awful taste.

"I told Tucker to watch the pancake, but he spent the whole time looking at you like a moron," Agnes mutters.

I turn to Tucker, my eyebrows raised. He squints as he stares at my little sister for a second, as if embarrassed by her admission.

"You were snoring so much," he mumbles in my direction, "I just wanted to make sure you weren't choking."

"That's not true at all," my little sister whispers as she resumes her task. "Well, I give up, I don't think you can eat anything in there. Too many shells."

I stare at her hair full of batter for a second. "Off to the shower before I really turn into an ogress."

She doesn't seem to take my threat into consideration at all, but obeys nonetheless. As for me, I return my attention to Tucker, wedged against the island, arms crossed on his chest.

"Do you often watch people sleep?" I ask with a teasing smile.

His gaze becomes more intense, more predatory.

"And make them breakfast—"

I don't have time to finish my sentence when he wraps his arm firmly around my waist and pulls me close. "Don't make fun of me," he orders me with a grumpy look on his face.

"Making food for a girl means a lot, you know that?"

He raises an eyebrow and plays along with me. It's rare that we're both so teasing. Normally, we'd be calling each other names or snapping at each other right before we'd throw ourselves at each other. The mood between us is different, and I'm not sure how to act. And I think he's just as lost as I am behind his tough-guy look.

"And what could that mean?" he whispers in my ear, his beard rubbing hard against my cheek.

I swallow hard with a lump in my throat.

"It means...that you really like me, I guess?" I whisper back.

His arm tightens around my waist. My breasts press against him. I need to feel his warmth, even if an inferno is already growing in my belly.

"Do you really like me?" Tucker continues, his nose nearly brushing mine.

My breath catches as I am caught off guard. For a moment, I want to push him away, to laugh falsely and ask him if he's losing his mind, but I would be lying to myself. Of course I like him, otherwise I wouldn't have admitted anything to him last night. But my pride prevents me from answering in the affirmative.

"I asked you first," I grumble.

I'm pretty sure he's going to respond with a mocking remark, because deep down, we're not that different. We put up such high barriers around ourselves that they are almost impossible to break through.

But Tucker surprises me. His mouth grazes my neck, then his tongue licks my skin. When he starts to nibble on me, I press myself against him a little more, forgetting everything else.

"Yeah," he admits seriously. "Really do."

His right hand presses against my ass, gripping me hard. What else can I do but curl my fingers around the back of his head?

"I think I do too."

There, it's said. Damn, look at us, we're like two confused 12-year-olds wondering what to say, what to do, and afraid of the consequences of their every word. My gaze is once again locked onto his. I believe that our supposedly insurmountable barriers are being broken down. It scares me, but I like it.

A rumble echoes in his chest as he lifts me up with a jerk, turns, and sets me on the kitchen island. I think I've just sat in batter, but I don't think about it anymore as his body slides between my thighs. My breathing quickens as my nipples harden. He seems to have noticed this detail because he runs his tongue over his bottom lip for a long time, his attention focused on my breasts. When he presses himself a little more between my thighs, I raise my legs and press him against me to feel his erection more. We still haven't kissed, like we're playing with each other to build up the tension between us.

We know perfectly well that we are going to succumb, to devour each other. But we want the other to give up first. A silent fight of domination. Who will jump on the other first…

His thumb caresses my cheekbone, stops on my mouth and presses my lower lip.

"Last night I dreamed I was thrusting into your little mouth," Tucker whispers against me.

He may think he's shocking me with his confession, but I part my lips and bite down hard on his fingertip before wrapping my tongue around his flesh. "Watch out, I'll bite."

He brings his thumb against his mouth and caresses it with his tongue, licking without any modesty the saliva I just put on it.

"That's really disgusting," exclaims Agnes, almost choking, a few feet away.

Feels like a cold shower. My eyes go wide as I push Tucker away abruptly, but he doesn't seem to be bothered at all. He slowly walks away from me, winking at my sister. "Next time, close your eyes."

Agnes walks into the living room, a pink vest in her hands, looking for the remote control. I glare at Tucker.

"Don't worry, I've seen Iris do worse," my little sister retorts. "When she was with Rafael, well, sometimes there were weird noises, and I was never allowed in her room."

My heart misses a beat. Agnes collapses on the couch and starts a cartoon, not realizing the bomb she has just dropped. I glance over at Tucker and discover that he is staring at me. This is the second time he's heard about Rafael, and now he's completely shut down. His gaze is no longer burning but has a different glow. Is it…shit, is it jealousy? I'm sure he's already imagining a lot of things between me and this Rafael he knows nothing about.

He moves away a few steps, arms along his body, while I try to regain my composure.

"An ex?" he almost spits.

I don't like the way he says that. As if he meant a piece of shit. "Yeah," I answer shortly.

"I see," Tucker continues with the same displeased expression on his face.

From the look on his face and the dryness of his tone, I don't feel like telling him anything more. He has no idea who Rafael was or what he meant to me. Nor does he know that he died, bleeding out while I was helpless next to him. Tucker takes a deep breath, understanding that I'm uncomfortable with this conversation, and seems to calm down.

"I'm sorry…I guess I get a little crazy when it comes to you."

How can he be so annoying and so attractive in the same minute? His confession calms me down inside. I know for a fact that a new feeling is developing in him, that this is why he's lost. I can see it in his eyes, damn it, and I'm pretty sure I'm giving him the same expression back.

"It's nothing," I whisper.

"No, it's something," he says gravely, in a low voice so that Agnes doesn't hear our little discussion. "You just shut down on me, and I don't like that. Last night, you confided in me, you trusted me, and I don't want us to become distant from each other again this morning. I won't allow that for us."

He swallows, his Adam's apple moving gently down his throat. His eyes are tired, and I wonder how long he's been awake, watching me sleep. He looks haunted and worried. So I approach him, unable to get angry, and press my mouth against his with a loud smack. "I think I already knew that…that you were a little crazy."

My voice is more relaxed, and his shoulders relax in turn.

"Oh yeah?" he asks, raising his eyebrows.

"Who calls himself a 'pack leader,' really?" I say mockingly.

He lets out a small laugh as his cell phone rings in his back pocket. He picks it up with a frown.

"My mom…um…I have to go."

"Is everything okay?"

He nods but now seems to be deep in thought. I watch him for the next minute as he collects his things. His jaw is clenched and his gaze locked. I doubt asking him anything else now would get me anywhere. If there's anyone on this earth more secretive than me, it's Tucker Bomley. When he has collected his bag, he walks towards me, uncertain.

"Thanks for staying the night," I finally say.

He frowns a little more, his shoulders tense. "You don't have to thank me, Iris. I was serious; nothing will happen to you."

I find it hard to believe his words, but I want to hold on to them.

"Tonight I'll—"

"It's okay," I cut him off. "I don't want you to be my chaperone."

"I don't mind. Some asshole broke into your house to write

that shit on this wall."

"And I freaked out last night, but I'm fine, really. I'll take care of Agnes. I'll be fine."

He seems divided. I can see that he wants to stay and prove himself, but that he is disturbed by the message he just received.

"I'll call you," he finally says before kissing me for a long time.

My breathing stops.

"See you later, the two redheads."

I send my fist in his direction to indicate that I don't validate this nickname but, already, he slams the door behind him.

"So," exclaims Agnes, passing her head over the sofa. "I like your boyfriend."

Your boyfriend. YOUR. Boyfriend. Tucker and I haven't really had a discussion about it. Officially, we're just self-proclaimed fuck buddies. Part of me is pushing away from the situation.

But this time, I don't want to be a coward.

TUCKER

I stop my car with a squeal of tires in front of the huge Victorian house. I get out of the car, my legs feeling numb. It's been a long time since I slept away from here and I feel…refreshed. I feel like holding Iris's little body against me all night has done me good physically but also psychologically.

Fuck, I can't stop thinking about watching her sleep last night. I wanted to take her so badly, the blood was boiling in my veins. And yet I felt satisfied just holding her against me.

Yeah, I'm really fucked up.

She confided in me, and I felt like the king of the world. The most secretive girl I know opened up to me. She revealed one of the many dark secrets she carries with her, and it made me want to make her mine, to protect her and to blow the head off of anyone who tried to hurt her.

I'm in so much trouble, I tell you.

I climb the stone steps and open the heavy door to the mansion. "Abraham?"

He comes up to me. He looks worried. "Sir," he greets me with a discreet nod.

"Where is my mother?" I ask him bluntly.

But I already know where to find her. I know she hasn't gone into Debbie's room because Abraham has locked the room. I hear crying and enter the huge living room on my left. The fireplace is lit, crackling sounds can be heard between the embers. On the floor, a crystal glass is shattered and a bottle of cognac is spilled on the fur rug in front of the fireplace.

Near the armchair, sitting on the floor, my mother is sobbing, her eyes lost in the flames.

"Mom?" I call out to her.

She hurriedly raises her head, and the sad look on her face hurts me. She is my mother. I will always take care of her, no matter what.

I kneel down beside her, taking care to keep my movements slow and calm so as not to frighten her.

"You haven't abandoned me?" she whispers in a small voice.

I shake my head, picking up the bottle from the floor.

"Why weren't you there last night? I thought you were gone, like your father," she sobs, "like Debbie, I was all alone."

"I didn't leave," I cut her off firmly so she'll understand my words and not question them. "I'm here."

When Abraham sent me that text earlier to tell me my mom was falling apart, no anger came to me, even though I know she drank alcohol last night. She agreed to meet this new doctor and go back on her meds.

"Did you see your doctor yesterday?"

She nods, a small smile on her face.

"I promised you I would. I didn't touch the alcohol." She cries again, wrapping her arms around her legs. "I resisted because I promised you," she continues. "I promised you that. I threw the bottle on the floor. But you weren't there. Not here...I thought you were gone."

I squeeze her shoulder as her head drops against my arm. "I'm here. I'm here."

TJ

I'm in the chapel with Dan.
Get your ass out here before it gets ugly.

A few minutes after receiving TJ's text, I walk down the stone steps of the chapel. I find Dan sitting on an old couch, a joint stuck to the corner of his lips, staring at the ceiling. He doesn't move, immersed in his thoughts. He runs a hand over his shaved head and inhales once more. I move towards him and, without a word, he hands me his joint.

I don't have time to bring it to my lips before TJ gets up from the other couch. His blond hair is matted and his mouth pinched.

"My father has withdrawn his complaint."

I drop into the chair next to Dan, and we exchange a look that only we can understand.

"You already texted me to tell me," I point out to my cousin.

"He wanted to destroy me, and all of a sudden he withdrew the charge. So, are you going to tell me what happened, or are you still acting like assholes?"

Dan lets out a little laugh but neither he nor I respond.

"Shit, guys," TJ says angrily. "He's thinking of taking a vacation to 'relieve the pressure of his job.' What happened?!"

"We're protecting our family," I just say. "We made it clear to him…by visiting him and his whore."

TJ stares at us, his mouth wide open. He drops back down on the couch in front of us, then raises his head.

"You guys are completely reckless."

"You're welcome, you little prick," Dan mumbles with a smile.

A silence fills the room.

"I tried to come by last night, but you weren't home," TJ continues, staring at me strangely.

My muscles tense up at once. I straighten up, elbows on my knees, and cross my hands after throwing the half-smoked joint on the floor.

"I was with Iris."

"Wait," exclaims TJ. "You spent the night at her place? I thought there was nothing going on between you two."

I look him straight in the eye but don't answer anything.

"You slept together, didn't you? Shit, you've been staring at her for weeks, eating her up. I know you don't want to share the juicy details, but I'll have you know that when you were fucking other chicks, you told us everything."

New silence. I have no desire to talk about Iris with them. What happened between us is none of their business. I don't want to talk about her body, her problems.

She is mine.

"We're hanging out," I say nonetheless.

They're going to see us together, and I don't want them asking her a lot of questions. Fuck buddies, nothing else, my ass.

"Shit, man," my cousin laughs.

Dan doesn't react, again, but I'm used to that. Ever since what happened to my sister, he's been withdrawn, but I know he's listening.

"Is there something going on between you two?" TJ continues like a busybody. "Did you fuck her?"

I want to smash his pretty little face because I don't like the words he's using, but I stand up straight.

"Man, every time her eyes meet mine…I think of one thing, her. Don't you get it? I'm the one who's fucked."

So he understands exactly what I'm saying to him.

"You're in deep shit," says TJ.

43. GET THE CLAWS OUT

IRIS

"But this word, 'killer,' it has a link with my past, and you know it!"

Since the beginning of my deposition, Detective Harrison keeps telling me not to jump to conclusions, that he has analyzed the files that the Portland police have made available to them on a database, that Joe Nelson apparently had no family, no suspicious contacts, no one who would try to find me…but I won't give up!

The detective runs a hand over his protruding belly, silently thinking for a minute.

"I'll investigate more thoroughly and contact the police over there. I'll call you back if I learn anything more. Until then, your university has been made aware of an intruder lurking around, and security will be beefed up."

I close my eyes and take a deep breath. He doesn't understand. I'm sure this intruder came into my house for a reason.

"Everything will be fine, miss," he says finally, with a faint smile.

An expression that I don't manage to return to him, my stomach twisting little by little and my body refusing to believe his words.

I walk along the corridor, Detective Harrison on my heels. I can only think of one thing, to join Agnes who is waiting for me in the small waiting room with another detective. My aunt called me several times, and I didn't have the courage to tell her what happened. I know that Agnes would have to leave Denver, that I would have to put her on the first plane to Portland, but I can't bring myself to do it.

I catch a glimpse of her little redhead tilted toward the detective, who is explaining something apparently funny. As I approach her, a voice snaps behind my back.

"Miss Foster?"

I dig my heels in and turn to the woman in the stilettos who's waiting three feet away, several huge files in her hands.

Professor Richards?! My criminology professor seems as surprised as I am by the situation. But after all, she's a lawyer, so it's not so surprising to see her here.

Her dark eyes analyze the slightest clue on my face, probably waiting for explanations from me that don't come.

"I'll get back to you soon," Harrison says, waving me off and heading back to the lobby of the police station.

My gaze remains fixed on Professor Richards, but I nod nonetheless.

"Is everything okay?" she asks as she approaches me, her heels clicking on the tile floor.

"Yeah, I'm fine, thanks. Just…just a little issue."

She nods in turn, searching through my words for what I'm not saying. Under her gaze, I feel like I'm being seen right through. I don't like it, this feeling that she can read me like an open book. But most of all, that look on her face, as if she understands why I'm here, as if she knows a part of my past that I try to hide from everyone. I don't think that's the case, but I'm getting paranoid.

I mentally shake myself and then stand up.

"I have to go," I announce as I walk by her.

I expect her to ignore me but she holds me back.

"Miss Foster?"

I turn to her, my eyebrows raised.

"I finished correcting the file you made with your classmate Tucker Bomley about the Larey case."

My heart misses a beat.

"Your analysis is good, but you'll see that once I get the notes to you when school starts again next week. No, actually, I want to talk to you about something else."

Oops…I'm willing to bet she's going to give me a hard time about what I said to her the other day in the lecture hall, that her friend who is Mikael Larey's lawyer should get off her ass and try to get him out of jail.

"You were apparently right to believe in Mr. Larey's innocence. I can't say anything, except that a new and crucial element has emerged."

"His lawyer has appealed the jury's decision?" I ask with a shred of hope.

Professor Richards stares at the Rolex on her wrist. "Oh, she didn't really need it."

I walk over to her. "What the hell happened?"

I see she hesitates between rolling her eyes or laughing at my language, but she doesn't and starts to back away, perfectly stoic, as usual.

"Have a good day, Miss Foster."

I leave the police station a few minutes later, with Agnes hanging on to me. I immediately text Tucker to tell him that I have just run into Professor Richards and that there is a change in the Larey case. As we pull up to Colfax Avenue, I listen to my little sister with a distracted ear, waiting for a response to my text that doesn't come.

I come out of my thoughts when I see Sanchez parking his car along the sidewalk. He notices me at this precise moment, and he smiles at me. His long black locks brush against the collar of his black T-shirt, and his piercing at the arch shines under the weak glow of the sun. His dark eyes quickly examine my miniature double who stands at my side.

Agnes stops when she sees me stop and is suddenly silent.

"Hey! Iris!" Sanchez greets me as he approaches me.

I raise my hand in his direction to greet him. "What are you doing here?" I ask him.

"I had an appointment," he answers. He raises his eyebrows several times, a suggestive air on the face, to make me understand that it was about sex in his appointment.

I roll my eyes and turn to my little sister. "This is Sanchez, a friend from school. And this is my little sister."

Agnes greets him with a wave but doesn't say anything, silently analyzing him. Her little frown doesn't look good to me.

"Oh, shit," Sanchez continues. "I didn't know you had a sister. Is she less of a pain in the ass than you?"

I hold back an expletive and punch him in the shoulder, which makes Agnes laugh. Sanchez spins his keys between his fingers, staring at me without saying anything. I wait patiently but eager to get out of there.

"I didn't know you were around. I mean, do you want to have lunch or…?"

I don't have time to answer when Agnes beats me to it by crossing her arms over her chest. "You know, my sister already has a boyfriend, and it's not you."

My jaw nearly drops. Agnes, damn it!

Sanchez stares at her, his eyes wide, before looking at me. "What?"

"Agnes," I sigh, warning her.

"His name is Tucker, and I think if you hit on my sister, he's going to hit you," Agnes continues.

Sanchez's stance changes. He stands up straight, his eyebrows slightly furrowed. This news seems to shake him completely. "You…"

"We just messing around, that's all," I cut him off to avoid starting a discussion that does not concern him in any way. We may be members of the same damn pack, but my life and my ass are my business.

"I see," Sanchez continues with an enigmatic look on his face. "I…I have to go. I'll see you later."

Why is he acting weird all of a sudden? I watch him walk away, then turn to my sister. "You're really a piece of work, you know that?"

She smiles at me innocently. "I don't like him," she says.

I laugh softly. I felt exactly the same way when I first saw Sanchez when we were both stuck in the old warehouse. But things have changed since then, and I think I misjudged Sanchez. He may be a bit of a jerk, but he's cool.

"You don't know him," I say to Agnes.

She shakes her head and continues her way with a little capricious pout. "He looks at you strangely. I don't like him, I tell you."

I stare at my phone again, but there's still no answer to my message.

TUCKER

I wake up with a start, push back the sheets that stick to my skin, and rush to the bathroom, not waiting a second to turn on the faucet and plunge my head under the icy water.

My memories go away, then come back. That fucking nightmare that keeps haunting me finally goes away, bringing me back to reality, then comes back suddenly.

I see my sister's little broken body in the hospital bed again.

My hands clutch the edge of the sink, my breathing ragged.

I end up rubbing my face energetically before going to my room. My eyes fall on the alarm clock next to my bed. Three past one in the morning. The covers are on the floor. I pick up my T-shirt and quickly put it on. It mops up water and sweat.

My broad frame fills half the mattress as I fall backwards, making the springs gently creak. I inhale deeply to try to calm myself. It's no use.

Nothing can slow my breathing, my nightmare claws at my skin with all its might, plunging its claws into me to hurt me eternally and remind me that I am partly to blame. That I shouldn't have cut Debbie out of this part of my life so drastically. Then she wouldn't have come to this stupid party out of curiosity and run into Matt. Before I even think about it, my instinct is to grab my phone. As I check my text messages, my thumb comes to rest over a name.

I haven't seen Iris in five fucking days, ever since I left her house after cooking like an asshole with her sister. She needed time to catch up on lost moments with her little sister. So I gave her all the space she needed to enjoy Agnes as much as possible.

I restrained myself from harassing her with texts and calls a good ten times. Hell, I needed to feel her body against mine. I wanted her close to me. To feel her, to hold her, to take her for hours. Like a fucking addict.

An obsession.

Is that what she is to me? Is that why she gets to me so much? Or is she the salvation I've been looking for all along?

I let out a curse, laughing inwardly at myself. I'm bullshitting. Just. Bullshit. Bullshit. Still, I can't seem to lock my phone. Acting without thinking, I quickly tap on the screen.

Iris

> I miss you.

I instantly regret sending that text. Iris is so surprising, so elusive, that she might laugh at me or piss me off. Or not even respond. Did she miss me? Part of me wants her to.

I don't want to be the only one completely addicted, completely affected. I can't get her out of my head. A second later, my phone vibrates.

Tucker

> You miss me, or are you missing a certain part of me…?

And just like that, I imagine her saying these words to me, with a defiant look on her face. Just like that, she pushes my past away. My nightmare slips away from me as I focus on her damn text, my heart lighter. I happily play along with her, eager to think of something other than my little sister's damaged body.

Iris

> A certain part of your body, in fact.

> My toes?

I burst out laughing in the middle of my room like an idiot.

Tucker

> Something else, babe.

I imagine her behind her screen, rolling her eyes at my answer. Knowing that I piss her off as much as I excite her makes me feel like a fucking king. I haven't been able to be reasonable when it comes to her for a long time. She opened up to me, and I swore to her that I would protect her. I wasn't lying. She woke up a part of me that had been asleep for a long time.

Life has been a bitch with her. Iris has an even more twisted past than mine, but she's a fighter.

And I think that…somewhere…her strength calls out to mine.

We're both damaged. Our souls are half destroyed. But isn't that what brings them together?

Iris
My nose? :)

I don't have time to answer her when she sends me another message.

Iris
I'd love to talk anatomy with you,
but I'm going to bed.
We're going back to school tomorrow.
Good night.

And that simple text puts a stupid smile on my face.

I've barely entered the lobby of Building A when Sarah stops me, her lower lip caught between her teeth. She undresses me with her eyes, lingering on my tight-fitting T-shirt. She is shorter than me, like most people, and I have to bend down to look her in the eye.

"Are you okay?" she asks me in a small voice. "You don't look like you slept well."

I glance at the black pleated skirt that clings to her legs and the sleeveless shirt, half open to reveal her breasts. Distant memories of me thrusting into her come back to me. She thinks she can get her hands on me again, but the only girl I want like crazy is sitting in the lecture hall.

"I'm fine," I mumble, trying to get around her.

I can't be cruel to her. Sarah is first and foremost a friend. She's part of my group, and she's loyal to me. But that's it. I will never lay a hand on her again, and she has to understand that.

Which doesn't seem to be the case, as her perfectly manicured hand grabs my forearm to hold me back. She raises her head to me, her long brown hair shining under the artificial light of the hall. Her eyes almost beg me to fuck her right there.

"I'd like to meet up after school. Maybe we could—"

"I already told you, Sarah, there's fucking nothing between us."

"I...I know, Tucker," she murmurs, falsely submissive, flickering her eyes. "But I miss you."

I feel like she just slapped me. I wrote those words to Iris last night, and they meant something else entirely. I don't have time to push her away when the door opens beside us. A vanilla scent fills my nostrils, and I know exactly who has just entered the hall. I turn slowly, my eyes roaming over the small figure that appears before me.

Iris takes a step and then freezes as she discovers me there with Sarah and analyzes our position. She stares at Sarah's hand on my arm with a curious, then angry look.

I don't know why I don't move as I continue to watch her. I want to make her react, I think.

She takes a step in our direction, unsure.

Come on, baby. Come dig your nails into me, come claim me, damn it.

The thought of it makes me hard as a rock. I need her. I want her. She drives me crazy, and I want her to get her claws out for me.

But most of all, I want to hold her as tight as I can. So that all the broken parts in her can finally come back together.

Sarah presses her chest against my arm, trying to bring my attention back to her. It fails.

Iris takes another step in my direction. We agreed to have a purely sexual relationship, and we both know that if she comes to mark her territory, if she openly shows me her jealousy, it will prove that things are much deeper than that. That feelings have entered the equation.

Iris reaches, and my breathing quickens.

"What do you want?" spits Sarah as she joins us.

Iris doesn't answer her, instead throwing herself at me. The students around us look on in amazement. I push Sarah's arm away and catch my redhead on the fly as she twists her fingers in my hair, knocking off my cap in the way.

I press her little body against mine, and her moan is lost between my lips. She bites my lower lip, a true conqueror. When her tongue mixes with mine, she reinforces the pressure of her hand on my neck and clings a little more to me. My erection is pinned between our bodies, trapped against her belly. And from the way she slowly undulates her hips, she seems to like it.

When she moves her head away a few seconds later, her lips are red and swollen. Her hazel eyes shine with satisfaction.

This is not a little lamb I have in front of me, but a she-wolf ready to bite at the slightest attack.

She pulls away from me with a small smile and turns to Sarah. "Don't go near him anymore."

Then she moves away towards the lecture hall without a backward glance, rolling her hips deliciously.

44. THE STORM

IRIS

I quickly climb the steps of the lecture hall and reach my usual place, in the center. What the hell did I do?

I close my eyes hard, cursing myself.

A part of me pulls me to the past, stopping me in my tracks, and an image imposes itself on my mind. And that image is Rafael, trapped under the car, taking his last breath and whispering that he loves me. Am I betraying him…?

NO! My conscience brings me back to the present moment and makes me come to my senses. I have had feelings for Rafael, he has been my first in everything, in every way. Yet I am not betraying him.

I think I am…just living. For the first time in a long time, I feel alive.

As if the breath of fresh air Tucker is blowing into my life is something I've been waiting for. As if this tall, dark-haired, different color eyes man was the push I needed to get my life back on track.

Someone drops down next to me, and I don't have to look up to know that it's Tucker. His scent invades my nostrils, strong and spicy. I feel his warmth brush against my skin. Damn it, I'm totally affected. Two of his fingers gently tug at one of my red hair strands to get me to react. I grumble and give his hand a little tap.

A deep laugh comes to me. The bastard.

"Retract your claws, angel, the threat is gone," he whispers against my ear.

I want to kiss him again, but I want even more to make him swallow his winning look.

"What threat?" I reply to tease him as I pick up my bag.

I take out my computer, but he doesn't move an inch, his so particular look attentive to the least of my gestures.

"Sarah," he says softly, teasing in his voice.

I ignore him and stare at the black screen in front of me, trying not to lose my temper.

"You kissed me in front of everyone," Tucker continues.

The masculine pride in him pleases me as much as it baffles me. I just took it to the next level when we were supposed to be just fuck buddies…And that seems to delight him?

"Yeah, I did that," I answer, trying not to lose face.

He leans toward me, his beard rubbing against my neck.

"You acted like a jealous girlfriend, Iris."

Girlfriend. Girlfriend. Is that what I am?

The next minute will be decisive. We haven't used those words with each other. Yet they are on my lips. I don't want to think about the future, but I don't want to push it away either. I turn to Tucker, looking for answers in his eyes. And what I find there reassures me. He wants me to admit my jealousy, to take the first step this time, me being so closed off.

This first step that will totally change the course of things.

I inhale deeply and whisper, "Yeah, I acted like a jealous girlfriend."

Surprise paints itself on his features before disappearing. I said it. Is he going to push me off, remind me that our relationship is only sexual, or is he going to follow me in this crazy adventure?

"I like it," he murmurs, confirming my second hypothesis. "But I think it's my turn, right?"

The little smirk on his face doesn't tell me anything.

"What do you mean, it's your turn?"

His muscles tense a little more, and he shrugs a shoulder. "You know, to act like a boyfriend too."

How can things get so much faster in such a short time? I feel like I have no control, like all my defenses are melting away. But I can't help it, this little voice is getting stronger and stronger inside me, and it orders me to let him do it without thinking about the consequences of our actions.

His lips are delicately placed on mine to never let them go. His tongue caresses mine in a sensual dance while his left hand firmly grasps the back of my neck. My breath hits his mouth as I try to catch my breath. Tucker doesn't let me rest, he presses himself to me a little more, his other hand squeezes my thigh, and I can only imagine the show we must be putting on for the other students.

"If you don't stop, I swear the next thing you'll be kissing is the door, Mr. Bomley."

I flinch as I recognize Professor Richards' voice. Tucker takes his time and licks his lower lip as he adjusts himself.

"I'm sorry, I just tripped," he replies with an innocent look and raises his hands in the air.

Our teacher raises both eyebrows, arms crossed.

"You tripped over your classmate's mouth?"

"Accidents happens so quickly…" Tucker sighs defeatedly.

I kick his ribs, glaring at him, but can't help but smile. Professor Richards purses her lips, no doubt wondering if she should really be fighting a battle against a student with raging hormones. She finally seems to give up the fight and turns to the dais to begin class.

"Be more careful next time," she finally says, "or I may send you out quite by…accident."

Tucker can't think of anything to say but still seems pleased with what has just happened between us. I continue to stare at his profile. Jealous girlfriend. Boyfriend. Did I just admit to Tucker that I felt more than sexual desire for him, and did he just do the same…?

Yes.

But what did I just get myself into?

Buck finishes pouring a draft beer, and I do the same on my end. It's Tuesday night, and yet High Peaks Bar is packed. I already miss Agnes, but if I'm to believe the texts I've received from Emma, she's constantly telling her about her vacation here.

I see movement to my left and hold back an expletive when I see that asshole Matt sitting at a table with his friends. The little smile he gives me makes me want to give him the finger, but I restrain myself and ignore him instead, not wanting to give him an ounce of importance.

As I grab a lemon wedge from the bin that's lying on the bar and slip it between my lips, I notice Dan pull himself up onto a stool right in front of me. Now there's a person I'd rather see here. If someone had told me a few weeks ago that I'd be happy to see a member of the Pack…

A tight-knit group, despite what some may think and what I myself thought, initially.

Dan seems as withdrawn as ever, running a hand over his shaved head with a blank stare. Since I've known him, he's been like this. It's as if an unhappiness was eating him up inside, destroying him little by little. This malaise is Debbie. I look at Matt, worried. If Debbie is in this state, it's partly because of that asshole, and if Dan sees him…let's just say I'm afraid that a brawl is coming.

A big one, in fact.

"Hi," I begin, walking over to Dan to get his attention.

He parts his lips, but no sound comes out. He smells of alcohol, making me realize he's already drunk a lot tonight. His eyes are glassy.

I feel a twinge of sadness because I'm sure that before Debbie's accident, he was a nice guy. But now he just seems…empty. A shell of flesh with no feelings other than sadness. The light inside him went out the day Debbie was taken from him.

"Would you like a glass of water?" I continue kindly.

I would like to help him, but how? I feel helpless and I hate it.

"A beer," he says through his teeth.

I stand still in front of him, unsure. He's already had quite a bit to drink. I don't want to watch him sink any further.

"Dan," I murmur, leaning towards him. "I've tried to escape with alcohol, too. It doesn't work."

He ignores the words coming out of my mouth.

"I want a beer, Iris…please," he finishes after a few seconds.

"Dan…"

After a minute of staring at each other, I finally pick up a small bottle and uncap it before handing it to him. I then grab a glass and fill it with water and put it next to him.

"If you're still thirsty."

He smiles at my gesture, but I know he won't touch it.

During my break, I decide to join him, my own beer in my

hand. Buck watches me from afar, wondering what the hell I'm doing. I sit down on a stool next to Dan and rest my elbows on the counter.

"Are you okay?"

He digs his heels in, and I can tell he doesn't want to confide in me.

"I thought you didn't drink alcohol?" he asks me.

"Yeah, I don't." It's only a beer. I can handle it. But I'll never touch hard liquor again in my life.

It's really dark tonight. He takes another sip and finally turns to me. "You and Tucker, huh?"

I raise my eyebrows, not knowing what to say.

"I knew you were going to sleep together, I've seen you from the beginning. But there's more, isn't there?"

I don't know why we're talking about Tucker and me. What am I supposed to say right now? We gave each other dating status the night before.

"Yeah. We're together." Saying it out loud makes me feel funny, but it's not unpleasant, actually.

"I'm happy for Tucker," Dan says, swallowing hard. "He's got you. And you've got him."

I understand what he's saying, but more importantly, I understand what he's not saying: he doesn't have anyone.

"I'm sorry," I whisper in his direction. "I'm sure Debbie will get better eventually."

He suddenly squints. Shit, maybe that wasn't the right thing to say. I've never been good at reassuring people.

"Do you want me to call Tucker?" I say to change the subject, hoping to calm him down.

"Call Tucker," he laughs softly, staring down at his beer. "Always him, right? But Tucker doesn't understand a damn thing."

"Okay…" I start slowly, "I think you've had a little too much to drink, man."

Dan feels anger, a lot of anger. And he wants to take it out on someone tonight. But it won't be on me. I need to get him out of the place safely, let him calm down and sober up slowly. I get up from my stool, looking for my phone. I've barely finished sending my text to the tall, dark-haired man who haunts my thoughts when Dan's voice hits me.

"It's his fucking fault too."

His fault too? Is he talking about Tucker? The fact that Tucker feels partly responsible for everything that happened to Debbie? Does Dan also feel that his best friend is partly to blame?

I turn around and realize that he's really talking about a completely different person. And that other person is none other than Matt, who is walking towards us with a big smile on his face. He winks at Dan.

Damn, I'm not liking this.

I approach Dan again, but he is already getting up.

"Okay, man, let's calm down," I exclaim loudly, looking around for Buck.

But he's taking an order a little further away, and his back is turned. Damn it. Matt approaches and stands in front of Dan with a nasty look on his face, but he addresses me.

"You fuck Tucker, and now Dan. Can I be next?" says Matt.

"Shut up," I spit. "Stop talking shit."

I don't want to play his game, that's what he wants. I hold back with all my being. He just doesn't need me to get him into more trouble.

I keep one eye on Dan. He takes one last sip, a strange smile plastered on his face.

"So, Dan, is her pussy is as good as Debbie's?" continues Matt.

Dan doesn't react, because he doesn't need to. A hand suddenly grabs the beer bottle he's been holding. I hardly have time to understand that this hand belongs to Tucker before he's already moving. His eyes are cloudy, almost crazy, as he brings the bottle down on Matt's face.

"What did you say, motherfucker?"

This is it, the storm is here. And there's nothing we can do but try to get away from it.

45. CALM HIM DOWN

IRIS

"Tucker!" I yell as I rush out.

He and Matt have just walked out, quickly followed by Dan. Well, more precisely, Tucker has pulled Matt out of the bar by his throat. Buck is already grabbing his cell phone. I don't have time to ask him not to call the cops before I rush outside.

I burst out into the parking lot and scan the area, trying to find them. Dan waits, arms crossed. He watches Tucker hit Matt without moving a finger. Why would he do that after what Matt did to Debbie?

But we have to stop them before something more serious happens. The streetlights allow me to make out what's going on. I run over to Tucker and yell his name again.

"Let him go," I yell.

He doesn't listen to me and slams Matt against the hood of a car. The latter throws his fist at Tucker's jaw with a grunt, then tries to free himself from his hold. But it doesn't work. My boyfriend is pretty pissed off, as if all the hatred he's been feeling for weeks is coming out in waves.

He's going to kill him.

"Dan!" I shout, shaking his arm. "Stop him! Do something, damn it!"

He runs a hand over his shaved head and turns to me. "The only thing I care about right now is Tucker finishing him."

I take a deep breath and close my eyes for a second. I can't count on him, he hates Matt as much as Tucker. But I can't wait with my arms crossed or there will be a murder. I walk over to Tucker, who is still holding Matt against the hood. He clutches his throat until he can't breathe. I try to remember my lessons, but everything is a blur in my head. When someone is so angry that they've gone crazy, you don't want to go near them.

I ignore this wisdom and raise my hand to Tucker.

"Listen to me, Tucker. You have to let him go. The cops are coming, and they're going to take you away. Let him go," I repeat.

But he seems to be completely unaffected by what I'm saying. He mumbles curses, tightening his grip on Matt's throat. His different color eyes are almost black now. I have to find something else, another way to reach him and make him come back to me.

With trembling fingers, I touch his biceps to show him I'm there.

This scene reminds me of another one in which I was trying to calm Rafael down, months ago. I had failed miserably, and he had violently pushed me away.

"Tucker," I call him softly. "Tucker!"

He turns his head towards me, his eyes squinting, his jaw contracted. He continues to hold Matt, who is trying in vain to free himself.

"Look at me," I order him. "The cops are coming, do you hear me?"

His breath comes out painfully from his chest, he looks like he's on the verge of exploding. I put my other hand on his shoulder. My skin is icy, his is hot, but that doesn't stop me.

"I don't want them to take you," I say, trying to convince him. "Don't waste your life on some worthless prick. You'll find another way to destroy this little shit. But not like this, okay?"

I stay silent for a second, then hesitantly add, "You're mine, and I'm not going to let you do anything stupid."

I insist on these words, and it seems to work. His nostrils quiver gently. He doesn't say anything but keeps his full attention on me. Matt is literally choking. His hands claw at Tucker's forearms.

"He's not worth it," I whisper to Tucker as I press myself against him. "You're worth it. Debbie is worth it."

I run my hand down his arm until I reach the hand that holds Matt. His fingers tighten a little more.

"You, you're worth it," he whispers.

I don't even have time to realize what he's just said when he suddenly lets go of Matt. Matt collapses to the ground, trying to catch his breath. I see the flashing lights a thousand feet away.

The cops are coming.

Tucker stares at Matt again, his fists clenched, as if he's hesitating to finish the job. I stand in front of Matt and lift my chin to look my tall, dark-haired self straight in the eye.

"Please," I beg him. "They're coming, go away."

He frowns, opens his mouth but no words come out. My eyes also beg him. After a second, and as a screech of tires sounds in the distance, he takes a deep breath and backs up a few steps before turning and heading back to his car, Dan following close behind.

A sigh of relief escapes my lips. That was a close call. Matt tries to get up but collapses to the ground again.

"Oh, no, you don't," I mumble, pushing him away.

Buck calls from the entrance of the bar, "Are you all right? I didn't have time to blink before everything went to hell. What happened?"

So he hardly saw anything. I take another look at the idiot on the ground. I'm not going to rat out Tucker.

"Matt tried to assault me," I lie. "He tried to come after me, and Tucker came to help me."

Matt looks at me, glaring. But I see something else in his eyes. He's scared.

And he'll shut the fuck up.

Worn out, exhausted, beat up—whatever you say—I arrive home an hour later. I almost want to rest my forehead on my steering wheel and close my eyes for just five minutes. But I'll fall asleep and wake up tomorrow morning with a stiff neck. I yawn until my jaw drops, turn off the ignition, and get out of my old car, eager to get to bed.

Two half-drunk college girls come out of the building as I enter, and I almost bump into one of them. Then I notice that there is a guy between them. One of the chicks has her thighs wrapped around the hips of the guy I recognize right away.

"Sanchez?"

He takes his mouth off the little blonde and turns his head towards me. The girl plunges her hands into his long black hair to try to kiss him again.

"Iris?" he answers me simply.

"What are you doing here? In my residence?"

For an answer, he glances at the two girls who accompany him, a coy smile stuck to his face. "Oh. OK. No need for details. Have a nice evening."

I quickly pass by them, ignoring the little laugh that comes out of his mouth. Sanchez has always seemed rather solitary and withdrawn to me since I met him, not the type to screw several girls at once. But appearances are sometimes deceiving, I know something about that. I think back to my little sister's words the other day. She had just met Sanchez and was already telling me that she didn't like him. Was it just a matter of appearances?

As I walk down the dimly lit hallway of my floor, my heart misses a beat. There's someone outside my apartment.

"Tucker?" I gasp when I finally make out the man.

He is sitting in front of the door, his head back against the wood, his eyes closed. At the sound of my voice, his eyelids open and he straightens up.

"What are you doing here?"

He shrugs his shoulders and looks at his hands. His knuckles are bruised. But something else catches my eye. He looks tired, weary, almost lost.

I kneel before him, attentive. I don't like to see him like this. He doesn't look like himself. He is usually so strong. I want to shake him, to help him get better.

"I don't know," he answers after a minute, his voice broken. "I needed to see you."

We look at each other for a long time, straight in the eyes, without moving. He tries to give me a message, but I can't understand what he really wants. I could tell him about the cops, tell him he's safe and that Matt won't say anything, but we want something else.

Finally, he stands up. My chest almost touches his, but he does nothing to pull me to him. It's as if he's afraid of my reaction and hesitates. So I take the step. I snuggle up to him, my nose pressed against his T-shirt. I inhale deeply his scent, and he does the same. I hear him take a long breath, his nostrils against my hair. His breath then hits my ear as his mouth slowly moves and he kisses my neck. Once, twice.

My arms tighten around his torso, my body perfectly molding his. I wanted to calm him down by doing this, but in reality, it calms me down too.

The heat from his body is slowly warming me up. I just need to snuggle up to him a little more. I close my eyes, letting myself go for a second, not fighting this bond that is starting to form between us.

Why fight the inevitable?

His mouth joins mine, and his tongue begins to caress me. His teeth nibble my lower lip. I let him take possession of me and of a part of my soul. My fingers twist in his hair, and I press myself a little harder against him. I don't care about anything, about my neighbors, about the moans that only want to come out of my mouth.

Soon we reach my room, and I find myself lying across my mattress, Tucker on top of me. He kisses my face then sucks on the tender skin of my neck, drawing a moan from me. I could let him give me pleasure, but this time I want him to succumb before I do. I can still feel the storm raging inside him, and I don't want to fight it. I want to dance with the storm that runs through him.

So I push him on his back, and he lets go. He pulls his shirt as I reach the object of my lust, the waistband of his pants. His hand immobilizes my impatient fingers.

"What are you doing, babe?"

I pass my tongue over my lips without answering him and return to what I was doing. He loosens his grip, attentive to my every move. When I reach his boxers and discover the prominent erection that was hidden behind the fabric, my breath stops. I need to feel his taste on my tongue. This sudden urge guides my movements. My tongue slowly titillates the tip of his cock, and a violent swear comes out of his mouth as Tucker twists his fingers through my hair. Realizing the brutality of his words, he releases his grip and gently strokes the back of my head.

"You decided to drive me crazy?" he asks me, short of breath.

I respond by parting my lips. My hot breath falls on his skin. When my mouth closes around his sex and his taste really invades my palate, I moan while rubbing my thighs against each other. The pleasure this act gives me almost shocks me. I'm not an expert on oral sex, and I didn't know that seeing Tucker take pleasure would feel so good.

"Yes, babe. Take me harder."

His tone is very different than usual. His semi-supplication draws a smile from me but I obey. I dig my cheeks a little deeper and swallow him more deeply, wanting to give him as much pleasure as I received when his mouth was between my thighs.

Half an hour later, I am lying on him, flat on my stomach, naked. My breasts are pressed against his chest and his thumb traces arabesques on the tender skin of my back. The difference in temperature between my room and our two bodies makes me shiver, but his warmth helps me not to feel cold.

A pleasant silence fills the room, interspersed only with the sound of the movie playing on the TV across from us.

"You want to talk to God? Let's go see Him together. I've got nothing better to do," I whisper along with one of the characters.

"Do you know the movie by heart?" Tucker asks me with a chuckle.

His voice makes his chest vibrate under my cheek, and I rub my nose against the few black hairs that dot his skin. "*Indiana Jones* was my dad's favorite movie. He could watch it five times in a row without getting tired of it, much to my mother's dismay."

Tucker's arms tighten around me as if he guesses that emotion is washing over me at the memory of my parents. He places a kiss on the top of my head. I feel good pressed against him, in a bubble that separates me from the world and all the shit that inhabits it. It's just Tucker and me.

A question pops into my head, and my mouth opens without me thinking. "Have you ever been in love?"

His thumb comes to rest on my back. "No. And you?"

I take a few seconds to answer. I don't know how to explain things but I have to answer him in turn. "I have…" I whisper softly against his skin.

His thumb starts moving over my body again, silently helping me to relax. "It was with this Rafael guy?"

I close my eyes for a moment. "Yeah."

"Why did you guys break up?" Tucker braces himself beneath me, attentive to my every word.

"We were in a car accident, a month after my parents died. I was rescued, but he didn't make it."

"Babe," Tucker whispers, pressing me a little closer to him.

We don't talk anymore. He leaves me in my thoughts, but I feel his breath on the top of my head reminding me that I am not alone.

I have been alone for a long time. But I am not alone anymore.

The next day at noon, I drop into a chair in the cafeteria, devouring the tray of fries I managed to grab. It's amazing how fast the trays go in front of hungry little students.

As I add salt—there is never enough—a hand enters my field of vision and tries to steal a fry. I smack the unknown hand.

TJ drops onto the chair in front of me, hastily withdrawing his fingers.

"Ouch," he squeaks, looking hurt. "Violation of my person! Help me, please!"

I stare at Tucker's cousin as I swallow my mouthful. "If you put your hand back in my field of vision, it'll be a homicide."

He laughs and rolls his eyes. "I'll have you know that you and I are in the same gang," he teases me, crossing his arms. "Come on, give me a little smile and tell me how much you missed me."

I really try not to smile, but in front of his happy face, I fail miserably. His scoundrel look gets a little stronger.

Noticing he's almost drooling over my fries, I roll my eyes and hand him one. "Here, choke on it."

A second later, he has swallowed it. "Have I ever told you that you are the best friend in the world?"

Taking it back wouldn't do any good, again. TJ is too jovial a person for me to argue with him at this hour. However, there are big dark circles under his eyes, and he really doesn't look his best. I hope it has nothing to do with his mother.

I open my mouth to ask him, but Sanchez appears near us, a tray of French fries in the hands.

"How did you get them?" exclaims TJ. "The lady who was serving told me that there was nothing left."

"I played with my charms," blows Sanchez, winking at us. He sits down close to TJ and gives him his tray. "Since I find you cute, you can take some, my dear."

TJ nudges him but takes some. There's only one seat left, next to me. I'm pretty sure another member is going to be added, but I don't mind the idea. Watching Sanchez and TJ bicker, I almost feel like I belong in this group that was unknown to me a short time ago.

"Did your night go well?" I ask Sanchez, remembering the girls he was with last night.

He nods, a cheeky look on his face. "*Muy bien,*" he replies in Spanish, his pierced eyebrow shining in the light of the room.

TJ receives a text on his cell phone, which makes him frown. Sanchez must also notice his expression because he asks, "What about your dad? And your mom?"

TJ seems to hesitate at first. He puts his two hands on the table, almost embarrassed. But it is with some relief that he answers us, "My mother is going to divorce that bastard."

And I share his relief. His mother will finally be able to free herself from the grip of her monstrous husband! I can't help but compare their relationship with that of my parents, and my heart sinks. They loved each other so much. My father would never lay a hand on my mother and vice versa. They loved and respected each other.

Not hesitating for a second, I grab TJ's hand. "That's great news," I whispered with a small smile. "She's going to be fine, it's going to get better."

He raises his face to me, his eyes shining. "Thanks, Iris."

One second, I have my hand on his. The next second, two strong arms wrap around my waist and I'm in Tucker's lap.

"Why are you touching my girl?" he mumbles, staring at TJ.

"I'm not a rag doll you can move around as you please," I grumble.

He smiles softly before pressing his mouth against mine with a loud snap.

"Your girl, huh," laughs TJ. "I don't want to say this, but it looks like 'your girl' is going to rip your balls off, man."

"I think my balls are too precious," Tucker laughs and kisses the top of my skull, as if his instincts told him to do so. He rests his hand on my lower abdomen, and I press my back against his chest. Why am I acting so comfortable with him?

I raise my head and feel a look on both of us. Sanchez stares at us. "I thought you were just messing around?" he says, raising an eyebrow and crossing his arms.

I remember telling him that the other day. But in the meantime, a few things have happened. I've decided not to be afraid and to let the moment guide me. I don't quite understand his frown and am about to answer him, but Tucker beats me to it. "We're together now."

We're together now. We're together, damn it. Hearing him say that word makes me feel weird. I'm not used to it.

"I see," Sanchez continues. "It's…cool."

He smiles at us kindly. But his eyes are not smiling. I feel like I'm missing something. I remember how he acted the other day when my sister told him almost the same thing about Tucker and me. One conclusion is coming to me.

Would Sanchez be…jealous?

46. TRUST

IRIS

Thirty minutes after my psychology class, I leave the lecture hall. The sun is low in the sky, signaling the end of the day.

I must admit that I couldn't follow my professor's explanations because I didn't really study this weekend. Let's just say I was busy with something else. Tucker crashed at my apartment, and I think he tried to break the record for the most orgasms I could have in less than two days. I ended up as exhausted as I was sated, with the image of his satisfied smile burned into my mind. He was damn proud of himself.

I have to admit that I'm feeling better. When I agreed that we were officially together, I was afraid that it would become awkward between us. I hadn't dated anyone since Rafael. But Tucker is exactly the same as he was before, except that now he allows himself affectionate gestures in public. When we went out to eat on Sunday, he held my hand. He didn't say anything, smile, or anything. His fingers just wrapped around mine. And strangely enough, I let him. I even enjoyed it.

Like a real couple, damn it.

My cell phone vibrates at the same moment. I look down to find a message from Tucker.

Ticker

Tonight. You, me, and my dick.

I almost burst out laughing. Told you nothing has changed between us. He's still as addicted to my ass and as vulgar. Does that bother me? Not at all.

I stop in the middle of the road leading to the parking lot. About ten yards away, Tucker is leaning against my car, arms crossed. His different color eyes are hidden behind a pair of dark sunglasses, but I know he's watching me. I know he's eating me up with his eyes because I'm doing the same to him. I put my phone away.

His legs are molded by his jeans. He's wearing a gray polo shirt that hugs his biceps deliciously. I want to run my hand through his brown locks and bite his lip furiously.

"If you ever scratch my car by putting your butt against it, I'll cut your balls off," I warn him with a little smile as I get to his side.

He raises his eyebrows, and I can almost feel his gaze intensify behind the smoked glass of his glasses.

"But you like my ass."

Not wrong.

Two students pass by us, laughing at his words.

"But I like my car even more," I say innocently.

A low sound comes out of his mouth, between grunting and laughing. Not very elegant but very sexy, I must say. That's when I notice the paper bag on the hood next to him. Seeing the fast-food logo, I can feel my stomach rumbling. I'm starving.

"What's this for?" I ask, pointing to the bag with my chin.

"Well," Tucker begins, straightening up, "it's to properly celebrate our relationship."

I let out a laugh. "You're thanking me for going out with you by offering me a burger?"

"The best burger you've ever had," Tucker replies, standing in front of me.

He takes off his sunglasses and looks into my eyes. I lift my head and stare at his mouth.

"Would you like me to buy you flowers?" he teases, letting me know that he's not the type to do that.

I'm glad of it. I'm not into flowers and chocolates.

"I already told you, I don't like flowers. But I hope you got extra cheese with the fries because if not, I'm not letting you sit on my couch."

He smiles softly as he grabs my chin between his thumb and forefinger. "Of course, I did. But I'm not going to sit on your couch, and neither are you."

He places his mouth on mine for a second, his warm breath hitting my wet lips. He kisses me again and I feel myself melting at his touch.

"Why is that?" I sigh, pressing myself against his chest.

"Because we're not going to your place."

I raise my eyes to him in surprise. "Where are we going?"

His right hand goes down my back until it stops on the top of my butt. He presses his mouth to my ear and whispers, "Let's go to my place."

At first, I think I heard him wrong. I know Tucker doesn't want anyone in his house. "We're going to the chapel, right? Are all the others waiting for us?"

He cuts me off again by pressing his mouth against mine and nibbles my bottom lip before shaking his head. "No, babe. We're not going into the chapel. There's no one waiting for us. We're going to my house."

So, he really wants to take me to his mansion, where his mother and sister are? He wants to invite me, *me*, when he refuses to let anyone go there, even TJ?

"You want me to come to your place?" I repeat stupidly.

He nods, uncertain. As if, deep down, he's afraid. I understand that he is apprehensive, and I feel privileged that, despite everything, he chooses to open his doors to me.

Because Tucker trusts me, I can see it in his eyes. He knows I won't judge him.

He steps away from me, slaps my butt, and joins my crate.

"Come on, move your little ass."

"Hey," I mutter, just to argue.

But I can't help but smile. I'll go to his place. I know that after tonight, our relationship will never be the same. It's really getting serious.

And for the first time in a long time, I'm not afraid of the future.

47. MEETING

IRIS

Tucker's pickup drives up the driveway of the huge family garden as my eyes wander in contemplation of the exterior. I'm pretty sure there are more shrubs here than people in the city of Denver!

Tucker squeezes my knee with his right hand, bringing my attention back to him. "Close your mouth, babe, you'll swallow flies. And look at what's really worth looking at."

I roll my eyes. I don't think we've been using that expression since the last century, but he's got a pretty good face, so I can hold my tongue.

"And what's really worth looking at?" I ask anyway in a mocking voice.

He turns off the engine when he pulls up in front of the big mansion and smiles gently as he leans towards me. "Me."

He stares at his cock hidden in his jeans, a masculine pride in his eyes.

"How do you expect me to look at it if I need a magnifying glass to do it, babe?"

I get out of the car, hearing him mumbling a curse. Another laugh escapes my mouth. I barely have time to think when I find myself pressed against the door, his face inches from mine. His breath hits my lips, but again, neither he nor I act. Building up desire when you want to jump on each other, fuck, that's one thing I'm starting to enjoy.

"I don't like what you just said," he grumbles like a kid.

I tilt my head to the side. Touching a man's ego is the worst thing you can do, but also the most delicious. Why deprive yourself of it?

"But you, I like you," he continues, his face a little closer to mine.

He places his lips on mine for a second before pulling back, releasing me from his grip. I ignore the panicked beating of my heart and lick my lips as I watch him grab the fast-food bag.

"Wow, that was almost too romantic," I murmur.

"I saw a guy say that once in a movie. Apparently chicks love that kind of line, did it work?"

I shrug, staring at the bag hungrily. "Some girls just love romantic words. Personally…offer me food every day, and I'll fall in love."

I laugh softly at my last words, but he doesn't follow me. I repeat what I just said in my head, finally understanding. We stare at each other for a second, not knowing what to say. Falling in love. Love. Isn't it too early to be talking about such bullshit? Of course it is. Probably…I don't know.

I've been in love before, and my heart broke when Rafael died in that car. Will I be able to love again? To put all those thousands of pieces back together and make them one?

Tucker keeps his eyes locked on me, as if he too is asking this question, but from a different angle. I scratch my throat, embarrassed. He snaps out of his thoughts. "Come on, follow me before you eat me because I didn't feed you."

I stare at his molded butt in his jeans as he climbs the few stone steps to the huge dark wooden door.

Biting into these two beautiful apples wouldn't be a bad idea…

I shake my head, trying to forget all the dirty thoughts that come to me.

My eyes fall on the large fountain and the statue in the center of it in front of the mansion. My discovery of Tucker's group and his pack seems so far away, today. A lot has happened since then.

"Are you coming, or are you going to keep looking at the garden? If you want, I have shears to trim the bushes near the path," Tucker yells from the doorway with a mocking smile.

I slowly move closer, looking angelic. "How about I cut the little thing hanging between your legs first?"

A growl comes from his mouth, making me burst out laughing.

"Twice you've referred to my cock in negative terms, I think you need me to refresh your memory."

I can't think of anything to say, remembering the last time he was on top of me, his cock deep in me.

Okay, "little" is not an appropriate adjective. But pissing him off is so much fun that I can't help myself. He smiles when I don't retort and opens the door, shifting to let me through.

I've barely stepped into the huge entrance when a wave of stress washes over me. How is this going to happen? What if his mother has a mental breakdown? How am I supposed to react?

I don't have time to think because Tucker puts his hand on the small of my back to move me forward. I hear footsteps to the right and recognize Abraham, the man who works at the mansion. He stares at me for a moment, his mouth wide open and his eyebrows furrowed. He doesn't seem to like my coming.

Not at all.

"Mr. Bomley," he begins softly as he approaches Tucker. "I don't think that—"

"I'll take care of everything, Abraham, just relax."

The man doesn't seem to be relaxing, quite the opposite. His eyes seem to be filled with panic. The two men take a few steps away, but I can't help but listen in on their conversation.

"Where is my mother?"

"She is sleeping in her room."

A certain relief comes over me.

"Great, so there's no reason to stress, right?"

"Yes…but, sir…"

Tucker doesn't listen to the old man anymore. His hand catches mine, and he leads me towards the huge wooden and marble staircase.

"Tucker," I murmur, pulling my hand away, "he's calling you."

He sighs and stops in the middle of the stairs.

"Would you like me to prepare something…decent, for your meal?"

Abraham points to the bag of fast food with a disgusted pout.

"What could be better than burgers with sauce and fries with cheese?" I exclaim, and Tucker explodes with laughter.

"We have everything we need, Abraham. Thank you."

Tucker backs away, staring at the paper bag with a dark look. My stomach rumbles loudly.

"Feed me, man," I mumble to Tucker.

Half an hour later, I'm lying on my back at the end of Tucker's bed, my head hanging off. I think I've eaten so many fries that I'm probably sweating grease and have gained at least six pounds.

Tucker is leaning against the headboard, staring at me without a word. I look around the room, trying to imagine him as a child here. It's unfortunate to say but this room feels empty, as if it holds no memories.

The sheets are black, the curtains too. Fortunately, the walls and moldings are light to offset this. There are no paintings hanging on the walls. The room is perfectly tidy, contrary to what I thought.

Finally, my eyes land on a desk that seems to be left abandoned in a corner. I straighten up when I see two small photo frames on it. I glance at the tall, dark-haired man, but he doesn't move, continuing to stare at me like a predator would stare at its prey. I walk towards the pictures, and a burst of laughter comes out of my mouth when I see the first picture of him.

"Damn, your cheeks are so round, I want to bite them."

My eyes then land on the second shot where there are four people, including Tucker and his mother, whom I immediately recognize. A beautiful young girl stands between them, smiling with all her teeth. Exactly the same look as him. She is full of life…

Full of life.

I raise my index finger to the picture but hold back at the last moment. I hear Tucker's footsteps behind me. He stops beside me, silent. I swallow my saliva and let out a few words.

"She is beautiful…"

He nods but says nothing for a while. "Debbie has always been beautiful, since she was young," he finally answers me, emotion piercing his voice.

My eyes finally fall on the last person in the photo: a middle-aged man with a craggy face, reminding me of the man standing next to me.

"Your father?"

"Yeah."

I turn to him, not knowing if he'll talk to me or not.

"He…he died of a heart attack."

He's already explained the basics to, me but I don't know much more than that and I don't feel like interfering in what's not my business. I turn to the picture again, analyzing his mother's features. She didn't look sick then. "And your mother…she…erm…"

"She was fine at the time this picture was taken."

He sits on the edge of the bed, his jaw clenched. I know he's trying to hide his emotions, to pretend that everything is fine. But I know that he is enormously affected by his mother's troubles. And that's okay. Who wouldn't feel something in a situation like this?

I expect our conversation to end there, but Tucker continues after resting his elbows on his thighs, his hands pressed together, "But it quickly got out of hand. We're not sure where it came from. But the night my dad had his heart attack, I wasn't there, and neither were Abraham and Debbie. Only my mom was there. By the time the emergency services arrived, it was too late. They said that…if they had been called sooner, maybe we could have saved him. But I wasn't there, and my sister wasn't there, damn it. Only my mother was in the mansion. My dad was unconscious while she watched TV three feet away. In her own world, in her own fucking bubble, oblivious to the fact that her husband was having a stroke a few feet away. She didn't even realize it. By the time she realized what was happening, it was too late."

A lot of questions are running through my head, but I don't know what to say.

"Why not have her committed? That's what you're wondering, right? Well, we did. She went to a center. But she…she was fucking dying there. She wanted her children back. So she came back and got treatment at the mansion. They wouldn't let her leave. Then… Debbie had her…her accident. And things got even worse. It's bad, right? But that's the fucking reality."

I watch him, trying to read him, which is impossible because he's completely shutting down his emotions for me now. Anger, on the other hand, is leaking out of him through his clenching fists and the quick breath that comes out of his mouth. I don't think for a second and approach him while removing my top. He raises his head, his eyebrows furrowed.

"Iris…"

"We've talked enough."

He doesn't move for a moment as I remove my bra under his intense gaze. A chill runs through my entire body, but I don't chicken out. The appetite I see in his eyes gives me courage. Not holding back any longer, I push him back on the bed and position myself on him, astride his hips. He lets out a husky sound, takes off his T-shirt, and tries to pull me to him.

"Oh no," I murmur with a small smile. "Let me do it."

I grab his hand and place it on the mattress, along his body. His eyes on mine, he seems frustrated but curious. I grab his other hand and place it on the other side, against his chest.

"You leave them there," I order him.

He smiles, obviously amused by the situation and by my role as dominant.

"I'm going to give you pleasure," I whisper in his ear as I lean into him. My nipples harden on his skin, making me want to rub myself against him, but I hold back.

"How am I supposed to enjoy myself if I can't caress you?" he mumbles.

His words hit me, but I try to ignore them and nibble on his lobe just before I run my tongue over it. His hands shake against me, but he doesn't move. I want to make him forget, at least for a few minutes, all the problems that rot his life. I straighten up, moving away from the warmth of his chest with regret. But I can thus admire it as I wish. The few dark hairs that dot his skin and the line that starts from his navel to disappear under his pants open my appetite a little more.

I tilt my hips slightly, feeling him harden under me. A muffled noise escapes from my mouth.

"Didn't you think it was little?" Tucker jokes, trying in vain to control himself.

Anything but little, but I hold back from answering him. His ego is big enough as it is. I move my hips again, undulating over him. His lips call to me. Then I don't resist. I lean toward him and gently lick the edges of his mouth, as if I'm lapping up some delicious liquid.

His right hand twists in my hair to immobilize me. I straighten up, displeased that he moved. However, his head ends up at my chest, and words die at the edge of my lips as his land on my right nipple and suck furiously. I hold my breath, forgetting my comment. A second before, his teeth were around my nipple, but I suddenly find myself pinned to the mattress, him on top of me. It's no longer time to play or tease.

His eyes are black. He spreads my thighs to make room between them, rubbing himself against me. Only our pants prevent our skins from coming into contact, but that doesn't stop him. When his mouth presses against mine, a beep sounds through the door. Completely in my bubble, I don't really pay attention to it.

"Holy shit."

Tucker jumps to his feet and rushes away from the bed, throwing the door open like a madman, still shirtless. I stare at the ceiling. What the hell just happened? Now that the door is wide open, the sound gets a little louder.

I grab my shirt and rush down the long hallway. Tucker is no longer in my line of sight, but I can hear the beeping still going on, a few rooms down. Only one door is open. I hesitate for a second but eventually move forward to the room. The beeping stops once I get there.

The first thing I see is Abraham looking at some kind of screen, puzzled.

"No problem on the screen, sir. The vitals haven't changed."

I turn my head, and finally, I see it. Or rather…I see them. Tucker is checking a bunch of wires connected to…to a young woman lost in the middle of a huge bed. He touches the side of her face, checking that everything is in place. After thirty seconds, he sighs, reassured.

"Everything is well connected," he continues, running a hand over her forehead.

Abraham doesn't seem in the least bit shocked by his naked torso. He simply straightens up, resuming his position as a butler.

"It's probably a problem from the machine. I'll call to have it fixed, sir. It's happened several times since yesterday."

Tucker looks at his little sister and nods silently. The butler leaves the room, but I am unable to do the same. I stare at this man leaning over this little half-broken woman, whose life is hanging by a thread. And my heart melts a little more, painfully.

Tucker turns his head in my direction and finally notices me, standing in his doorway. I swallow and take a step towards him, seeing that he doesn't reject me at all.

For a long time, we don't talk. I look at Debbie, trying to recognize the girl I saw earlier in the picture. Her features are delicate, as fine as those of a doll. A doll that looks broken, lost in the middle of these white sheets, her eyes closed.

Tucker is standing next to her, gazing protectively at her. It's like…like he's waiting for me to speak.

The truth is, I want to cry and hug him. Why the fuck did life try to hurt us so much?

Finally, I spot a men's baseball shirt hanging by the bed. A small, forced smile comes over my face.

"Really, huh?" I begin in a slightly shaky voice.

Tucker laughs softly. "My sister was…is my biggest fan. At least, before I got kicked off the team."

He crosses his arms over his bare chest. I know the memories are flooding back to him. I then approach the bed.

"She's beautiful, Tucker."

He nods, silent. When I'm only a step away, I see him tense up again. But I want him to understand that he wasn't wrong to trust me.

"Hi, Debbie," I whisper softly. "I'm Iris, the one who puts up with your unbearable brother."

A small sound comes out of his mouth, but his eyes shine with contentment. I watch his sister again, praying to the gods that she will wake up one day.

48. THE DARKNESS

IRIS

A few hours later, I'm singing the lyrics to Lady Gaga and Bradley Cooper's "Shallow" like crazy while Tucker mumbles that it's going to rain.

I should be home working. Instead, Yeleen called us earlier and finally convinced us to join the party at her house. It's a great day, and I want it to end on a high note. After the emotional time we had tonight, Tucker and I needed to clear our heads.

"'In the shallow, shalloooooooow,'" I continue while staring at the ceiling of the shower.

"Somebody get me a rope," my boyfriend mutters.

I straighten up and throw my fist into his shoulder while he pretends to scream. "That's good, die silently."

"Please, join me in silence," he begs me as I give him the finger while continuing to sing, not offended at all.

I know I have talent…it's just hidden. Very, very deeply.

We arrive at a house that's quite small if you compare it to the Bomley property but with a huge garden. From here, I can see that the party is happening at the back of the property. Tucker parks in front of the house, gets out, then puts his arm around my shoulders as I join him. The alcohol seems to be flowing. I can see a canopy of sorts on the east side of the house but no lights are on inside.

"This is the indoor pool," Tucker tells me as he walks towards the entrance of the house.

Oh, how lucky! An indoor pool. Who wouldn't dream of that? Well, the bathtubs are already very good…

The first person that we cross is Sanchez, who greets us from afar, a chick on each side. I return the wave out of politeness while

Tucker doesn't even seem to notice. He stares at Dan, sitting on a couch, which seems to have been put in the middle of the garden just for the occasion.

Something is happening between the two of them. Dan closes up a little more each day, as if broken inside. I exchange a glance with Tucker and understand that they need to talk alone. He kisses me quickly and then whispers against my lips, "I'll be back soon."

Understanding, I simply nod and watch him walk away towards his best friend.

"Well…" starts a sour voice behind me. "Look at that. You've managed to get your hooks into him."

I turn in Sarah's direction, giving her my best smile. "Don't waste your time trying to put me down, I really don't care."

She squints a little more and throws back a long brown lock of hair. When she crosses her arms, my eyes land on the sparkling watch she wears on her wrist.

"Pity. I pity you," she laughs falsely. "I have no idea what he sees in you."

I walk towards her, keeping a smile on my face even though I inwardly want to hit her. "I blow divinely well. What do you want, I have a tongue that does wonders."

Her mouth opens but no sound comes out. She doesn't have the time to answer me when steps are heard.

"My best friend!!"

I turn and see TJ, Yeleen on his heels. She practically jumps on me, stars in her eyes. "You guys are so fucking cute together. And I want you to make babies, lots and lots of babies, for fuck's sake."

I burst out laughing at her ridiculous remark but let her kiss me loudly on both cheeks. Sarah holds back from retorting and straightens her chin. TJ comes up to me, his mouth taut.

"I'm sooo happy," he begins, imitating a girl's voice. "Come and celebrate this soooo cute couple by kissing Uncle TJ."

I mutter a curse and push him away gently, smiling nevertheless. What a bunch of crazies…I think I really like them. I look around but see no sign of Trey, Yeleen's boyfriend. I know how hard it's been between them. "No Trey tonight?"

The beautiful woman shakes her head gently with a contrite smile, and I understand that something happened between them.

"Come on, I'll buy you a drink," I say, pulling her after me.

"You're at my place," she laughs with a sad look.

"It doesn't make any difference."

TUCKER

Dan was gone before I got to him. I find him on the other side of the house, dragging on his joint. He stares at his feet, uninterested in the party going on a few feet away. He's going off the rails again, just like the days after my little sister's accident.

I know how much he loved her and how much he still does. When Debbie had her accident, at first he wanted to kill Matt. Then he started walking away from me and doing drugs.

I walk up to him, looking for his eyes.

"Aren't you with your girl?" he asks me, handing me his joint.

I hesitate for a second but finally get it back and drag it. "I'll join her later."

He nods, taking the joint back and putting it in his mouth again.

"You okay, man?" I ask.

Stupid question, but damn, I feel like I'm losing my brother a little more every day, and it's killing me. Because he's my brother, he's the one who's been watching over me since I was a kid, and vice versa. We've lived a wild life together, and there's no way I'm letting him go down again.

He laughs softly. "Of course I'm okay. Don't worry about me."

I position myself in front of him. "Dan, fuck…"

He runs a hand over his shaved head. "Do you ever think about it?" he asks.

I swallow hard. "Every second of my fucking life."

He finally plants his dark eyes on mine.

"That night, it just keeps going round and round in my head," he murmurs, tapping his temple with his free hand. "Debbie wanted to go to that stupid party so bad. A fucking party like the one tonight, right?" He throws his joint to the floor and rubs his head again. His muscles tense the fabric of his T-shirt. "We fucked up, Tucker. You screwed up. Maybe if you'd let her come to that stupid party, she wouldn't have snuck in and ended up with Matt. She wouldn't have run away and she…she wouldn't have had that fucking accident."

His words send a chill down my spine. I blink several times, trying to register his words. "So what? Everyone was sleeping with everyone else. We used to fuck chicks in public. Is that why you wanted my sister to come, damn it?!"

He stares at the sky, shaking his head. "No but…you…I…we should have known she was still coming."

Neither he nor I speak. The gnawing pain is all around us. Does he think I don't blame myself every day? Damn, the regrets keep eating me up. I should have tried to find my sister instead of hitting Matt. I should have known she would come to this stupid party even if I told her not to.

I KNOW IT.

"I miss her, man," Dan mutters. He pulls a new joint from his pocket and lights it. "She's broken on her fucking bed, but so am I."

And he walks away into the night.

After ten minutes of thinking, I finally join the crowd, looking for a redhead in it. But I can't find Iris.

Dan is gone, and I didn't want to hunt him down now. He is in pain, but he doesn't understand the pain that is killing me a little more each day. Every day I see my little sister lying still. Sometimes I think that maybe she would be happier if she joined my father, and then the next second I insult myself for having such thoughts.

I find TJ, hitting on a little blonde.

"Hey, where's Iris?"

He turns to me, putting his cap back on. "Making out with some random guy over there."

My body suddenly tenses up.

TJ explodes with laughter in front of me, holding his stomach. "Relax, man. I am joking with you."

I have absolutely no desire to laugh. Faced with my seriousness, he points to the covered swimming pool, opposite the party.

"She closed herself in there with Yeleen and some beers."

I don't listen to TJ anymore and walk quickly towards the indoor pool. The glass door is ajar. I hear splashing. I enter discreetly and discover Iris and Yeleen sitting at the edge of the pool, their feet in the water.

Then I hear crying.

"Why do I always have to fall in love with dirty bastards?" mumbles Yeleen, finishing her beer. "You know what? He chose his studies over me, he's moving to another city. Well, good riddance. I hope he finds a girl who will break his heart."

I suddenly stop. Is she talking about Trey?

Iris finally sees me. She smiles gently at me, as if asking if everything is okay. I nod automatically. Yeleen notices me, too, and waves at me with a loud sniff, then gets to her feet.

"Hi, handsome. I'm totally tipsy but I want you to know that I love her, OK?" she tells me, pointing at Iris. "So if you hurt her, I'll break your knees."

Then she passes by me, not leaving me time to answer or ask her any questions.

Iris still stares at me intently, and I do the same. Why would I hurt her when she makes me feel so good? I rub my chest unconsciously, not really understanding how such a small thing can have so much influence on me.

"Hey, you," she says softly to me as she straightens up.

I watch her come to me and see her breasts bared again, her nipple in my mouth. It was just sex between us. Then we started dating. Why the fuck do I feel like there's so much more?

A sensation knots my throat. It's not unpleasant, but it's... weird. Something I've never felt before.

"Hi, babe," I say, welcoming her and pulling her to me. When her body is pressed against mine again, I feel complete. I needed this.

I'm totally nuts about this girl. Oh, yes, I am.

She puts her hand on the back of my neck to pull me to her and kisses me fiercely, her eyes shining. Her tongue wraps around mine just before she backs away, an impish look on her face.

"Come back here," I order her, but she shakes her head.

She pulls off her top in one smooth motion. "I'm hot. So hot. Aren't you?"

I analyze her body, which makes me desperately need her.

"Oh, yes, I'm damn hot. So come here."

She shakes her head again and then strips down to her underwear. She laughs and tosses her pants away. Then, after one last look at me, she jumps into the pool, swimming back to the center.

"Get out of the water," I snap, not feeling like playing at all. "I don't want someone to come in and see you like that."

"Yeleen closed the door on her way out. But you can totally leave…or…join me."

She splashes water in my direction, soaking her hair in the process. Her body jiggles under the water as she keeps herself afloat. Would I leave her alone here? Never in a million years.

I quickly undress to my boxers and dive into the water. I don't surface until I reach her. I try to grab her arm, but she pulls away at the last moment, a smirk on her face.

She drives me crazy. Completely crazy.

She swims quickly to try to escape me again, but I am faster than her. I grab her right foot and pull her toward me. A howl mixed with laughter comes out of her mouth as she finds herself pressed to me.

"Found you," I whisper.

The rest of my sentence dies on my lips as she wraps her legs around my hips, pressing her little pussy directly against my already stiff cock. I reach a spot in the pool where I have my footing, Iris still clinging to me.

A muffled grunt escapes from my throat, but already she's putting her lips against mine and we're having a hell of a time making out for long minutes. Her hips move against mine. I can't hold on anymore, I can't keep control.

My right hand twists around her tiny thong, and the fabric rips between my fingers. My mouth muffles her moan.

It's no longer possible to stop. I wouldn't be able to. I pull down my soaked boxers and position her perfectly around me. She gently pulls her face away, her index finger brushing against my short beard. As the tip of my cock penetrates her, she looks into mine. A thousand and one emotions run through us. I can't look away, not when she stares at me like that, and her flesh contracts around me to draw me deeper into her.

"I'm starting to be crazy about you, can you feel it? Completely crazy."

She doesn't say anything, but her eyes reflect my words back to me. She puts her mouth on mine. Once. Twice. And I twist my hand in her hair to keep it there. I move her up and down on my cock, her eyes still on mine.

"It feels so good," she whispers in my ear. "I don't want you to ever stop."

I don't answer because I tell myself that I will surely never have enough of her. When I feel her cumming around me, her nails digging into my neck, I pick up the pace.

"Come on, babe, make me cum," I whisper.

Fuck, she's going to kill me. A few seconds later, I cum inside her, letting the pleasure wash over me. Her mouth sprinkles kisses on my neck and I tighten it against me. Then I realize what we've forgotten.

"Condom…"

"I'm on the pill, and I'm clean."

"I'm clean too." And it's true. I've always worn condoms and I got tested during summer vacation.

I hear my cell phone ringing in the distance, but I ignore it. Whoever it is, fuck that person.

The next few minutes pass with the same feeling, a mixture of euphoria and something much, much more intense.

When the door swings open, I don't realize. I don't understand that everything is about to shatter.

I pull Iris against me and wrap my arms around her. "What the hell is going on?!"

It's just TJ. He walks towards me, looking grim. His lips are trembling and his eyes are filled with tears.

"Tucker…" he whispers, not caring about our nakedness.

"What's going on?" asks Iris, trying to cover her body as best she can.

I keep my eyes on my cousin. I get out of the water, pulling my soaked underwear up over my hips. I hear Iris doing the same behind my back.

TJ doesn't give her a single glance. He continues to look at me, his lips trembling. He swallows with difficulty. Deep down, I think I know. I know what he is going to tell me. I think a part of me feels it.

Just when you think you've found a piece of the light, the darkness is always there to cover it up.

"Tucker…it's Debbie. She…she…she's dead."

49. SAYING GOODBYE

IRIS

Saying goodbye to my parents was the hardest thing I've ever had to do. I stood there with my little sister pressed against me and watched them disappear underground, locked in wooden coffins.

I cried my eyes out and prayed to wake up. But it didn't work, they were gone. I collapsed in the middle of the cemetery, whispering their names.

Again. And again. And again.

They were gone. Agnes and I were left to take care of ourselves. I felt as if my heart had just broken. The following days were even worse. I didn't eat anything and cried every night in bed. Unfortunately, this was only the beginning of the nightmare. No light in my darkness, only sadness. And hatred for their killer.

Soon after, Rafael died. Then weeks passed, months passed, and the pain began to diminish. But the void that my parents' death left in my heart will never disappear. A part of me will always be broken, although the other part wants to live and try to get through it.

Today, it is Tucker's heart that is broken.

Four nights earlier, Debbie Bomley died.

It wasn't a machine malfunction, it was simply her life being extinguished…while Tucker was having fun with me at a damn party. TJ came up next to us, his eyes filled with tears, and he gave us the horrible news. At first, Tucker didn't move. He stood still, staring at something. Then I quickly realized he was staring into space. He was like…disconnected from reality.

And then he inhaled sharply and left, shoving TJ in the process. TJ shouted at him, but he ignored him.

By the time I came to my senses and ran after him into Yeleen's garden, Tucker had already disappeared in the middle of the party that was still in full swing. I went to join him at his house, but TJ held me back. He shook his head and asked me to leave him alone. That's what I did.

But finally, I gave in that night. I tried to call him, but it went straight to his voicemail. The next morning when I tried to go to his house, the huge gate to the property was closed. Tucker did not return my other calls. Over the next few days, I hoped to run into him in class, but both he and TJ were absent.

I need to support Tucker, to show him that I am here for him, even if I don't know how to do it, how to reach him. He opened up to me, but his little sister's death closed him off completely, and these four days have passed in radio silence.

This morning, my cell phone vibrated. I jumped on it, thinking Tucker was trying to reach me, but it was TJ. Simple phrases that broke me in turn. This morning Debbie will be buried, and TJ asked me to come over.

I lay my head against the steering wheel of my car, my heart beating wildly, my throat tight. The rain is starting to fall. The sky is gray, not a single ray of sunlight. I straighten up and look outside. I don't know what I'm doing here, but I know I have to be here. For Tucker. I hesitate for a long time, afraid to show up at the funeral when he didn't ask me to be there. But I want him to understand that I am there for him.

I get out and slam the car door behind me. I walk forward and take a huge path. The gravel crunches under my heels, but I keep my eyes ahead, trying not to look at the graves around me. Ever since I saw my parents disappear underground, followed by Rafael, I have hated cemeteries. Maybe it's a phobia.

Fine drops fall on my hair, but I ignore them. I follow the path, my hands sweaty. There is a small crowd of about twenty people at the end. Like me, they are all dressed in black. I quickly spot TJ. Yeleen and Sarah press against him, their eyes red. Abraham supports Tucker's mother as she stares at a large hole in the ground.

My eyes scan over the other people. A little ways away from the group, a tall, dark-haired man with lightning eyes stares at a white wooden coffin. Tucker. Black pants and shirt, hands in pockets, he stands straight, letting the rain fall on him. We are the only ones without an umbrella. It's as if the water flowing over him represents the tears that don't want to run down his cheeks, locked deep in his heart.

A man says a few words. I hear a muffled cry. It's Yeleen who can't hold back her tears anymore and collapses against TJ. The latter turns his face towards me and finally sees me. His eyes are red. He nods gently as if silently thanking me for being there. I nod my head back and then turn my attention back to Tucker. He doesn't move an inch. I want to approach him, but I don't dare. I'm afraid of his reaction.

The minutes pass silently. He doesn't show any expression, but from time to time, his jaw contracts and it looks like he is holding his breath. Finally, the most painful stage arrives. Debbie's coffin is gradually lowered into the ground.

Tucker steps forward, bends down to the upturned earth, takes a handful, straightens up, and drops it on the white wood. His features are hard, but his look does not lie anymore. He expresses all the pain that eats away at him and will continue to eat him up for a long time. His mother follows his lead and I can only wonder how will her madness evolve? She seems strangely lucid today.

Other people do the same. I stand back, not knowing if I should participate. Tucker hasn't noticed me yet, or maybe he has but he doesn't care. The ceremony is coming to an end. They all start to walk away. Tucker suddenly looks up, and his eyes meet mine. I try to give him my silent support, but I'm met with a wall. No expression from him.

The next second, he heads in the opposite direction of me. It's raining more and more, and my vision is getting blurred little by little. I try to follow his steps, but the rest of the group is between him and me. By the time I cross the lawn without jostling anyone, Tucker is gone. I see his pickup truck drive away. And disappear.

"Damn it," I mutter through my teeth.

I'm starting to feel cold, soaked to the bone. I turn around to return to my own vehicle. Yeleen is being held by TJ, who is taking her to her own car. I start to follow the same path as them but stop at the last moment. Everyone has left, even Tucker's mother.

But a new person has just arrived.

Dan.

His back is to me, though I recognize his massive shoulders and shaved head. He's staring at the hole in the ground, his head down. My teeth are chattering—I'll probably be sick as a dog—but I can't ignore him. Not when I can imagine all the pain he must be feeling.

I cross the muddy lawn again and approach Debbie's grave. Dan tenses at my arrival but does not turn to me. I stand beside him, as silent as he is. I glance at him and notice his red eyes. Even through the smell of wet grass, I can smell the alcohol coming from him. He's as soaked as I am but seems completely weathertight.

"Are you okay?" I whisper between my lips.

Stupid. Do you really think he's okay? He lost the person he loved most in the world, of course he's not okay.

He doesn't respond. In fact, he doesn't even react, as if he doesn't see me. I move a little closer to him, as if the faint heat emanating from my body could wake him up and help him. But he still doesn't say anything, staring at the grave with his tired, bloodshot eyes.

"I'm sorry, Dan. So sorry," I whisper, looking back at the grave. I know he's locked in a dark room right now, and will be for a long time, but I hope that one day he'll find the key to get out.

Like I tried to do. After a minute of silence, I slowly walk away.

"It's his fault."

I freeze. Did he speak or am I going crazy? I turn to him, eyebrows raised, unsure. "Did you say something?"

His face turns towards me and his features crack. He no longer seems indifferent. His eyes are as sad as ever, but he seems overcome with hatred. "I said, 'It's his fault.'"

I frown, confused. "I don't understand…"

He stares at me for a few seconds but says nothing. Finally, he walks away without turning around once. He also disappears from my sight and I find myself alone in the middle of this cemetery.

Sitting in the center of the lecture hall, I scan the rows around me. No sign of Tucker. No sign of him. He's not responding to my text, or my calls. I know he needs space and time. I try to give him some while reminding him that I'm here for him. I've been there, I know how hard it is.

How tempting it is to get lost in the darkness. It's true, it's so much fun to stay in the dark rather than be blinded by the light. But light is essential to our lives. It drives out demons.

Our demons.

But Tucker isn't here. Richards explains several morbid cases that took place in Miami in the 1990s. I listen with one ear, preoccupied with so many other things.

Finally, the class ends. I pick up my papers, on which I have not written anything down, and walk quickly down the stairs.

"Miss Foster!" someone yells behind me.

I brake abruptly. and a student nearly runs into me.

"Watch out, damn it."

"Fuck," I mutter through my teeth as I turn toward the stage.

My teacher, perched on high heels, beckons me to join her. Her little smile makes me ask myself many questions.

"Yes?" I asked as I reached her, my bag pressed against my chest.

"Larey case." She approaches me. "Where is your classmate, Mr. Bomley, who was working with you?"

My lips open but no words come out. I swallow hard.

"He had…a problem. A family problem."

She nods, not looking for more information.

"I recently saw my colleague, Larey's lawyer. Now that things are coming together, I can tell you one thing. Two things, actually. First…"

My heart misses a beat. "What?"

"We have a new witness."

I widen my eyes, increasingly interested. "What kind of witness? A witness who could clear Mikael's name?"

My teacher doesn't answer directly but smiles at me, silently confirming my theory. "I can't tell you anything concrete, but Helena had mentioned her suicidal desires to her own mother several times."

The suicide hypothesis. The one I had considered myself.

"What's the second thing?"

"This new witness—the mother—has concrete evidence accusing Helena. She refused from the beginning to cooperate to protect her daughter—even though she is dead—but she finally agreed to help us.

"What evidence does she have?" I know she won't tell me what it's about, not right now, anyway. "Is it possible that he will eventually be found innocent? Released?"

Professor Richards crosses her arms and purses her lips.

A lot of questions come to mind as hope is reborn in me.

"I won't say anything more. Have a nice day, miss." She dismisses me openly, apparently in a hurry.

I walk away from the stage, my heart a little lighter. I believe it. If an innocent man is behind bars, I pray that justice will be done and that Mikael will be released, cleared of the crimes he did not commit.

Two hours later, I pull up to the Bomley property. Thank God the gate is open this time.

I know I shouldn't be here, but I'm totally consumed with pain and stress. I'm probably doing something wrong, but I need to see Tucker. I need him to listen to me, to know that I'm here. That I will be there when he needs me.

We are a couple, he and I. At least we used to be. What about today? What's going on between us? Another unanswered question…

I stop my car in front of the mansion and take a deep breath.

"Come on, you can do it, you sissy," I mutter through clenched teeth.

I open the door and get out of my car, looking at the huge wooden door. I fiddle with my fingers, stressed, and climb the few steps leading to the entrance. The door swings open.

Tucker frowns at the sight of me. He stares at me, but I feel like he's not really there, like he's just a body shell with no soul. The thought scares me but I ignore it. I stop on the first step, unsure.

"I…hi." My voice is a whisper.

He closes the door behind him and walks towards me. His beard is longer than before, his eyes darkened.

"Hi."

His voice is hoarse and broken, like he hasn't spoken for many days, which I'm not sure he has. Seeing him like this breaks my heart a little more. I swallow hard to get my breath back. I need…need to feel him against me. I walk up the rest of the steps to get to his level and wrap my arms around his chest.

His body is ice cold when it's usually boiling.

His arms stay by his side. He is completely sealed to my gesture. I pull him a little closer to me, rubbing my face against his chest.

"I'm sorry. So sorry, Tucker," I whisper, my voice hoarse.

He inhales deeply over me. His muscles tense a little more and then he braces himself completely. He tries to pull away from me but I don't move an inch. I don't let go.

"I know what you're going to do. You're in great pain. You want to push me away, hurt me to get away. I've been there too. I know how you feel. I know it, Tucker."

I straighten my head, and he tilts his towards me, his eyebrows furrowed.

"I know you're hurting, but don't try to hurt me back, please."

He still doesn't answer but watches me in silence. His breath hits my face. Then his mask cracks little by little. His jaw almost starts to tremble.

"I don't want to hurt you but…this is not the right time, Iris."

He tries to pull away again, and this time I let him. I watch him put distance between us, helpless. A silent minute passes. Finally, he sits down on the step under our feet, his eyes lost on the huge garden.

"I wasn't there, Iris."

I close my eyes tightly, feeling all of his pain seeping from his pores. I settle down next to him, not saying a word.

"I thought her device was malfunctioning, but it wasn't. She was dying. And she died while I was at a stupid party with…"

With me.

He doesn't say those words, but I can guess. And they hurt. I try to take it in. I've been there, I know how much pain he's in and can't see anything around him. But it's fucking hard. I turn to him and put my hand on his forearm.

"You couldn't have known, Tucker. It's not your fault. It's NOT your fault."

He doesn't say anything back to me, and I understand that he thinks it is, he has some responsibility.

"I wasn't near her. She left on her own," he finally whispers.

"You stayed with her all those months. She wasn't alone. Debbie knew you were there for her."

He shakes his head and stands up. I do the same.

"She was all I had left, you know? I have nothing left."

I try to take another step towards him, being careful not to touch him. "Me. You have me, Tucker. I'm here. And I'm yours, just like you are mine, remember?"

He closes his eyes and inhales once more. He opens his eyelids again and his mask is back in place. He's completely closed. "I can't be yours. Not after this. I need time."

I reach for his hand, but his words chill me.

"It's over."

My heart misses a beat. I swallow, not sure I heard correctly.

"Don't say that," I whisper between my trembling lips. "You can't fucking say that. Don't hurt me, Tucker."

He doesn't answer me. Unable to take it anymore, I cling desperately to him, my heart beating wildly. My arms go around his neck, and I press my face into his neck.

"Don't do this to me now. Not when I've fallen in love again. Do you hear me? After my parents died, after Rafael died, I felt nothing. It was you who made me feel something again."

I reach out and grab his jaw with both hands. For the first time in a long time, I open up completely. I need to bring him back into our world, close to me.

"I love you. Let me help you, let me make you feel something in turn."

He puts his big hand on mine. "I am completely numb. I feel nothing, Iris."

"Not now, not for a while. But Tucker...I..."

He pulls my hands away from his face, gently.

"You deserve better, Iris. You've been through too much, too. You deserve someone who will love you."

"But you love me," I whisper, a lump in my throat. I try to hold it in, but my tears run down my cheeks. After all these days, I finally let go. I'm not hiding anymore, my lips are trembling softly. "I know you love me," I continue a little more forcefully. "And you're punishing yourself. You refuse to be happy because you think you don't deserve it. You think you're partly responsible for Debbie's death. You're hurting yourself. But you're also hurting me, Tucker."

Tucker puts his mouth on mine for a second but doesn't answer me. But he doesn't need to. I don't like this. His kiss…it's like a goodbye kiss. He thinks he doesn't deserve his happiness, but he's wrong.

He pulls away and walks to the door.

"Don't do this."

My voice breaks on the last word.

"Don't do it," I repeat. "If you break what's between us tonight…you're breaking me too, damn it."

He turns to me, a sad little smile on his face. "I could never break you, babe. Not me, not any man. You're the strongest woman I know. Go home and don't come back."

And he walks into the house, abandoning everything.

Abandoning me.

"I love you," I whisper again. "Don't do this."

But he's not there anymore. I'm alone on the front porch.

Once again, love is not enough.

50. DROP THE MASKS

IRIS

Getting up, going to class, going home, sleeping. Having a lump in your throat.

And do it again.

Again and again, trying to forget the pain. Trying to get past this feeling that tears me apart inside.

I'm tired of pretending. I just…want this pain to go away. My conscience had warned me though. I shouldn't have fallen in love again. Love brings happiness but can take it away at any moment.

So why did I fall in love with that damn bastard? Why did he trample on my heart? Why does love hurt so much?!

The rational part of my brain gets in Tucker's shoes, understands why he did what he did, but the other part wants to shake him until his teeth rattle and he suffers as much as I do. I didn't plan on falling in love when I came to this damn town. Tucker chased me for weeks. I fought it, then succumbed. And before I even realized it, he had made a place for himself in my heart. Until I broke it last week. And yet, I still love him.

I hate this feeling, but I know for a fact that it won't go away anytime soon.

Yeleen has been texting me nonstop for the past few days. I wonder if she knows that Tucker has dumped me like a hot potato. I hope in my heart she's yelled at him.

I've tried to think of something else, to get him out of my thoughts. But part of me hopes he'll text to apologize or to talk.

Stupid girl, what did you expect?

I decided not to let it get me down. I have to accept his decision. Tucker has made it perfectly clear that he doesn't need me. He needs to fight his own demons, grieve…away from me.

I throw back my covers and get out of bed. It's over, I have to pull myself together and move on. I don't have the right to mope. The shower I take does me a world of good. It clears my head and allows me to finally think about something else.

A few minutes later, I leave my apartment, my hair still wet. It's time for a new day. Everything is going to be fine. I take a deep breath, clutching my car keys in my hand.

Everything is going to be okay.

The following hours pass before my eyes. I'm a spectator of my own life. I smile at those who say hello to me and take notes in my cognitive psychology class like a perfect little student. But inside me, it's a big mess. Everything is not going well at all. I can't wait for this damn class to end so I can get the hell out.

Twenty minutes later, my ordeal ends. I am one of the first to leave the lecture hall. I take a deep breath as I walk down the hallway filled with hungry students. I walk quickly, eager to leave.

"Iris!"

I stop and half turn, watching Yeleen come to me. She gives me a slight, uncertain smile.

"Hi…"

"Hum, hi," I just say back to her.

"I tried to reach you yesterday…"

"Yeah, sorry, My phone died."

She nods at my lie, as if she understands me. As if she understands my need to withdraw into myself, to push everything and everyone away to avoid facing this shitty reality.

"Are you okay?" she asks me softly, putting back a lock of her hair.

So I understand. She knows.

My look must speak for me because she doesn't give me a chance to answer. "I stopped by Tucker's house a few days ago. I still hadn't heard from him so I dropped by. He was…bad. Really bad. In between a couple of incoherent words, he told me that he dumped you. I'm sorry."

I'm having trouble swallowing. "It's okay, Yeleen. I'm okay. He needs to grieve on his own."

Again, she doesn't seem to believe my lie, but she gets over it.

"He's being a jerk," she finally says. "He pushed you away

because that's what he does best, Iris. He lost the person he loved most in the world. He pushed you away because he loves you but he doesn't think he deserves to be happy. That he doesn't deserve his happiness with you."

"Is that what he told you?"

"It's Tucker…he didn't tell me, but I saw it in his eyes, Iris. He needs you. He's just too stupid to realize it. And I hope he gets his fingers out before it's too late."

"It's already too late," I mutter through my teeth. "I wanted to show him I was there for him, but he pushed me away like a piece of shit, Yeleen. I'm not going to cry for crumbs. I accept his decision. I have suffered too much in the past, I don't want to suffer in the future, understand?"

Yeleen doesn't answer me. A small grimace appears on her face. She stretches her hand towards me for a second before letting it fall along her body.

"I'm here for you, like you were for me, Iris. Know that."

I nod but don't answer. I'm about to walk away but Yeleen adds, "Matt's in the hospital."

Her words stop me in my tracks. "What?"

Yeleen shrugs.

"Who sent that piece of garbage there?"

She doesn't answer me. I feel that she is keeping a secret. That she knows the truth. Eventually she says, "I think he…fell down the stairs."

"Fell down, huh?"

She nods, but her eyes tell me she is lying. Someone sent him to the hospital. Someone who has a lot of anger in him, resentment too. And I'm convinced that someone is Dan. Or Tucker. Maybe the whole pack? Debbie's dead, Tucker feels partly responsible, but he's also mad at Matt, no question about it. The son of a bitch hurt his little sister.

"Was it Tucker?" My voice sounds like a whisper.

Yeleen straightens up, her eyes hard. "I told you, Iris, Matt fell."

"Fell…" I repeat sarcastically. "Or someone helped him to fall?"

The man is scum, I'm not saying he's not…but part of me wants to know what happened. How far did we get back at him?

"I have to go," Yeleen exclaims. "I'll see you later."

I watch her walk away and back toward the bathroom. The door to the right, the one leading to the men's room, opens. A tall figure walks through the door. A figure I know very well.

Tucker.

With his eyes locked straight ahead, he hasn't noticed me yet. I watch him on the sly from a few steps away. His beard is longer. He apparently hasn't shaved since the last time I saw him. I didn't expect to see him at school today. His eyes are no longer ringed like the other day, but his eyebrows are furrowed, making his gaze stern and cold. Seeing him like this makes me want to pull his hair to hurt him and then ask him if he's okay.

I'm stupid. After everything that happened, after his rejection, I'm still worried about him. I can't see it any other way. He lifts his head, and his eyes meet mine. He frowns a little more just before he stops. Still, he looks me up and down, thinking deeply.

That's right, think, asshole.

I keep a neutral expression on my face while openly staring at him in turn. One detail catches my attention. A few feet separate us, and yet I can see the state of his hands. The knuckles of his fingers are completely raw.

I raise my head and stare at him, my lips half-open. It looks like I was right. Matt is in the hospital. And he didn't fall. Tucker's posture changes slightly at my behavior.

He knows that I know what he did.

He takes a step in my direction, his gaze still cold.

"You hit Matt. You sent him to the hospital."

And he had to make sure we didn't know it was him.

He says nothing in his defense.

We stare at each other for several minutes. Neither of us speaks. Part of me wants to ask him if he's holding it together. That said, I mentally replay our last conversation. I told him I loved him and he left me, unable to even look me in the eye.

Because I know what I would have seen in his eyes: love for me. Fuck, he decided to take away our happiness and I can't do anything. I was serious with Yeleen, I don't want to suffer anymore.

I don't have the strength anymore.

Finally, he breaks the silence.

"Hi."

I raise an eyebrow. Seriously, did he just give me a stupid greeting?

I walk away without a word, but he stops me. "Iris, wait."

"Let me go."

He doesn't listen to me, blocking my way with his body. I cross my arms over my chest, waiting for him to say what he has to say. Looking at him hurts. So many conflicting feelings. I don't fucking know what to do.

I don't know if he notices the dark circles under my eyes but his posture changes slightly.

"Are you okay?" he asks.

I can't hold back the joyless laugh that comes out of my throat. "Are you fucking serious?"

I can't believe it. Did his mother drop him his head as a baby?

I don't let him answer and continue, "Do I look okay? You're not fine, but you hurt me too. I told you I loved you, and you turned your back on me. So no, I'm not okay."

"I told you my reasons," he mumbles through his teeth as if suddenly upset.

I put my hands up, telling him to be quiet.

"It's okay, I understand your reasons. You don't think you have the right to be happy, so you threw me away like a piece of shit. I'm not going to chase after you. I've been through a lot, Tucker. I don't want to be unhappy anymore, okay?"

These words hurt, but they are necessary. Necessary for me to move on.

He grabs my elbow as I pass by him to leave. His hand wraps around me, his skin on mine electrifies me for a moment, but I contain my emotions. My heart rate speeds up though.

"I know you're mad at me," he whispers beside me, "but don't hate me. I won't stand for it."

"I don't hate you. Because despite the pain, I'm stupid enough to still love you. But my feelings will go away, Tucker. And I won't be here anymore."

He doesn't answer me.

"I hope you get better," I whisper, pulling his hand away and walking around him.

I feel his gaze burn my back, but I ignore it.

This is the end of our conversation. Full of unspoken words. Happiness destroyed. Support gone. This time, it is not him who rejects me, it is me who leaves.

A few hours later, I finish my shift at the bar. There weren't many customers, normal for a Monday night. My head was elsewhere all evening, and my colleague Buck had to correct me several times because I had made a mistake in the orders.

Anyway, there was one thing I did see tonight…it was Dan, at the back of the room, drinking beers, with a blank stare. He didn't let anyone get close to him, locked in his bubble. On his face, there was no more pain, only hatred. Did he help Tucker beat up Matt?

When I finish my shift, I sigh in contentment and drop my cleaning rag on the bar. Buck leans next to me, looking concerned.

"Are you all right, honey?"

I open my mouth, unsure. "It's been a rough few days. I need some sleep."

He finally nods. "Then go and rest."

And that's my intention. I leave ten minutes later, stifling a yawn. It's only 11:30 p.m., but fortunately for me, my shift was ending early tonight. I cross the half-lit parking lot, in a hurry to get to my car.

I get to my car and take out my car keys, but what I see leaves me frozen. The right front tire is completely flat. Damn, did I run over something and get a flat tire without realizing it on the way here?

Damn it. That's the way to end an evening in style.

Headlights shines on me from the right, a horn blares, and I hold back an expletive while jumping.

A huge red Dodge is parked in front of me. Someone is rolling down the driver's window.

"What's wrong?" Dan asks me, leaning over to me.

I kick my tire to show him. "My tire is completely flat. I must have gotten a flat on the way here."

He makes a little face. "Do you have a spare tire?"

I shake my head and massage my temples. If my father saw me from up there, he'd yell at me. "No, I don't. I'll get a cab and take a look at it tomorrow."

"Don't be silly. Get in, I'll take you home."

I hesitate to accept. He had two beers tonight. Not enough to be drunk…but I've been there once before.

"I'll be fine, thanks."

He leans out the window, eyebrows raised. "You're not taking a cab. You'll pay a fortune."

I know that, and I don't need to lose money like that. I think for another minute, under his insistent look.

"So?"

"Okay…I accept."

He pulls his head in. I pick up my bag, walk around the vehicle and get in. "This is nice of you," I say as he drives away.

"I'm always here to help save money," he replies simply.

I lean back against the headrest, feeling a headache take over. Dan keeps his attention on the road, his driving rather calm. I don't know why I had a bad feeling, but he's driving very well. I don't know how to start a conversation, and talking about Debbie is not the thing to do, so I keep quiet and look outside.

My phone vibrates in my bag, and I frown at who is calling me.

Detective Harrisson.

"Aren't you going to pick up?" asks Dan.

I snap out of my thoughts, nod, and put the phone to my ear. "Detective?"

"Miss Foster? I'm sorry to bother you late. When we last spoke, I told you that Joe Nelson had no immediate family, so there was probably no connection between him and the break-in at your apartment, but I also told you that I was going to ask for confirmation from some police friends who just happen to be in Portland, your home town."

"And have you heard anything else?" I ask, my heart racing.

I hear him take a deep breath through the receiver. "I thought Joe Nelson had no family. But my contacts there gave me other information. According to the subsequent investigation by Portland officers, Joe Nelson had a child that he never officially recognized. That's why he didn't show up in the database for him. I think he never recognized his child to keep his life from being disrupted by all the arrests of his father."

"He had…a child?" I whisper, wondering if I'm dreaming. "You think his child was trying to find me? Is it possible that he was the one who came after me?"

The cop waits a second before answering me. "Nothing is confirmed yet, Miss. But his son—"

"His son?" I cut him off without saying a word.

Dan stares at me out of the corner of his eye, surely disconcerted by my conversation.

The detective says, "Yes, his son, Sanchez Yerez."

Oh, my God.

The cop pauses for a moment and then continues. "Twenty years old. He would have left Portland a few months ago. They don't know where he is right now."

My heart misses a beat. An unpleasant chill runs up my spine. The detective keeps talking into the phone but I can't hear anything. It's like I'm numb.

Sanchez.

Sanchez Yerez.

I could tell myself it's a coincidence, but I feel like it's not. The last few weeks and months are racing through my head. The first time I ran into Sanchez in the abandoned factory. He was new this year…like me. His dark look that reminded me strangely of someone else. And everything that happened afterwards…our friendship. Me running into him going out with some girls in front of my residence. He was always trying to get closer to me.

No…it's not possible…and yet, I think it is.

How could I be so stupid?

Is Sanchez the son of the man who killed my parents? The son of the man I killed?

With trembling hands, I whisper before ending the call, "I'll call you back."

My phone slips out of my hands and falls at my feet. I feel like I'm in another world, like I'm in another nightmare.

"Are you okay?" Dan asks me.

I'm too stunned to answer for a moment. "You have to take me home, Dan. I have a huge problem."

Dan remains silent at my remark and then finally replies, "You'll be back at the Sky residence soon."

I press my forehead against my window. Dan's words stick in my mind.

"How do you know what dorm I'm staying at?"

"Tucker told me."

Something in his attitude calls out to me, but everything is racing through my head.

Sanchez…my God. But that's impossible.

"Where are we?" I ask as we drive through a huge forest. I've never been here before.

Dan still doesn't answer me. Another bad feeling rises in me. The air is escaping from my lungs.

"Dan, what the hell are you playing at?! I have to get home immediately."

The car stops with a squeal of tires. I think there's an old cabin a few feet away but I'm not sure. Suddenly, I see someone approaching the car. A male figure that I quickly recognize.

Sanchez.

I sit still, petrified. I don't understand what's going on but my survival instinct is to move. A breath near my ear. A whisper from Dan.

"I don't think you're going home just yet."

And then suddenly, darkness.

51. REVENGE

IRIS

Thirsty…I'm thirsty. So thirsty…my throat burns, the back of my head hurts so much…what is happening to me? Why don't my eyelids open? What happened?

Slam.

A door that is brutally closed.

I'm choking…I'm choking…I'm trying to get air into my lungs, but again, my body won't obey me!

I breathe in sharply and blink my eyes as I gradually regain consciousness.

What the…

It is dark in the room, very dark. There is a strong smell of dampness. My eyes are acclimating to the darkness. I raise my head and the back of my head hurts even more. Memories come back to me little by little, along with the pain.

I was hit!

The detective called me…Sanchez…Joe Nelson's son…I was in Dan's car that was supposed to take me home, but he hit me! Oh, my God!!!

Panic overtakes me, but I try to stay calm. I pull on my arms, but my movements are limited. I am tied to a chair. My hands are sore, but I don't feel like I've been drugged. I don't understand what happened. Why would Dan do such a thing?

I hear footsteps on an old, creaky floor. I straighten my head to study my surroundings little by little. I am in an old cabin that looks like it's been abandoned. There is only an old lamp which works half, hung on the right wall. Aside from this chair I'm sitting in, there's no furniture. I heard footsteps though I slowly turn my head towards the only window that lets in a few rays of moonlight.

Dan is standing in front of the window with his back to me. He runs a hand over his shaved head and lets out a frustrated sigh. I want to scream, to ask him to untie me, but Dan isn't a good guy. For some reason, he took it out on me. He took me straight to my nightmare, to Sanchez. Before I passed out, I saw him outside the car. My pulse quickens, an unpleasant shiver runs through me. Where is he? Where am I? What is the connection between Dan and Joe Nelson?

For years I've been studying human behavior and didn't realize that monsters were around me every minute. The real question I ask myself is what will they do to me?

A new crack. Dan turns to me and stands still for a second, seeing that I'm awake. Bile fills my mouth. I want to scream insults at him but, weakened, I simply whisper, "Where am I?"

"In an old abandoned cabin."

My lips almost tremble but I find the courage to continue. "Why, Dan? Why you? Why me?"

The only answer I get is a throaty laugh. His gaze pierces me from where he stands. He moves quickly towards me but stops just before he reaches me, looking crazy.

"Do you know how long I've been suffering because of Tucker?"

Dan crouches down in front of me. His gaze becomes distant, as if he is reliving a memory.

"I've always been in love with Debbie. From the time I was a little boy, I was fucking crazy about her. Tucker knew it, he knew I was hooked, but he kept me from getting close to her. I finally started a relationship with her, even though he wasn't really down with it. I wanted to bring Debbie to our parties, to our world, but Tucker refused. He thought he could decide everything about everyone. Like a little chief with his soldiers. A pack leader? Give me a fucking break."

He straightens up and paces back and forth, looking at his feet.

"On that fateful night, he stopped her from coming to this party. Fuck, he knew for a fact that Debbie would come, that she wouldn't listen to him! But once again, he decided for everyone, as if he was the king. He's also responsible for her accident. He took her from me."

"It's not his fault. It was Matt who abused her."

"And I'll deal with him in due time."

"You're out of your mind, Dan! It's not Tucker's fault!"

"You shut your mouth! Do you hear me?! You shut up!"

But I can't keep my mouth shut. I'm trying to talk some sense into him while I still can. "Debbie had an accident, it's not Tucker's fault. He's in as much pain as you are!"

But Dan can't hear me, my words go in one ear and out the other. He is so certain of what he is saying that he never doubts himself. "He had only one thing to do: take care of Debbie and watch her until she woke up. But he let her down. He let her die while he was in your arms."

Was he watching us?

Dan brushes his index finger across my forehead. I try to get as far away as possible, but it's nearly impossible.

"He let the only woman I loved die! He never knew how to protect her, because he's just fucking weak. He broke me. Today I'm broken, Iris. I want to destroy them all, destroy all of YOU. I realized how important you were to him before that fool even realized it. From the moment you met him, you had an almost magnetic fascination with him. So I found the perfect way to hurt him in turn…you. And what better way than to use you to hurt him? To draw him to me? I want him to understand what it feels like to lose the woman in his life!"

"So, to hurt me, you decided to go with Sanchez?! Do you know who he is?! What he did to me?!"

"Yes, I decided to go with Sanchez. You were so obsessed with Tucker that you didn't see the danger around you. I knew right away that Sanchez was out to get you. He came to town for no reason except to find you. But you know what? Sanchez also understood my hatred and my need for revenge against Tucker. He really understood me. A shared need for revenge against two different people that came together. You and Tucker. So I decided to team up with him."

How is this possible?! How could Dan agree to help Sanchez?!

"He told me that you destroyed his father," says Dan, "and that he wanted revenge for that. You became our target. He would get his personal revenge, and I would get to Tucker through you. Kill two birds with one stone."

"You don't know anything," I spit out. "Sanchez is the son of the man who killed my parents and almost raped my little sister! Did you know that?"

Dan doesn't answer, apparently surprised, and I have my answer.

"Of course, you didn't know! He told you I broke his father? Yes, I killed him, but it was in self-defense. And you're going to help him hurt me, in spite of it all, just because you want to get to Tucker?!"

"I want to hurt Tucker, to hurt him as much as I've been hurt. I don't care about the rest," he says strongly as if trying to convince himself, although he seems a little less sure.

"That's not true," I reply, shaking my head from side to side. "You can't *just* not care. Please, listen to me…don't let him hurt me. You are completely out of touch with reality, mad with grief and resentment. You hate Tucker, I get that. But—"

"Just shut up. I'm not falling for your doe-eyed tricks. Thanks to you, Tucker's gonna swoop in thinking he can save you. When he finds out you're in danger, he'll want to protect you. And while Sanchez takes care of you, I'll take care of your man."

"Dan, listen to me. Don't do this! Don't let your hatred blind you!"

He doesn't listen to me, takes a step back, and crosses his arms over his chest. But his eyes are still as empty as ever.

"Debbie doesn't—"

He squints, ready to attack me. "Don't say her name," he cuts me off. "Don't say it! You have no right to do it!"

I try to calm down. I have to be quick, try to bring him back to reality. With trembling lips, I look him straight in the eye and say, "Tucker tried to protect her. You think he wasn't hurt by her accident? By her death? She was his little sister! And he suffers for it every day. He feels responsible. You don't know him, Dan. You're blinded by your jealousy, by your resentment. Have you ever considered your own share of the responsibility? While Tucker was beating Matt for abusing his sister and she was running into a tree, where were you?!"

"Shut up! Shut up! Shut up!" he yells, pacing back and forth, rubbing his temples and forehead like a lunatic.

"Listen to me, I'm begging you. You're better than this. Debbie wouldn't have wanted this."

At the mention of this name, he doesn't move, as if hanging on my lips. He finally listens to me, without yelling at me to shut up this time.

"She loved you so much, and she loved her big brother so much. If she saw you today, how would she react? Don't do this… please. Let me go. I don't—"

The door suddenly opens. Sanchez enters, a small smile on his face. His pierced eyebrow shines softly in the weak moonlight. I was wrong about him. But now his mask has fallen off, and I see him for who he really is. And the more I observe his face and his features, the more I recognize in him his monster of a father.

"So, surprise, my pretty?"

"Don't call me pretty. Don't call me anything, asshole!"

He approaches, me and I don't have time to think when his hand meets my cheekbone with a thud.

"Did you think that changing cities would make you untouchable? That I wouldn't try to find the woman who killed my father? He was a monster, but I loved him."

"Sanchez…she says your father killed her parents," Dan begins, confused. "That's not what you told me. You told me that she was the one who destroyed your father, her and her family, but I didn't know that he had…that he had…killed and abused—"

"*Cállate*, shut up," exclaims Sanchez. "Do you want to get back at Tucker or not?! Do you want to make him suffer?"

"Yes, but…"

"Then call him. Tell him his little bitch is here and we're going to take care of her."

Dan takes another breath, and his eyes meet mine.

"Don't do it," I whisper in his direction.

He doesn't say anything, he just turns away and leaves the old cabin. Sanchez then turns to me, his attention focused on my face. He takes something out of his jacket. A gun!

"You should have been suspicious of me. After all, even your little sister looked smarter."

"The day she met you, she told me she didn't like you," I challenge him despite my fear.

Sanchez lets out a little laugh. "You see? Very clever."

Another thought comes to me suddenly. "It's you who wrote the word 'killer' on my wall, wasn't it? It was you who called me on that unknown number, who was watching me?"

"Bingo."

He smiles at me a little more, and I inwardly pray for help. I don't want Tucker to come because Dan would come after him… but a part of me is calling for him with all my might.

I need him.

TUCKER

Sitting against the stone of Debbie's grave, I take another sip of beer. The can is empty so I send it waltzing away, not caring about anything. I'm drinking like a fish, in the middle of the night. I'm sinking, and I don't know what to do to get my head above water. The one person who was helping me not to drown is no longer in my life. All because I pushed her away, like a moron.

I sent her packing, I told her to get out of my sight, I left her because I'm just a fucking loser. If I couldn't take care of my sister, how could I do it with her? How can I be happy when Debbie is in the ground? I don't deserve it.

While I was having fun with Iris, she fucking died. She died and I wasn't there. And it's eating me up, it's destroying me completely. I don't want to destroy Iris, I don't want to drag her down with me, drag her down into the darkness. She deserves to be happy.

Something runs down my cheek. I touch my skin with my forefinger and wipe away the single tear that runs down.

I think back to our conversation. She told me she fucking loved me. Her little body was pressed against mine, and I didn't know what to say. I wanted to tell her the same thing, but my mouth couldn't say it. I couldn't think. All I could think about was suffering alone and pushing her away so she wouldn't suffer with me.

My phone rings, pulling me out of my thoughts. It's Dan. I don't have time to greet him when he tells me, in a voice from beyond the grave, "Meet me at the cottage on the old Littleton Road. Iris is with me."

His tone makes my blood run cold. I don't recognize him at all. A bad feeling is rising in me. I haven't heard from Dan since Debbie died because he wouldn't talk to me. And now he calls me to tell me that he is with Iris, in that old abandoned cabin where we used to go hunting with our fathers? Something is wrong, I feel it. Many assumptions come to me, but I refuse to believe them. Dan is my best friend…he would never hurt her, not when he knows what she means to me.

"What did you do?" I murmur between my lips.

"I wanted to hurt you like you hurt me, *brother*."

He spits out the word like an insult before hanging up.

52. LOVE

TUCKER

I've never driven so fast in my life. The minutes are going by too fast and the miles too slow, damn it! I pass an old van that moves like a snail. I nearly graze its side mirror and the driver honks at me, but I ignore him, stepping on the gas a little more.

Worry consumes me as the questions loop in my head. I'd like to tell myself that everything is fine, that Dan is with Iris in that old shack, just…talking. But I know it's much more serious. Something's going on…something's not right.

He said he wanted to hurt me like I hurt him. What is he talking about?! I'm hurting as much as he is right now. I have lost my sister and I feel that I am losing Dan, who's like a brother to me. I can't lose the woman I care about too. Not now.

I arrive five minutes later at the old cottage on the road to Littleton. I immediately recognize Dan's Dodge parked a few feet away. Memories come flooding in, and I see us coming here with our respective fathers.

My muscles tense as I stop and get out of my car, leaving the door open while my eyes slowly get used to the darkness. I find Dan smoking a joint in front of the old shack, staring at me. His eyes are black, his eyebrows furrowed. I see the pure hatred in him.

No more sadness, only anger…directed at me. I'm discombobulated for a second, but I move towards him with a determined step as he takes a few steps in my direction, too.

"What the hell is this shit?" I spit out right away. "Where's Iris?"

He throws his joint on the ground, looking at me with disgust. I don't have time to think, all I can think about is her—whom I apparently failed to protect from all dangers as I had hoped.

"Let's play a little game," Dan begins in a gentle voice.

"I don't want to get into your bullshit, I just want my girl back."

My angry tone doesn't seem to get to him. He even seems to be enjoying himself. "I was sure you were going to come and rescue her like a perfect little dog. But it's too late, Tucker, you'll understand what it feels like to have the woman you love taken away from you. You're going to suffer like I suffered when you let Debbie down."

I stand still, frozen in place. "'Let Debbie down'?! You better shut up before I really lose it." I say.

I try to walk around him to the cabin, wondering if Iris is really inside because I don't hear any noise. I glance over at Dan's car but she's not in it. Maybe she doesn't want to see me? Considering the way I treated her, that would be possible. But no, I think it's much more serious than that.

"Where is Iris?! Iris, are you in there?!"

No answer.

"She is with Sanchez."

I swallow roughly, my brain thinking at full speed. My muscles tense up a little more. "What the hell does Sanchez have to do with this?"

"She broke his father, so he will break her."

I begin to connect the dots. The questions swirling around in my head are slowly being answered and my concern is growing.

Iris broke Sanchez's father...no, don't tell me that...that Sanchez has a connection to her past?! I never trusted this guy even though he was part of our circle of friends. As soon as he came out of the third challenge, almost clinging to her, I had a bad feeling about him. I could see how much he wanted to get close to her like a little dog. I thought like a guy and figured he was interested in her.

What if his attitude was hiding a lot more than I thought?!

"You won't be able to do anything but watch her be destroyed, like Debbie! Because of you, she is dead!" spits Dan. "She became a vegetable because of you, and you let her die like a piece of shit while you were screwing Iris! Look at you, the great Tucker Bomley reduced to nothing, doesn't that hurt?"

Hatred slowly fills me, and I approach him, getting right in his face. My nostrils quiver at these words and insults. "You think I don't blame myself for Debbie's death? For her accident?! I never gave up on her. But I'm starting to realize that you and I were never buddies. As for Iris..."

Dan laughs sourly and glares at me, not impressed at all.

"Is our alpha about to hurt me too?"

"You want to get back at me by hurting Iris?" I say again, but I don't let him respond. "I swear that if you or Sanchez touch her, I'll kill you."

I've always considered Dan my brother, all these years. But I'm realizing that he had some resentment buried inside him, resentment towards me. He wants to hurt me by touching Iris, by leaving her in the hands of that son of a bitch Sanchez? Very bad idea.

Dan tries once again to block my way, but I push him roughly, which makes him move back a few steps. I hear a crash inside the cabin, and I run towards it, furious.

I haven't taken more than a couple steps when Dan tackles me. His frame is as large as mine, we have both spent dozens of hours at the gym. But I'm full of anger. A storm is brewing inside me, ready to devastate everything in its path.

Dan may be strong, but I'm as powerful as a bear tonight, adrenaline coursing through my veins. He slams into my side, making me wobble, but I stay on my feet. I send my fist in his direction, his nose cracking fearfully under my fingers. His upper lip is split in two, he spits a mixture of saliva and blood on the ground.

"I'm going to break you so badly that you will never recover. Did you leave her with that bastard?!"

A new scream from behind him.

Iris.

Dan and I rush toward each other. I think a blade grazes my side but I don't feel anything. My forehead meets his nose and a growl comes from his chest. Then my knee hits his ribs as he bends down.

I hit him in the face again with my elbow, and he collapses to the ground with a muffled sound, unconscious.

I don't think for a second. I have to help Iris. The most horrible scenarios run through my head, but I refuse to believe them. I refuse to tell myself that I am too late. An unpleasant voice echoes in my mind: if I hadn't pushed Iris away, nothing would have happened like this.

I can't lose her. Not when she means more to me than anything. This little piece of woman has brought me completely to my knees.

I throw the old door open, slamming it against the wall of the cottage. I immediately see who is there and what is going on. I can't think of anything else.

Iris is tied to an old wooden chair. Sanchez, who had his back to me, turns to me, apparently unhappy to see me here. He probably thought Dan would overpower me while he was dealing with MY girl.

Noticing the trickle of blood coming from Iris' nostril, I see red. I barely have time to notice that she has fortunately not been undressed before I charge towards Sanchez.

And nothing will stop me.

"You shouldn't have come in here," he says with an evil smile.

I understand what he is getting at when I see him raise a gun in my direction, but he doesn't have time to finish his gesture when I run at him. A shot rings out near my head. A few inches to the left and it would have blown my face off. The bullet grazed my ear, and I feel the blood running down my neck. I can't hear anything on this side, but I try to hold Sanchez under my weight.

"Tucker!" screams Iris, half hysterical, half crying, from behind me.

Seeing her like this and hearing the distress in her voice breaks me down a little more. They tried to lure me here hoping to have his revenge on her to hurt me.

Big fucking mistake on their part.

A wolf will always defend his she-wolf.

Sanchez is thinner than Dan, but he's faster, more skilled. I slam him to the ground with all my weight, but his knee meets my thigh muscle. I swallow a grunt of pain as he tries to clock me with his gun.

"I'll kill you, I'll kill you both," he says with difficulty.

My hand sends the gun flying and I slam him back down.

"I'll send you to meet your father instead, you motherfucker," I mutter between my lips. "You messed with the wrong people."

He tries to pull away, but my fingers wrap around his throat and I squeeze with all my might.

"Tucker!" shouts Iris from behind me, still locked in the chair.

She wriggles and nearly falls, taking the chair with her.

I'm bleeding and my muscles are tired, but I don't let go. I need to vent all my hatred in turn. I was betrayed. Iris was betrayed by trying to shatter the new life she was trying to build here. Why would I let him live?

But I think of my girl begging me not to kill him.

"He deserves to die in prison," she continues in a weaker voice. "Don't let him win, don't let him destroy your life by killing him. I want him to rot in a cell."

I hear her words and part of me wants to listen, but that would be too simple. My revenge isn't over. He hit her! He made her bleed! He deserves to have me take care of him.

"I need you," Iris gasps, struggling to breathe. "Don't let me down."

These words immobilize me. Don't let her down.

I know what she's trying to do, she's getting inside my head and into my pores to make me see reason. She doesn't want me to end up behind bars for killing Sanchez.

The latter loses consciousness in my grip, and I turn my head towards Iris. Seeing her in this state, her face damaged, hurts me more than the blows I received tonight. Her eyes are filled with tears.

Sanchez is not dead yet. I know he's only passed out, but I release him and drop down in front of Iris's chair, struggling to untie the rope that holds her wrists.

"Iris," I whisper, pulling her to me after freeing her. "I'm so fucking sorry. I'm sorry, I'm sorry."

I don't even know what I'm apologizing for. For letting her down a few days earlier. For pushing her away when the only thing I needed was her. Because I couldn't see how else to do it. Because I still can't see, despite all my feelings for her threatening to boil over.

She clings to me, her head buried in my neck. I don't let her go, unable to pull her away. Her chest presses against my torso, and I feel like I'm stabilizing a little bit.

If I hadn't gotten there first...I...no, I don't want to think about it!

I hear footsteps at my back just as Iris stiffens in my arms. I know it's not Sanchez, he's still passed out beside us.

"Dan..." Iris whispers.

She tries to push me away, so I release her and straighten up, turning to the one I considered my best friend a few hours ago. He sniffs, blood and tears on his face. He has retrieved the gun I had knocked away and holds it in his hand. He stares at Sanchez for a few seconds, then at me, then at Iris, longer. He looks at Sanchez's swollen face, as if disoriented…as if he was trying to stay connected to reality but had no grip on it.

"Put the gun down," I articulate through clenched teeth.

"Please, Dan. Think back to our conversation, think of Debbie," Iris begs him, sitting up with difficulty beside me.

"I didn't know that Sanchez's father killed your parents," Dan begins, raising his gun in our direction. "I just…I just wanted everyone to suffer like I did. I wanted to break you, Tucker. You killed Debbie, we killed her. I…I killed her, too. She should have woken up, Tucker! But she's dead! I killed her."

He sobs softly. He seems to be finally reconnecting to reality. Guilt is choking him. I raise both hands in the air, trying to appear calm when I am absolutely not. "Her accident wasn't our fault, Dan." I don't really mean that, but I try to calm him down as best I can. "And after she died…the doctors said that…they told me that she wouldn't have woken up anyway."

"I miss her." Another tear rolls down his cheek. He wipes his nose with his free hand, sniffing constantly.

"And I miss her too," I say. "I miss her every day that she's gone. But I also know that she would have liked us to live, Dan."

A heavy silence fills the room, and he finally shakes his head. "No, I can't live without her. No, I can't live without her," he murmurs as he turns the gun on himself, placing it against his temple.

"No!" I shout, leaping towards him.

"Dan!" exclaims Iris behind my back.

But it's too late. Dan pulls the trigger.

He collapses to the floor, dead, with a bullet—HIS bullet—in his head. Drops of blood splatter me, and I fall on the old floor, my knees hitting the ground.

I stare at his body, silent. I feel an immense cold, but I can't move. I hear Iris crying. She falls in front of me and clings to my shoulders. She sobs while clinging to my T-shirt, and I press her face against my chest. I let her little body collapse into mine. She warms me up and tries to snap me out of my lethargy.

But she doesn't succeed.

Sanchez still hasn't moved, yet I know it's only a matter of time before he wakes up. But I still can't do anything but hold Iris. I bury my head in her hair so I can't see Dan's body and sniff her scent like a drug addict in need of a fix. It's the only thing that helps me escape from this reality.

"I thought I was losing you."

These are the only words I can say, so I repeat them a few times, and Iris runs her hands through my hair, pressing herself against me a little more. She consoling me gently, as she would with a child, as she would with her little sister. In fact, she calms us both.

"I can't lose you," I whisper again.

She stares at me as she slowly pulls away, sniffing a few times. I run my thumb under her eyes to wipe away her tears and brush her mouth gently.

"I love you," I finally say. "I fucking love you."

I managed to say it, to finally put words to what I was feeling. She doesn't answer me at all, but I don't need an answer, I just need to feel her against me, to let her heart cradle mine.

Just for a moment.

IRIS

I finish packing my bags in the trunk of my old Chevrolet. It's full to the brim with everything I've accumulated over the past few months in my little student apartment.

It's been a rough few days, and I'm still not fully healed. My lip is bruised and I still have bruises all over my body, but I've escaped the worst. Tucker didn't let go of me. He was by my side while the doctors examined me, and at night he held me close. But even though we were physically there, we were mentally elsewhere.

He was seeing his best friend blow his brains out. I was seeing my parents dead on our living room floor.

At first I thought about staying in this town, but I couldn't. Not after this. Even though Sanchez is now behind bars and I'm safe.

So I've decided to leave.

I need to see my sister. To go back to Portland, at least for a while. Away from all this. Tucker has to stay here and look after his mother. We need to rebuild each other.

We were two parts of a whole, and I know we'll probably get back together as one again someday.

But not now. Not after everything that's happened, what I've been through. I'm not ready, and neither is he.

I hear footsteps at my back, and I know it's him joining me. I close my trunk, ready to write a new page of my story, far from all these nightmares, all these horrors. I need to get better.

Thanks to Tucker, I have learned to love again and to live. A unique love. The one you can never forget.

I turn around and find him standing there with his hands in his pockets. I didn't have the strength or courage to say goodbye to the others—TJ and Yeleen—but I'm really going to miss them. When I came here, I didn't think I would make any friends. And yet, they have managed to create a place for themselves in my troubled existence.

"Hi, Redhead," Tucker begins with a small smile.

Hearing him call me that, the first nickname he ever gave me, takes me back weeks and plunges me into my memories.

Our relationship has been a game of chess on a human scale. A game that neither he nor I won.

"Hi…"

I swing back and forth, contemplating one last time the features of his face, engraving them in my memory. His unique look will haunt me for a long time to come, I know it, I prepared myself for it.

"My mother had an appointment with a new doctor this morning," he says after clearing his throat. "She's agreed to go to a new center. I'm going to visit her as much as I can over the next few weeks so that she understands that I'm here, so that she can get used to this new environment."

My mouth opens by itself. "But no?! Oh, my God, that's great,

Tucker! I'm happy for her, for you."

He nods, appreciating my words. "I've also decided to do some major sorting of Debbie's things."

We stare at each other but neither he nor I speak. The memory of his sister is still too painful to talk about much.

"Is Agnes excited about your homecoming?" he asks me afterwards.

I let out a small laugh as I think about my sister. "Oh yes, she's really excited. I decided to sort out my parents' things. I finally feel ready for it."

"You're ready," Tucker whispers, staring at me intently. "You're free now."

A silent minute passes. I look at his face one last time, not really knowing what to say. I slowly say, "So this is where we say goodbye, huh?"

Tucker nods but doesn't say anything more, as if he is unable to. I nod in turn and walk to the door. I barely take a step when his hand wraps around my elbow and he turns me toward him. His pale eyes meet mine as he kisses me for the last time.

His tongue caresses mine, his lips graze my cheeks, my chin, my forehead, then the tip of my nose. He inhales my scent, capturing my perfume for a moment more.

I long to snuggle up to him, but I have to resist because if I let myself go, I won't have the strength to leave. I need to find myself again, to rebuild myself, after all this, before I can think of anything else.

"I'll always be there for you," he whispers in my ear before kissing my skin one last time. "Anytime. For whatever reason."

I inhale sharply and look into his eyes. "I believe that a part of me will always belong to you, will always love you, no matter how far away or how much time passes."

His index finger grazes my cheek and he smiles softly before stepping back. "Go on, get out of here, beautiful."

I nod again, tears trapped under my eyelids. But I swallow them and smile back at him. I open my car door and get behind the wheel. "Don't kill TJ, even if he annoys you, okay?"

"I won't promise you anything," Tucker replies with an innocent shrug.

I laugh again and conclude, "Bye, Tucker."

"See you, babe."

I shake my head as if exasperated, and he lets out a small laugh. I start the car and drive away. I turn a page in my life to discover a new one. I see him in my side rearview mirror, motionless. His silhouette, his broad shoulders disappear little by little from my sight.

Today, we say goodbye. But it is not a farewell.

Deep inside me…deep inside, I know that I will see him again one day.

And until then, no matter how much time passes, I won't forget him.

EPILOGUE

IRIS

THREE MONTHS LATER

The hardest part was sorting through our family photo albums. Seeing the happy faces of my parents next to Agnes and me was heartbreaking. While tears rolled down my cheeks, a smile remained on my face as many memories of my childhood came to the surface.

I found, among the things stored at my aunt's house, my mother's favorite shirt. It smelled of her. I couldn't leave it locked in a box. To tell you the truth, when it's a little too hard, when the loss is a little too much, I hold it close to me just for a few moments. Even after all these months, it still has a touch of her smell.

Contrary to what I expected, my Aunt Emma helped me sort through all their stuff.

It actually broke the ice for us, in a way. Our relationship improved dramatically. Behind my aunt's coldness is a surprisingly understanding woman. When she heard what happened in Denver, she broke down in my arms. Her attitude changed. Everything that happened helped bring us together. For the first time in a long time, she has really acted like a family member, supporting me, letting me talk to her about anything and everything to clear my head. In fact, she has been taking care of me for the last three months.

Agnes doesn't quite understand this new connection. But she doesn't know the whole truth. I want to preserve her as much as possible.

I have spent the last three months learning to live with new memories, not necessarily pleasant ones, but they are part of me. I am stronger now. I am free of my past, free of any connection to my parents' killer.

Leaving Denver was the right thing to do, but I would be lying if I said it was easy. It's not easy when someone comes back to haunt you every minute of every day.

I needed to get out of town, to get away from it all. To rebuild myself. But my rebuilding is not complete. I miss Tucker, damn it. I miss him more than I should. A part of my heart has stayed with him. I know I should try to ignore it, but it's hard.

I snap out of my thoughts as I walk into my new—and tiny—bathroom.

"Agnes!" I yell as I find her soaked shirt on the tile floor. "I told you before that your clothes should not be used as a mop."

I know she can hear me because she's in the small living room a few feet away, but she keeps her eyes on the TV, pretending to be innocent.

"No, carry on; it's fascinating!" I mumble, throwing the laundry into the basket. "You'll end up killing me."

She still doesn't say anything, but a small smile appears on her face.

Little devil.

I walk towards my room, stifling a yawn. The bar I got a job at is super nice, but the hours are pretty random. I need a good shower and twelve hours of sleep.

As I walk into the room and turn on the lamp next to my bed, the doorbell rings. I frown as I stare at the clock. 9:17 p.m.

"I'm going to open the door!" shouts Agnes.

"Check who's there before you open the door! It must be Aunt Emma."

She must have made a mistake and thought my little sister was sleeping at her place tonight. Agnes spends every weekend here but lives with her the rest of the time.

"So who is it?" I shout to my little sister.

She doesn't answer me, so I listen carefully. I stopped looking behind my back to check that no one was following me, I'm not afraid anymore, but I'm still careful.

I come out of my room, eager to check on my little sister. There she is, leaning against the wall, arms crossed over her chest with a devilish grin on her face.

"Who was that? I don't—"

I lose my words as I discover who is standing on my doorstep. Tucker.

This can't be…what is he doing here? In my new apartment?!

I had sent him a message when I arrived in Portland to tell him that everything was OK. And he answered me immediately. But afterwards, I held back with all my might because I knew it would be too hard. I tried to forget him, but I couldn't. Tucker came to haunt my every dream. I was unhappy despite my little sister's presence, unable to move on.

Could he, on the other hand? I've asked myself that question many times, but I think I have my answer tonight.

Because here he is…in front of me.

And it's no longer a dream. This is reality. *My reality.*

"Tucker…" I whisper in his direction. "What the hell are you doing here?"

He takes a step towards me without saying anything and frowns, as if he didn't really know what he was doing here. I stare at him helplessly. His hair is a little longer than when I left him. He's put on some muscle. But his gaze…his gaze remains the same, intense and entirely focused on me. He looks like a wild beast ready to jump on its prey, and I am the prey.

Do I really have the strength to fight against the invisible cage that he is placing all around me, just with his look?

"Hi," he says, a little awkwardly.

I walk over to him and cross my arms over my chest, as uncomfortable as he is. "What are you doing here?"

"Mikael Larey has finally been cleared. New evidence has been discovered. In the past, Helena Larey had told her mother several times that she sometimes had suicidal urges. Her mother was never really alarmed because she knew that her daughter was seeing a psychologist, but Helena's mother had hidden something fundamental from us."

I remember talking to Mrs. Richards months earlier about how evidence had been found that would surely turn the tide.

"Helena's mother had in her possession a suicide letter from her daughter, which she eventually turned over to the police after Mikael's trial. In this letter, Helena explained what she planned to do to herself and her daughter. The mother didn't intervene to save her granddaughter because…fuck, Helena sent the letter the same day as the tragedy. So her mother didn't receive it until a few days later, and it was already too late. You were right, Iris."

"Mikael was innocent," I whisper.

Tucker nods several times before running a hand over the back of his neck. "The mother didn't disclose the letter at the trial, damn it. She didn't tell the police because she wanted to protect her daughter, even though her daughter killed herself and took her child to the grave."

Shock overwhelms me. I didn't expect him to tell me such news.

"So it was Helena who abused their daughter and strangled her before killing herself. That's why Mikael's fingerprints weren't on the knife. Oh, my God…" I whisper, not believing it. "I…I fucking knew it! I knew something was wrong."

For the first time in weeks, a joy comes over me, and I don't try to contain it. An innocent man is going to be set free. "And you came all the way here to tell me that instead of picking up your phone?"

He shrugs casually. "I needed to…tell you in person."

I nod as he eyes my legs shamelessly. A lot of time has passed, but the attraction remains. The bond that united us has not disappeared. He's there, even stronger, even more invasive.

"And how is your mother?"

He comes out of his thoughts and stares at me, straight in the eyes this time, trying to relax. "The first few weeks were very difficult but I was there for her. I visited her every day. And now she's doing well. Great, in fact."

"That's great, Tucker."

Like three months earlier, we stare at each other. I remember the last words we exchanged. I can't think of anything else. I didn't think I'd see him again…But here he is.

For me?

"Well, you caught me off guard, I didn't expect to see you here. You came all the way here to tell me all this?"

He doesn't answer, so I go on. "Why did you come, Tucker?"

He takes another step in my direction, running his tongue over his lower lip. "Officially? To tell you that Larey has been released."

"And…unofficially?" I ask in a whisper, feeling a lump in my throat.

He stops a few steps away from me, and I feel the warmth coming from his pores. It caresses my skin and makes it electric. I try to fight the electric current that runs through me but I can't.

"TJ screams at me every day that he misses his best friend."

"Oh, really?"

He smiles gently at my skepticism. "You want the truth?" he finally says.

His smell invades my nostrils, exactly the same as I remember. I nod my head. I can't talk.

"I know you needed to come back here for a little bit, but I realized I made a mistake letting you go."

He takes another step in my direction. Only a handful of inches separate us now.

"I tried to leave you alone, but I couldn't get you out of my fucking head. I spent most of my time at my sister's grave. And the more time passed, the more I understood that she would have wanted me to be happy. But I couldn't be happy because I wasn't whole."

My throat gets a little bit lumpier and I'm hanging on his lips. Because I too have felt his unhappiness.

"I thought about it for a long time, and I understood that I needed you to be happy, to be whole again, Iris. So I decided to stop being a coward. I want you back. I want you back with me." He swallows before continuing, "When I met you, I was afraid I would fall in love with you. I was afraid to love you, but it was too late. And now I'm afraid of losing you. I don't want your memory to haunt my thoughts, to be present only in my head. A great man once said that just because it's in our heads doesn't mean it's not real. But I don't want this reality."

Behind the tears hidden under my eyelids, I laugh softly to hide my true emotions.

"Are you quoting *Harry Potter* to me again?"

His eyes shine intensely as I lift my head to make eye contact with him. His hand brushes my cheek.

"Will you get out of my thoughts and back into my reality, Iris?"

My heart beats furiously. So many things are racing through my mind, but when he touches me, I can't think. I can only stare at his gaze, which pierces my soul, which destroys all my barriers, once again.

"C'mon kiss him!" Agnes whispers furiously behind my back.

Tucker raises an eyebrow, appreciative. "The truth always comes out of the children's mouths."

He doesn't say anything more, but I know he's waiting for my reaction, my answer.

Finally, I nod several times, my throat too knotted to speak.

"Yeah?" he pushes with a childish smile on his face.

"Yes," I finally whisper. "I want to become your reality."

I thought I had to get away from him to rebuild myself, to live again, to be free. I didn't want to get lost between my heart and my mind.

But the truth is that I wasn't living. I was just surviving, these last months. I needed him to be complete again.

He is the key to my reconstruction. And I am his. Because in the end, this whole thing is just about him, about us.

Just about you, Tucker.

Then his mouth lands on mine and never leaves it.

Two parts of a whole—the king and queen—destined to become one. One and the same heart. One and the same love.

Our love.

Acknowledgment

I hope that you have enjoyed the journey with the wolf and his redhead. I entrust them to you, place them in your hands and let you cherish them as you wish.

What was only a sweet dream has come true. Getting into Iris's thoughts was not easy, but I believe it is a journey that will stay with me forever. Tucker has a special place in my heart. Julie D., I know he has a place in yours too. I leave him in your care.

Tucker and Iris started their adventures on Wattpad but they have come to life today, and it is partly thanks to you, my dear readers. Thank you for being by my side, for following my adventures, for supporting me, for talking so well about my writing, for sending me messages sometimes late at night to tell me about the emotions that went through you while reading my story. Thank you to my first readers who have followed me since the beginning and who, I hope, will be by my side until the end.

Thank you to the great authors who supported me in this new adventure. Lou Marceau, you have been a great help to me. Ana Klis, you proved me that solidarity and kindness exist more than anything else among authors. Kentin Jarno, the more time passes, the more you become a cornerstone for me. Thank you, Anne Cantore, for agreeing to discover this universe in preview and for having reassured me at the same time. And so many others, that I don't forget.

Thank you to the great reviewers who communicate on the networks and to the group moderators who help us discover our babies. Aly, a special hug to you.

And finally, thank you to the Addictives team. You guys are the best. Juliette, working with you has been a great adventure. You have made the story and the adventures of Tucker and Iris even better.

Myrina Holmes Demons and Wonders
by *Anna Triss*

I'm Myrina Holmes, the top Tracker of Infernum, tasked with neutralizing supernatural creatures who disobey our laws.

In my world, demons have legions. Fourteen to be precise: seven dedicated to the cardinal virtues and seven ruled by the deadly sins.

As a marginal hybrid, I belong to neither camp, which suits me just fine. I love my job and my life on Earth when I'm not on a mission. Except, of course, when mysterious corpses literally fall from the sky to torture my brain and when my succubus half-sister starts hanging out with the most detestable Hybresang there is, Kelen Wills.

A supremely powerful sinner, commander-in-chief of an elite army, he doesn't embody one deadly sin. No, he possesses all seven-with a penchant for lust, anger, pride, and gluttony. But keep that detail to yourself...

Anyway, this guy has made it his mission to seduce me, probably because I'm the only woman who can resist his dubious charms.

This Hybresang can go to hell, because I have other midnight demons to deal with.

My Hipster Next Door
by *Mag Maury*

In Liverpool, the barbershop Hipster Maniac is an institution. Run by three bearded, tattooed friends, it is the place to listen to great rock, get a trim, and have a drink.

But for Line, it also spelled trouble. For starters, when she first got to the neighborhood, she rear-ended Jordan's car, who turned out to be one of the three barbers. Then she discovered that they were neighbors in business and residence! So no way can she escape this muscle-flaunting, smoldering man who is covered in tattoos and... completely insufferable!

He draws her near only to push her away. He toys with her shamelessly. But worst of all he hates Christmas whereas that is Line's very favorite time of year!

Beneath a backdrop of festive fairy lights, intoxicatingly passionate kisses, and blistering banter... It's on!

The Cocky Heir
by *Ana K. Anderson*

She is about to get married. But not to him.

Quinn MacFayden, an accomplished expat businessman in New York, is set to return to Scotland in extremis to protect the precious family legacy. His 91-year-old grandfather is about to marry a perfect stranger sixty-six years his junior... And that is out of the question! Quinn swears it. Over his dead body will Dawn Fleming ever be part of the family!

But Dawn is not a future bride like the others. She is nowhere near the gold digger he imagined and, above all, she knows just how to stand up to him. And so a game of cat and mouse begins between them. A war with no holds barred and where surrender has never been so tempting...

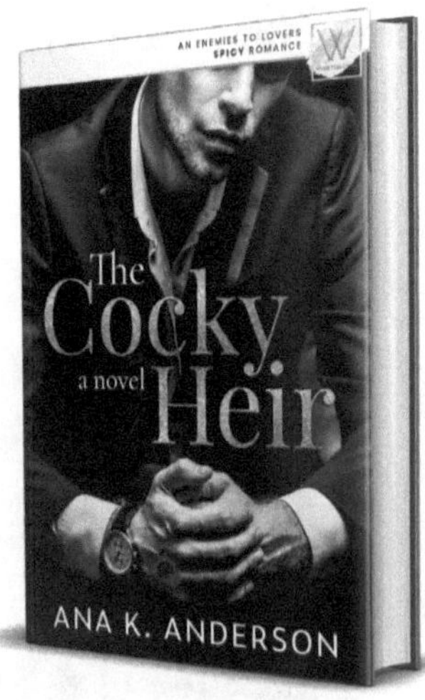

My Stepbrother: A Sexual Revelation
by *Sophie S. Pierucci*

Cassie is a highly intelligent young woman... Too much so for her own good!

And she is as daunting as she is intriguing. Carl, the son of his father's second wife, would hardly say otherwise!

Carl is the exact opposite of his steady father. He is a player and a slayer. Afraid of nothing and no one. Except for Cassie when she asks him to introduce her to the pleasures of the flesh.

And when the situation gets out of control, it is too late to turn back, and the two lovers find themselves ensnared in forbidden passion. Forbidden by everyone: society, their parents, their friends.

But how to resist the desire that consumes them?

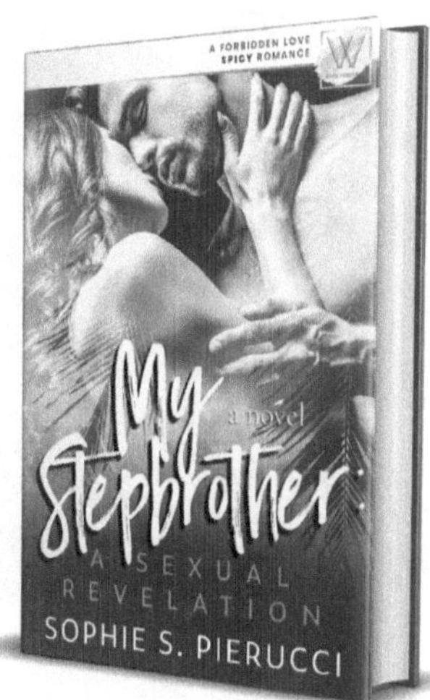

Your Power Over me
by *Missy Heart*

A family home heavy with secrets, a dangerously charismatic owner.

Will her arrival at Iron House be the end of her?

Ever since she was a teenager, Lovisa has known it: at Iron House, anything can happen, especially the worst.

However, when she is forced to return to the family home for her stepfather's funeral, her heart races: she is going to see him again, this "brother" who she never wanted and who yet turned her whole world upside down.

Now at the head of a drug cartel, authoritarian and brutal, Niklas is nothing like the teenager she knew nine years ago. At his side, Lovisa finds herself immersed in a harsh, ruthless—but fascinating—world.

Irremediably attracted to this man who wants her as much harm as good, will Lovisa manage to fight her unmentionable desires? Or will she give in to Niklas' magnetic darkness?

Touchdown
by *Sonia Birdy*

She's a runner, but the campus star quaterback runs faster than she does!

Rocky has had a chaotic life from which she concluded three fundamental things: life is a succession of problems to be solved, men are assholes to be avoided and promises are only binding on fools who want to believe in them. So, unlike the other girls on campus, boys are not a priority for her. Worse, she sees them as an obstacle to her success!

But during a student party, she meets Jude. Freshly transferred from Harvard to play on Brown's soccer team, Jude is the new star on campus. Handsome and inaccessible, he is the type not to get attached: the perfect candidate for a one-night stand.

But the chemistry is too strong. And though Rocky is determined to run away from him, he is determined to conquer her heart.

Kalliopee: A Princess's Sacrifice
by *Koko Nhan*

After years of violent battles, Kalliopee agrees to sacrifice her freedom by marrying the prince of the enemy kingdom in order to bring peace.

In a world where women are treated as slaves rather than wives, she is still delighted to be reunited with her first love, Karel.

However, life is unpredictable, and the horrors of war have transformed Karel into a tough and ruthless heir to the throne, who despises the Viridians more than anything. While he has no qualms about mistreating Kalliopee, his determination wavers when confronted with her striking eyes. In the midst of desire and animosity, schemes and plots, dreams and disillusionment, will the princess's heart endure the price of her liberty?

The Private Garden
by *Oly TL*

The most disturbing and transgressive of contracts...

Tiger Sexton seems to have it all. Charisma. Respect. Relentless business acumen. More fortune than he could spend in a life and a sublime wife, Sophia.

When Oceane is invited by Mrs. Sexton for a job interview in one of the restaurants that her husband gave her, the young French tourist knows nothing about this couple. Their name means

nothing to her, people are not her thing. She just wants a job, a place to live and to move on with her life... Sophia's proposal comes at the right time: the Sextons are looking for an *au pair*.

But by opening their doors to her, many other locks are likely to open. Is Oceane ready for this? And what about Sophia, and especially the Tiger lurking in this Secret Garden?

Keep in touch with Anita Rigins

Instagram:
https://www.instagram.com/anitarigins/

ABOUT THE AUTHOR

Anita Rigins has always had a passion for the law, so she studied criminal business law. At the same time, she needed to dream, so she started writing. Today, she writes physiological romances with thriller backgrounds. Worlds created from dreams or nightmares, which she shapes to break and then reattach the hearts of her readers!